DEDICATION

When the light burns and burdens
When the 'truth' twists and knots, choking your eyes and voice
When the day has no place for you
May the Darkness gather you up, offering you solace and rest
in Her kind arms
May rage warm your soul and strengthen your heart

This book is dedicated to the survivors. You know who you are. I wrote this for you.

CONTENTS

TRIGGER WARNING

This book deals heavily with themes of death, grief, loss, abuse, trauma, mental health, violence, justice and revenge – particularly among women and people of color. There are many scenes of violence and gore. Notably, there are two brief mentions of child sexual assault that occurred in the past in relation to the events of the book – one in flashback and one in the aftermath. There are also mentions of rape, the graphic depiction of a potential hate crime and cannibalism.

PROLOGUE

The coastal town of Sunset Cove thought it knew fog. It swept in every few days – bringing that clean rain feeling without the hassle. It was a welcome visitor, cooling the hottest summer nights and adding mystery to dreary winter days.

The fog that stalked into Sunset Cove the evening of September 28 was different. Instead of the light feeling of clouds on the ground, this fog was sharp – full of oppressive tendrils – not unlike that of a cocoon.

They say that when a caterpillar enters a cocoon, it has no idea what is happening, and that before the creature turns into a butterfly its entire body liquefies, insides turned out, a mass of goo and confusion.

This new fog began its journey through the county of Sunset Cove at 7:01 pm. By 9 pm, the entire town and outlying areas were engulfed and pulsating with the truth that had swept in from the water.

The screams started at 7:15.

HOW'S THE WEATHER OUT THERE?

7:16 pm, Saturday, Sept. 28, 2020, 15 minutes after The Fog

Jimmy St. Clair knew three things at this moment.

1) The thing snacking on his intestines used to be his buddy Ronnie.

They'd gone downtown to get some beers and watch the game at Molly Hannigan's on Mission. The Irish pub had just enough burnished wood to mute its patrons' shouts of excitement. He and Ronnie were still pretty hungover from their trip to the city the night before.

2) From his vantage point on the cold, gray concrete, Jimmy saw the silhouette of his right arm dangling from the underside of the faded, yellow awning of the candy shop next to Molly's – or maybe some other poor bastard had lost an arm in this chaos. Either way, it was wedged perfectly beneath the second "D" in Benedict's Candy and Ice Cream Shop.

3) Being eaten alive wasn't as awful as he'd thought it would be. Maybe it was shock? But he wasn't in excruciating pain. He still knew his name, who was president, Sammy Sosa's batting stats and his top picks for fantasy football. In fact, he didn't really even feel like he was dying. He knew he should. He knew that having an arm ripped off and seeing your best friend chew on your intestines after turning into some kind of giant man/dog/wolf thing was epic bad, but mostly he just felt annoyed. And cold. So very, very cold.

"Come on, bro," Jimmy said. "Knock it off."

He took a swipe at Ronnie's snout. His hand connected. Ronnie squealed like a stepped-on Pomeranian.

Jimmy sat up and assessed himself. The one hand he still had turned an ashy gray. This disappointed him more than anything else. He'd always secretly loved his skin. His grandma said it reminded her of black star calla lilies – her favorite flower. To see it change in death hurt his heart. But he still didn't feel dead. He felt… fine. Strong, even. Ronnie, on the other hand, hackles raised, keening and howling, was yacking his giant, gnarly wolf-dog guts out.

But still. None of this was cool. None of this was chill.

*****

7:05 pm, Saturday, Sept. 28, 2020, 4 minutes after The Fog

Sam Bridger had a wandering soul. She spent decades moving from town to town. At the time, she thought it was her nature – the need to see what was over the next hill – to explore. Then she landed in Sunset Cove and realized she had serious Goldilocks Syndrome. Colorado was too conservative and she hated skiing. Texas was too… Texas. Utah didn't have enough alcohol – or anything else. Minnesota – too cold, and North Dakota… Jesus, North Dakota was a fucking nightmare. But Sunset Cove was just right.

On paper, Sunset Cove was a quaint beach community – a college town nestled between the Pacific Ocean and redwood forests – home to both Silicon Valley gurus and Cal State professors. It had a thriving downtown that complemented its beach tourism. The place *should* have been idyllic. The reality was actually kind of terrifying.

In the 70s, it was the murder capital of the country because three serial killers operated out of the area – a fact locals *loved* telling tourists.

Multiple horror movies and television shows were either based on or shot in the area. The Big Foot museum claimed that several cryptids live in the dense, thickly-shadowed woods. Meth and homelessness were rampant. The city council, through decades of sheer passive aggressiveness, had managed to repel all chain hotels, restaurants and shops from the city proper. The only nod to the American culture of homogeneity was a Denny's off the highway that, in and of itself, was the setting of most nightmares.

Yet Sam loved every wannabe hippie, hermit survivalist, mountain bike snob, granola yoga instructor, skater dude, surf chic, 420-obsessed, meth head, eco terrorist, pseudo-intellectual, Angela Davis lives here, veganism cures all ills, no ACUPUNCTURE cures all ills, how many tattoos can you fit on the human body?, La Cucina on Portola has the best burritos, Nah man, Gordo's on Seventeenth has the best burritos, are you going to the Pear, the Blue or the Cat Saturday, hey, did you hear about that guy who got shot outside the Pear?, aging goth, clueless techie, half the county is Mexican, this land belongs to the Ohlone, scary mountain inch of the place.

From the salt-bleached Vietnamese restaurant signs on the West Side, to the dilapidated clapboard coffee shops in the mountains (some with actual giant redwoods growing inside them), the whole county had more personality than it knew what to do with. In fact, sometimes it had several – changing drastically from block to block and moment to moment.

While most of the United States had given in to the idea that if it stomped the uniqueness out of its citizens and its locations life would be safer, Sunset Cove stood, or rather stumbled up out of the gutter after a three-day bender as a monument to humanity's glorious and terrifying strangeness. Sam, after all her travels across this dysfunctional nation, understood how special that was.

If she were being honest with herself, she knew that downtown Sunset Cove was her favorite part of this mad place and that she particularly loved Sunset Cove Bookshop.

At 7:05 pm the night of Sept. 28, she stood smack in the middle of the SciFi section. After nearly a decade in Sunset Cove, Sam had developed what she felt was a sound theory that downtown was, in reality, the home of a very hospitable but incredibly short-tempered Old God.

Upon entering the twelve-block radius that comprised Sunset Cove's downtown, people felt a euphoric welcoming – as though being greeted by an old friend who missed them terribly after a long absence. The average buildings surrounding downtown opened up into a tree-lined street of equally average 30s-era, gray, concrete architecture dotted with tasteful yet cheerful signage and the condensed, distilled insanity of the humans within the area. Then said visitors would immediately get lost. It was well-documented that even the most 'local' of locals got turned around after a block or two. This confluence of events was made all the more delightful by the endless parade of unfiltered humanity.

Sam felt the twitch to leave downtown about ten minutes prior. A baby screamed just so. A homeless woman's rant used the word 'cunt' one too many times. It all grated along Sam's spine. She could tell that the Old God had become tired of her and she needed to get the fuck out of downtown.

By Sunset Cove calculations, she had twenty minutes before said homeless woman attempted to shank her the second she walked out the door. That gave her ten minutes to peruse the new releases before heading to the bus stop. This was not her first rodeo.

Sam's hackles continued to rise. Bookshop was sacrosanct. Tweekers avoided it. If a tourist came in, even they had the good sense to know they'd wandered into sacred space. The shelves were just tall enough that Sam had to stand on tiptoe to reach the top. They were light wood and expansive – large enough to muffle noise but not loom. The seating was plentiful and appropriately uncomfortable. If a patron was going to sit and read, they had to commit to it, damn it. The staff was knowledgeable enough to leave regulars alone and make amazing recommendations when asked.

She felt the need to run. Sam tried to drop back into the solid hardcover in her hands but the commotion outside escalated. Screams echoed against the floor to ceiling windows to her left.

Fuck. How had she miscalculated?

The man in the far corner of the shop dropped his book with an obscene thud. He stared at his empty hand like he'd never seen it before. In a town that shut down every year on April 20, his behavior wasn't entirely out of place, but the horror in his face told her that things were going sideways much, much faster than she'd anticipated.

Sam's eyes darted around the room – searching for a clear exit. What she'd failed to notice in her search for a new paperback was the hazy light, like a fog, winding its way inside.

Sam bonded with the man next to her as only strangers can when looking for reassurance at an insane moment.

"Is it a fire, you think?" he asked.

"There's no alarms," she said. "No fire trucks."

Sirens blared to life. She flinched not just at the sound but that she would, of course, be proven instantly wrong.

Sam stared at the man – at all the moonlight and lies crossing his face.

"You okay?" he asked her. She saw both the kind hazel eyes and something *else* lurking beneath them.

"No," she replied. She was usually never so blunt with strangers, but it seemed appropriate considering how very not okay she had become with no warning. "Neither are you."

"What're you talking about? I'm fine." He scratched his beard. His fingers caught in the bark and he stilled. "Oh."

The circle of his lips hardened into a knot. His hair grew wild and vast as it burst into branches and leaves. She ducked in close to his trunk as his branches broke through the roof. Leaves and ceiling tiles crashed around her.

Water.

The thought came unbidden as the world broke.

I am not a tree. I don't need to be watered.

Sam often argued with herself.

Ceiling dust clattered up – choking her. The thought popped in again but this time with Technicolor urgency.

Water. Water is safety. Get to water. Now.

The membrane changing Sunset Cove's nature stretched taut. Yet, the screams, the carnage had only just begun.

Sam scrambled out from under the tree and ran for the back exit. A four-foot-tall witch stood between her and the door. On a "normal" night in Sunset Cove, a child dressed in a black cloak and pointy hat would have been a mere amusement.

"Where are your adults?" Sam demanded as she weighed her instinct to run against her need to not be an unredeemable piece of shit.

"Adults? I don't have adults," the child spat out in disgust as a giant, mottled, gray tentacle smashed the bookshelf beside her.

Something important inside Sam shattered – the absurdity, the noise, the smoke, the tiny witch and the *fucking kraken*? It was all. Far. Too. Much.

The child disappeared. Sam turned to the direction the tentacle came from and ran after it. She needed, with every fiber of her being, to find the owner of said tentacle and give it a piece of her mind. She did not care how ridiculous, suicidal or fruitless her new mission was. For some reason, yelling at a giant, mythical sea monster made sense and she'd be damned if she wasn't going to hold onto that.

She rushed through the crumbling main entrance of Sunset Cove Bookshop and turned toward the retreating tentacle.

As Sam ran into the night, it hit her like a brick wall. The Darkness surrounded her. It engulfed her. The infinite potential of the night surrendered itself to her. She knew, in a way she had never known anything else – not love, not comfort, not even her own sense of self – that the night, the Darkness, belonged to her.

Despite the shrieking chaos on the street before her – contorted bodies projected through the diffused fog and the pile of picked-clean human bones clattering beneath her feet, Sam relaxed. Her shoulders unclenched. She sighed, closed her eyes and reached out to claim what was hers.

No.

The sensation was akin to a sharp, quick slap on the wrist.

"Oww." She tried again – stretching her senses into the void.

I said NO. Knock it off. You're not ready. You'll die. Get to water now, young lady.

The hell?? Young lady?

For the first time, Sam doubted that the voices she'd spent a lifetime arguing with were actually her own. That scared her more than the fifty-foot, slimy, gray cephalopod booking it over low buildings, heading west on Mission Street toward the Pacific ocean.

Who are you?

She did not really want an answer from the voice that had told her not to take the job from the guy with the excessive, red chest hair and that she couldn't pull off a pencil skirt.

I'm you from before.

Me from before what?

Before we died the first time.

We died a FIRST TIME?

Sam ducked as a golden, white-winged angel buzzed her in pursuit of a giant, horned bat woman.

We have died a thousand times. The important part is to not die this time. Get to the river.

I'm not going anywhere until you expla- but Sam couldn't finish the thought. The glorious and beautiful night wanted her. The Infinite pulled at her soul. The void needed to be filled and it would fill itself with her.

She bent double, puking out the white chocolate, chicken pot pie from the place next door. It had been a treat after a long week.

The remnants of white chocolate gravy dribbled down her chin as the voice stated with the smuggest of satisfaction: *That's why.*

Fuck it. Fine.

Sam hated few things on this earth more than running. Her boobs were too big to do it without being obscene and honestly, it struck her as an antiquated exercise leftover from before bikes were invented. Still, as the Darkness tore at her, she managed a light jog. The anarchy that greeted Sam reminded her of the punk shows of her youth. Snarling rage took most of the attention. A few combatants burnt themselves and each other out in the center while a lot of innocent bystanders wondered if they should join in, but mostly just enjoyed the show.

Half a dozen buskers called downtown home. Most were pretty normal by Sunset Cove standards. The violin guy played classical music in front of Bookshop on Saturdays. On Sunday afternoons, that became the blues guitar guy's spot.

The most famous busker was the Mad Martinelli. He dressed from head to toe in whimsical bright patterns and tights. He never revealed his face behind the multitude of masks and between accordion versions of pop songs he made jokes about being a fat, sixty-year old Puerto Rican transplant.

As Sam struggle-jogged, the Mad Martinelli morphed into an emu, then a crocodile, a standing desk, and a Rolls Royce. As she passed him, he settled himself into his suitcase as a pale slurry gurgling in distress.

She darted left towards the wide, meandering river that cut through Sunset Cove. Sam's dart was more of a fast-paced walk with an occasional skip interspersed with a gasping: "Dear God, my lungs." The night continued to dig into her mind and heart. Its whispers slid against her skin. It begged her to stop and play. The voice screamed, cajoled, and taunted her into moving faster.

Sam's reality swung wildly between the new nightmare of Sunset Cove's transformation, the night's darkness trying to rip out her eyes and what felt like flashbacks to ancient, bloody land.

I swing my sword, sweet and true, piercing the final interloper's throat. His blood pours over my body and I am free. My people are free. Still, the legions of men do not stop. They must know who I am. They must know what I will do. Her combatant falls backward. She leans over him – his blood a holy baptism. Covering his left eye with her mouth, she sucks it from his dying skull. Then she stands and pops it in her teeth for all the world to see. His visions, his blood belong to her. Her soldiers scream in delight. The celebration of this triumph will last for many days.

I did not suck out that guy's eyeball and eat it.

Yes, you did. Keep going.

Where?

Turn right at the zombie.

A desiccated corpse of a man in basketball shorts with black socks and slides groaned as he banged his head over and over into the locked, sliding door entrance to Trader Joes.

Why?

Why what?

Why would I eat his eye?

I don't know.

Why don't you know? You were me in the past.

That one wasn't me. I was before her.

Sam could still taste the rotten fish and death of the eyeball melting in her mouth.

Well, it was disgusting.

Yes, yes, it was. We're here.

Sam wasn't even sure how she'd gotten here – let alone where '*here*' was. She stopped in the middle of the bridge spanning the Saint Augustus river – such as it was. The concrete arch spanned a quarter mile over the shallow water. This late in the year, it was barely more than a glorified mud puddle. The bridge had several inlets that the unhoused residents of Sunset Cove used as sanctuaries.

Sam had never seen the human who lived in the four-foot by four-foot bridge alcove. They never seemed to leave their blue-tarped palace. The architect shored up one side with a wheeled suitcase and the other with a shopping cart. The floor consisted of layers of cardboard. By Sunset Cove homeless standards, it was pretty nice. As she stared, swatting at the Darkness buzzing around her head, the plastic structure expanded. The walls turned to stone and grew upward. While Sam was distracted, the night closed in.

"Leave me alone," she shouted at the Darkness.

"*You're so… strong,*" it buzzed in the air.

Sam swore she felt something grab her ass. She spun, her back against the bridge edge.

"NO."

She shoved back with her mind. The force of the shock wave, her will pushing against the night, threw her backward off the bridge – now crumbling under the weight of the castle. She tumbled into the sluggish water below.

"**Ow,**" said the ancient voice in Sam's head. The water closed in and she lost consciousness.

*****

5:32 pm, Sept. 28, 750 B.C.E., 2,769 years before The Fog

Her father had gone mad. Under normal circumstances, you'd just throw the old goat in a room without sharp objects, feed him, wait until he wandered into the bog and call it a fucking day. But no, her father was chieftain and still charismatic enough to hold the weak-willed and stupid prisoner with his rheumy, blue gaze.

Twenty men stared, slack jawed and lost in his manic glory as the daft geezer rattled off tale after tale. 'The goddess is coming,' he said. 'The crows speak to me,' he said. 'Look at this weird boil on my foot. It's proof of the goddess' favor,' he said.

Fuck me. Anand couldn't take it anymore.

"Da," she said, ever so quiet.

"Da." Still nothing.

Oh, for fuck's sake.

"DA! The fields, Da!"

"Ya dinna need to shriek at me, daughter."

He teetered back on the high stool that substituted for his throne during these informal adoration sessions. He brushed beer foam from his grizzled mustache and smiled at her.

Anand softened. He was probably going to get them all killed, but he was still her Da.

"Da, with all respect to the goddess. Those fields aren't going to harvest themselves."

Her father trembled as he rose.

"Oh, yes. Of course. Of course." He patted her cheeks. She smelled the decay wafting from his bones and breath. "My level-headed daughter. Thank you for looking out for us, dear. Yes. Yes."

*****

7:09 pm Sept. 28, 2020, 8 minutes after The Fog

Chiba Leary hated her dog and her husband and her kids. She was then consumed with self-loathing for hating her dog, her husband… and her kids.

No, dammit! She was working on this! Her feelings were valid. Danny said his back hurt too much after dealing with the girls all day to take Ridley for a walk. It's not like she hadn't spent all day fixing computers in cold, dusty rooms. But no, he needed the rest.

She'd picked up Mexican takeout and her youngest had a meltdown because the beans in her burrito were the 'yucky' kind. They were the same beans as last week. Chiba knew it. She still had the receipt. Her eldest, well, her eldest just stared at her screen and shrugged – at everything – a jaded sixteen-year old in a seven-year old body.

So yeah, right now, she hated her family, including the dog. Except, that she didn't. It wasn't her dog's fault that he needed a walk. It wasn't Malak's fault that she was five and everything is weird when you're five. It wasn't her husband's fault that he had flat feet and a bad back.

She sighed, rolled her shoulders and checked her phone. This part of Sunset Cove was as suburban as it got. The streets were cleaned every third Thursday. All the streetlights worked and a homeless, heroin addict was only found passed out in the slide at the park across the street once every six months or so. Chiba's best friend called it a pocket dimension for normals.

To the untrained and unwise, Chiba Leary was scary as hell. She'd once made a male doctor cry for refusing to give her kid a strep test. Retail clerks took one look at her five-foot-three-inch frame, triangle jaw, square shoulders, resting bitch face and ran to the back room, leaving the less-experienced clerks to face her loud voice and razor-sharp opinions.

The few select humans who knew Chiba Leary best understood that while all the bluster and rage was absolutely real, it was only used as a weapon she wielded to protect herself and those she cared about. As far as she was concerned, most everyone else could fuck off – as long as they were safe and sound. Chiba didn't wish ill on anyone. She just didn't need them anywhere near her, her family, her friends or her business. Thanks very much.

With all these conflicting emotions about having to walk the damn dog, Chiba failed to take heed of the thick, slightly glowing fog swirling around her.

Ridley, on the other hand, freaked the fuck out. He jumped like he'd been bit on the butt by a judgmental chihuahua. The scruffy gray dog yipped and whined at the air.

"Jesus. What in the hell?"

Chiba looked up from the article on the origins of Crab Rangoon. She saw nothing. She felt nothing – except cool, damp fog.

Her dog continued to dance in a way that made her wonder if the sidewalk had turned to lava. She bent to touch it. It was as cool and as damp as the gray air.

"Seriously. What is it?"

She leaned to check if he'd been stabbed.

No blood. No needles. The little dog vibrated under her hands.

"The hell, Ridley." She rubbed his chunky side.

We really need to put him on a diet, she thought.

"It's okay, buddy. You're okay. Shh. You're okay."

Then the taupe and brick, two-story five houses down, the one with the mini skate ramp out front, exploded.

*****

The Liminal Space

The Goddess of Death tells herself that she does not dream. That is a lie.

She thinks, she plans and she learns. But, most importantly, she remembers.

She detonates into waves upon waves of agony spreading through galaxies. Lost in the chaos of dark remembering. Time is unable to exist.

Screaming, she cannot find herself and the ancient mother is upset.

You're not ready.

She is in the middle of a diligent and protracted search for her left arm. She'd managed to piece the rest of herself together but that damned arm is nowhere to be found. The 'self' is not much – a hollowed-out husk and dry, rattling bones stitched together with stubborn sinew and nightmares.

"People will die," she said as she tears through the couch cushions. Nope, not there. She does find fifty black hair ties, though.

You can't save everyone.

"Watch me." She shines a light under the bed.

It's not a matter of will. You know that. It's math. Probability. There are rules.

"Don't care. Have to try."

The arm twitches at her from the farthest corner beneath the bed. She lays down and stretches her right arm but she's both too short to reach and too broad to fit.

She sighs and stands. Then she looks around for a long thing to use to push her arm out from under the bed.

You could ask for my help.

"I could, but I'm not going to." She pauses and thinks for a moment. "Probably."

Isn't saving them at the expense of your well-being another symptom of your abuse? They didn't ask for your help.

Sam faces the woman. Those burning eyes do not relent.

"They didn't ask to be in this situation."

Neither did you.

"I don't know what you want from me. I have to do this. I can't *not* be this. It's not my nature. You know that."

I want you to be honest with yourself and me. I want you to ask for help and accept it when offered.

She gave Sam her left arm. The woman's pale, slender hands glittered with stars. The heat death of the universe was embedded beneath her fingernails. Sam growled and snatched the arm away. She snapped it back into place

"I'm sorry," Sam said. "I'm sorry for how I am. I am sorry for what I did."

I have no need of your shame. I need you to return what you took.

Those burning eyes hardened and drilled holes deep into her skull.

Her consciousness fell through nebulae, bacteria and tardigrade stampedes until arriving within the body lying halfway in a fetid pool on the eastern edge of the Saint Augustus river ten feet before it spilled into the ocean.

Sam awoke. She gasped and puked up four weeks worth of mud and river water.

*****

Oct. 28, 2020, 30 days after The Fog

In the last month, Chiba built a kind of fucked up routine, in an admittedly desperate attempt at normalcy.

7 am - Wake up. (Fight nervous breakdown.)

7:15 am - Brush teeth. (Scream quietly with toothbrush in mouth to mute sound.)

7:30 am - Greet family. (Do not think about the state of the house.)

Through some miracle Chiba refused to question, the electricity remained on so the girls could watch the three kids' DVDs they had in peace while Danny made breakfast.

8 am - Danny attempts to home school.

8:15 am - Danny has nervous breakdown during homeschooling.

8:16 am - Go outside and have an actual shrieking nervous breakdown at the edge of the driveway before biking off to 'work.'

8:30 am - Park ass in front of the Clocktower for new job as a courier.

8:45 am - Lean against the southeast edge of the Clocktower and try to feel casual. There's no need to advertise. Everyone down here knows everyone else's sales pitch these days.

9:15 am - Repeat customer shows up for safe passage up the mountain. They make her show the black band around her forearm again.

Chiba hated this part – the band, the mark, whatever. The thing that simultaneously let her and her whole family stay safe, gave her a semblance of gainful employment in these mad times and kept her up at night wondering who or what had marked her and her family and why had they done such a thing.

She noticed the black band minutes after the explosion and Chiba knew it was the reason she survived.

The solid band circled her forearm – exactly three-quarters of an inch wide, yes, she'd measured, and it was such a deep, inky, black that in certain lighting her hand appeared to be disconnected from the rest of her body.

Every member of her family had one. Half her friends had one. Every child under the age of eighteen in Sunset Cove had one. No one knew what the band meant or where it came from – other than it offered near-absolute protection.

Chiba discovered this the night The Fog came. The explosion knocked her backward five feet, ass over tea kettle. She smacked her head hard on her next door neighbor's picket fence. As she came to, shaking off the ringing in her ears and the dust in her nose, a burning figure ran from the wreckage.

Chiba could tell by the pink tracksuit that it was her neighbor, Sue Something-or-other. The same woman who had a 'Coexist' bumper sticker and kept inviting Chiba to come over and smoke a bowl over a glass of wine on Friday afternoons.

Sue Something-or-other sprinted away at an inhuman speed – shrieking as flames consumed her clothes, melding them into her skin.

Chiba screamed.

Sue snapped towards her.

Horror consumed Chiba as she slowly realized that Sue Something-or-other wasn't stopping, dropping or rolling. The flaming woman charged at Chiba – her hands charred down to bone.

She couldn't make herself run away. Chiba pushed back into the fence as though she could move through it.

Sue Something-or-other's pale blond hair burnt black and crisp into her skull. Her right eye exploded out of her face from the heat. Chiba stopped screaming and clawed at her own throat. She gasped for air through the terror. She wanted to close her eyes but didn't dare.

Sue Something-or-other got within three feet before she was yanked back like a giant, invisible hand had snatched her around her blackened, skinless torso and tossed her into the night.

9:30 am - Take her customer up the mountain.

Not a day went by that Chiba wasn't grateful that Sam left her electric bike in their garage the night before The Fog rolled in.

It was their usual Friday game night. Sam rode the bulky, orange monstrosity over in case she'd wanted to get drunk – something her best friend did a little too often for Chiba's taste. Chiba gave her a ride home the next morning. Sam planned on taking the bus to get her bike on Sunday.

9:45 am - The night creatures are all tucked away and dreaming in the chasms, corners and crypts of Sunset Cove.

The mountains were no more or less safe in the morning than the rest of the valley. But no human, carrying the band or not, would be caught alive west of the Whispering Pines exit after sunset. Here there be vampires, trolls, werewolves, fae and all the wild things too far gone for the semi-polite society that had formed in the blood-soaked days following The Fog.

Her passenger, a small being, who used an ancient quilt as a cover to try to hide its obvious feathers, never spoke to Chiba. Every transaction was written in bold, black marker on an old newspaper and passed over with mittened hands. Chiba suspected claws but didn't care enough to ask. Her passenger was quiet, paid in canned goods and had never once tried to eat her. They were Chiba's favorite customer.

The Orange Monstrosity, while short on looks, was long on utility. The impossibly bulky frame held Chiba's weight and allowed for an attached cart that her customer barely fit into. Chiba managed to get the whole contraption halfway up the mountain without sweating her ass completely off.

Thank you, Sam. Wherever you are.

Sunset Cove county was home to the city of Sunset Cove as well as several attendant mini suburbs. Her passenger always asked to be dropped off in front of the remains of a grocery store in Redwood Valley, the 'squarest' suburb in the county. The flat building used to take up the lion's share of a strip mall. Before The Fog, Redwood Valley had an active, well-paid and very bored police force. All the bars closed at 10 pm and the most exciting thing happening after midnight was the rumble of trucks driving past on their way to Silicon Valley.

Chiba never understood why Sam lived there.

"I'm hiding," she'd said, the one time Chiba tried asking about it.

10:45 am - Arrive at the fritzing stoplight in front of a brown, brick coffee shop – barely visible beneath the thicket of vines and scrub.

The rain forest that sprang up in the minutes after The Fog had shoved aside concrete slabs and titled buildings, as if stating, in no uncertain terms, who and what belonged here, and who and what wasn't welcome anymore.

Chiba could go no further with the bike. She stopped and her passenger delicately crawled out of the basket, clutching the quilt around their neck.

They handed Chiba a newspaper.

Three days
Same time
Same place

"You want me to pick you up here in three days. Same time of day."

The quilted head nodded. They turned then stopped. Chiba heard rustling under the quilt.

The passenger turned back to her with another piece of newspaper.

I will have fruit for you

Chiba smiled.

"Thank you. My kids will love it," she said and froze – terrified she'd somehow put her family in danger.

Her passenger paused to write again. They did not notice Chiba's plastic smile.

I will bring extra for offspring

Touched, she couldn't find words. Her passenger shuffled into the jungle, the quilt dragging over vines until Chiba lost sight of them in the damp gloom.

10:55 am - Danny kept telling her to stay away, but Chiba couldn't help herself. Sam's place was only three miles north of the Coffee Shop Jungle. She disappeared the night The Fog rolled in. Her last text messages to Chiba read:

At Bookshop. Bored. You?

Hey, is shit getting weird there too? Earthquake weather?

"Honey," Danny would start.

Don't start.

"Okay, then," he relented the way he did every time because he couldn't bear it either. "Then we find her."

Then we find her.

10:30 am - Redwood Valley was known for being a quiet, bedroom community. After The Fog, the silence became sepulchral. Chiba didn't want to think too hard on why. She rubbed the black band around her left forearm. The skin was slightly raised like a tattoo. Yet, the band always felt cooler than her skin. She swore it had a scent as well – like a crisp autumn night. Zara said hers smelled like old books. Danny's reminded him of his Karate class and Malak…

"Blood, Mommy. Mine smells like blood."

Sam rented a studio over a two-car garage. Her ancient landlady had gone blind in The Fog, yet she waved to Chiba from ten feet away, cloudy eyes staring through her. In every horror movie, this white-haired crone would have been the harbinger of doom. Yet, she had smiled with real warmth when Chiba first mustered up the courage to drop by Sam's apartment after The Fog.

"It's fine, dear," she said. "Here's the spare key. She'll be happy to know you're watering her plants. I can't climb the stairs, you know."

"You haven't seen her?" Chiba cursed herself for asking a blind woman what she'd seen but the landlady, Jane, (maybe? Chiba couldn't remember what Sam said her name was.) chuckled.

"No, I haven't but you're welcome to stop by anytime."

Chiba didn't want to ask the next question but she did it anyway.

"Are you OK here? How have you survived?"

"Oh, it's fine," she said and pointed to the roof. "My son's a gargoyle. He takes care of any evening interlopers."

Jane patted Chiba's shoulder.

"I'm going to take a nap," she said.

Chiba looked up at the stone creature, frozen, massive wings spread over the gabled rooftop. His fangs seemed to drip with blood and ichor even in stone.

"Is that a Hawaiian shirt?"

Jane didn't bother to turn back.

"It was Aloha Saturday," she said.

Sam's place creeped Chiba out even before The Fog.

The narrow street didn't have curbs. A brook ran next to the garage. Massive oak trees in various states of collapse reclined over Sam's apartment. Dry autumn leaves blew across the street. A lone raven yelled at her from some tree. Chiba fought off every chill running down her spine and pulled Danny's baseball bat from the sling he'd made for her.

Just a quick pop in and out, water the plants and head home. Right, Chiba?

The landlady was nowhere to be seen and the gargoyle must have taken up residence in the backyard.

Chiba parked the Orange Monstrosity next to the rickety, bleached, wooden stairs that led up to Sam's cramped studio.

"I like a nest," she'd told Chiba one game night a few months after moving in.

Something felt different. Chiba couldn't put her finger on it. She'd thought it felt different before when she'd tried to will her best friend back into existence. So far, it hadn't worked. She imagined letting herself in and there'd be Sam – book in one hand, casual as hell, wondering how she'd gotten a key – somehow not even aware of the insanity of the past month.

Normal. The same. Familiar. The way everything was before.

Chiba realized as soon as the door swung open that something was very, very wrong.

The tangy, metallic scent of blood filled the air – so much that it edged into sickening. Her stomach roiled. Water poured over her shoes when she stepped through the doorway.

And the air – Chiba knelt down on the balls of her feet – terrified she was about to be struck by lightning. She'd read that's what you were supposed to do. Chiba perched there, staring at the black smear on Sam's yellowed linoleum kitchen floor, water up to her ankles before it struck her that she was inside and lightning was not coming.

She stood up too fast and heard the sound of running water from Sam's bathroom. Chiba glanced around the mismatched room. Nothing else was out of place. The plants wilted and sad – took up too much space in the tiny apartment. The white walls were bare except for the stupid painting Sam's awful mother gave her. It had accusing eyes that followed Chiba around the room.

"I need to remind myself," Sam said when she asked her why she kept it.

"I don't think you do, love."

Chiba brought the bat up to her shoulder and wanted, with every fiber of her being to leave, to go back through that door and act like none of this was happening. She'd had this same feeling the second night of The Fog, the desperate cellular ache to retreat.

The same damn thought popped into her head as it did that night:

What if I can help?

FUCK.

"Fucking hell, Sam," she whispered in the gloomy dappled light. "Fucking hell."

Chiba did a little shaking dance, squared her shoulders, set the bat firmly in both hands and crept towards the bathroom.

FUCK.

Sam's apartment, like everything in Sunset Cove, was cobbled together with leftovers that didn't fit any place else. The wooden hallway floor creaked with each splashing step and looked like it had been part of an abandoned barn in a past life.

Chiba froze. Whatever waited for her in that bathroom could hear her coming. She inhaled. Her heart pounded through her rib cage.

She nudged the bathroom door open with the bat.

In the damn near cheerful fucking morning light, sat Chiba's best friend, sprawled out, missing her left shoe, skin gray and hanging from her bones. What appeared to be sticks, leaves and mud matted her hair. She'd passed out over the shower drain. Water streamed over her muck-caked face. Still clad in that ubiquitous gray hoodie she wore like armor, Chiba feared she was looking at her best friend's corpse.

"Sam?" Chiba yelped.

Sam cracked open one sunken eye, shoved her hair out of her face and squinted up at her.

"Hey, Chibs, how'd you get in?"

10:57 am - We find her.

MY BEST FRIEND HAS LOST HER DAMN MIND

1:42 pm, Oct. 28, 750 B.C.E., 2,769 years before The Fog

Her mind reeled at the scene. She knew her eyes did deceive her and yet.

"Da!" she shrieked.

The naked old man climbed off the bed.

"Go away, Anand. Get out!"

Anand clawed at her stomach. The truth rose up from her gut. It threatened to burst from her mouth unbidden.

The other occupant of that bed was also naked, crying, and less than eight years old.

Anand drew her weapon.

She met the little girl's eyes.

"Get dressed and go to your mother. _Now._"

"Anand." She heard pleading. He raised his hands. "Wait. There's no need."

She kept the weapon and her eyes on him as the little girl ran out.

Anand heard his pleas as if from a distance – his anger, his cajoling.

"I am the chieftain," he said. "They'll never believe you. They'll think you're after the title."

She wasn't capable of weighing her odds at the moment. She stepped forward, herding him towards the door.

"Move."

He was yelling – threats and curses. His goddess would avenge him.

"No. She won't."

She didn't think he heard her.

Her body felt far away. As they left their low wood house, the rest of the village took notice.

They started yelling at her, demanding to know what was going on. Anand couldn't have answered. The details of this moment existed just beyond her fingertips.

When they finally reached the center of the little village, a crowd had gathered. She shoved her father to his knees.

"Tell them," she croaked.

He babbled at the sky. She inhaled and screamed:

"I command you to tell them!"

Her father stilled. The crowd hushed. He turned and looked up at her – reality settling into his aged body.

"It's you, my sweet girl. Isn't it? It's always been you."

"Tell them." She didn't understand what he meant. She could barely hear his words over the roaring in her skull.

And he did. He looked over the crowd and somehow embodied both the leader he once was and the abomination he'd become.

Anand gazed out at the crowd as he spoke. Her weapon rested in her right hand. When he finished, she scanned the crowd, one by one they looked up at her and nodded. The people she'd grown up with. The people her father had protected and loved. They knew the law as well as she did.

She gripped the weapon in both hands. Her father bowed his neck in anticipation. She brought it down, quick and heavy using all her weight to make it fast.

Blood spat back at her, getting into her eyes.

She turned from what she'd done, dropped to her knees and keened.

This is how you became a goddess.

*****

10:48 am, Oct. 28, 2020, 30 days after The Fog

Chiba pointed the bat at her.

"Are you a zombie? Vampire? Troll? Werewolf? Fae? Lych? Demon clown?"

"No."

Sam struggled to push herself off the shower floor. Her feet were stuck behind the toilet. Her mind couldn't solve the riddle of how to get them out.

"Are you going to try to eat me or any member of my family?" Chiba demanded, half yelling, half pleading.

"Oh, for fuck's sake. Look at me. I can't even get out of the fucking shower."

Sam's arms fought valiantly in their battle to let her sit up. They failed.

Chiba paused.

"That wasn't an answer. You could be trying to lull me into a false sense of security."

Sam met Chiba's wild eyes.

"No. I am not going to eat you or your kids or your husband."

"Or the dog?"

"Or the dog." Sam tried to laugh but her lungs rebelled. She coughed up black water and mud. She tried and failed, yet again, to turn over or get her feet out from behind the toilet.

"Oh, love, what happened?" Chiba flipped from grizzly to momma bear.

The two women were of similar, average height, dark hair and going a little soft around the belly in their middle age. Although, Chiba's was more from having two kids and Sam's was from general laziness. Sam's face was rounder, her skin paler and her eyes were an off-puttingly light, yet indescribable shade. While Chiba's soft brown eyes shone out of her warm brown complexion and resting bitch face.

After a decade of friendship, spending holidays together and both of them coming from shitty families, they had informally adopted each other as sisters.

Chiba wrapped her arms around Sam, pulled her up and dropped her onto the toilet.

"Honey, what happened?" She rubbed her back.

Sam pointed to the wood shelf just out of reach on the other side of the cramped room, unable to catch her breath. Her red, white and purple inhalers rested on the top.

"Which one?"

Sam made a panicked gathering gesture which Chiba understood to mean "All of them NOW."

Sam took hit after hit then leaned over the shower and puked more black sludge out of her lungs.

"The fuck. How are you alive?"

Sam didn't bother to answer, because, honestly, she wasn't so sure herself.

"Izzz okay," Sam gasped and took her first full breath in a month.

Oh, sweet oxygen. How I've longed for thee.

A glass of water appeared in her peripherals. Sam rinsed the mud out of her mouth and gulped the rest.

"You know I want to know where you've been for the past month but I don't want to pressure you and I'm a little afraid to ask."

"I was in the river. Sort of stuck."

Chiba picked a leaf out of her hair.

"Hey, I think I have protein bars in the cabinet," Sam said. "Could you get me one? Then I should have the energy to shower."

"Okay."

Chiba returned with three energy bars, a low step stool and a pile of clothes. She dropped the stool in the shower and put the clothes on the shelf.

"Here." She peeled open the bars and handed them to Sam one at a time.

"I can open them myself."

Chiba ignored her.

"You're not gonna be able to shower on your own."

"What? No, I'll be fine."

"Take off your shoe without falling over."

Sam stared at her remaining shoe – a sensible black mule. It felt several thousand miles away.

"You paused."

"Yes. Yes, I did."

"Can I help you, please?"

The food burned warm in Sam's belly and her breathing was almost normal but she couldn't unbend her spine. Sam wanted to relent but her base, pigheaded nature wouldn't let her.

"How 'bout this? I'll help you undress, put you on that stool, turn on the water, hand you soap and stand over here."

"Okay."

Sam's defeat filled the tiny room with immeasurable sorrow.

Chiba knew how much she hated this and said nothing as she gently but unceremoniously pulled off the ruined hoodie, jeans, then dropped her onto the stool.

Sam could feel Chiba's worry over her sagging skin.

"I'll be fine. I just need some food and sleep."

"Uh, huh."

Chiba handed her the soap without looking at her.

"Really. I'm fine."

"Uh, huh."

"You don't believe me."

"Can you blame me?"

"I cannot," Sam said, trying to shampoo her hair around the leaves – hoping somehow they would rinse out.

"Here. May I?"

"Okay."

Chiba picked leaves and sticks out of Sam's hair.

"I get that this looks bad."

Chiba snorted.

"And my explanation for where I've been for the past month isn't great."

Chiba snorted louder.

"And that the world has become a scary shit show since you last saw me."

Chiba sobbed a little.

Sam grabbed her friend's hand, and turned to meet her eyes.

"But I'm okay and I will help. It'll just take me some time to…" she gestured,

"Get stronger? But it should be better at night."

Chiba handed her a towel and faced her, hands on hips.

"I know you're not telling me anything but I can't tell if it's because you can't face it yet or haven't figured out how to tell me."

"I haven't figured out how to tell you.”

"Is it bad?" Chiba asked.

"Not exactly."

"Is it bad for me or my family?"

“Kinda, sorta, but not really."

"Sam. Not really?"

Sam pointed to the band on her wrist.

"Chibs, with that thing you're damn near immortal. Like there's two things it doesn't protect you from."

"Wait. WHAT!? What do you know about this thing!?"

This was when Sam realized, too late, that she had lost control of the conversation.

"Chiba, I'm exhausted. I have literal shit in my hair and I'm naked. I will tell you everything about that, where I've been and what happened, when I have clothes and some rest."

Sam knew Chiba wanted to vibrate out of her skin. She hated waiting, loathed not knowing and abjectly despised uncertainty.

Not that Sam could blame her, but she didn't have an explanation – at least, not one that would make sense in her current condition. What Chiba lacked in patience, she more than made up for in compassion. Sam could see the internal battle and when the light bulb went off over her head Sam knew she didn't have a way out.

"Okay, but can you at least tell me that it's not bad? It's not going to give me cancer or my soul hasn't been sold to some demon that's waiting to collect?"

Sam sighed.

"I need a towel for this," she said. Chiba handed her the big rainbow beach towel on the back of the door.

Here goes nothing.

"That," Sam waved at the black band again, "means you are under the personal protection of a *very* powerful being."

"Like, I'm their property? Like they're coming to collect."

"No." Sam rubbed her hair and configured the best way to break this to Chiba. "Okay, so less 'powerful' beings can't hurt you. Hell, they can't even get near you because that mark sort of loans you the 'powerful' being's protection. To other powerful beings, it's a warning. It means that to mess with you would provoke… well, would provoke war."

Sam shrugged.

"That's all."

Sam's Dad used to take her fishing. Chiba's slack jaw and empty eyes reminded her of the poor fish he'd haul out of the frozen lakes back home.

"That's all!!??" Chiba's voice got louder and higher with each syllable. "That. Is. ALL!? Sam. Who the FUCK put this on me?

Who put this on my kids? What "powerful" being are we talking about here??"

"Well." Sam met her best friend's gaze with bleary, exhausted eyes. "Me. We're talking about me, Chiba. I put that on you, and the kids, and Danny. Hell, even the dog has one."

*****

The Liminal Space

The Darkness has her.

It expects her to surrender, to be torn asunder and like it. Saying yes please and moan in compliance while dissolving into nothingness. Bashing itself against the insides of her skull.

This was the beginning.

She breathes out 'no.' It is a small thing. Tiny. A gasp... It is the music of a song she doesn't like. A voice that annoyed her. The very definition of what she is not.

No.

A whisper. And it got louder. And louder. The kernel of no got harder and grew, solid and smooth, spreading from the inside of her heart to the edges of her fingernails – slick and impenetrable.

The Darkness no longer had her. So she grabbed it by the throat and inhaled it – in defense, in revenge but mostly because she *could*. It wriggled in her lungs, fighting its way through her veins, her blood, her very cells until settling into an enraged, sleeping NO. Waiting. Waiting to burst forth from her sunken chest and reduce it all to ash – the lies, the shame, the pain.

The Darkness fears her.

*****

11:10 am, Oct. 28, 2020, 30 days after The Fog

Chiba didn't believe a word of it. Her therapist had once told her that PTSD could cause all kinds of delusions – like delusions of grandeur. The world may be fucked six ways to Sunday but there was no way the dirty, dehydrated mess in front of her was a god.

"Goddess."

"Okay, so what are you goddess of?"

"Lots of stuff," Sam said with a yawn.

After a protracted wrestling match, Chiba had managed to get her mostly dressed in shorts and a tank top with her new hoodie wrapped around her shoulders. Her shoes and purple compression knee socks were in Chiba's Mom Bag because the water was still ankle deep and wet socks were the worst.

"Darkness, Death, Justice, Abundance, Battle, Foresight, Lakes, Magic, Vengeance," Sam said. "There's more but those aren't very interesting."

"You're a goddess? Of death?"

"*The* Goddess of Death, but yeah." Sam's eyes crossed as she worked to pull another twig out of her hair. "You don't believe me."

"How many leaves and twigs do you have in there?"

"All of them."

They laughed, too hard and too long. The anger and awkwardness disappeared into the familiar.

"Wherever you were, you couldn't get out, you couldn't call?"

"They do not have cell reception in the Liminal Space, Chibs."

Chiba's bravado dropped.

"I was so worried about you. I was so scared."

"I know, love, and I'm so sorry," Sam said. "If I could have reached you, I would have."

"I don't know what happened to you, but I believe you believe it and that's what's important," Chiba said. She reached across the table and patted her friend's arm. "And when you're ready to talk about it, I'm here for you."

Sam wanted to tell Chiba that everything from here on out would be a lot easier if she just had some faith in her, for once, but she knew this was not in Chiba's nature.

Sam chomped down on the rest of the granola bar.

"Thank you," she said around a mouthful. "I will."

Chiba stood back in Mom Mode. She put her hands on her yoga-pants-clad hips.

"We should head back down," she said. "I don't want to get stuck out there at night."

"I'm going with you?"

"Of course, you are." Chiba grabbed more bars from the counter and shoved them in her Mom Bag. Then she refilled Sam's water bottle. "I'm not leaving you up here all by yourself. You need to come home."

"This isn't my home?"

Chiba snorted.

"This is your lair, or nest, or whatever you want to call it," she said. "Your home is with us. You know that."

Sam swallowed and fought back tears. It had been so long – thousands of years – since she'd heard that.

"Okay, Mom." Sam chewed the granola harder to push down the sobs.

"Yup." Chiba rubbed her hands together. "I'm still your mom/soul sister/daughter/best friend. Can you stand? Or am I carrying you down the stairs?"

Sam stood.

"I can walk." She took two steps, toppled into the table and puked up the last of the black water from her lungs.

The clash of metal and screams. The metallic blood in her mouth that she isn't sure is her own. This feeling. This feeling of swinging axes at her back, dodging knives. The rush of wind telling her she's in danger. Being in this moment and this moment alone. All the triumphant murder. Her enemies weeping at her feet. She... she... she loves this.

Sam wiped the dregs away and rubbed her hand off on her hoodie before Chiba noticed the blood mixed with river water.

"Oh, honey," Chiba rubbed her back. "Do you want me to try carrying you?"

"Naw, I'm good."

"Sam." Chiba's tone of voice made it clear that she was not going to tolerate her bullshit in this matter.

"Okay," Sam said. "How about you help me?"

They managed to not fall down the stairs or over the skeletal railing. Chiba deposited Sam gracelessly into the Orange Monstrosity's pull cart.

Chiba unlocked the bike and settled in.

"Hey," Sam waved her arms, "don't shakensmoncreekshammointon."

"What?"

Sam poked one eye out from under the black hood. She was three-quarters asleep already. The same thing happened the last time Sam got a lung infection. Chiba had to drag her down the stairs. Then she tucked Sam in beneath five blankets in her guest room and mom-guilted her into eating chicken soup until she was strong enough to run away.

"Don't. Take. Stone. Creek. Down. The. Mountain. Izshangerous," Sam said. She nodded as though she'd just said something deeply profound, pulled the hood over both eyes and passed all the way out.

The fuck is that supposed to mean?

Chiba had a terrible sense of direction – even when there wasn't an apocalypse. Stone Creek was the only route she had memorized. She knew of other routes but she wasn't comfortable with the idea of getting lost in the dark. Vampires hunted around here at night. While the band protected Chiba, it only protected Sam if she was within a few feet of her.

Also, vampires bounced. Chiba shivered. She remembered the first night of The Fog. Dozens of shrieking wraiths ran at her so fast they left after images burned into her retinas, bouncing off the invisible shield around her. It reminded her of birds flying into picture windows. Even the sound was the same: **THONK**.

Chiba hated vampires. So she decided on Stone Creek.

How could Sam know anything about it anyway? Right?

She ignored clanging internal alarm bells and peddled down the steep hill leading from Sam's house to Stone Creek drive.

Redwood Valley had always been a sleepy burg. The town existed because it was conveniently located between Silicon Valley and the ocean. As a result, it didn't have a heart but two main arteries the commuters used to get to either work or Sunset Cove. The veins of neighborhoods shot off from the main roads but were disconnected from each other, cut off by mountains, valleys, forests or rivers – all jammed into ten-square miles.

Chiba always found Redwood Valley disturbing, perhaps even more so now because The Fog hadn't changed it all that much.

Demon kids still ran up and down the hills. Parents eyed her from their driveways but kept to themselves. Only now the people judging her had scales or were dead.

If it hadn't been the end of the world, it would have been a lovely autumn day.

Chiba tried to focus on the crunch of orange and red leaves under the bike tire and the crisp, dry smell of wood smoke so she could ignore the dread creeping up her spine.

Her therapist would have lectured her for ignoring her friend's boundaries.

Is it a boundary if she's delusional and I have to get her to safety as quick as possible?

And what if she's right?

Chiba glanced behind her. Sam's head lolled off the edge of the cart – nodding in agreement with each bump in the road. She realized she'd never seen that hoodie before. It glinted and rippled like a patch of moonlight in the middle of the afternoon.

So she was a little distracted when the metal cage dropped over them.

Chiba yelled as the front tire slammed into the metal bars. She stood on the brakes but the inertia propelled her forward. Her face smashed into solid metal. She bounced back, sitting hard on the Orange Monstrosity's top tube – bruising her vulva.

"Yaaaaaaaaaggggghghh!!!"

Chiba pinwheeled, and through several feats of balance and strength that included minor internal organ damage, managed to keep the bike upright.

"The fuck?"

Sam pulled the hoodie off and sat up.

Chiba did not handle surprises well. Chiba did not handle pain well and Chiba very much did not handle being trapped well. She yanked the baseball bat out of the sling and swung at the bars.

"What the FUCK is this bullshit!" The world around her clanged. She set up again.

"Get me out of here! Mother fucker! I hate this. Do you fucking hear me! I will rip your face off and feed it to you."

"Chiba!"

She beat the cage until her arms hurt.

"Chiba!" Sam yelled again. She grabbed the top of the bat. "Who are you yelling at?"

"I don't know!" Chiba said. "Everyone? Where the hell did this come from?"

Sam looked around.

"This is Stone Creek, isn't it?"

Chiba's mouth fell open.

"Uhh…"

"You didn't listen to me?"

"Are you saying it's my fault we're trapped? Is that what you're saying?" Chiba felt tears coming on.

"Chiba."

"You're right. I didn't listen to you because you're saying you're a god," Chiba said, throwing up her arms in frustration.

"... Goddess, actually," Sam, oh so unhelpfully, interjected.

"And you know how much my sense of direction sucks."

"You do get lost everywhere."

"And now we're going to die and it's my fault," Chiba said. "This is a vampire trap isn't it?"

She wailed on the bars a few more times because it made her feel better, and really, the times called for it. She was also avoiding looking at Sam. It was her fault. She'd just gotten her back and now she was going to lose her again.

"Would you stop, please? The whacking is giving me a headache."

Sam leaned against the Orange Monstrosity, rubbing her temples and assessed the situation. They were trapped in what appeared to be an over-sized birdcage. The more Sam examined it – from the solid edges to the bent ceiling, the more she was convinced it was actually a birdcage spelled to giant proportions.

The vampires have a witch. A strong one too - if this is any indication.

The cage had been suspended from one of the old redwoods. Likely, a giant held the rope and let go at just the right moment. Sam heard massive rumbling as the giant ambled away. They had to be at least fifty-feet tall by the sound of snapping branches.

The fuckers are organized. I'll give 'em that.

"I'm so sorry," Chiba said and gave her a determined, yet fatalistic look. "I will get us out of here. I promise."

There was not a snowball's chance in hell she was going to do that, but it was cute of her to think so.

"We'll be fine."

Chiba held up her arm and rolled up her sleeve – flashing the band.

"I'll protect you," she said. "You just have to stay close to me. Don't get further than three feet away and they can't touch you."

Sam didn't tell Chiba that the vampires were probably going to try to smoke her out, using one of the band's few weaknesses, until she was so disoriented that she lost sight of Sam or gave her up to save herself.

"Do you remember the time we went to that Indian place?" Sam asked, as she settled back into the cart.

Chiba wedged the bat between the bars trying to make the opening between them larger.

"Why are you bringing this up now?"

"Because I'm going to ask you to do everything you hate," Sam said.

"Sam…"

"We were driving to the Indian place -"

"And you couldn't remember the name so I couldn't look up directions," Chiba interrupted.

"And I told you to trust me," Sam shot back.

"You couldn't even tell me the street it was on. I was not being unreasonable."

Sam leveled her steeliest gaze at her best friend.

"Did you, or did you not, have the best butter chicken of your life that day?"

"You cannot compare this," Chiba said and spun around, pointing at the twelve-feet of real estate within a sixteen-foot tall, cheap, gold cage planted in the middle of abandoned tarmac, "to me not trusting you about getting *us* to *the* Indian place."

Sam pointed at her.

"It's exactly the same," Sam said. "I am The Morrigan, Chiba. I will get us both out of this just fine. But first, I need a nap. I have to sleep and rest to be strong enough to get us home. So I'm going to ask you to sit tight until nightfall and let me take care of this."

Chiba stared up at the top of the cage. Sam knew she was fighting tears and a panic attack.

"I hate everything about this. As a trauma survivor…"

"I know."

Sam's gaze was not unsympathetic.

"I think you might be delusional," Chiba said. "I think you just went through so much trauma…" The dam holding it all together for the past month cracked.

"I didn't, Chiba," she said. "I was fine. I was safe."

If Sam had the energy, she would have pulled her sorry ass out of the cart and hugged her because she knew about all the times Chiba hadn't been fine and wasn't safe.

"If you're a god-"

"Goddess."

"Why are you so weak?" Chiba wiped away tears with her jacket sleeve. "Why do you have pneumonia again?"

Sam tilted her head back against the cart. The sun spat its rays at her. She glared at it.

Fucking Day Star.

No, wait. Blessings on my brother and his house, or whatever.

She met Chiba's worried brown eyes and pursed lips.

"It's like being born, right?" Sam said. "Becoming a goddess takes time and you have to marinate in the Liminal Space. Well, I left early. I left marinating early."

"Are you saying you're a preemie goddess?" Chiba smiled.

"Basically, yes."

"Why did you leave early?"

Sam pulled the hood tighter over her head to ward off the sun's accusations.

"I forgot to do something and it was time sensitive."

Fuck, did she sound lame. It was the truth though. She'd forgotten something so important. It was a debt she couldn't leave unpaid, but it sounded like she'd ducked out of Goddess School early because she wanted to play hookie.

"Did you leave the oven on? You left the oven on didn't you?"

"I'm going back to sleep now, Chiba."

"So you want me to just sit here and wait for pointy, vampire death while you sleep?"

"Yup."

"I hate everything about this," Chiba said.

"I know."

"This is torture, Sam. This is literally torture for me. I can't just sit here. I'll go insane."

Sam knew then that the battle was won.

"You can talk to Carl."

She pointed without looking from under the hoodie.

"Carl?"

CAAAAW.

Chiba jumped, spun and grabbed her heart. Behind her was the biggest fucking raven she had ever seen. At nearly three feet tall, it glistened in every oil slick shade of black.

"Carl, Chiba. Chiba, Carl." Sam waved like a drunk orchestra conductor.

The creature, because Chiba wasn't sure it could be classified as a bird – with its razor claws and giant, curved, snapping beak seemed to be … judging her.

"Carl, Chiba's having a rough time right now," Sam said from within her hoodie. "Please take care of her. I'm going to rest."

Caww. CAAAAW. caw.

The sounds coming out of the creature's maw could only be described as a dying cat puking up rusty gears.

"Don't be judgmental," Sam said. She pulled her hood away from her face to lecture him. "This is stressful for her. Be nice for once."

Caaaa.

With every verbalization, the bird shrugged and the ruff under its chin doubled in size.

"Sam????"

"No, that's a good idea," Sam said through a yawn. "You should get her some branches. She can make stakes. That'll keep her occupied. She'll need a knife though."

Chiba could not stop staring at the raven.

Sam contorted and pulled a six-inch, death blade from the inside back of her hoodie.

CAAAAAAAAAWWW.

"This? This is the Blade of a Thousand Cuts? Are you sure? I thought it had a brown handle." Sam examined the serrated knife, sheathed in black leather. "I really need to label these."

Caw.

"Okay, well, get her a knife too, then, and a label maker for later, please."

Caw. Cawwww. Cawwww.

"I can *so* be trusted with a label maker, *Carl*!"

"Sam!"

Sam was pretty sure Chiba's eyes weren't ever going to go all the way back into her skull.

"Please don't freak out."

"I am not freaking out," Chiba said, freaking out in every corner of her soul.

"Carl'll take care of whatever you need. He can be a pretty good listener when he's not being an ass."

Caw.

"You heard me."

"Sam…"

Chiba had never wanted anything in her life as much as she wanted this entire situation to go away. She'd spent most of the day needing something normal, ordinary even. She missed her kids. She was hungry and tired. Her vulva hurt like she'd given birth two weeks ago and now her best friend had lost her damn mind.

"This is some fucked up bullshit, Sam."

"I love you."

"It's still bullshit."

"Yeah, I know."

CAW.

*****

3:33 pm Nov. 1, 750 B.C.E., 2,769 years before The Fog

They came to her under the guise of concern and helpfulness. These men with gray beards, big robes, short swords and junk, shifty eyes.

"We heard about what happened. I am so sorry. Please let us know if there's anything we can do to help."

Arthmael the Red had once knocked her father unconscious for looking at his daughter sideways. In retrospect, that seemed way less crazy than it did at the time, but now he was *sorry*?

Rutting dogs had more subtlety.

"We are fine, Arthmael," she said. "I do appreciate the concern."

She sat on her father's stool, holding court and damn Arthmael's eyes for expecting anything less of her.

"Well, my dear child."

"I am not your dear child."

Anand had zero time for his bullshit and even less patience.

"Last I checked, I have a birthmark on the side of my ass just like my father before me and his mother before him," she said. "Do you have a birthmark on the side of your ass, Arthmael the Red?"

In the squinty half light, she could tell she played a game of wits with an unarmed man. But he was a big fucker. His neck was thicker than the post holding up the ceiling.

"No…"

"So then, I canna be your 'dear child' now can I?"

Her father had told her that when a man is about to hit you, his entire being pulls into a point, like a storm gathering, like the tip of a knife, like the pinpoints of rage in Arthmael the Red's beady blue eyes. Anand was quick – always had been. In moments of battle, the world around her slowed. She grinned to herself as his meaty fist brushed a strand of her curly, dark, brown hair when she sidestepped. He put his full mass into the punch and expected to land the blow. The lack of connection over-balanced him. He stumbled into the heavy, wooden dining table and cursed a blue streak when he barked his shin.

"So help me, girl," he said. Then Arthmael the Red reached for her throat. She swerved again as a giant raven, black as night, and shrieking like the souls of the damned, landed on the table.

Colman, one of her father's men, bless his drunken, half-blind ass, gasped and pointed.

"The Goddess is angry! She does not approve."

Anand took advantage of the distraction. She drew her long knife from behind her back and set it at the old man's throat.

"The Goddess does not approve," she said. "Get back."

Arthmael the Red put his hands up, consolation dripping from them.

"Now, girl."

"Call me a girl one more time and I'll bathe in your heart's blood."

Arthmael the Red and his lackeys backed away. His four men appeared to wrestle with the common sense need to listen to the woman with the knife and their 'manly instinct' try to overpower her. Lucky for them, common sense won out.

"You'll leave us and never return," she said.

They backed out of the door into the cool autumn light where their horses stood, an invitation for them to leave.

Arthmael the Red grinned at her. His crooked, rotten teeth were a threat to her life, her people and her very soul.

He mounted his horse.

"Oh, I'll leave, little girl, for now," he said. "But when I return, you'll regret crossing me and mine."

As they rode away, the raven flew over their heads and shit on Arthmael the Red's back.

*****

6:15 pm, Oct. 28, 2020, 30 days after The Fog

The bird was much better company than Chiba anticipated. It brought her several stout branches and a decent enough knife. He even brought her a couple apples to munch on. Sam, true to her word, passed out in the fetal position inside the cart with as much of her body tucked beneath her hoodie as she could manage. Her feet were still bare. Chiba took off her jacket and draped it over Sam's legs.

The Morrigan, huh?

All Chiba knew of The Morrigan was that she was some kind of ancient, Celtic goddess – very dark and war-like. Chiba pictured a sharp-featured, clear-eyed, statuesque woman with a hooded cloak and a raven on her shoulder. If Sam was The Morrigan, Chiba was a burrito. The bird and the new hoodie were coincidental. She'd known Sam for almost a decade and had once seen her move a caterpillar off a picnic table and take it to a tree forty feet away because "it looked hungry and somebody might squish it." On more than one occasion, Sam had stated that she wasn't fond of birds because they were "tiny, angry dinosaurs."

Goddess of Death, my ass.

But … where had the knife come from? Why didn't the bird fly away?

Maybe Sam had gained the ability to talk to animals in The Fog and wherever she was, whatever had happened to her, she'd picked this identity of The Morrigan as a protection against trauma? Or Carl was a human who had been turned into a raven? Maybe, he and Sam had escaped whoever had kidnapped her and that is why he understood her and wouldn't leave? Maybe, Sam told her not to go this way because this is where she'd been kidnapped?

Oh, fuck. Oh, fuck. Oh, fuck.

The sun dropped below the horizon. Like some obnoxious postcard, the trees were perfect black silhouettes against the blazing orange, yellow and red sky. The temperature fell ten degrees. Chiba really wanted her coat back. She glanced at Sam and realized she looked better. The hollows of her cheeks filled out and in the muddled, gray light her skin became taut and healthy. Even her breathing eased. The wheezing, asthmatic rattle disappeared.

Unless. **Unless.** *The vampires bit Sam and she was changing into one of them. That's why she could barely move during the day. It was a trap! She was trapped in a cage with a turning vampire – who was also her best friend.*

Chiba pulled the stake close to her chest and pointed it at Sam. The supposed vampire in question rolled over, sat up and stretched.

"How are you holding up?"

She twisted her neck, like she was just some normal person rolling out of bed after a nap.

"Fine," Chiba said in the World's Tiniest Voice.

Sam glanced at the stake and Chiba's posture.

"You decided that I'm a vampire and you might need to stake me, didn't you?"

"Yes." Miraculously, Chiba's voice got tinier.

Sam stood up on her own which did nothing for Chiba's peace of mind.

"I told you, Chibs." Sam pointed at herself and twirled. "This guy? Queen of the Darkness and look, look at you, you glorious darkness."

Sam radiated joy and vitality as she spun again.

"Oh, such a beautiful night." She threw her arms up. "Yes, I mean you. Look at how beautiful you are! All these twinkling stars. So glorious!"

"Sam?"

Chiba pointed a stake at her. Sam could feel her tension vibrate the cage around them.

"There's a simple way to check that I'm not a vampire." She stepped towards her, hand outstretched for a shake. "If I'm dangerous, I'll bounce right off, right? No harm? No foul?"

Their world shifted. A clang rang through Chiba's bones. The vampires had arrived. They tipped the cage on its side and formed a half circle around them. Sam and Chiba were trapped. Without a thought, Chiba grabbed Sam's hand, yanked her close, wrapped her arm tight around her waist and pointed the stake at the vampires.

"Stay the hell away from her!" Chiba yelled.

Sam couldn't help herself. She grinned at Chiba.

"What?" Chiba demanded, seeing the look.

"I'm just really proud of you. I'm so glad you're my friend." Sam fought back a tear.

Chiba tightened her grip on Sam's waist.

"Family. You're my family."

"Family," Sam agreed. Then she gave up and shed a small tear.

The vampires, it seemed, were not having such a sweet moment. Sam focused on the half dozen creatures. The month since The Fog had not been kind to them. She wasn't sure how they could talk let alone move. The sinews holding their bones together were visible through their translucent skin. Their clothes were distant gray tatters. The speed of their movements burnt through most fabrics. All of the vampires were bald. Their hair had fallen out ages ago.

Starving. They're all starving.

"Leo said the one without the band was sick! He said she stank like death."

Sam couldn't tell the difference between any of them – except that this one was a little shorter and less translucent than the one they were yelling at.

"Well, she's not dying, is she? Look at her."

"But she's human, right?"

The six of them sniffed the air. They pointed at Chiba.

"That one's human."

"And scared." It grinned. All of its teeth except the top incisors had fallen out – a cross between a meth addict and a rattlesnake.

From the back, came the voice of reason:

"Doesn't matter if she's sick or not," it said, sounding less snake-like and younger than the others. "We're starving. If we don't drink soon, we'll die."

"How do we separate them?"

They writhed closer then retreated – intoxicated by blood but still together enough to be afraid of the band on Chiba's arm.

The tallest one closed his eyes and swayed.

"That one smells." He pointed a skeletal arm at Sam. "She… something's not right, Cora."

Cora stepped forward out of the shadows. She was small, shorter than Sam and Chiba but clearly the leader.

"What do you mean not right?" Cora asked. "Can we eat her or not?"

"Over my dead body!" Chiba yelled.

Sam flinched because she knew what the response would be.

"Fine," Cora hissed. "We'll burn this forest and smoke you out. When you're dying, you'll hand her over or pass out and we'll eat you both."

Sam gave herself a mental pat on the back for figuring out their plan. She assumed the really bad element in town would have figured out the band's weaknesses and learned to exploit them. She loved it when she got it right. Although, she didn't love being talked about like she was on the evening's menu. Chiba sobbed and dug her hand into Sam's side.

"I have a compromise," Sam said and held up her hands. She wasn't sure why, but it seemed like the kind of thing a hostage negotiator would do.

"No one cares, snack!" The tallest vamp spat at her.

"Okay," Sam said. "One. Thank you. Two. I'm a whole meal and you know it."

She tried to step away from Chiba, but she followed her – snagging her hoodie.

"Nononononononono," Chiba said. "You don't understand."

Sam pulled her hands away from the garment.

"Chiba, it's okay. I got this."

Sam stepped outside the ring of safety. Chiba screamed.

What happened next went by faster than Chiba's brain could process. She couldn't be certain it was real or not but the after images were burned into her eyes. Sam flung vampires hundreds of feet in the air and shoved them back. Sam dropped one into the ground so hard he was half buried.

All Chiba really knew was that in the time it took her to blink, the vampires stopped attacking. Sam held the tallest one by the throat. Her fingernails penetrated the waxy skin of his neck. He clawed at her. His feet couldn't get purchase. In the dim light, black tendrils crept from Sam's nails and spread through the flesh of the vampire's face.

Chiba had never seen her look like that – the blank coldness, the utter apathy at calculating the end of him.

Cora stepped out of the shadows.

"Don't," she pleaded, without sentiment or hope. "Please. Don't. He's starving. We're all starving. We try to only take the sick or the dying but we're so, so hungry. He doesn't deserve to die. It's not his fault he's like this."

Sam turned and leveled that blank stare at Cora. She dropped the tall vampire.

"You're right," she said.

As quick as that, Chiba's best friend came back. Sam reached into her hoodie and pulled out a metal thermos.

"The compromise," Sam said. She tucked the thermos under her armpit. Twisting, Sam pulled out what appeared to be either a really long knife or a really short sword and dropped the thermos.

Chiba laughed – too loud and nervous. She clamped a hand over her mouth to stifle the hysterics bubbling over.

Sam picked up the thermos and tucked it under her armpit again. She angled the knife over the center of her forearm and slashed down. Inky liquid spilled out in long ribbons. The vampires hissed and writhed. Sam held up one finger.

"Stay," she ordered.

Sam let streams of blood dribble into the thermos. She spat into the metal canister. Then she etched a strange symbol into its metal side with her fingernail, spun the lid shut, shook the bottle three times and knelt over the vampire. Threads of darkness crawled up his neck. Unable to speak, the undead, desiccated creature dug his claws into his throat trying – without success – to cut the tendrils out of him. Chiba never imagined they could die, let alone that it would bother her so much to see one suffering.

"Here," Sam said as she held the thermos to his lips. He tried to push her hands away. The vampire coughed up black sludge. The rank stench of decay made Chiba's stomach recoil. Any more stress and she would lose her guts too.

Sam sat back on her heels.

"You're right. I'm sorry. I shouldn't have done that. I lost my temper. I'm sorry I did that to you but if you don't drink this soon, you'll die. It will not be a good death."

Sam held out the canister to him again. He nodded and sipped. The sipping turned to gulping. The vampire fell backward as he poured the contents down his gullet.

The transformation took less than thirty seconds. Stringy hair began to shine. Gaunt, hollowed out cheeks became flush. It reminded Chiba of a balloon filling with air. Muscles fleshed out and flexed. Everything about the vampire went from decay to vibrant, seductive health. Chiba stepped towards the tall, now-handsome, red-haired man before her.

What am I doing?

The other vampires wailed in frustration. Cora seemed both happy and despondent in her quiet little way.

"Thank you," she murmured to Sam as she bent down to pick up the discarded thermos.

The male vampire was too busy admiring his arms. Sam held it out to Cora. The object made a mysterious gurgling noise.

"It has unlimited refills."

Cora snatched it out of Sam's hand quicker than Chiba could see. The vampires passed around the blood canister with strange shrieking noises.

Sam noticed Chiba's look.

"They're talking faster than you can hear."

Chiba couldn't help herself.

"What are they saying? Can you tell?"

"They're talking about how good it is. 'I'm getting cherries and chocolate.' 'You think? It's completely different for me. I keep tasting lemongrass and sour apple.' 'That's so weird. I think it tastes like honey-oat cereal.'"

Chiba turned green.

"But that… but that's your blood," she said and grabbed Sam's arm.

"Sort of…" Sam hemmed and hawed. "It's kinda hard to explain."

At that, Chiba took a long, silent look at Sam and screamed. She screamed out all the rage, the uncertainty and pain of the past month.

The vampires jumped and started. Sam held up a hand to them.

"Nope, it's okay," she said. "She's earned this."

The undead shrugged and drank their fill.

Chiba's scream eventually wound down into a coughing fit. Sam handed her a bottle of water.

"Feel better?"

"Thank you. No, not really."

Chiba drank from the bottle, wondered where Sam had gotten it and decided to give up on figuring anything out until morning. She shivered – exhausted and done.

"Can we go now?"

"Sure," Sam said. "Sorry. I just need to finish up with them for a minute "

She stepped back towards Cora and took on the attitude of a football coach.

"Okay, Cora," Sam said. "Couple things: One: You can pour that into a metal container that is touching the Earth and that container will always be full. *However,* that metal container can never be moved after that. Never. Not once. Got it? The thermos will always be filled but I figure you all could use some extra.".

"Thank you," Cora said.

The blood meal turned her into a small, young woman with long, curly, dark hair and a serious expression.

"Two," Sam said in that overly gruff tone. "I expect you to share with your fellow vampires."

The shrieking angst started from all corners with that. Cora held up a hand.

"We don't have a problem with sharing with most of our community but..."

The lanky redhead finished the thought:

"Some of them are Nazis."

"There are rumors that some of them are Nazis," Cora said.

Sam didn't seem surprised.

"I will take care of that tomorrow," she said. "Any vamps that show up will not be Nazis and I'll try to make more of these," she waved at the thermos "in the coming days..."

Sam stared off into the distance.

"Was there something else?" Cora asked.

"Oh, right. Yes. Try to help people out where you can and when the full moon starts round up all the werewolves, bring them to the cemetery off Whispering Pines and keep them there."

"All night?"

"Yeah." Sam rubbed her eyes. "All night. I should have something figured out by then. Oh, also, I don't know what you've got on the witch and the giant helping you but let them go."

Sam was losing steam by the second. She stumbled back but caught herself.

Chiba felt panic rising again. She blinked and the tall redhead was at Sam's side.

"Here." He held out his arm for her. She took it and leaned in.

"Okay, thass all I got right noww."

"The witch and the giant are my parents," Cora said. Sam wobbled.

"If you wouldn't mind, he can escort you both home." Cora nodded to Chiba.

The redhead was already leading Sam back to the bike.

"I guess…?"

"You'll be safe," she said "We're only a danger when we're hungry. Tynan will be glad to make sure you get home safe."

Sam patted his arm as she collapsed backwards into the bike cart.

"Thass a good Tuna…"

The trip back down the mountain was, shockingly, uneventful. Tynan ran ahead of the bike a few times and seemed bored by his escort duties. He tried to make idle chit chat with Chiba but she shut that down quick. Making small talk with a vampire after the apocalypse was beyond her at the moment. Tynan gave up and speed walked in silence. Sam open-mouth snored the entire ride.

Chiba could not collect her thoughts. They ran around inside her skull – bumping into one another and falling down. About halfway down the mountain, she stopped thinking altogether and breathed the cold mountain air.

When they turned onto Chiba's street, Tynan gasped and stopped.

"Whoa," he said.

Chiba braked.

"What?"

"You don't see it? You can't feel it?" He rubbed his head, like he was fighting a headache. "Right, you're human."

"What is it?" Chiba had enough of "it" for several lifetimes.

"Is that your house?" He pointed at her two-story, ranch-style house with white stucco and brown shutters.

"How did you know that?"

"It's lit up like a Christmas tree," he said. He put his hand out and turned his head away from it.

"What are you talking about?"

The house looked like it always did – porch light, patch of lawn, two car-garage and a doormat that read: "GO AWAY!"

"I dunno," he said. "I don't think I can get too close to it. I'll take you as far as I can, okay?"

"Okay," Chiba said and filed this under the ever growing list of: 'I'm too tired to deal with this right now but I will grill Sam about it in the morning.'

They got to her driveway and Tynan became more agitated. He hissed and fluttered.

"I can't go any further."

"Iss okaaa, Tuna," Sam piped up from the cart. "We're good from herrrrrre."

Tynan waved and disappeared into the night.

Chiba rode up the driveway, hit the garage door opener and parked inside. Danny rushed through the door as she stopped.

"Chiba!" he said. "Are you OK? What the hell? I was out of my mind."

Chiba's six-foot, three-inch tall, bearded-bear of a husband was an absolute mess. His brown eyes were red from tears and his voice was too loud and high pitched.

"Issss it my fault, Danny," Sam said and waved her hand in that extravagant way. Vanna White would be jealous.

The color drained from his face.

"Sam!" He ran to her as she tried to stand up.

In the ensuing chaos, Sam fell out of the cart and scraped her hand on the garage floor. Danny then picked her up. He wrapped one arm around her and the other around Chiba in a big hug. Chiba warned him not to be so loud as to wake up the girls.

He wiped away tears and kissed the top of Sam's head.

"I'm just so happy to see you," he said. "Did Chiba tell you how worried we were? We were so worried. How did you find her? Where were you? What happened?"

He squeezed Sam until her back popped.

"Okay," she patted his arm, "bones are fragile."

"Sorry." He pulled away. Sam tilted towards the ground.

"Oh, Danny, help her please," Chiba said. "She's not very stable."

"What's wrong?"

"She's got pneumonia."

"Again?" He wrapped his arm around Sam's waist and held her up.

"Can we stop with the 'again' please?" Sam's head lolled against his shoulder as she fought for consciousness. "Isss not like I get pneumonia all the time."

Chiba followed them up the steps into the house.

"Is it three? I'm counting three times. Guest room?" he asked Chiba over his shoulder.

"Guest room," she said with a nod.

"Maybe four?"

Sam held up a hand to count but gave up as Danny dragged her up the stairs.

"Fffff, it's not four," she said. "I don't remember exactly and I'm too tired to count, but it's not four."

"You're too tired because you have pneumonia."

"Your face has pneumonia."

"Your actual face has pneumonia," Danny said.

"It's my lungs, not my face."

"Like that's better?"

Chiba listened to their banter fade away up the stairs. She collapsed onto the couch, shoved her face into a pillow and sobbed.

*****

1 am, Nov. 2, 750 B.C.E., 2,769 years before The Fog

Anand knew Arthmael would take the path home that led around the lake. He and his six clansmen would camp overnight at the lake's edge.

She had watched the men disappear into the forest and made a show of feeling poorly and needing to rest. Not a soul believed her and not a soul said so out loud.

She waited until sunset and rode her horse at full gallop along the same path as Arthmael and his goons.

She stopped more than a mile away from the edge of the lake.

She pulled her horse off the path and tied him to a branch out of sight. Anand paused. She drank in the night and its sounds.

Arthmael the Red would not stop trying to take over her lands and he was deeply stupid. Half his people died last winter for lack of food. Anand learned of it all too late to help. She knew his fields were well-appointed but he'd let his ego get the better of him and had sent his people off on stupid skirmishes instead of farming. Her people would starve under his rule. He would then tell them their hunger was the fault of their neighbors and use his piss-poor judgment as an excuse to attack.

The problem of men is their arrogance. Their lack of care.

Anand pulled her hood over her head and hurried to find the path that circled to the far side of the lake. Navigating in the darkness had always been easy for her.

When she reached the water, she stripped off her clothes, bundled them into her cloak and tucked it behind a rock at the edge of the forest. She took a handful of mud at the edge of the lake and smeared it around her eyes and cheeks.

Anand waded into the frigid water, sword clenched in her fist.

Arthmael the Red's guards, she knew, were as big and dumb as he was. She was betting her life that the one man on guard would watch the forest and not the lake.

Anand slunk low in the water, walking until the iciness covered her chin. Their fire burned cheery and warm a hundred yards away.

She went numb after a few excruciating minutes. The cold stabbed at her arms and made her teeth chatter. She breathed deep, calming the icy panic in her body.

The numbness would make her reaction time slower. She would need to factor that into her calculations. Cold fish brushed her legs and water grass tried to trip her. Rocks and pebbles dug into the flesh of her feet.

She had never believed the stories that something terrible lived in these waters. Anand refused to indulge the idea that a thing she had never seen nor touched could stop her.

The camp was still. Anand waited for a moment. No one came. She tilted her head back, looked at the stars for what might be the last time and in a silent murmur asked the night, the lake and any ancestor that might be listening, to please, please help her do what must be done.

She stalked out of the water – pushing slowly to not make waves and crouching so her head was just above the surface until the last moment.

The night air blasted her body and she bit her cheeks bloody to keep her teeth together.

Their low fire beckoned. A half mountain of a man sat before it.

The rest of the party lay still just within sight of the flames. Anand stopped just outside of the ring of light and listened. Then she heard it. The man at the fire, the one standing between her people and slow, agonizing death – *snoring*.

She snickered.

Still, she crouched low and slow behind him. Anand angled her arm just so and pulled her blade's tip in and across his throat.

He never woke up.

She lowered his massive torso to the rocks and went for her next victim. This one was already on the ground. His eyes fluttered and a gurgle escaped his lips as steaming blood spilled down his throat onto the muddy ground.

Anand did not enjoy this. Nor did she dislike it. Death was a task to be done – like sweeping or planning the harvest.

None of the men stirred. She slit Arthmael the Red's throat and moved on to the final sleeping man.

He was awake.

His thin face turned white in the firelight as he shrieked. All elbows and knees, he scrambled away from her, slipping on the slick rocks. He bolted for the horses.

It dawned on Anand how she must appear to him – naked, covered in blood and mud.

She pointed her sword at him, rolled her eyes back in her skull and screamed.

He keened and fell backward, crawling to the horses.

She waited by the fire until the sound of hooves and shrieks disappeared into the night.

Anand straightened her spine and walked back into the water.

Somehow, the return trip was colder and harder. The water weighed on her limbs. Every movement was torturous. She knew this meant trouble and pulled at every ounce of her will to get to her clothes. Her hands shook so bad she almost couldn't get dressed.

The ruckus, thankfully, hadn't disturbed her horse. She found him right where she'd left him.

By the time she'd returned him to the stable, gotten into her night clothes and into bed, the fever raged in earnest. Anand greeted the next day coughing and aching. The sickness she'd faked for an alibi became real.

The lone survivor ranted to anyone about how a naked goddess had appeared and slit his companion's throats. His clan assumed he'd murdered Arthmael the Red in a bid to take over.

They stoned him to death a few days later.

Anand took months to recover.

No man came around asking if she needed help again.

This was the first time you got pneumonia.

*****

9:35 am, Oct. 29, 2020, 31 days after *The Fog*

The door to Chiba and Danny's guest room did not lock. Its simple door knob was woefully ill-suited to provide any privacy in a house with two little girls.

About two years ago, on the first night Sam crashed over at this house, she put her backpack in front of the door in an abundance of caution and foresight. She was awakened, promptly, at 9 am the next morning by Zara who pushed open the door and began lecturing her, in a way that only a five year old who isn't mad, just disappointed, can.

"Why is there a backpack here, Auntie?" Zara didn't stop to hear the answer. "I could trip."

Chiba and Danny's guest room, like every guest room, was a repository of all the crap that didn't fit any place else in the house. It also had an air mattress.

Danny's board games sat on the top of the high shelf in the corner. Nothing matched. A lamp with four bulbs was the only light in the room – only two of them worked. Chiba's action figures cluttered the rest of the shelves and desk space. A couple cardboard boxes sat below the lone window.

Last night, she'd moved a desk chair in front of the door. It was, admittedly, a half-assed effort, but she was the Goddess of Battle. Men wept in terror at the mention of her holy name and she would be *damned* before she surrendered.

"There's a chair."

"Malak, we're not supposed to be here."

A brief scuffle began as the elder sister tried to pull the younger back before realizing the door was open already anyway and since she didn't do it, she wouldn't get into trouble.

Bang!

Malak shoved the desk chair aside so hard it hit the wall.

"Whoopsie," said the Tiniest Voice in the Universe.

"I don't think we should be here, Malak, Mom said." Zara's perpetual concern got louder as she walked further into the room.

"Ooh, what dis?"

Sam opened one eye at that, checking to make sure she hadn't left any sharp, pointy things lying around. Malak held her hoodie in one hand and a sparkly cupcake in the other. Sam closed her eye.

"What!? Where'd you get that? I want one."

"I dunno."

Sam could hear Malak shrug The Shrug of Lies and another scuffle, this time for Sparkly Cupcake Dominance, commenced. Sam sighed, rolled over and girded her mind to enter the fray.

"Hey."

She sat up and rubbed her eyes.

Each girl held the decimated remains of a purple, sparkly cupcake. Glitter frosting decorated Zara's long, straight, brown hair. Her big, blue, eyes were huge with maniacal glee over the sugary treat. Purple frosting was smeared over Malak's cheeks and forehead like some insanely adorable war paint. Thus, a rare stalemate in cuteness was achieved.

"You sure you should be eating that?"

"Auntie!" they yelled – way, way too loud for nine in the morning.

Sam was surrounded. Little arms circled her neck and shoulders and tried to squeeze the life from her. A tiny knot in her soul loosened.

"Okay," she said and put an arm around each in surrender and squeezed back.

"I missed you so much."

They detached in unison and Malak jumped around the room. Her chin-length, brown bob flew around her head in excitement.

"I'm so happy," she said. "Hippity, hop, happy,"

Zara remained next to Sam – her small face far too serious for someone in a "Bee Cool" T-shirt.

"I was really worried about you, Auntie," she said. Then she grabbed Sam's arm and head butted her shoulder.

"Aww, thanks, kid. I'm okay and I'm back now."

Zara tilted her head, triangle jaw and wide eyes so like her mother's. She studied Sam in the exact same way Chiba did when she knew Sam was full of bullshit but was too much of a mom to confront her about it.

Zara squeezed her neck again.

"I love you, Auntie."

"I love you too, Zara."

Malak continued hopping around the room. She picked up Sam's hoodie again – spinning and hopping in circles trying to get both arms through the holes.

Danny walked in. He pointed at Malak.

"Is that dangerous?"

"Only in the obvious way," Sam replied.

"Okay, girls," he said. "Breakfast is ready. Why don't you give your auntie some privacy, please? Malak, give her back her hoodie."

He stopped his spinning top offspring, pulled the garment over her head and tossed it at Sam. She caught it as the girls ran out the door and down the stairs, a swirling gale of taffeta and purple, dancing and singing about how much they loved breakfast.

He towered over the air mattress, his hand on his hips.

"So. The Morrigan, huh?"

"Yup."

She rubbed her face and flinched against the sunlight shrieking at her through the blinds.

"Goddess of Death?"

"Yup."

"You have frosting in your hair."

"Not surprising."

"Do you need help downstairs or are you good?"

"I'm good. Thank you," she said and pulled her hoodie over her head.

"You want the blood of your enemies on your pancakes or is maple syrup okay?"

"Maple syrup is fine, thank you." She glared daggers at him.

Danny bent over and kissed the top of her head.

"I'm glad you're back, Your Majesty."

"You're never letting this go, are you?"

He sauntered out of the room.

"I will not."

He left the door ajar. Sam used her inhalers and snapped her fingers. Ridley wandered in and laid his head on her leg.

"Report," Sam ordered.

The dog failed to respond.

"Report, please," she pleaded.

The unwavering devotion and absolute silence in Ridley's gaze would not be moved.

"If I scratch your butt, will you please report? Ugh, okay fine."

She scratched the top of his butt and the sturdy mutt snuffled in ecstasy.

"You're such a good boy." Sam scritched behind his ears and the dog sighed.

"Do you have anything to report, my sweet, sweet boy?"

Front door scary

She stilled.

"Do you mean going outside is scary?"

No, front door scary

"Anything else?"

No.

She kept up the butt scritches.

"Thank you, my sweet handsome."

Love you

"I love you, too." She made kissy noises.

Sam toddled downstairs.

The Learys lived in a two-story, four-bedroom, two-and-a-half bath, two-car garage, suburban, stucco, everything-standard, everything-average home. The walls were white. The carpet beige. Like all homes inhabited by children, the place was a catastrophe. Toys littered the floor. Mysterious red and purple paint splatters dotted the carpet. Tiny gray hand prints decorated most of the walls.

She had to use the wall to steady herself but she made it all the way down to the final step on her own when a flying five year old tackled her.

"Auntie!"

Sam landed hard on her ass.

Chiba hustled over to run interference.

The Leary's living room had not changed in the apocalypse. A bright red couch, which was the perfect width for naps and for hiding candy wrappers between the cushions, sat against the wall next to the front door. It faced their over-sized TV. In front of the couch, an ancient coffee table held the twenty plastic cups the Leary women drank from during the course of a day. Two beat up recliners book-ended the couch. Behind the TV, A high counter separated the kitchen from the living room.

"Okay, your auntie isn't feeling her best right now." Chiba wrangled Malak back to the couch. "How about you girls take it easy until she feels better please?"

Danny emerged from the kitchen and handed her a plate.

"Pancake?"

With a flourish he poured a few drops of syrup onto the small pancake.

Sam stared at it and sat down on the couch. Zara got her puzzled look from her spot on the recliner.

"We're running out of food," she said, far more dour than a kid in purple polka dot leggings had any right to be.

Chiba put a plate in front of Malak, who snuggled up to Sam when she sat down. Chiba cut Malak's pancake into pieces – plate resting on the low coffee table.

"We are not running out of food," she said and straightened. "We just have to conserve right now. We're having pancakes as a treat because your auntie's back. I will get us more food in a couple days."

Sam waved her left hand at the kitchen.

"No, you're not."

"Yes, I'm getting us more food soon," Chiba said and nodded in the way that said 'for fuck's sake play along.'

Sam swallowed some pancake.

"I mean you're not running out of food. Check the kitchen."

She had forgotten Danny was still in there.

He yipped.

"What the FUCK!?"

"Danny." Chiba rolled her eyes as the girls giggled uncontrollably.

"You're not supposed to say that word, Dad," Zara said.

He leapt out of the kitchen.

"Food!" he yelled as he danced around. "We have food!"

He ran back into the kitchen.

"WE HAVE A DEAD PIG!? Why is there a whole dead pig on my counter?"

"Was this you?" Chiba asked Sam.

"Goddess of Abundance," she replied with a shrug and took another bite of pancake.

"Ooo, I wanna see," Malak said. She hopped off the couch only to be blocked by Danny. Ridley ran into the kitchen and barked his head off at the corpse.

A dozen emotions collided in Chiba's chest. Relief. Gratitude. Absolute fucking irritation that she'd busted her ass for scraps and Sam came in with a wave of her hand and fixed it. Pride in her friend. Relief. Shame that she hadn't been able to provide for her family. The release from the terror that her kids would go hungry. Relief. Gratitude that they wouldn't have to eat the dog. Joy.

A tear fell down her cheek.

"Hey," Sam whispered and reached for her hand.

She'd already doubled then tripled the girls' pancake haul so they were too busy to notice.

Chiba wiped away the tears and shook her head.

"It's okay," she said. She was pretty sure she meant it. "I'm okay."

"Sammmmmmmm!" Danny yelled. "Why do we have a pig? What am I supposed to do with a dead pig?"

"Sorry, I'm a little out of practice. The diet the last time I did this was… different."

Zara stared at her.

"What the fuck, Auntie?"

Malak fell off the couch giggling.

"Zara," Chiba warned and handed her small pancake to Sam. "Could you?"

"Sure."

Sam waved her hand. At close range, Chiba thought she could feel the magic of it – the shifting of atoms, the weird scramble of reality rearranging itself at one woman's whim.

"Hey," Sam said. She had inhaled her pancakes and settled back into the red couch. "So, where are the food people?"

Malak crawled onto the top couch cushion and took that opportunity to use the top of Sam's head as a footrest.

"The cooks?"

"Nope." Sam coughed and fought the rising tide of exhaustion. "The people who make food, like, with magic and stuff. I forget what they're called." She yawned and her head lolled back, displacing Malak's feet.

"You know," she waved an arm at the faceless, food-creating masses, "those people."

Danny and Chiba exchanged a look.

"There aren't any people like that, Sam," Danny said.

Her eyes fluttered closed

"Yes, there are," she muttered. "I can feel them." She stuck her tongue out in disgust. "They're … sunny … never mind, I'll figure it out."

Sam put her feet up on the coffee table and stretched. Malak slid off the couch cushion, rolled herself up in a blanket and leaned her head onto Sam's arm. Zara claimed Sam's other side as she shoveled pancakes into her face.

Soft snores emanated from Sam's mouth. She snorted and jerked awake.

"Hey, Chibs."

Chiba paused, fork loaded with four layers of pancake dripping with maple syrup stopped inches from her lips.

"Yeah?"

"Has the power been on since The Fog?"

"Yeah, the power's been on this whole time," Chiba said. She smiled with pride. "Was that you?"

Sam's head dropped back onto the couch.

"Nope, that was *not* me."

Someone who had not known Sam for the better part of a decade, and who had not heard what her voice did when she talked about her mother, might not have felt a chill go down their spine at the way she said, "*not* me."

But Chiba knew. She checked to make sure her kids weren't paying attention.

"Fuck," she whispered.

NAZI SMITING

10:35 am, Oct. 29, 2020, 31 days after The Fog

On jagged cliffs above the Pacific Ocean, six miles northwest as the crow flies from Chiba and Danny's house, stood a gleaming, white stucco, glass-box of a mansion.

The desperate creatures of Sunset Cove avoided this place. Although, none could explain why, exactly. The pristine edifice looked ripe for the taking. The perfunctory landscaping of waxy-leaved, manicured shrubs, blue and white clusters of agapanthus and Bradford Pear trees were quietly being taken over by slender golden threads of dodder that wafted serenely in the ocean breeze. The effect was lovely, but the parasitic dodder plant sucked the very life from everything it touched. The gate was nothing more than metal – easily bent or broken. There wasn't even any blood on the alabaster exterior walls… and yet, and yet, the center of a hurricane is a noxious calm – steeped in ozone and dread.

Were a creature inclined to peek through the second-story windows of this place, they would see a dozen or so humans lying in various states of repose: one man sprawled over a billiards table, a woman passed out on a couch, book in her lap, in the bedroom, another woman lay on a bed, legs spread, dress hiked up around her waist. A man lay unconscious on the floor before her.

Not one of these people had moved a millimeter in thirty days. Yet each was, in their own way, very much alive.

If a soul were brave enough to enter this silent monument and walk through its cold, calculating halls they may stumble upon a small bathroom in the back. Here they would find the only movement among these living statues.

On the toilet in this bathroom, white dress pants around his ankles, a white-haired man sat frozen while tiny, blue, electric volts jumped from his hands into the electrical outlet.

*****

1:30 pm, Oct. 29, 2020, 31 days after The Fog

Sam dreamt of her old life – drinking at the Purple Pear downtown with the shipping crew. Every Friday night for years, they met at this grimy altar to Sunset Cove.

The crowd in the Purple Pear depended on the day of the week. Fridays were, unfortunately, Metal night. Thursday was Queer night. Sundays it transformed into a goth club. Sam had tried to get everyone to switch to Thursdays as much out of a hatred for Metal as a love for being queer, but she failed. Mostly, because it was easier to get the pool table on Metal night. So every Friday, they gathered around shooting stick, drinking two-dollar Bud Light cans and yelling in each other's ears so they could be heard over the shrieking.

Sam bent over the wobbly table and made a combo shot.

A man in all white appeared at the edge of the crowd. Dre, Chiba, Danny, Jimmy, and Brix were all there. He stared at them like they were bugs in need of dissection.

Sam stood between him and her friends.

"Where have you been?" His voice was too high with odd dips and turns. "I couldn't find you. All these years. Were you asleep?"

"It's still my turn," she told him. Her pool cue transformed into her short sword. Blood dripped from the tip onto the Purple Pear's sticky floor. They both knew it was his.

"Cheater," he said, staring at the blood. "You took what's mine. It's easy when you cheat. But you can't cheat me this time. It's mine."

He backed away.

Sam hated his voice – the way it bounced off the dirty, black walls and cracked, plastic tiki idol decorations.

"What are you talking about?"

He studied her.

"You don't remember?" he asked, eyes raking over her skin. "You don't remember cheating on the battlefield? The Fog that stole my magic? And left yours? How come she helped you, huh? What did you do?"

He laughed and laughed – hollow and mean.

Sam jerked awake. Hours had passed. She'd developed a wicked crick in her neck. Tiny, idle hands had painted her fingers and toes bright, mismatched colors. Then they stuck flower stickers on the drying paint. Someone (probably Chiba) had thrown a soft, gray blanket over her.

She sat up, stretched and tried to pull the stickers off. She heard the girls playing upstairs.

"Hey," Chiba said and came over with a glass of water. "How are you feeling?"

"Better, I think," Sam said. "It's almost sundown isn't it?"

Chiba nodded.

"You can tell?" she asked, with all the gentleness in her heart.

"I can tell."

The silence between them widened into canyons of empty, awkward space.

"It's okay," Sam said, thinking how hard this all must be for her. "You know. It's okay to be freaked out by this – by me, I mean. I get it."

Chiba sighed and settled into the couch.

"I-I'm a little freaked out."

"It's okay if you're a lot freaked out," Sam said.

"Are you sure?"

"Chibs, yes." Sam sat up and faced her. "This is nuts. The world's fucked up. Everyone has changed. Everything has changed. If I were you, I would have lost my shit a thousand times over by now."

"I started drinking again," Chiba confessed.

Damn, okay, so it is that bad.

"Okay."

"It's not. It's not okay. I'm trying to be better."

"You're doing that thing where you beat yourself up and I don't support it."

Chiba stood and paced.

"I should be doing better," she said. "This isn't good for me. For my health, for my kids I need to be better."

"Oh, for fuck's sake," Sam said and sipped the water. "A zombie nearly killed you a month ago. You were running out of food. You lived through the apocalypse and your best friend disappeared. You didn't know how you were going to survive. You did what you had to do."

Chiba stared at her.

"I want a beer," Chiba said, and gave Sam a look.

"So have a beer. I'll have one, too."

"Sam." Chiba sat back down and put her hand on hers, so her best friend understood the severity of the situation. "We are out of beer."

"Oh," Sam laughed and waved her arm. "Okay."

A cold six-pack appeared on the table. Then she reached into her hoodie and pulled out a bottle opener. She popped open the tops and handed one to Chiba.

"Cheers," Chiba said as they clinked bottles.

"Sláinte," Sam replied.

They took long swigs and contemplated.

"I dreamt about the Purple Pear."

Chiba laughed so hard beer spilled onto her shirt.

"I haven't thought about that shithole in forever," she said and wiped off the alcohol. Then she stilled. "I wonder if everyone is alive."

Sam glared at the middle distance.

"They are," she said, but didn't add, *for now.*

"That's something, at least," Chiba said. "So what's it like? Being a goddess?"

Sam sipped her beer and tried to find the words to describe it: *singed singing blood, the shapeless void, burning twisting responsibility. Hope.*

"It's okay."

"Yeah?" Chiba asked. Sam could tell that response worried her.

"It's… it's not something words were built for. I don't know. I wish I could describe it."

But I'm worried anything I say will freak you out more, or worse, you'll try to stop me.

Chiba pulled herself together, sat up straight, fixed her face and became determined.

"I'm gonna say it," she said and cleared her throat. "I need to say it. Are you still… you?"

"What do you mean?"

"I dunno," Chiba said. She had already downed half her beer. Her courage and thoughts were slipping away. She exhaled.

"Chiba," Sam began, "before I am anything – before I am Death, before I am a goddess, before all that – I am your family."

Chiba started crying into her beer.

"Does that help?"

Chiba nodded.

"I'm going to hug you now," Sam told her.

"Okay." Chiba nodded and sobbed in relief while Death patted her back.

*****

6:10 pm, Oct. 29, 2020, 31 days after The Fog

Sam begged off the evening meal – telling everyone she wanted to go for a walk. She could see Chiba's moment of panic, wanting to warn her of the dangers out in this new world. Then the New Reality of Sam set in.

"I'll be fine," Sam said, trying to reassure her, but they both knew Chiba would worry until she came back.

Malak wrapped herself around her leg in a futile effort to hitch a ride.

"I'm sorry, kid," she said and patted her head. Then she tried to extricate herself from the vice-like grip of those tiny, tiny arms.

"No, Auntie," Malak said. "Stay. There are scary people out there."

"I'm sorry, baby," Sam said. "I just need some fresh air. I'll be back soon."

Lies. These were bold-faced lies.

Zara decided to join her sister and pile on the guilt.

"Are you sure, Auntie?" Zara asked. "Mommy told us to never go outside at night. That it's too dangerous."

Chiba and Sam exchanged a look. Neither had a clue how to explain.

Sam knelt down to Zara and Malak eye level.

"Well, girls, your auntie is really strong," Sam told them – for some reason, describing herself in the third person like a psychopath. "I'm so strong that any scary, bad thing out there should be afraid of me."

"Really?"

Zara's concerned disbelief was written across her small round face.

"Yeah, baby," she said. "Really."

Sam's heart cracked. Though she managed to exit the front door without anyone throwing a tantrum. She stopped dead the second the door clicked shut.

Then she looked to her right and left to make sure she wasn't hallucinating and exploded.

"What, in the LEGIT FUCK, are you two doing here?"

Flanking her, two Wraiths guarded the Leary's front door. They were foul creatures pulled from the depths of the Darkness. The stench of their crimes followed them through eternity. The air around them reeked of hate and disease. They could neither be seen nor heard by humans – dogs, on the other hand, knew exactly what they were. Nine times out of ten, a dog freaking out about nothing was actually barking at a Wraith. Like the Ravens, Wraiths had been bound to her service in atonement for their crimes. Their souls tattered and torn. Sam could see through their paper thin forms.

They came to earth hungry for the flesh denied them so long, but they were only allowed to consume humans as vile as they once were.

These two looked particularly juicy.

She stepped away from the door and faced them.

"Again, what the fuck are you doing here?"

Their voices were globs of wet flesh hitting concrete.

"Queens' orders, Your Highness.

"I am the Queen and I don't want you anywhere near this place." Sam's hackles rose.

"Respectfully," the Wraith to her left began, "you're not really the Queen yet, are you? You're more like a …"

The Wraith to her left tried to warn his counterpart with aggressive flapping.

"Princess."

Sam closed her eyes and reminded herself that she couldn't kill what was already dead.

"Leave," she barked. "Leave. Now."

"We can't," they replied.

Sam swore their wispy darkness trembled.

"Queens' orders. We're here to protect the house and the neighborhood."

Sam studied the fullness of their shadows.

"Have you *eaten* recently?"

"Yes, Your Highness," they said in unison – equally proud and happy. Sam held back the bile rising in her throat.

"Who? Who did you eat?"

"Some bloke, Your Highness. He followed the man of the house. We split him. Right up the middle."

"Gross," Sam said.

She contemplated ordering them to drop the honorifics but she couldn't bear the thought of hearing her name in their gaping maws.

"Danny left?"

"Yes, he went to the market with bags of food."

Danny must have discovered the automatic refills on the food in the pantry and wanted to share.

"Okay, who did you eat?" Sam asked. "Can you tell me anything about him? Was he tall or short? A witch? A troll? Shape shifter? Anything? Anything at all?"

"Short. Funny hat. Not much meat. He was chewy. Tasted sweet."

One of the Wraiths blew a bubble out of the residual flesh they'd been gumming.

It snapped between their jaws.

"I will talk to my Goddess Mothers about this," she said and walked away from the wretches.

"Good luck with that, Princess," one of them called after her.

Sam stopped and turned back.

I am the Goddess of Revenge.

"Do you think I don't know who you are? Do you think I don't know what you've done?"

"That was a long time ago, Pr..." its voice had become blood splatters on wooden planks, the last gasp before the gallows. If it had eyes, they would have turned down in shame.

"And yet here you are," she said and stood too close. She examined every inch, breathed in the stench of hatred and shame. Her stomach roiled but she held fast. "Soul bound to Darkness, consuming the filth of this realm."

His compatriot stilled and tried to make itself invisible. She knew that one's crimes as well. To be bound was to have one's essence ripped apart and sutured back together with threads of the Darkness. One must commit acts so heinous that they tear the fabric of Life itself.

"The last man you beat to death, what was his name?"

"Wh, wh.. why?" The Wraith stammered at her. "I don't… I don't see how that's relevant. Why do you need to know?"

She smirked at him.

"Do you not remember?"

"I remember."

She felt the rage push forward. The task ahead of her made her nervous and this creature more than deserved torment.

"What was his name?"

"T-T-Thomas," it whispered.

"You beat him for hours, didn't you?" she asked. "Then you set dogs on his unconscious body to rip him apart, yes? When the dog tore his foot off, he woke up. Thomas screamed. He begged for his life. He cried. And you LAUGHED. You thought it was funny – because you could, because you felt joy at another human being's pain."

"I WAS DOING MY JOB! IT WAS MY JOB. I WAS GOOD AT MY JOB. HE NEEDED TO LEARN."

Sam held up a hand. The creature shrank from her. It repeated the lies it told itself. She drew it closer with the flick of a finger.

"For the next ten hours, I command you to experience every second of what you did to him over and over."

The Wraith screamed. Agony twisted through it.

"Silently."

She turned to his companion.

"I see you," she bit out through clenched jaws. "I see what you are. The things you've done – equal or worse than his. Do not make the mistake of thinking otherwise."

It bowed.

"Yes, Your Majesty."

"You know what? You can experience Thomas' pain as well."

It shrieked. The night around her rippled and stilled in response.

"Silently."

She rolled her eyes and stalked away.

"Princess, my ass, you over-blown shower curtain."

By the end of the Leary's driveway, the 'new' Sunset Cove overwhelmed her. Chiba's neighborhood of neat, boxy, suburban houses was so close to the way it had been when she left – if she ignored the burnt ruin of the house a few doors down, all the boarded up windows, the odd quiet and the plume of smoke wafting from the skeletal remains of the boardwalk. Sam couldn't take the time to mourn or remember. Her appointment was time sensitive. She hadn't lied about that.

She hurried to the crossroads, then turned to make sure she couldn't be seen from the house. Her need to be out of sight was not only because she didn't want the Learys to know what she was doing, but also because she was about to slice a small tear in reality and if she fucked up all matter within a thirty-foot radius would dissolve.

She stopped, facing the park across the street. It was unchanged. Somehow, that creeped Sam out more than anything. She shook her left hand, reached for the sure knowledge that all of time and space existed simultaneously, and found the thin fold that separated this point from where she wanted to be. The nail on her left pointer finger grew sharp and black. Inky fluid dripped from its tip.

Sam took a deep breath and with her nail pierced the folded reality just above her head. Exhaling, she dragged her finger down and grabbed the delicate edges. Then she pulled with her will, not her hands. The opening hiccuped and she ducked through to the forest on the other side.

The tear closed behind her and she did a little dance of triumph.

This forest, nestled in the mountains above Sunset Cove, had felt enchanted before The Fog. It was a popular, local hiking spot. The trail head was less than one hundred yards from a high school parking lot. A charming stream ran between the high school and the path that wound its way deep into the redwood forest. Sam had spent many Sunday afternoons wandering these trails – exchanging her deepest, darkest secrets with her friends. This place always felt nice. After The Fog, it still felt welcoming, like the kind of forest a little girl in a fairytale would run away to only to be taken in and cared for by fairies or gnomes or bears.

Sam knew what she was about to stop would have changed that. It would have wounded this innocent place.

She found a picnic table on the school side of the stream. Sam knew this was their designated meeting place. She tried to give herself plenty of time to prepare. Her stomach gurgled in anticipation. The timing left no room for error.

"Carl, come. Bring half a dozen of your kind."

The birds, each two feet or taller and cloaked in shimmering darkness, landed on the picnic table before her.

"Carl, you're on look out. Let me know when the Lords of Ire are on their way."

"Yes, Boss," he squawked without a smidge of sarcasm. Sensing her stress, he kept his smart mouth to himself – for the moment.

He should have a word with those fucking Wraiths.

"You lot," she addressed the remaining Unkindness. "You will draw the werewolf and vampire up the mountain. If one of you is eaten, another raven will replace it. Keep them occupied for hours - but end well before sunrise. Do you understand?"

Choruses of 'Yes, Boss' rang out.

"Repeat it back to me."

They did, in screeching voices.

She held her hand over them, changing their nature. One of the five birds shrieked and folded into a rabbit as black as night.

"You. Hide in that shrub and lead them up the mountain. Got it?"

It nodded.

"Good. Take your places."

Her throat felt scratchy. She dried her palms on her hoodie. Sam sat on the top of the picnic table and rearranged her sitting position four times.

Look natural.

"They're coming!" Carl called down.

"Who?"

"The werewolf and the vampire."

Thank the Holy Darkness.

She hopped off the table and braced herself against it.

The pair emerged from the trees. It had been about three months in "real time" since she'd seen him, but in the Liminal Space it had been thousands of years. She had watched him die bad over and over. She replayed every detail in her mind, because she'd be damned if she screwed this up.

"Sam!" he yelled, incredulous with joy.

"Hey, Jimmy," she said his name the way she'd always said it, with all the wry fondness in her heart. She practiced removing all the grief.

"Oh, my God! I can't believe it! You're here! You're alive."

It never occurred to him to not hug her. He had half a foot on her so he leaned over and wrapped his arms around her shoulders for a couple seconds before stepping back.

"Ronnie, this is my buddy, Sam." He gestured for the giant werewolf to come over.

Six minutes. Maybe less.

He waved with that shrugging Sunset Cove attitude. The giant, wolf man dwarfed Jimmy, at ten-ish feet, gray fur sprouted everywhere from his body. He wore board shorts and an open Hawaiian shirt.

Jimmy noticed her staring.

"He's cool," he said. "I promise. He just ate."

Sam made herself look back at Jimmy. *Alive. Smiling. Acting like she was still human.*

She dug her nails into her palms to keep from screaming.

"It's cool," she said. "I've just never seen a werewolf in a Hawaiian shirt before. Aloha Saturday?"

Jimmy grinned at her.

"You know it," he said and nodded. "It's good to see you. What have you been up to? Since you know?"

Sam tried her damnedest to remember how to be a normal person.

"Since Brix dumped me, we got super drunk at the Purple Pear, I threw up on your grandma's lawn and passed out on your bathroom floor?"

He laughed.

"Classic, Sam," he said. "Naw, dude. I mean since this." He gestured to the world so impossibly changed.

"Oh," she blinked. "Not much. I spent the past month lying in the river downtown."

"Wait, by the bridge?"

"Yup."

"Fuck, that was you? I thought it was a dead body."

It kind of was.

"That was me."

"Shit, Sam. I'm so sorry." He genuinely was. She could tell by the hang of his shoulders.

His eyes bulging. Squirming. Vampires don't need to breathe but their brains need blood. One half of his face a mass of pulp and gore. He could still feel pain. Less than five minutes now.

"I should have pulled you out," he said.

"It's okay." She patted his arm. "There wasn't anything you could have done. Truly, Jimmy. It's okay."

Change the subject. Reassure him. Time. Tick FUCKING tock. So little time.

"Hey, what are you two doing up here?" she asked, pretending to be casual. "Is it a full moon?"

"Oh, we come up here to chase rabbits," Jimmy said. "My uncle has a pig farm. I drink the blood. Ronnie eats the bones. It keeps us from going crazy and hunting people. I know – kinda gross."

I've eaten eyeballs. You have no idea from gross.

"No, I get it, dude. We all do what we gotta do." She looked at the werewolf again, something not computing. "But it's not a full moon."

The werewolf shrunk a bit.

"He can't change back," he said. Then Jimmy lifted his shirt, showing her the thin silver scars across his abdomen. "We think it's 'cause he ate vampire right after changing. It didn't agree with him."

He slapped his friend hard on the back.

"Right, buddy?"

The beast nodded apologetically.

They'd pulled the werewolf's arms off. He howled and howled.

She dug her nails in so hard, half moons appeared in her palms,

"What about you?" Jimmy asked and sniffed the air. "You smell human – sort of. Wait. How come you're still alive. She smells kinda human, right Ronnie?"

The beast nodded.

"Sam, what are you doing out here?"

So soon now. Just a few more words.

"I have an appointment I have to keep."

Your grandmother. She'll come out here trying to find you. Your body turned to stone. She touched your hand just to make sure. She couldn't believe it was real.

Flies dropping in and out of Ronnie's corpse. She's old. Collapses with the weight of her grief. Sam could never make herself look past this moment – to see if the woman who fed her cinnamon rolls the morning after one of the worst nights of her life survived her heartbreak.

She memorized her face instead. The lines around her mouth, the crown on her bottom incisor. The map of veins on the backs of her hands – the ones she hid behind to escape sight of her dead grandson.

"Sam, you shouldn't be out here," Jimmy said. "It's not safe. I don't think you know what's out here. I mean we're cool but there's way scary shit out here."

Yeah, I'm one of them. Less than two minutes now. They need to go.

"Truly, guys," she said in her most reassuring and commanding voice. "I'm fine."

The men spoke to each other without words.

"I think you should come with us," he said with the same aura of protective concern he had the night she'd downed three vodka tonics in thirty minutes.

The patchwork werewolf sauntered to her. He was over it and eager to hunt rabbits. He carefully wrapped his giant claws around her upper arms and lifted.

"What is he doing?"

She didn't move.

"He's trying to pick you up and take you with us."

Sam smiled, patted the furry man's arm, and because he meant well, didn't rip it off for touching her without permission.

"Dude, why can't he pick you up?"

She gazed into Ronnie's eyes and let the Darkness slip for a moment.

"Do you understand now, Wolf?"

The beast inhaled, nodded and stepped back.

"I'm not *that* human," Sam said. "I'll be fine."

"Really?"

Carl screamed over head.

"Truly," she said and waved two fingers of her left hand. "I'm fine."

The men's heads swiveled. Jimmy licked his lips and hissed.

"I'll be totally good here. Do you two need to go?" she asked with every ounce of fake innocence she could muster.

Jimmy swayed, human instincts fighting with animal.

"I'm fine," she said brightly. "Go ahead." She waved again to double the pheromones. The men howled. "Have fun."

With one last glance, Jimmy and Ronnie rushed into the night, up the mountain.

Sam exhaled and damn near fell over. She gripped the edge of the picnic table for support. Sweat dripped into the small of her back.

Too close. Too. Fucking. Close.

Sam pulled her staff from her hoodie. She heard them coming from the opposite direction of where Jimmy and Ronnie ran off to – the laughing, genial, happy men, a dozen or so, playing grab ass and chuffing about. She rushed to the shadow of a nearby redwood and pulled her hood low over her forehead.

The desperate need to fill the night air with the red mist of their blood rose up within her. She could taste their death and it was sweet.

In the Liminal Space, the sliver between all worlds, the connection between all realities, she'd seen this night – studied it until her eyes burned from knowing. The Morrigan has foresight in battle. She knows her enemies' every move. Every play was memorized.

This moment was to be the opening salvo in the battle. Her enemy's opening act had been to torture and slaughter her most vulnerable ally – the man she forgot to protect. When her soul entered the Liminal Space, she chose who to guard and who to leave behind.

Jimmy didn't have a band because Sam forgot to give him one.

She told herself it was because she hadn't seen him in months, that she was embarrassed for puking on his lawn, that she was trying to blot out the memory of Brix and what he did.

In the Liminal Space, she'd watched Jimmy die hundreds of thousands of times. Sam rationalized all the reasons she'd forgotten and why it was okay.

"What if I leave early?" she asked. "Before I'm fully cooked or whatever?"

From the Celestial Mothers' expressions, this was a shite idea.

"Too many variables," Nemain muttered. "It cannot be calculated."

"But I can leave?" she asked. "I can stop this? I can keep it from happening?"

Nemain shrugged. She didn't know and she *despised* not knowing.

"It is a bad idea," Nemain said.

Anand, all bunny slippers and chocolate chip cookies smell, grabbed her arms.

"I know this is hard for you but you cannot save everyone," she said, her kind eyes held depths of sympathy and understanding. "You will learn to live with it."

She paused and squeezed.

"Also, my dear, if you leave, you may not be able to come back."

Sam met Badb's eyes and faced the seething depths of chaos and rage within them.

"What do you think?" Sam asked her.

Badb grinned, sharp teeth pressing into full, wide lips.

"Two questions, daughter," she said in that voice that made battle-hardened warriors shit themselves. "One: What do you want to do? Two: Who, or what do you *really* think you're saving?"

Sam thought about it for several moments.

"Huh," she said.

"Yes," Badb replied.

Sam looked around the Liminal Space, which Nemain had fashioned to resemble a vast, ancient library.

"Okay," she said. "How do I get out of here?"

"If you do this, you will need allies," Badb said.

Sam didn't know how she returned to the reality of Sunset Cove. She decided to leave and then she was lying on her kitchen floor, covered in river slime a day before a white supremacist mob would torture and murder Jimmy.

The mob in question, who called themselves the Lords of Ire, gathered around the picnic table. Six, she counted. She wouldn't set the circle until seven stood there. She counted again and again. Rage burned in her throat.

Sam scanned their ordinary faces. Of the six, there was one vampire and a troll. From this distance, the others appeared human. She fought the argument with herself whether she should just deal with these assholes now and find the leader later, when he sauntered up.

Sam hated that if she hadn't known what he was, she would have found him attractive. He had thick, ropey muscles, small waist, broad shoulders, slicked-back gray hair and a well-trimmed beard. Bright ink ran across his skin. He looked like the kind of guy who owned a craft brewery with his brother-in-law. He looked like he used scented beard oil.

She ran from the shadows. The end of her staff kicked up pine needles as she sank it into the earth to draw the circle. She stepped through the final foot, turned, connected the ends and stabbed her left hand. When her heart's blood sprayed on the line, the circle closed, trapping them inside it with her.

"The fuck …?" They gawped.

Sam set the circle at a circumference of thirty feet or so with the picnic table in the center. Someone brought beer. The twelve pack sat at the edge of the table. The blue box was torn at the corner and missing a couple cans.

Their crimes echoed through her mind at this close range. Sam closed her eyes against the clamor of voices demanding justice.

"Who called the stripper?"

They laughed.

"Naw, dude. Look at her. She's too old. Too fat."

She knew her presence made them nervous. It activated their fight or flight instinct. Not one among them had the self-awareness to resolve the cognitive dissonance.

"I wouldn't fuck her if you paid me."

"I hope you got a discount on that."

"Does she talk?"

"I fuckin' hope not."

"You look lost," the leader barked at her. Sam opened her eyes.

She lights a black candle whenever he leaves. She holds a piece of red cloth and begs me, praying, praying with every fiber of her being. Make him disappear. Please.

"Are you lost?" he repeated. "Because if you're not lost, then we're gonna assume you want to be here and we're gonna treat you like you want to be here. I don't think you wanna be here. Last chance, sweetheart."

Sweetheart. That's what he called her when he walked out the door.

Sam had a plan. It was intricate – a subtle dance of vengeance. It included drowning each and every one of them in the blood of their friends. Their screams and cries for mercy would be hers to cherish. But now, in close proximity to these "people," Sam wanted nothing more than to be done with them so she could shower their literal and figurative stench off her. Apparently, personal hygiene was the first casualty of the apocalypse.

"Yup," she said and raised her arms above her head, "We're gonna do this instead."

As she dropped her arms, thick black tentacles burst forth from the ground. They wrapped around the Lords of Ires' wrists and pulled their hands straight down to their sides.

"I know why you're here," she said. She stared at the ground because she didn't want to look at them. "I know what you were gonna do."

"You fucking cunt, let me go!"

Sam stepped to the man besmirching her. She raked her eyes over his scraggly handlebar mustache, sleeveless Confederate flag t-shirt, faded cross tattoo on his scrawny right bicep.

"Jesus, you can't help being a cliche, can you?"

"Fuck off, cunt," he said as spittle frothed from his lips, dripping onto his sagging chin.

Sam met his eyes.

"Say it again."

"What?" He blinked.

"Call me a cunt again."

His eyes dropped from hers. He looked about sixty but was probably forty or so. Meth did that to a person.

He mumbled under his breath.

"What did you say, Travis?"

Sweat broke out across his forehead. The stench of him – stale beer, failing kidneys and pungent chemicals he ingested regularly irradiated the air. Sam coughed in defense.

Their bonds glitched and disappeared.

The vampire got to her first. It slapped her so hard she hit the edge of the circle. The invisible barrier shimmered and she bounced off.

Dazed and hacking up a lung, Sam tried to stand but the vampire yanked her up by her hair. A stringy, black mustache and breath like rancid meat overwhelmed her senses.

"Hello, lunch," he said and clamped down onto her neck. His teeth slid into her carotid artery. Over his shoulder, Sam could see the Lords of Ire high fiving and laughing. Sam closed her eyes, calmed her rioting lungs and consoled herself with the fact that this would be all over soon.

The grimy vamp's tongue lapped her blood into his mouth. He coughed and threw her aside. The Lords of Ire stopped laughing.

The vampire wiped inky blood from his lips. He gazed at his own fingertips.

"Dudes," he said as he belched up noxious black ichor. "I don't feel so good."

His slender body exploded. Chunks of him flew around the circle. The right half of his blackened skull landed on the beer box.

Sam wiped the excess blood from her neck and flicked the droplets away.

"Next!" she yelled. His scent was still in her nostrils. She wanted to burn it out with their blood.

The fucking troll lumbered up. Battle thrummed through her veins. It thumped in time to the low insistent beat of her pulse.

It squared off to her, thick, green hide riddled with pockmarks and warts – hunched back, knuckles dragging in the dirt. It stood a solid seven-feet tall. Beady, yellow eyes burned in its twisted skull. The creature smelt of lilacs.

Sam noticed the flower print half shirt that didn't cover its belly.

"Oh, shit!" Sam exclaimed. "You're a girl?"

In response, the troll swung one massive claw at Sam's face. She ducked and noticed that its talons were covered in a cute, neutral pink polish. She swung the other hand, rhythmic and unrelenting. The troll backed Sam toward the edge of the circle.

"I'll kill you," she muttered, gray tongue lolling between blocky, yellow teeth.

Sam glanced at the barrier behind her. It held strong and steady. She pulled her short sword from her hoodie. As the woman swung her arm around, Sam slammed the weapon down with all her weight.

The troll's arm dropped. Bright, green blood burst from the stump, covering Sam in foul liquid. The troll shrieked, spraying gore everywhere and passed out.

Sam grinned. She wiped goo from her face and neck.

"Next?" Sam yelled.

"Enough!" their leader barked. The muscles in his torso roiled and skipped.

"Now you're gonna get it," Travis murmured, but he didn't sound as confident as he did a few minutes ago.

The leader of the Lords of Ire barked and howled. His bones cracked and elongated.

"He's gonna eat you alive," Travis said.

Claws burst from the man's fingertips. Hair sprouted over his tattoos. Saliva dripped from his elongated jaw and serrated teeth.

Sam was unimpressed.

The dudes in this town. For fuck's sake. Every fucking idiot with hair on his chest thinks he's an alpha.

The murderous ring leader of the Lords of Ire (trademark pending) was not, in fact, a werewolf. He was a shape shifter who managed to get about halfway through this lengthy and obviously excruciating transformation before Sam got bored.

"I'm going to chew you up and shit you out," he growled.

"Yeah, someone said that already," Sam said and held up a hand. "Stop."

To his great surprise, his transformation just stopped.

"What the fu-"

She closed her fingers.

"Shhh…"

He went silent and it *finally* dawned on the remaining members of the Lords of Ire that they just *might* be fucked.

"Sit," Sam said.

He sat, shocked. His face went gloriously slack in confusion.

"Rollover." Sam snapped her fingers. With all the obedience in his heart, he rolled on his back and stood up.

"Beg."

"Help me," he pleaded. "I can't move. She won't let me."

Sam closed her hand and he fell silent. His eyes rolled and panicked. He was trapped inside a body he no longer controlled. Blood sweat broke out along the visible patches of his skin.

She raised her arms again. As she lowered them, the dark tendrils wrapped around the four remaining Lords of Ires' wrists – not that she expected much fight from the rest of them. But as Nemain always said, "Prepare for the worst."

"Four years ago, Michael Seamus Flannery, you offered yourself 'mind, body, and soul' to The Morrigan," Sam said as she paced. She swung her sword back and forth as she bit out the words.

"'Let me be your instrument of justice' you begged." The temperature around Sam dropped several degrees. "'Let me right the wrongs of this world in your honor, sweet Annie, oh Kindly One, my Beloved Goddess of Justice.' Do you remember your vow? Michael Seamus Flannery?" She spun, hoodie flying in rage.

"*I* remember because you then proceeded to commit hate crimes IN MY NAME!" Sam ended her tirade screaming – the sound of a thousand ravens shrieking in the darkness.

"But I'm going to deal with you later. Now!" She slapped the top of the picnic table in her best imitation of a used car salesman. "Who's ready to lose a hand?"

Travis cried. Big, sloppy tears fell through the dirty creases of his face.

"I didn't do nothing," he said to Sam. "I didn't hurt nobody. I don't deserve this."

Sam stood before him. She tucked the sword back into her hoodie and put her hands in her pockets.

At her whim, his left hand moved in front of his face.

"You have three small scars on your knuckles," she said. "How did you get them?"

He somehow got paler.

"What?" His milky, hound dog eyes widened.

"How did you get those scars?"

His eyes rolled back in his skull. He could not avoid the truth written on his very skin.

Sam leaned close to him and lowered his hand with a thought

"I see you, Travis Herbert Thompson."

Flickering through her mind like a Sunday matinee, Sam saw the truth of him – the abusive childhood, drug addiction, the desperate yearning to belong and be loved twisted into fear and rage. If she thought about it too much, she might be reminded of herself.

"I punched someone," he admitted.

Sam smiled without humor or kindness.

"Oh, you punched someone?" She grinned – teeth white exclamation points in the darkness. "Why did you punch this person?"

"Go ahead." Sam lost all patience with his bullshit. "Explain to me how you beat a sixty-two year-old Chinese man into a coma for bumping into you on the street.

"What was his name?"

"What?" he asked.

"Do you know the name of the man you almost killed?"

Tears pooled onto the front of his white t-shirt.

"I don't know," he said, snot running into his mouth.

"Haoyu Zhang. His name was Haoyu Zhang."

Sam wanted to hate him. She wanted to feel the righteous fury she'd felt when this night began but all she could see was Travis as a seven year old while his greasy father whipped the snotty child into a bloody mess.

"You know that man you beat?" she asked. "Who you nearly killed, he's still afraid to go outside sometimes, Travis? He has a scar in his skull, where you cracked his head on the pavement."

He blathered.

"I shouldn't a done it." His mind was long gone. It ran away to protect itself. "I shouldn't a done it."

Sam grabbed his chin.

"Look at me." She met his eyes. "Justice demands you pay today. You were hurt and you passed that hurt on to someone else. You must pay for that but…" She shook his chin to make sure it sunk in. "Harm no other, or I will find you. You don't want to see me again."

Sam licked the index finger on her left hand and drew a line from the corner of his eye to his jaw – a curse dependent on intent.

Travis nodded too hard. His eyes rolled up and down in his head.

"I shouldn't a done it. I shouldn't a done it."

He said it over and over again. He did not stop when Sam sliced off his left hand and sent him on his way into the night. She maimed the other three without much thought or care. They screamed at her. They told her that she had betrayed her race. She would be seeing them again.

Sam surveyed the carnage around her.

I was not prepared for all these bodily fluids… that's what she said.

"Don't think I forgot about you," Sam said. She advanced on the fuckwit hybrid who claimed he would 'chew her up and shit her out.'

The blood sweat had dried and crusted in his matted fur. He was seconds from passing out from the pain.

"You will stay awake," Sam said.

Like a wet dog, he shook himself.

Sam pulled up the picnic table so she'd have a place to sit.

His animal jaw protruded from his human face. Michael Seamus Flannery's eyes, at this moment, were all too human as he tried to answer her through her own curse of silence. She couldn't imagine a more pathetic bastard.

"Please," he begged through massive canines. "I have a wife."

Something was very wrong. He shouldn't have been able to disobey her like that. She glanced down at her left hand. It was shaking. The cold air, the adrenaline, the viscous sickness in her lungs conspired to rob her of stamina and vengeance. Not even the Sacred Night could save her. Sam didn't have much time.

"Yes," she said as she stood and got in his face. From these close quarters, she could smell that he had shat himself. "I know your wife. Yvette's her name, yes?"

He whimpered.

"Hold up your left hand."

He obeyed her this time. She stood too close to be ignored. Sam pried the gold band from his finger.

Snot dripped from his malformed nose. She put the ring in the palm of her hand, feeling the simple, powerful magic of it against her skin.

"She prays to me too, you know," Sam said. She closed her fist over the band. "Do you think I don't know what you did to her? After all this, you think I wouldn't know what you did to your wife?"

He dry heaved in her face. Sam fought revulsion. Her lungs spasmed and jerked. She let out a small cough.

"A few days after The Fog, you discovered that you could transform."

She held her palm under his nose and refused to look away.

"You told her you want to have sex in this form. 'You'll love it,' you said. 'I'm huge like this.' She wasn't into it. She said no."

The ring vibrated.

"So you raped her. You raped her for hours. She *tore* and you raped her."

The ring snapped in half.

Michael Seamus Flannery tried to turn away. He tried to escape the justice in her eyes. Sam grabbed his jaw and forced him to look at her.

"She prays to me. Every time you leave, she lights a black candle at my altar and she prays that you will disappear."

Sam held the broken ring to his eye. It turned to dust in the darkness.

"Do you know whose prayers I'm answering tonight?" she asked. "Do you have any idea how fucked you are? Do you?"

He shook, trying to fight her, trying to fight the vow he made. She held on to her will and bent him to it.

"Do you know how fucked you are? Tell me you know how fucked you are."

"I know how fucked I am," he whispered.

She could tell from his tone that he didn't – not really, but he would. She would show him.

"Transform into a giant, black dog."

He shrieked as his bones broke and twisted.

"Quietly."

The shaking in her hands spread to her knees.

"Faster."

The man disappeared. Sam addressed the hound before her.

"You are now my faithful servant. You will do my binding with absolute, blind loyalty and you will love every second of it. If I say jump, you jump."

The dog jumped.

"But, deep within this beast's mind, you, Michael Seamus Flannery, will see and know everything that I make you do. You will never be able to stop me. Do you understand?"

The dog yipped in agreement.

"Great."

Sam pulled a collar from her hoodie. Affixed to the collar was a mini food bowl and a blank bone where his name would be etched. She sighed.

"I'm too tired to name you," she said. "You're Dog. The bowl will drop twice a day and fill with food. That is the only food you'll eat. Drink, piss and shit at will."

She patted his head.

"Go away and wait for further instructions."

The dog licked her hand once and ran away.

Sam collapsed back onto the picnic table – so, so glad that was over. Sweat draped her body. She tried to focus on the strength she would need to get home. She coughed, low and short.

Oh fuck, this is so bad.

Sam knew from experience what those little coughs meant.

She scuffed the drawn circle with the toe of her left foot. It dropped away in a foggy, glittering crash.

So did Sam.

It was raining in the world beyond her circle.

She fell to her knees on the soft forest floor. The sickness in her lungs wracked her body. Deep, hacking coughs could not clear her airways. She found her inhaler and tried to use it.

Carl swooped down, landing with a soft pat on the pine needles next to her.

"You sound terrible."

Sam bent over like a cat hawking up a fur ball.

"It's not that bad," she breathed at him, when she could.

The bird tilted its sharp head at her.

"That was dumb - not telling your friends to come back here and check on you. You should have thought of that."

Sam leaned back and cursed the rain, this fucking bird, all white supremacists everywhere and, last but certainly not least, her traitorous lungs. Icy droplets soaked her hoodie.

"Will you die?" Carl squawked. "If you die, can I eat your eyes?"

She glared at him.

"Fuck you, Carl," she breathed. "Go get them. Bring Ronnie and Jimmy back here."

He picked a bug from the forest floor and gulped it back.

"Maybe I don't want to," he said. "Maybe I want to eat your eyes."

The world got fuzzy and dim.

"Maybe you have to do what I say," Sam heaved.

"What do your intestines taste like?" he asked as he flapped and strutted. "You look like you eat a lot of cheese."

"Eat a bag of dicks, Carl."

"Happily, where are they?" The bird looked around. "If you die, who rules the Darkness?"

Sam crawled toward the corvid until they were eye to eye.

"I rule the Holy Darkness," she gasped, but it felt like a lie. "I have always ruled the Holy Darkness. I will always rule the Holy Darkness. Now, go get help."

She met the black pool of his eye and held him. He hopped from one foot to another.

"You don't even know what the Holy Darkness is," he replied.

From the primordial depths of her soul, Sam commanded: "Fuck off, Carl."

The bird turned to face the trail, as though something far away called to him. He flew off.

Sam knelt on the forest floor. Pine needles dug into her hands and knees. She half-coughed, half-puked. Her wrenching marred the simple quiet of the rainy forest. Sam tasted the sharp tang of blood. Shivering overtook her again. The stubborn, violent need for survival in her soul urged her to crawl under the picnic table.

Sam, anointed Goddess of Death, was *pretty* certain that she couldn't *actually* die but when the music floated her way she had a doubt.

The singer's voice, high, ancient and filled with the rage of the dying, pierced the quiet.

Sam swore she heard a steel guitar accompany him. She pulled herself off the ground and using her staff as a cane she stumbled along the stream up the mountain toward the sound.

On another night, in another life, she would have loved this – the pitter patter of the rain, the way the trees sighed and expanded. The sacred quiet brought low and human with music.

He sat, long legs propped up on a rock beneath a massive oak. Its branches offered shelter from the rain. Thick, snarled, inky hair reached his chin. The man's skin was as pale as a vampire's. He wore all black – jeans, t-shirt, jacket and boots. His small, white teeth flashed when he caught sight of her.

"Death, welcome," he said. "Please sit."

He nodded to a tree stump. Sam, too exhausted to be suspicious, sat. Two pigs sidled up to her, one on each side. She nearly cried at their warmth. She leaned her head onto one of the pig's round bellies. The man played on – hypnotic and low. She closed her eyes.

"Is this your forest?" Sam asked in an effort not to be rude.

He smiled and kept playing. Sam couldn't decide if he was tragically beautiful or a gothic villain.

"I guard this forest," he said.

Visions of an ancient land, riddled with mist, crooked trees and cattle swam in Sam's mind. This man stood in the midst of it all, although he looked different than he did today with a long, flowing, gray beard and mane, giant horns protruding from his forehead.

"Veles… I missed you," she murmured.

"I missed you too, lady." The guitar got quieter. "You can rest now, Anand."

A thought nagged at the corner of her mind and she jerked awake.

"Wait, I know you," she said, but consciousness floated further and further away. "You're that guy. You play Don Julio's in the valley…." Sam lost the battle with exhaustion. "You're Jakob

Blanc. Dre loves you. He keeps trying to get me to go see your show."

"Yes, Sam," he told her. "I'm him too. Rest now."

And he sang her to sleep with a lullaby.

*****

Midnight, Nov. 3, 648 B.C.E., 2,666 years before the Fog

Water sluiced down her face. Lightning arced and raced across the sky. Thunder dropped and shook her skeleton. She'd clawed her way up the pile of bodies to him. Lightning killed half of them. She'd slaughtered the rest. The stink of ozone mingled with the stench of blood too thick to be washed away.

The fucker would not stop laughing even though the tip of her short sword stuck out his back.

It was a miracle he still stood.

He smiled that cruel smile – hands on hips, blindly triumphant, acting like his every breath wasn't borrowed from her hands.

"But you can't kill me?" he asked. "Can you, woman? I am greater than death. I am a force. You cannot kill me. I am a GOD."

Would you please just fucking die already? I'm cold, wet and direly in need of a cup of tea.

Lightning flashed and thunder rumbled.

It crept behind her. He was too smug to notice the strange clouds drifting up from the ground. They lazily caressed the corpses beneath them. Lightning illuminated the scene – the tendrils pulling from the earth.

He looked suddenly terrified. The Fog surrounded him. The lightning stopped. An after-image of the grimacing planes of his face burned into her memory.

She yanked the sword from his gut. Feeling it catch on his ribs, she shoved it with every ounce of her strength straight up through his jaw out the top of his head.

He fell over dead.

Try me, asshole.

*****

The Liminal Space

Sam awoke to the deep, rich smell of cooked meat. She inhaled and sat up when she realized her lungs worked.

The room she found herself in was small. A bright fire pit burned in its center. Jakob Blanc stood over the fire, a living shadow in the dark room. He tended to the roasting meat.

Something wasn't right. Sam felt uneasy in her bones. She didn't know how she got here and the room tilted at odd angles when she moved. She struggled to sit up in the pile of animal hides surrounding her.

He turned.

"Rise and shine."

He plunged a tankard into a barrel a few feet from the fire.

"Here," he smiled and handed it to her, "you're going to need this."

She took the small metal cup. Its high alcohol content was clear from the smell.

"Why do I need…"

All three of her Celestial Mothers emerged from the shadows behind him. They were clearly pissed. Black droplets fell from Badb's fingertips, hissing when they touched the wooden floor.

Sam had zero fucking clue what was happening.

"Where was the error?" Badb demanded.

"What are you talking about?" Sam asked.

Dark tendrils spread from the Goddess of Battle's fingertips.

"You could have died!"

"Yeah?" Sam clamored out of the pile of furs. "And? So what? I'm the Goddess of Death. It's not like I can *actually* die."

Nemain's gaze didn't rise from studying the floor.

"You can," she whispered. "In this state, you can."

"Where was the error?" Badb thundered.

What's wrong with you? Why aren't you perfect? Why can't you be perfect? I need you to be perfect.

Sam's breath came in quick, frantic bursts. She backed away from the women and searched for the exit.

Anand strode forward.

"Sisters, stop," she said. "Look at her."

A part of Sam's mind stepped away from the rage and panic and looked at herself.

Stand up straight, it said. Look them in the eye. Laugh. Pretend like it's fine. Then get the fuck out of here.

"She's terrified," Nemain murmured.

Badb's rage softened.

"She split herself in two out of fear."

Sam had never hated anything in her life as much as she hated these women right now. She dug her fingers into the wall, splinters broke through her flesh. No one was allowed to see her like this – this crazed, cornered animal. Sam clawed at the wall. Her entire being shivered. Shrieking screams climbed out of her throat. The wall gave way.

You need to learn what's wrong with you. You need to understand why you're a terrible person.

She stepped back, the parts of herself resolved into one. She hurled herself at the wall. The second before crashing into it, a shivering overtook her, reality pulsed and she transformed into a raven.

Sam flew away.

*****

Midnight, Oct. 30, 2020, 32 days after The Fog

The moon rose high overhead and as the clock struck midnight in a world where time no longer mattered.

A tall, slender woman with thick, auburn hair rummaged around in the back of her guest room closet. She hid these objects from her husband.

"What are you praying for, sweetheart?" he would ask. "I give you everything you need."

"I'm praying for you, baby," she repeated. "I'm praying for you."

She pulled the black candle, a raven's feather, and a red piece of cloth from the box and arranged the objects on a low, wooden table against the western wall of the room. She opened the thick, black curtains to let in what moonlight she could on this overcast night.

She tried to ignore the burning inside her body, and the bruises on her neck and head, to focus on her goddess as she knelt before the simple altar.

Yvette inhaled, centering herself, before placing her hands upon the table. The pain faded away and the rage of her goddess flooded her. She opened her eyes.

Between her hands, sat the two burnished halves of a man's gold wedding band.

Yvette covered her mouth to muffle the scream – a habit she developed early on in her marriage.

Long moments she stood there, eyes darting back and forth, breath coming fast and low, mind racing. She couldn't move, couldn't act.

The scream welled up in her throat again. This time she didn't quell it. High, shrieking sobs burst out of her mouth. Yvette clawed at her throat, scratching her skin raw. She flung the altar across the room, threw herself onto the bed and tore the sheets. Yvette picked up the rocking chair in the room and heaved. She beat it against the walls until exhausted. Then she collapsed to the floor.

Between hiccuping sobs, she panted out:

"Th-th-thank y-you. Thank you. Thank you." Until her voice was gone.

A TERRIBLY LONG AND SUNNY DAY

1:10 am, Oct. 30, 2020, 32 days after The Fog

Sam emerged from the tear in the wall to find herself lying under an oak tree in the forest. Jakob Blanc lay next to her, holding her hand. His deep-set eyes were shut.

She jerked her hand out of his. He didn't move. Sam grabbed his shoulder and shook. He gave no response. She tried and failed to lift him up.

Sam understood that his body needed to remain in this forest – that this was how she must have looked floating for a month in the Saint Augustus river, but abandoning a man passed out on the forest floor felt wrong. She studied him in the darkness. She decided that the harsh angles of his cheeks and razor thin lips were beautiful.

Even her short time in the Liminal Space had restored her. Plus, she'd gained a nifty new skill. Rolling away from the tree's shelter, she stood.

The edges of her skin – the lines between herself and the world – blurred and shook. Her form folded in on itself to become feathers and claws.

The world settled into sharp technicolor. Sam cawed and flew into the night.

Once in the air, she tried to ignore the fresh scars on the landscape of her town – the boardwalk in smouldering ruins, monsters and coral palaces half-submerged off the coast, flying angels and demons circling the night sky with her. Great swaths of town ran red with blood. Mythical forests and rivers dotted the edges of the county.

Sam's heart broke with the knowledge that she couldn't fix it. She couldn't undo what had been done, but she could keep it from getting worse. She banked left and in slow descending circles landed on Chiba's driveway. Sam unfolded herself into human form.

The Wraiths, shivering in agony, greeted her.

"You have a message from your Celestial Mothers," the right one intoned.

"Great," she snarled and tried to brush past. The Wraith refused to move. Sam could not bear to end her evening passing through Wraith sludge. She gagged at the thought, but so help her, she'd do it to avoid this conversation.

"I don't want to hear it," she said. "Move!"

To her eternal gratitude, the shower curtains parted and she opened the Leary's door with the key Chiba gave her only to be hit by a ballistic missile disguised as a hyperactive five year old.

"Auntie!" Malak yelled.

"Oof." Sam managed to keep her legs under her this time. "Hey, Tiny Hurricane. Can you keep your voice down, please? Isn't it *way, way* past your bedtime? What are you doing up so late?"

Malak leapt away. Sam sat down on the gray armchair so she could remove her wet socks and shoes.

"Uh, huh," Malak said in what she considered a whisper, which meant yelling in a whispering voice. "The angry bird lady woke me up. She said if I told you to see your brother, she would teach me to fight."

Sam peeled off her left purple sock and grimaced at its sogginess. Ridley huffed in his sleep in his crate behind the chair.

"What angry bird lady?" she asked. "You need to go back to bed, Malak."

"The angry bird lady in my dream." Malak twirled and chewed her hair. "She said I can fight. I wanna fight, Auntie."

Sam stilled. She tilted her chin at Malak and stuffed the terror down low so the little girl wouldn't notice.

"Does the angry bird lady have a name, honey?"

"Bad," Malak giggled. "But she's not bad. But her name is bad."

She fell backward onto the floor laughing – her footie pajamas covered in pink and purple giraffes. The night had been too long and exhausting for Sam to fully process this development. She leaned over and held out a hand to Malak.

"Okay, Goofy Giraffe Girl, time for bed."

She wrapped her tiny hand in Sam's and made a show of trying to yank her over.

"You have a brother, Auntie?" Malak asked. "Is he your brother like Mommy is your sister or is he your brother like Zara's my sister?"

Sam pulled her niece to her feet and herded her up the stairs.

"He's my brother like your mommy is my sister."

She stopped a few stairs ahead of Sam and turned around so her face was level with Sam's.

"'Cause you picked him?"

"Yes, baby, because we picked each other."

Malak poked a sharp, tiny, bony finger at her face.

"Why did you pick each other?"

"Because our mommies are alike."

"Why are they alike?"

"Malak," Sam said in warning.

Her niece blinked and ignored her.

"What's that?"

"That is someone stalling because she doesn't want to go to bed," Sam said.

Malak yanked at her hair and pulled out a chunk of dried, green troll blood.

"No, dis."

"That's yucky." Sam held out her hand. "Give it."

Malak made a cross-eyed, slow motion show of placing the hunk of goo in her mouth.

"Malak Samara Leary, do NOT eat that," Sam ordered in her Most Commanding Voice. "That is yucky. It will make you sick."

"Aww." She hung her head in defeat and handed over the contraband. "Fine."

Malak slumped over. Her arms drooped to signal that the gross injustice of bedtime weighed heavily upon her poor, innocent soul. Then she stomped down the hallway to her room.

"Night, Auntie."

"Night, baby. I love you."

*****

4:03 am, Oct. 30, 2020, 32 days after *The Fog*

Miles away, near the top of the mountain, almost to the edge of Sunset Cove county line, Jimmy and Ronnie ran amok.

They'd chased rabbits up and down these mountains. They were too far gone into blood lust to notice that every rabbit they devoured was jet black and had fur vaguely reminiscent of feathers.

Jimmy felt a little at war with himself over these hunts. He had never fed on a human – not even that first blood-soaked night, but he still felt both guilty and exhilarated hunting and eating these small creatures.

As the hours of chase, capture and consumption wore on, Jimmy got bored. The night was winding down and it was almost time for them to head back to his studio, backyard in-law unit at his grandmother's house when he realized they had reached the edge of Sunset Cove county.

Since the night of The Fog, it hadn't even occurred to him that he could leave. As he and Ronnie dropped out of their blood lust and he realized that the county line had become just that – a line. A two–foot-wide depression separated Sunset Cove from the rest of the world.

"Hold up," Jimmy told Ronnie and walked toward it. Even the trees and vegetation were split at this exact point. Some part of Jimmy's brain, the same part that told when to leave downtown during a night of partying, screamed.

Still, it's just a line, right?

He reached out slow and steady – to reassure himself that it was no big deal.

As his hand hovered inches from the barrier, Jimmy noticed a wide, black band around his forearm.

Where did that come from?

He lurched forward a bit in surprise. His hand hit the barrier like a bomb. The blast knocked over all the trees in a mile radius. A cacophony rose up from the forest as wildlife and woodland creatures scuttled in fear.

The force of the shockwave flung Ronnie two miles away.

When the werewolf awoke, he smelled the first rays of morning peeking over the mountain.

Ronnie spent ten minutes, hackles raised and howling, low and desperate, searching for Jimmy. He found him unconscious, wedged between two downed trees.

The werewolf slung his vampire friend over his shoulder and raced further into the forest. He found a soft patch of dirt and dug until his claws bled. With seconds to spare, he threw Jimmy into the four-foot deep hole and shoved dirt over every inch of his friend.

Then he circled the patch of dirt three times. Ronnie moved a bit of dirt away to create a pillow for his head and settled in for guard duty until sunset.

Maybe this'll make up for the intestines, he thought before drifting off.

*****

10:16 am, Oct. 30, 2020, 32 days after The Fog

Sam left the Learys' house the next morning with a belly full of blueberry waffles and a heart full of dread. The strength she'd gained from visiting Jakob in the Liminal Space was waning and her brother lived on the other side of the county.

"Scum," she greeted the Wraiths.

Sam hopped down the driveway and tore a hole in reality before she lost her nerve. She tightened the black hood over her head and tried to think Dark Thoughts.

"This is gonna suck," she said and leapt through the shimmering tear.

Sam landed face first in a sand dune. Her left shoe had disappeared in transit. She brushed the sand from her face and sat up.

The ocean roared behind her. Before The Fog, a few scraggly locals would be found walking their dogs or communing with the sea on this mile-long stretch of sand. This was one of the few areas of Sunset Cove with a traditional beach. The ocean usually met the land in craigy cliff faces and rocky outcroppings. The lone corpse of a monstrous, beached goldfish was her only company today. Sam could have walked into its mouth with twenty feet to spare. Rows of foot-long teeth dripped with rotting flesh. The stench of it made her eyes water.

The sea was gray and moody, with little difference between it and the sky. Mist whipped through the air. This was the first time she'd seen the ocean since returning. Like all humans, she stared at it for a moment, breathing in its nature. Her lungs rebelled and a coughing fit ensued.

The morning mist offered little protection from the incessant glare of her brother's kingdom. Even this diffused light burned through her clothes. It sapped her strength and fed the sickness in her lungs.

Sam climbed the large dune to the highway. Dre and Gracie's farmhouse sat about two miles due east. As she reached the top of the dune, a massive shadow loomed over head.

Where the two lane highway had been, stood a fifty-foot tall thicket. The living wall was straight out of a fairytale. Thick. green vines with inch-long thorns wove together into an impenetrable barrier that ran in either direction as far as the eye could see.

"Damn, Dre," Sam muttered. "You are not fucking around."

She stood before the living wall and feeling like the Biggest Idiot in the World, announced:

"Hello! I am," she cleared her throat, "The Morrigan, Goddess of Death, Queen of Darkness..."

She felt stupid in her bones.

"I seek audience with my brother, Ama, Sun God, Creator of All Life, the man responsible for this godforsaken sunlight trying to rip my eyeballs out."

The critters scurrying among the writhing vines went silent.

"Anybody? Dre??"

The air around her stilled and then, in the farthest corner of her mind, a gentle bemusement and one relentless thought: *prove it.*

She stepped back and looked at the massive wall before her.

Prove it? Seriously?

"Okay, fine," Sam said and reached out. Her left hand hovered above the thick vines. She closed her eyes. The life, beautiful and pulsing through their cells, burned bright in her mind. Death and Darkness coiled around her heart. She let an infinitesimal fraction of it loose and wrapped it around her. Death radiated from her very being. The vines withered and shrank. Sam stepped forward. Her presence killed every living creature from single-celled amoeba to giant rat within a three-foot radius. As she walked into the crevice she made, the vines grew back around her.

The barrier was about ten-feet deep. Sam paused halfway through to admire the intricacy of the latticework of life. Patches of sunlight streamed into the most impenetrable inner layer. The half-rotted corpse of a raccoon was suspended five feet above her. All sound was muffled and peaceful except the buzz of vibrant, exotic insects. The creatures of this ecosystem kept well away from her. They poked their heads out a bit, eyes glowing through the beautiful gloom.

"Hello," she said and nodded to their uneasy presence. "Just passing through. I'll be out of your hair in a minute."

Sam emerged from the cool shelter of the hedge to relentless sunlight and overwhelming heat. A fourteen-foot-tall bull elephant stood before her. His tusks brushed the ground, when, in a delightful impression of human etiquette, he bowed.

"Hello, beautiful!" Sam said. The animal's thin tail wagged. The tufted end flicked bugs as it swished back and forth. "Are you my escort?"

He lumbered his weight around in a slow circle until he faced Dre's house and waited for her to follow.

"Brother, you are spoiling me," Sam said. "Thank you!"

Sam kept up a running commentary of her admiration for the elephant. She was desperate to ignore the stress of traversing her brother's kingdom. Sunlight punched through her skull. It disrupted her thoughts. She could only concentrate on the next step. Her stupid lungs labored and wheezed.

This stretch of land had been populated with low scrub trees and grass before The Fog. Now, she caught glimpses of a savanna – when her brain could process the sight.

"I love your ears," she said. "I love everything with big ears. It's a thing. Chiba has big ears so I assume everyone and everything with big ears is as cool as Chiba. Gray is my favorite color. Your wrinkles are amazing. Do you actually eat peanuts? Would you like some peanuts? I can get you some peanuts. I rode an elephant when I was a kid. I'm sorry. I didn't know it hurt them. Do you need anything? You have my heart. Do you need any tacos? The soul of your mortal enemy tortured for all eternity? I would do that for you. Can I hug you? I'm serious about the mortal enemy thing. You might be the most beautiful being I've ever seen."

She took one step after another, dizzy, but too stubborn to stop. A cough burst from her throat. Sam snuck two quick shots of her inhaler. The elephant's left eye assessed her. Its perfect wrinkles conveyed concern and disbelief. He sat, blocking her path through the copse of trees and low shrubbery. None of this was native to Sunset Cove. She'd seen pictures of these umbrella-like trees, thin trunks and uplifted branches in photos but never in real life.

"What?" Sam demanded. She didn't want to be cranky with this beautiful creature but the tiny sun daggers hurt her mood.

He refused to turn and look at her.

"Dude, it's fine," she said. "I'm fine. Don't worry about it. Let's go. I can totally do this."

Sam wondered if she'd lose the title of 'Goddess of Truth' if she kept lying like this.

The elephant, who she called Dashi for no real reason, would not budge. Sam crept to his back and poked him.

"Seriously, I'm okay."

The elephant, smartly, did not believe her.

"Fine, I'm hugging you."

Sam maneuvered past Dashi's back haunch and stepped over a twisted tree trunk. She leaned into him and splayed her arms wide across his belly. His hide felt rougher than sandpaper. She inhaled his clean muddy scent. He turned his massive head, wafted his ears and patted her head with his trunk.

"I would take a bullet for you. Do you need my kidney for any reason at all?"

A gangly thing crashed through the bushes behind her. Sam, too exhausted to care, didn't bother to turn around to see what it was.

The humming sunlight tried again and again to tear her body into bloody chunks. It nestled into her cells. As it burned them, it bounced back, finding another layer to destroy. It didn't just kill her – it erased her.

Without her volition, her hoodie grew into a robe that covered every inch of Sam's body. The Darkness within the garment expanded in an attempt to protect her, but the light proved too strong. In the dim, barely functioning corners of her mind, she considered particle physics, feedback loops and that Dre owed her a beer.

Dashi wrapped his trunk around her waist and lifted her high in the air. He deposited Sam between the two massive humps of a camel.

So that's what that was.

She wanted to speak but her tongue had turned to a dusty lump stuck to the roof of her mouth.

Her guardians took off at breakneck speeds. Dashi used his mass to clear a path and Mo (which is what Sam decided to call the camel for no real reason) galloped behind.

Her soul scorched and burnt. Pieces of it broke off and flew away in the breeze.

The animals skidded to a halt in front of a low structure. Dashi peeled her from Mo's back and placed her in the opening of the shelter. He nudged her until he found her desiccated hand and moved it until she touched…

Sam inhaled and screamed – blind and burning in the mad winds of the Sun.

"Tell her she is welcome in your Realm. Say it! Announce that she is protected and to be left alone. Say it!" The distant voices would have been loud if her ears hadn't seared away.

A second voice – softer, not so 'it's my way or the highway' repeated the words.

Silence.

Andre Sussex Damascus stared down at the black pit lying before him and wanted a cigarette – badly. His fingers twitched with need and memory. A figure, clad in a robe so dark no light penetrated or escaped it, had appeared in his garden. It screamed with Sam's voice.

Some instinct told him not to reach out to help her. He knew it would hurt her more.

Four skeletal fingers peaked out from the left edge of the abyss.

One damn cigarette. He wouldn't even smoke it. Just smell it.

As he watched, fascinated, ribbons of black emerged from the robe and knit sinew and skin on to exposed bone.

Nope, he'd smoke it. Gracie'd understand. Hell, he'd smoke packs while lying in a field of wildflowers for days and days. Just laying there watching the sun drift across the sky.

The hand, pink and fresh, disappeared back into the robe and popped back out holding an unlit cigarette.

"Sam!" He exclaimed and reached for her.

His hand passed through hers.

"Is this a joke?" Dre asked.

"Tell him he is welcome in your Realm," Ama said. "Announce that he is not a threat and is protected."

"He is…" Sam's raspy voice heaved from beneath the darkness. She choked but didn't drop the cigarette. Sam sat back on her heels. Her strained face appeared within the inky folds. "He is welcome in my Realm. He is not a threat and he is to be protected."

"Excellent!" Ama said and pounded his cane into the ground. "You may take the offering."

Dre leaned over again to take the cigarette from her – without incident this time.

Sam pushed herself up to stand but swayed with the effort.

"That?" she breathed, trying to pull oxygen into her lungs. "Sucked."

Dre wrapped his arms around her and lifted her several inches off the ground.

"Hey, Big Brother," she muttered into his chest tattoo. She tried and failed to wrap her squished arms around him. He kissed the top of her head.

"I missed you," she said.

She seemed more fragile than he remembered. A hacking cough erupted from her lungs. Dre set her down and patted her back as she retched.

"Pneumonia again?" he asked.

"I really" *cough* "wish" *cough hack cough* "people" *hack hack* "would stop" *cough cough* "saying 'again.'"

"Imagine how we feel," Dre replied.

"Fair," Sam wheezed. "Fair."

As the hoodie pieced her organs back together, and self-awareness returned, she realized they stood in a field of riotous flowers.

Purple. A LOT. Of purple.

Deep scarlet Amaranth, star-shaped, lavender California borage, elegant pinkish-purple milkweed, mulberry tree limbs reached toward the sky laden with juicy, dark red berries, wild – almost alien – patterned passion flower. Purple cones of anise hyssop emerged from bright green triangular leaves, long waxy leaves of healing yerba santa, odd, gangly yet nutritious snake gourd, a few bright sunflowers, delicate periwinkle heal-all, medicinal earthstar mushrooms, extravagant scarlet emperor runner beans.

She'd never seen anything like this assault of life and color. It was tranquil and heartbreaking. Red and purple were Dre and Gracie's wedding colors.

In the center of his Kingdom, in the middle of his testament to his love, was his home garden. Seven or so above-ground beds (accursed gophers, he told her at lunch one day) of black kale, green beans, mint, thyme and others. Handmade wooden trellises bracketed each end. Fat orange and yellow pumpkins and squash dripped from them. Dre's pride in the height of these hanging vegetables knew no bounds. He bragged about them endlessly and took any excuse to show her pictures of their steady progress.

Nothing about this place made sense to Sam – the angles of tree branches, the quality of light, the odd, stinging hum of unfettered life. While she loved it and couldn't tear her eyes from the wonders it held, she fought the innate urge to kill everything and start over with a semblance of order.

The Fog did nothing to change Dre's outward appearance. In fact, Sam was almost certain he wore that same outfit the last time she saw him – open-toe sandals, knee-length jean shorts, gray tank top and a lavender Hawaiian shirt. His loose afro and long beard were shot through with gray.

He was the kind of man who smiled and nodded to every single person he passed on the street and not one of them could stop themselves from returning the courtesy.

"Your Death Bringer is a mess."

Sam came to several horrifying conclusions all at once:

1 -   Her hoodie had transformed from a perfectly normal, cotton poly-blend sweatshirt into a silky, black cloak. It slithered when she moved and was three times too large. It made her look like a small child playing dress up in a real goddess's clothes.

2 -   The man speaking was Ama – the God Creator of All Life on Earth and she wasn't one hundred percent certain she'd gotten all the troll blood out of her hair.

3 -   She had lost her other shoe.

"Ama," Sam said and bowed. Her hood flipped over her head, burying her face in fabric. She shoved it back and pretended, with all her might, to be a queen.

A small man, he stood a foot shorter than Dre. Yet, he seemed to take up more space than his stature implied. He wore sandals like Dre, dark, knee-length shorts, a black tank top and a brown and black Hawaiian shirt. Within the deep planes and angles of this man's burnt umber face, Sam saw … everyone. All people came from him and in some way everyone looked like him – from the shape of his eyes to the curve of his lip, the high jut of his cheekbones. Sam could see not just every person she'd ever met, but everyone who had ever and would ever live.

You're so beautiful, Sam thought.

"Thank you, Death Bringer," Ama said. "You are very kind."

Dre met her surprised gaze.

"He's a mind reader," Dre said.

Oh! That's so obnoxious! I bet you hate that!

"Yes," Ama said. "My heir finds my abilities unfortunate."

The old man studied her. His eyes rested on her forehead before scanning every inch of her face. Sam tried and failed not to freak out.

"You're sure about this one?" he asked Dre.

Dre folded his arms and didn't utter a word. Sam knew that look. Once he made up his mind, no power in this world or the next could sway Dre Damascus. The old man shrugged.

Ama tapped her forehead.

A long, vibrating black string stuck to his finger. The other end remained in her skull.

"Huh," he said, examining his finger.

"The fuck!?" Sam touched her forehead but felt nothing but skin.

"He did it to me, too," Dre said, appearing nonplussed by the situation. "Mine is purple."

"Of course, it is," Sam said as she flailed at the air between them. Her hands passed through the black line connecting her to the God of Life.

Ama twisted the thread between his fingers and examined it. His face inches from a piece of what she assumed was her soul.

"You are dying, Death Bringer," Ama said. "Your lungs will fail before the sun sets."

Sam straightened.

"I am the Goddess of Death," she said and fought to breathe through the cough erupting from her chest. "I am the Queen of the Darkness."

Sam was about to list her titles but he interrupted her.

"Is that what she calls you? Queen of the Darkness?" Ama's mouth quirked in a smile for a split second as he studied the string. "That's cute."

A chill passed through Sam's bones.

"Is that what *who* calls me?" she asked.

Ama's milky, brown eyes, ancient and not unkind, met hers over the cat's cradle of her soul in his hands.

"You still can't remember? Interesting."

Panic rose up from her belly and out of her mouth.

"Can't remember what?" Her lungs seized. She couldn't breathe. Shallow hiccuping coughs replaced inhalations.

"Who don't I remember?" Sam gasped and dropped to her hands and knees. Dre knelt beside her, patting her back.

"Ama," Dre said, his voice full of reverence and fear. "Help. Please."

"I'm trying to, my heir," he said. The tangled clump shook in his hands. He searched it until he noticed the minuscule blue shard disrupting the flow of her existence. Ama pursed his lips and blew. The little, blue thorn flipped end over end out of the frantic mass of black string. It disintegrated in the sunlight.

Sam's coughing fit stopped.

The jumbled string in Ama's hands calmed, vibrating happily.

Ama untangled her soul from his fingers and tapped her forehead. The line disappeared.

He held her face in his hands.

"It is good we finally meet, little Death Bringer," he said and patted her cheek. "Give her my regards when you return to her."

Sam stood, fists clenched at her sides. Oxygen filled her brain at a dizzying speed.

"Who? Who are you talking about?"

The sadness in his face terrified her.

"Death Bringer, so many versions of you left behind in so many places," he said. "Which one is the truth?"

"What?" Her mind would not wrap itself around the question. "I don't understand."

His voice dropped in a way that was meant to be soothing but her blood ran cold.

"You will."

With that, the old man spun on his heel and jaunted away with far too much vigor for someone of his advanced years.

Dre stood next to her watching him speed walk away.

"Pneumonia?"

"Gone."

"Good," he said, exhaling in relief. "I would love to imbibe to celebrate but I don't have any…"

Sam reached into her ridiculous robe and pulled out a six pack.

"I missed you." He bumped his shoulder into hers.

"Missed you too, big brother," she replied. Sam leaned into his side, squashing down the memory of the future she had seen.

*****

The Liminal Space

This is how it ended.

He stood before her. For one shining moment, she'd been so proud of both of them – her big, heroic brother. Her power echoed through every molecule around them. How far they'd both come.

And then it dawned on her. The emptiness of him. Hollowed out and wrecked. He couldn't look at her. No quick darting jokes. No sly grin. His soul as heavy as the earth around them.

She hadn't even noticed the desiccated corpse Sunset Cove had become in her triumphant joy.

"They're gone," he said. "I need to follow them. I can't be here."

Sam had emerged minutes ago and ran straight to him.

"Who's gone, Dre? I don't understand. What are you talking about?"

It was then that she noticed the burnt hull of the farmhouse.

"No!" She gasped. Two dirt mounds scarred the ground fifteen feet behind him

"No!"

But it was true. Sam felt their bodies rotting beneath the earth. She closed her mind against the knowledge of Sohlie's tiny corpse.

"Send me to them, please." He touched her arm. He still had rough farmer's hands.

They were gods now. How did this go so wrong?

Tears raced down her cheeks.

She looked around for an excuse, anything to save her from this moment, from his request because she didn't have a reason to refuse him. It was then that the details of this new world sunk in – once verdant hillsides scorched and bleeding. Sam reached out with her goddess mind and felt it all, her beloved home a gutted and smouldering wreck. Its people murdered, enslaved, starving and behind it all … him. Laughing.

She didn't yet know about the pieces of her best friend strewn across town or the tiny starved body lying in a gutter on Wilson or the white-hot outline of a man cradling his daughter etched onto a garage floor, or the scruffy, gray dog that had just disappeared. None of the truth of this reality had revealed itself to her yet.

She doubled over and couldn't catch her breath.

"Sister?"

She met his soft brown eyes.

"I don't think I can do this."

"Sam, I need to be with them." He knelt down to meet her eyes. "I miss my wife. I miss my little girl."

And she knew. Every part of her knew. The calluses on her little toes knew.

"Okay," she said. She yanked him up with her before she could stop herself. "Stand up." Sam shook off the grief and rage and loss for a moment.

"You're sure?"

"Absolutely," he said and that sly smile flashed and disappeared again.

Sam reached up. Her left hand hovered over his heart. They had become gods and he still wore that ridiculous Hawaiian shirt. In her mind's eye, she saw the molecules of him – masses of patterns, electrical activity and that indefinable essence. She searched until she found it. The thread of hope holding him to this reality. She reached through his heart and snapped it.

Sam stepped back to open her eyes. His body disintegrated into gray dust over the earth. A purple flame burned bright and cheery in her left hand. An ill wind tossed her hair and cloak about as the remaining life and color in Sunset Cove raced to her open hand.

The fire grew until it engulfed her. For one last moment, she held onto the bright, warm life. She heard it – the giggles, the cries, the joy, the terror. It surrounded her. Yet, it was nothing she could touch.

She straightened her left arm, tore open reality, and the Life of Sunset Cove swept through the opening – leaving her, or so she thought, utterly alone.

She had become Death.

*****

Dre's Kingdom, The Liminal Space

"Thank you for my escorts," Sam told him.

They sat across from each other at the weather-beaten picnic table.

"You're welcome." Dre drummed his fingers on the table's surface and pulled the dark gray rectangle vape out of his pocket and set it on the table. Sam knew it held THC for his anxiety. "I thought you'd enjoy them."

"Does that even work here?" Sam gestured to the pen.

"Sadly, it failed many moons ago."

She waved her hand over the mechanism.

"Try it now."

His eyes lit up. Dre took a deep pull from the pen. The muscles in his shoulders and back unlocked as the vapor did its job. He turned his head and exhaled away from her.

"Glorious!" He exclaimed, clapping in relief.

"Better?"

"Much. You're wonderful. Thank you."

Sam struggled for something to say, to bridge the gap of time and change between them. She stared off into the distance at the mountains of lavender, violet and crimson plants – the color so intense that it made her eyes ache.

"It's beautiful," she said.

"I was going for subtle. Understated," he deadpanned, a dancing twinkle in his eyes.

Mother fucker.

Sam nearly spit out the swig of beer she'd just taken. Her shoulders shook. She fought and almost failed to keep beer from shooting out her nose. The battle won, Sam swallowed.

"Mission accomplished," she said. "It's a perfect whisper of purple with a hint of red."

He leaned back, making a show of assessing his kingdom.

"I was thinking of adding a couple more wisteria over there but I'm afraid it will be too much." Dre made a steeple of his fingers. He gazed at her over them. A smirk played at the corners of his mouth. "What do you think? Too much? Or should I do it?"

Sam wiped beer from her mouth with the back of her hand to hide the giggles.

"I think two or three would be fine. But no more, like, you couldn't do five."

He nodded solemnly.

"You're absolutely right. That would be too much."

"Yes, practically ostentatious."

He snorted. She giggled, wiping a tear from her eye.

When the God of Life and Goddess of Death hungout, they had the combined age and sense of humor of two twelve year olds on a sugar high.

"Dare I ask how it is out there?"

Sam pulled her knee up to her chest. She hugged it – debating how honest she should be with him.

"What do you want to know?" she asked and chugged half the bottle.

"You see anyone?" He gazed beyond her shoulder and she knew what he was really asking. "This place? It feels… " Dre shook his head.

"It's kinda fucked," Sam said. "I feel it too, more now. Probably not to the level you do. It feels…"

"Out of balance," he finished – diplomatic as ever.

She finished her beer and popped open another.

"There's too much death. It's okay. You can say it."

"What's the plan?"

So many things I can't tell you yet. Don't ask again because the weight of this is killing me but sharing it with you would be a burden even you couldn't bear.

"Your Life Bringers have disappeared," Sam said. "There's not enough food. I know they're not all dead. Do you have any idea what's happened to them?"

"Are you going to kill them?"

She knew why he asked but the question hurt.

"No," she said, willing him to understand all the things she couldn't say. "The lack of balance hurts me too. I'm still me, Dre."

He studied her – the wild hair, over-sized robe and deep shadows beneath her eyes.

"You are, aren't you? Somehow that scares me more than anything. Tell me, sister, how did you get out of the Liminal Space?"

Sam shrugged.

"I decided to leave and I was out." *This*, she didn't have to lie about. The cacophony of birds and rustling of animals around them went silent. He slammed his empty beer down onto the table.

"You think I haven't tried?" he asked - his soft brown eyes full of rage. "Get me out of here, Sam."

She pulled a flat, square stone from her hoodie and touched his hand.

"I will try. I don't think I can, but I will try." She slid the stone across the table. "In the meantime, I can do this."

The stone, about half an inch deep, two inches high and about four inches across, had two perfect holes in it. Dre wiped away tears of frustration.

"It's beautiful," he said, and picked it up, examining it from every angle. He had studied geology in college before beer took over his life. "Metamorphic slate. Looks like it's been in the ocean."

"Nerd," Sam said. She tapped the rock with her nail, black ichor dripped onto it. "It's also a magic cell phone."

He glared at her.

"You're jo-"

Through the largest hole, Dre's house appeared. It was quaint as fuck in Sam's opinion – one-story, ranch-style, navy blue with white accents. Lush and well-kept bushes guarded the walls and doors. Huge, ancient trees stood guard overhead. A couple smaller oaks grew in the yard – nearly the perfect height for a child to climb. A two-story, wire, chicken coop that Dre built over two weeks, sat a few hundred feet from the house next to the goat pen.

A tiny human, legs too small to do more than toddle ran out of the house – faster than it seemed possible for someone that size.

Sohlie threw back her head, short, black curls forming a halo. She stopped and waited. Gracie followed fast on her heels. Sam could almost hear the slap of her sandals against the sidewalk.

Gracie's long, black braid swung behind her back as she chased her daughter, full, brown skirt flowing in the wind.

Gracie caught the ruffled strap of her little pink romper and swung her daughter up into her arms. Sohlie's face lit up with joy as her mother covered her face with kisses.

Gracie turned to the house and Sam caught a glimpse of the slick, silver machete strapped to her back.

Tears streamed down Dre's face. He didn't bother wiping them away.

"Better?" Sam murmured.

He nodded.

"I'll give one to Gracie. The second opening is for sound."

Dre nodded and pulled a purple, cotton handkerchief from his pocket.

"My people are congregated on the West Side," Dre said. He blew his nose delicately. "Remember where we used to store hops during the busy season?"

"The big, scary warehouse that used to be a gum factory?"

Dre nodded.

"The one where I stepped in a hole, almost broke my leg and you had to take me to urgent care?"

"Your favorite," Dre said, and folded the handkerchief up into a neat square. He tucked it back into his pocket.

"Well, fuck."

Sam tilted her head back and squinted at the blue sky – not cursing it for the first time in a month.

"Some of yours are there too," Dre said.

"What?" Sam's head swiveled back to him.

His hands rested on the table.

"You can't feel them?"

"No?"

She reached her consciousness out to the other side of town, imagining the building, rusted, yellow, corrugated walls, acres of concrete floor, decrepit idle machines and the …

Zzzzzzz

Like a live wire touched her brain.

Zzzt

"Oh, I don't like that," she said, touching her temple.

Dre took a hit from his vape pen. He stared off into the middle distance.

"So this plan of yours…"

"What makes you think I have a plan?" she asked, too quickly.

"*This*," he gestured to the world at large, "is not the kind of shit you tolerate." He laughed. "Also, when don't you have a plan?"

How well he knew her got pretty fucking obnoxious sometimes.

"Yeah, okay, I might have a plan," she admitted, rubbing the back of her neck. Sam prayed to the Holy Darkness he wouldn't ask the next question.

"And how do Gracie and Sohlie fit into this plan?"

She met his eyes – level and true.

"They don't," she said. "Not if it can be helped."

In this she could be honest, but with the opening right there…

"I wouldn't do that. But, I would like your permission to add some additional security to the farm. Nothing major: a couple Wraiths, a little protection spell here and there."

She shrugged and willed nonchalance to ooze from her pores.

"I can protect my family," he replied.

His fucking stubbornness would be the death of all life everywhere and he would fucking shrug about it while she screamed behind gritted teeth.

"Of course, you can," Sam said, and held out her palms and pulled her shoulders up to her ears. "No one's saying you can't. And you're doing an excellent job – if I may say. This is more for my own piece of mind. Like I said, nothing major, a couple of Wraiths, little spell here and there. No big."

He paused and leveled her with his gaze.

"Does your plan include me?"

"Not unless absolutely necessary."

"I can protect my family, *sister*," he shot back.

Sam was both touched and terrified. She ran the calculations and knew she wasn't gonna win this one.

"Fine, the plan includes you."

He raised one eyebrow and waved a hand in dismissal.

"Do as you will."

The animals surrounding them went back to their noisy business and Sam released the breath she'd been holding out of the side of her mouth.

"Cool."

Be. Casual. Do not bawl.

"Hey, so guess who I saw last night who's also a vampire?"

She took a swig and went back to their old routine because they were both, deep in their hearts, gossipy bitches.

He pretended to contemplate for several seconds.

"Hmm… Jocelyn?"

"Ew, no," she said. "God, I haven't thought about her in forever."

She paused for effect:

"Jimmy."

"Jimmy's a vampire?" he replied, slamming his beer down.

"I know right??"

She widened her eyes and pretended to be shocked by the news. They spoke like this for some time. Trading gossip. Rehashing old stories they'd told a thousand times before, making up stupid jokes.

"And that's why you never use a hair dryer on a goat."

"I warned you she was a biter."

"Okay, but don't you remember the hula hoop burlesque dancers?"

"Look, I've got half an ab."

"Like, I'm pretty sure there was fire."

Sam!

For one brief, terrible second Sam's consciousness split. She saw Dre sitting at the picnic table in his purple garden overlapped with him lying unconscious on the ground.

Sam!

The world shook and tumbled.

*****

12:30 pm, Oct. 30, 2020, 32 days after The Fog

Graciela Ines Smith Gutierrez-Damascus made a point to eat lunch with her husband everyday since The Fog. She packed the little wicker basket with a blanket, toys for Sohlie, a book to read aloud, water and food. Today's meal was butternut squash and leek soup with a roasted beet and spinach salad. Dessert was leftover pumpkin pie.

She arrived at the lean-to she built from planks of wood Dre was going to use for Sohlie's tree house. Gracie held her daughter in one arm and the picnic basket in the other.

She damn near dropped both.

In the opening of the shelter, lay a figure covered in black so deep and endless it sucked up the light around it.

Gracie put down the basket and tightened her grip on Sohlie. She slid her grandmother's machete from behind her back. Step by step, she inched forward, weapon extended, trying to see inside the narrow opening. The dark figure obscured her view of Dre.

Gracie remembered the night of The Fog. They were both early risers. They'd been asleep. Dre awoke sweating. He mumbled about sunshine, thirst and smashing a vase into the universe.

She tried to drag him back to bed but he wouldn't listen. He ran, barefoot, to the garden and collapsed. Gracie couldn't move him, couldn't even roll him over. The Earth had claimed him.

Then the world split open and that Damn Wall sprung forth from deep underground.

Gracie thought, at first, they were having an earthquake – the kind of temblor that shook this town when she was a kid. The earth turned to waves, heaving and writhing, Sohlie woke up screaming. Gracie tried to run back to the house to calm her but the ground rose up and dropped away beneath her feet.

When it stopped, the house was intact. Gracie ran inside to comfort Sohlie and tried to call... anyone. Her mother, her father, her brother, her best friend, Lynn. Anyone. The line went silent after a couple of rings.

She spent that night wandering between her daughter's crib and her husband's body. His chest rose and fell. A low steady pulse beat in his neck but Gracie wasn't able to lift his hand from the ground.

They settled into a mad routine once she realized that she couldn't leave the farm. She couldn't get within twenty feet of that Damn Cursed Wall. A herd of elephants, of all things, stood between her and the living edifice. They were prisoners in their own home and Gracie didn't know why. Nothing since that night made any sense.

Her garden grew without tending. Plants bore fruit out of season. Animals she'd only seen in a zoo wandered by her every day without sparing her a glance. Her husband lived without food, water or moving for a month.

None of this made sense.

So she created order where she could – with a picnic basket and a story book.

Gracie tapped the figure with the dull side of the machete. She knelt down to get a closer look, Sohlie whined in protest. Gracie put her down and reached out. She was certain her hand would pass through the darkness. Her breath caught when she touched something solid.

Gracie patted the inky blackness. The hair on her arms stood up. The fabric under her fingers brought to mind stars, ancient, exploding galaxies and the vast emptiness of space. The form beneath the fabric… Gracie realized was a person's back. She noticed the pale hand peeking from sleeve the touching Dre's. Gracie pulled the hood away from their face.

La Muerta.

"Sam!"

Sam, but not Sam, her friend's eyes flickered as ripples of power ebbed and flowed from her like a storm about to break. Sohlie whimpered. Gracie stepped back, swooped up her daughter in one arm and kept the machete at the ready.

Sam's eyes popped open. She rolled over and yanked the mass of cloth from her head.

"Hey, Gracie."

She wiped her eyes and squinted up at all five-feet, three-inches of the Most Intimidating Woman Ever. She'd once seen Gracie put together a four-course dinner party in under an hour with no warning. The woman had baked a pie from *scratch* and called it *easy*. Sam had once microwaved aluminum foil trying to nuke a potato.

Some women become goddesses after a weird fog takes over their county and they spend a month stuck in an alternate dimension. Gracie had been born a goddess.

"What the hell, Sam?"

Sam struggled to stand up through yards of fabric.

"Could you please turn back into a hoodie now?" she asked the garment engulfing her. "This is-this is embarrassing."

Sam inhaled her first true, real, full breath as a goddess. Oxygen flooded her brain as her synapses sizzled and hissed. She understood, in this moment, the weight of Death within her.

The cloak retreated into itself, becoming a harmless hoodie once more

Gracie didn't drop the machete. Sohlie clung to her, peeking her head out from her mother's chest.

ZZZZZZZZTTTTT

The buzz Sam heard in Dre's realm got louder and more insistent.

The electrical wire touched her facial nerve.

"Hi, Sohlie," Sam said, eye twitching uncontrollably.

The little girl retreated further into her mother's arms.

"Sam!" Gracie said, and waved the machete. "Focus, please. Please tell me what is going on."

And Sam couldn't. Maybe it was the electrical wire at the base of her skull. Maybe it was Gracie's kindergarten teacher manners. Maybe it was that all the thoughts of the past month built up and got caught in Sam's throat. Maybe it was the hazel eyes of the toddler in her arms. Maybe it was the vision of her tiny body rotting in a grave that haunted her every second of every day but she just … couldn't.

Sam fished the magic stone cell phone from her hoodie.

"Here," she said and handed it to Gracie. "He'll explain."

Their hands touched in passing the object. Gracie would not notice the brand new black band on her arm until much, much later. Her husband's voice echoed from the stone.

"Hello, my love."

She almost dropped it.

Sam leaned over to be eye level with the God of Life's daughter, held up her left hand, tilted her head to the side and asked the one question no toddler could refuse.

"High five, Sohlie?"

The little hand hit hers and the child jumped in excitement. Sohlie noticed the band on her arm but got distracted.

"Dada?"

Rendered virtually invisible by the rock in Gracie's hand, Sam muttered something about coming back later and took off.

She ran to the edge of the tree line near the house and sat, pulling a device from her hoodie. Biting her lip in concentration, she had to start over twice. Sam snapped her fingers without looking up.

"Carl."

The bird appeared at her side.

"Yes, Your Majesty." He tilted his head in servitude.

"I want five Wraiths patrolling the perimeter," she said. "None of the gross ones."

She didn't bother to look up from what she was typing.

"Dahmer's available," he responded promptly.

"Yeah, Dahmer's fine." She nodded. "But they don't kill anyone or anything. Only subdue."

"Understood, Your Highness," he said.

So agreeable. So compliant. Does he think I forgot?

Sam finished her chore and leaned back against the sheltering tree behind her.

"Put up a rod now. I'll come back tonight to check it and add the others."

Carl squawked in obedience. The bird hopped back and forth.

"Is that all, Your Highness?"

She put the device down and gestured to him.

"Come here."

He tried to assert his will against her. She felt the resistance and overrode it.

"Come here," she commanded. "Now."

He hopped forward to stand before her crossed legs. Sam leaned over and placed a small, white sticker on his beak.

It declared, in bold, black letters:

CAW

Sam sat back against the tree and admired her handiwork.

"Do not take that off."

"Your majesty…" He wanted to protest.

"Don't call me 'Your Majesty or 'Your Highness. I fucking hate that."

"I understand, Boss," he said. "Anything else?"

"Yeah. Fuck you, Carl."

*****

12:50 pm, Oct. 30, 2020, 32 days after The Fog

Jimmy awoke in a tunnel – not entirely sure how he got there. His body lay twisted beneath rocks that slid from the collapsed ceiling. His vampire cells told him daylight raged outside.

He clambered over the detritus and landed on his feet. Dust rose up around him.

The tunnel arched fifteen feet above his head, jagged stones stacked against each other kept the earth behind it at bay. Ancient, rusty railroad tracks led away from the collapse.

In the distance, Jimmy thought he heard the sounds of a party – loud voices and the faintest whiff of alcohol.

He picked up his baseball cap, patted the dust off it as best he could, placed it back on his head and took off toward the noise.

*****

12:55 pm, Oct. 30, 2020, 32 days after The Fog

Birds chirped cheerfully around Sam. A light breeze frolicked in from the ocean. The forest swayed in a delicate dance.

She tried to turn into a bird so she could fly over the wall and out of Dre's Kingdom but **ZZZZZZZZTTTTT**

"Motherfucker!"

The electrical wire would not let up from the base of her skull. She couldn't concentrate.

ZZZZZTTT

"Fuck off!"

Her right arm flailed without her permission. A large, red-eyed marsupial pulled apart an apple on the tree branch to her right. It gnawed on the fruit while watching her like she was in the latest episode of its favorite telenovela.

Zzzt

"Fine!" Sam yelled to no one. She pointed to the furry creature. "Can you not, please?"

The animal blinked twice, nibbled the apple and continued judging her from a safe distance.

Sam tore a hole in reality. She willed it to take her to whatever was doing this to her skull so she could murder it and be done with this nonsense.

Sam shook her left hand and drew a line in reality.

ZZZTTTTT

She dropped her hand too far. The tear went through the earth. The ground beneath Sam's feet disappeared and she stumbled into the gaping hole. She may also have been, upon further reflection, a little drunk.

Several cubic feet of dirt and organic matter followed her as she face planted onto tarmac. The Old Beeman Building, architectural nightmare that it was, stood before her. Rusted, yellow-painted, corrugated steel wrapped around the one-story rectangle like a candy wrapper. Dre told her once that it was several football fields in size. Sam hadn't cared enough at the time to remember how many.

Giant eucalyptus trees guarded the building from the street, their tan and silver bark peeling away from the trunks to suffocate everything on the ground below them.

The parking lot alone was large enough to accommodate the several thousand residents of Sunset Cove currently milling about it. Not one of whom blinked an eye at her graceless arrival.

The last time this town turned out in numbers like this, Karol's was giving away free ice cream because their freezer broke.

"Get to the back of the line," the cat person next to her hissed.

Sam picked herself up, dusted dirt from her socks and got a head rush from standing up too fast.

"There's a line?" she asked, gazing at the mass of creatures around her.

"Yes," said the calico with mismatched eyes. It licked the back of its hand with the bored wariness of a local who'd dealt with too many drunk tourists to find her shit interesting. "It starts on Maple."

Five blocks away.

"Holy shit," Sam said and wobbled beneath that knowledge. "What's everyone in line for?"

The people, who included a svelte elf, a ghost (sheet and all), two mermaids in wheelchairs and a six-foot-four-inch tall, pot-bellied, middle-aged man in a bear costume shifted and glanced at each other.

The cat speared a flea with its claw and licked it off.

"Food," it answered without looking at her. "Now get to the back of the line before the goons see you and we get in trouble."

Too late.

"You!"

Sam swung around to see the troll she'd dismembered the night before booking it towards her.

"Hey, I know you!" Sam said and pointed.

The troll charged her, simple floral dress flapping behind her. She barreled through the crowd to Sam. Green spittle formed at the corners of her mouth. She swung.

"Hey there, Bertha," she said as she dodged and weaved. The crowd around her fell back. A small circle opened around them.

"You sure about this? You wanna lose the other arm?"

"My name," the troll swung, missed Sam's face and exhaled, "is Tanya."

"Honestly, you do not look like a Tanya."

The wire in Sam's brain tweaked and her left leg went out. Sam landed hard on the concrete. Tanya leapt on top of her and wrapped her hand in Sam's hair.

She grinned, jagged teeth showing against her crooked lips.

"Conal said you'd be easy to kill in the daytime." Tanya giggled and tried to smash her head into the concrete. Sam didn't move. The troll levied her massive weight to push her skull into the black tarmac.

"Oh, he said that, did he?"

She grabbed Tanya's chartreuse wrist, squeezed and yanked her hand out of her hair. Tanya's eyes watered.

"You wanna lose this arm too?" Sam asked. She stood up with ease, keeping hold of the Troll's wrist. They were the same height with Tanya still on her knees.

"Do you?" Sam asked and pulled the troll's arm harder. She'd already sewn shut the now empty sleeve of her dress.

"Please," Tanya begged. "He has my sister."

Those thick nails pulling out Jimmy's fangs. Slowly. Breaking his fingers off and tossing them in the dust. He begged her to stop too. Pleaded for his hands, his teeth, his very eyes. She ignored him.

The crowd fell heavy and silent. Sam imagined what Tanya had done to them for fun, or out of boredom.

She pulled the troll's arm and leaned in close.

"I offer you mercy, Tanya Eleanor Evans," Sam said. She ran a finger across the troll's forehead, casting the spell she'd forgotten the night before. "Remember, I know your heart. I know your soul. Harm another and my eyes gleaming in the darkness will be the last thing you see."

Sam let her go. The troll scrambled away. The silent crowd parted around her. Tanya glanced at the building. She picked herself up, brushed her dress off and squared her shoulders.

"My sister," she said and met Sam's gaze. "S-s-s-ave her." Her eyes dropped. "Please. S-s-s-heee's not like me. She's a good person."

For a brief moment, Sam admired the courage it took for her to say that.

"Okay," she said and shrugged.

"P-p-p-p-p-promise."

"I don't make promises," Sam said. "I keep my word."

The troll's green eyes searched her face, trying to find reassurance and, not seeing it, the troll pressed her luck. Again.

"Please."

Sam sighed.

"Tanya," she gritted out. "I will get her out of there intact and alive – if it's within my power. I will do everything that I can. Okay?"

The troll nodded her pointy chin, turned on her warty, bare heel and lurched to the edges of the crowd.

Sam's buzz dipped perilously close to hangover territory and the wire in her brain wrapped around her skull throbbed.

The hunger, desperation and resolute will to live of the crowd set in. She wiped away a tear and breathed. Focusing with every cell, she pulled two, large, folding tables from her hoodie. Sam set them up and turned to the cat person.

"What are people eating nowadays?"

"I eat fish and birds mostly," the cat said, shrugging furry shoulders.

Carl, who landed on one of the tables, pranced and cawed in absolute outrage.

Sam ignored him. She assessed the crowd.

"Pizza? Do people still eat pizza?"

"I'm gluten free."

"I'm vegan."

"I'm a pescatarian."

She rubbed her forehead and shook off the pain.

Focus on the problem, Nemain would say. What is the problem?

People are starving. I don't know what to feed them. There are so many of them. I'm tired. I'm sad. I want pizza and I'm overwhelmed.

So you have more than one problem. How do you begin to solve them? What is the obstacle to solving the problem?

Sam waved her hand over one table. A white, flat rectangle with red lettering appeared. She popped it open and grabbed two, giant, slices of Hawaiian. Chewing on the gooey, cheesy, sweet, salty, messy gorgeousness, Sam contemplated the problem.

The crowd muttered and shifted.

"I'm gonna need a minute," she told them, around a mouthful of pizza. She held up a finger. "Gimme one minute."

"Hey, we're hungry too!" some dude yelled.

The cat shushed him.

"She said she needs a minute. Leave her be."

"Okay, well, I didn't hear that."

Sam shoved the pizza into her mouth and chewed, feeling her molecules fill up. The solution that had seemed impossible presented itself.

She brushed crumbs from her lips and hands. Closing her eyes, she imagined every company party, every barbecue, every potluck, every time she felt nourished by this ridiculous community.

Waving her arms, she brought forth pizzas, salads, all the fruits and vegetables she could think of: squash, spinach, bread, cakes, roasted chicken, piles of hot dogs, hamburgers, a vat of Chiba's haleem, Gracie's peach pie, and a keg of Dre's sour ale. Sam set the feast to replenish itself. On the other table, she formed a square, wooden box.

She tapped the feast table with her staff, then walked a few feet and hit the concrete with it. An identical table appeared, she repeated the multiplication five more times and then duplicated the table with the box three times over.

"CAA-RRRRLLLL!" she yelled, looking around for that damn bird.

"What?" He appeared at the table next to her.

"Make sure no one's an asshole," she ordered. "Soup's on! Help yourself!"

He bobbed his head, white sticker on his beak flashing in the sun.

"And how do you suggest I do that?" he said, dripping sarcasm. "Flap them into submission? How are they supposed to eat this food, or carry it home, *Your Bossiness*? With their hands?" He glared at the cat and squawked in outrage. "Or claws?

Sam wondered, fleetingly, if she would lose the title of Goddess of Justice if she strangled him.

"Fine," she said and waved her hand, adding tables, plates, bowls, utensils and wagons. "DDDDOOOOOOOOGG!!"

The giant hound bounded out of the shadows. Strings of drool crossed his massive jaws. She patted his head with reluctant approval.

"Make sure no one's an asshole… gently," she ordered. "Herd them. Don't *hurt* them. Got it?"

His bark of understanding bounced around the parking lot.

"You!" Sam pointed at the cat. "What's your name?"

"Kit," the creature said and continued to study its nails.

Sam sidestepped the landmine that was Kit the Cat.

"You look responsible."

"God, I hope not."

"Okay fine, just tell the box your order and food will come out," she snapped. "Okay? Spread the word. I need to get inside that building."

Kit stabbed another flea.

"You should make a sign."

The throbbing in her skull, which had dulled, flared to life.

"Fine!" Sam exploded. She waved a sign in all caps into existence and stalked off.

"Wait," Kit said and grabbed her arm. "Don't go in there. It's dangerous. This Conal guy, people do whatever he tells them. He's got traps all over the building. No one leaves. You either die or become his bitch."

The crowd cycled through the tables of food, flowing around them like water.

Sam met Kit's amber cat eyes.

"Thank you for your concern but I'll be fine."

"Kit's right." The guy in the bear costume chewed through a chicken leg. "Mm, this is delicious, by the way. Thank you." He swallowed. "We've seen the heaviest hitters in this town walk in there. They never come out."

The wire around Sam's skull tightened, threatening to pop her eyes out.

"No, you haven't," she said.

"Haven't what?"

"You haven't seen the heaviest hitters in this town. Not yet."

A fifteen-foot-wide perimeter around the building was completely dead. No grass, weeds, scrub or even microbes lived in the soil. Any creature crossing this Dead Zone would, depending on their strength, be weakened, sicken or die. It struck her then that this was the work of one of her own acolytes. A Death Bringer built this little murder moat.

She inspected the quality. It was as impenetrable as it was impeccable. Sam felt a flash of pride.

The guards either bailed or were told to retreat after her run-in with Tanya. Sam circled the building once, trying to find a decent entrance.

The wire burning into her skull. She found a door that felt right. It was an ordinary gray maintenance door with a silver handle on the far side of the building from the crowd.

Sam stepped into the Dead Zone and sucked Death into herself like a margarita.

She dissolved the handle with her nail and opened the door. It clicked shut behind her – mechanical, final.

Sam found herself inside a narrow hallway. Green, industrial lights illuminated the concrete floor and corrugated walls. A thin figure in a long, black cloak stood about twenty feet away, between Sam and the door at the end of the hallway.

Thin, pale hands drew back the hood revealing a young woman with a pointed chin, freckles, and hair that had been dyed to a delightful, rosy, orange. Her hair was tucked behind a blue, flower headband and styled into perfect, winged waves.

"Prepare to meet your doom," she intoned in a voice that was trying real hard to be two octaves lower than it actually was. Sam leaned back against the door. Her left eye twitched.

"Are you fucking serious right now?"

"Deadly serious," the baby Death Bringer answered, bringing her hands forward and pushing a wave of Death at Sam.

It washed over her like a refreshing ocean mist. The twitch eased.

The girl was clearly confused.

"My name is Raven."

"Of course, it is."

Raven gathered power around her.

"And I am death incarnate," she spat out, sending waves of it at Sam.

This time, Sam got notes of sunscreen.

"Look kid," Sam said and stepped away from the wall. "I respect your talent but you're punching *way* above your weight."

"But I'm Death." The girl sobbed and tried again.

Sam caught her hand before she hurt herself.

"No, sweetie," Sam said and patted her forearm. "You're not."

It dawned on her that the girl should have recognized her already.

Raven pulled her hands away and flailed at Sam. The green overhead light caught a silver thread coming out of her left ear. Sam caught the delicate line and snapped it.

The young woman collapsed. She touched her ear.

"He's gone! Praise be to the Goddess, he's gone." She looked up at Sam, a flurry of emotions passing over her face. "The things he made me do..."

Her face went blank.

"Okay." Sam reached down to help her up. "We're not doing that."

"I should have been able to stop him. I should have been strong enough. Why wasn't I strong enough?"

Raven planted her hands on Sam's shoulders and jumped back.

"Holy shit!" The girl looked at her hands and back at Sam, jaw slack, eyes wide. She dropped to the floor again. This time on purpose.

"Your Majesty." Raven bowed her head.

"Nope, no. Hell, no." Sam panicked and gestured for her to stand up. "We are definitely *not* doing that."

"But."

"Listen, kid…"

"Forgive me, please," she begged.

"Raven," Sam gave up and knelt in front of her, "there's nothing to forgive. You did nothing wrong"

The girl wiped away tears.

"But…"

"Raven, please look at me.”

"I should have been stronger. I should have stopped him. He made me hurt people. I killed people." The words poured out of her.

"And he hurt you, too?"

"Well… " The girl shrugged her thin shoulders, still not looking at her.

Sam's middle-aged knees ached. She shifted to sit cross-legged on the floor with her back against the wall.

"And you didn't want to hurt people? But he made you because he's a piece of shit Silver Tongue and I should have gotten here sooner and stopped him?"

Raven met her eyes then. Sam could see the sweet, tortured soul within.

"Oh, no, don't blame yourself, Your Majesty."

Sam smiled.

"One: call me Sam. That's a … royal decree or whatever. Two: so I shouldn't blame myself but you should?"

Raven's face went blank.

"Yup, got ya there, didn't I?"

"I…"

"Here's the deal, kid." Sam tried to pull her aging and exhausted bones off the cold floor but couldn't get the will. "I would love to talk to you more about your powers, how that abusive shit gibbon is going to rot in eternal torment and how you did nothing wrong, also that you should find a therapist or Healer or whatever they're called now to work through this, but whatever is behind that door is screaming at me and I have to go deal with it. Okay?"

Raven stood.

"The dead are behind that door, Your – Sam." Raven helped her off the floor. "I tried to help them but he wouldn't let me. I am so sorry."

Sam's numb legs protested. The wire flared.

"Nothing to be sorry for, remember?" Sam waddled toward the door.

"I can help you." Raven rushed through her words. "It's the least I can do."

"You can help me, by going outside, getting something to eat and drink, finding your people, a therapist and going wherever you call home."

"But…" She tried again.

"You can summon me in a few days when things have settled down and we can talk about your powers and such. Okay?"

Sam reached the door and paused.

"Hey," Raven said softly.

"Yeah?" Sam half turned.

"May I ditch the cloak? You won't be offended or anything? It's not really my thing. He made me wear it."

Sam sighed and banged her head against the metal door.

"Naw, it's all good."

Raven shed the cloak, revealing turquoise corduroy cutoffs, a yellow, flowered shirt, bright red combat boots and mismatched knee socks, one with cats, the other fish.

"I think it looks great on you by the way." Raven turned and skipped away.

"Thank you."

"I like your socks though."

"Okay."

"Permission to share a hug?" Raven held her arms wide.

"Permission granted," Sam answered, a flicker of a smile on her lips. The girl wrapped her skinny arms around her and squeezed.

"Okay." Sam patted her back and broke the hug.

Raven skipped to the exit, waving as she went.

"Bye!"

Sam sighed and jerked open the heavy metal door to confront the endless, rotting dead.

Zombies.

*****

2:15 pm, Oct. 30, 2020, 32 days after The Fog

Byron Masaru Tanaka was the first person killed by The Fog.

His divorce had been a nightmare. Recriminations, lies, lawyers and tears.

She cheated on him. So he cheated on her. Then she slept with her lawyer. They both wanted the dog. No one wanted the vacation house in Tahoe.

After three years and two glasses of ice water thrown in his face at mediation, he just wanted peace. He needed to sit in front of the ocean for three days and do absolutely nothing.

A gangly crane of a man, his legs were skinny and his chest broad. His shoulders were permanently hunched from pouring over spreadsheets. He had a one-inch-diameter bald spot on the crown of his head and a meticulous, borderline-obsessive knowledge of feudal Japanese history.

Byron drove down to Sunset Cove late in the afternoon on Sept. 28. His hotel, a towering mix of sixties retro and hipster chic, sat right on the beach. He checked in at about 6:15 pm. Traffic from

Fresno had been okay – not nail-biting but not a cool breeze over the winding mountains and reservoirs either.

He settled in and left the hotel at 6:45 pm.

A stroll. He just wanted to take a stroll along a sandy beach.

He grabbed a light jacket against the fall cold and damn near sprinted out of the hotel down a steep little hill, past the railroad tracks and the rickety wharf jetting out into the ocean, to the line of garish, boardwalk fun house fronts.

He passed through the gates of Poseidon's Kingdom – wrought iron, sea kelp strands painted electric green.

Families straggled out, carrying exhausted kids. Couples and young people ruled this time at the boardwalk. The crowd was thin enough to walk through easily but still good for people watching.

At this time of day, all the rides were closed but the flashing lights of the rollercoaster and the ship drop stayed on all night.

Waves crashed in the distance. He could feel the water before him.

Byron hopped down the sandy, stone steps. Beyond the wide beach, black water rushed in and retreated. The crest of the waves reflected the lights of the boardwalk.

Nothing in this world could ever be more magical, more pure to him, than this.

He jogged to the water's frigid edge – not that he cared so much about the cold.

The Fog rolled in without warning like a nuclear blast. The force of it picked him up and flung him. Byron landed hard on those same stone steps, cracking his skull wide open.

It took him five minutes to die.

The obscene carnage seared his fading vision.

Shadows above him, screamed and snarled. Tears fell from the corners of his eyes. He gasped for air, struggling to move but his limbs wouldn't respond. The inhuman shrieks and thunks, tearing of flesh, thunderous falling of buildings built into a crescendo of madness. He couldn't escape. His vision faded. His breath accelerated and stopped.

Byron awoke alone on this very beach. He sat up. His spot was the perfect distance from the water – just far enough to feel a light, cooling spray. Behind him the boardwalk stood empty, hollow and silent. Not a soul in sight.

He knew he was dead. He knew of the horrors he committed on behalf of the man in the red shirt. He knew others like him surrounded him in a dark warehouse.

So he sat and looked at the water, remembering his first date with his ex-wife. She wore that yellow striped dress and a straw hat. He wanted to touch her. The way the fabric played around her knees. The way her hair swung about her shoulders. She was a drug to him.

The wind shifted and got colder.

A black-hooded figure approached. It glared up at the sun before glancing down at him.

"Nope," he said.

She pulled her hood back revealing riotous dark hair.

"Whaddya mean, 'nope'?" Death asked him.

She was magnetic in the scariest of ways - strange eyes burning with cosmic fire.

"Take the others first," he said. Turning his eyes back to the water, he licked salt from his lips. "I'm not ready."

She rolled her eyes, sighed and sat next to him. She stared out at the crashing waves,

"You know you can't stay like this forever, right? You have to move on."

He nodded, avoiding her terrifying gaze.

"I know. I need more time."

Byron glanced back at the boardwalk. A pair of lovers flirted and frolicked. The woman's yellow dress played in the ocean breeze.

"Hey, why are we like this?" he asked her. "Was it The Fog?"

She sighed again. Death dug a little pit in the sand with a stick.

"Yeah… no… sort of. That's on me, honestly." She didn't sound happy about it. "Once The Fog hit, the door to the other side closed until I, well, until I became this. So everyone who died in Sunset Cove before I became…"

"Became Death," he finished for her.

"Yeah, you all got stuck and I have to walk everyone across." She squinted at the sun.

They sat in silence for a few moments. The waves crashed with slow reassurance. "For what it's worth, I am sorry."

Her eyes, he decided, terrified him because they were so compelling. They called him into the unknown, that feeling he got at the edge of a cliff telling him to jump or drive into oncoming traffic.

He craned his neck to look at the boardwalk.

"Did she ever love me, you think? Or was it all an act?"

She turned with him and studied the couple.

"I think you should see how she looks at you when you're not looking at her," she replied after a moment. "She adores you. She's looking at you like you hung the sun and the moon. She has stars in her eyes."

He turned back to the water, tears falling from his cheeks.

Death stood. She shook the sand from her cloak. Then she pulled off each shoe, dumping the sand from them one at a time, balancing like a bird on one foot.

"I'll come back once I'm done with the others."

She turned to leave.

"Hey," he stopped her, "you ever feel like that about anyone?"

She grimaced in the relentless sunlight.

"Death doesn't get a love story," she said and disappeared.

*****

The Liminal Space

It took thousands of years.

Sam lost count after the first hundred.

The stench of rotting bodies saturated her pores. Blood and viscera covered her hands. She had to touch them to walk them out of this purgatory.

Some went quick – eager to leave. Others shattered her heart into thousands of pieces. The toddler who didn't understand why mommy hurt him like that. The houseless vet reliving desert bombings, the shaking earth, disintegrating houses, the silence after mass death – unable to look away, unable to stop blaming herself.

Sam took to visiting Byron when it all got too much. After the third or fourth visit, he stopped asking how it was going. They sat on the beach in companionable silence. She brought out an icy six pack, created an umbrella for shade and willed herself to wade back into the naked, needy humanity around her.

"I don't understand."

"Why didn't anyone help us?"

"I'm fine. Leave me alone!"

"Where were you? Why didn't you stop this?"

"Where's my daddy? I want my daddy."

He packed them into a vast, empty room in the Old Beeman Building. Acres of hungry dead. They didn't know why they wanted flesh and brains – the gateways between life and death. The still point that trapped them, leaving them starving. He used them to destroy his enemies.

Do as I say or they'll eat you alive.

Sam sat with them all, listened to them, cried so hard she got dehydrated and imagined all the slow, excruciating ways she was going to kill the man in the red shirt.

Dark clouds gathered over Byron's beach. She appeared next to him.

The fire in her eyes had dimmed.

They stared at the sea per their tradition.

"So that's it, huh?"

"Yup," she replied with her shoulders bunched up around her ears.

"It's not your fault, you know."

She rubbed her face and tried to smile.

"You sure about that?"

Sam didn't mention the dozens of teeth torn bodies littering the space around them.

Byron stood, holding out his hand to help her up. No couple frolicked in the low buildings behind them now.

"Yup." He met those eyes, finding comfort in them for the first time. "I'm glad it was you."

He disappeared, leaving Sam cradling his desiccated skull in her lap. The bottom half of his face had rotted away, revealing teeth and sinew – perfect for tearing flesh. Dried blood crusted his neck and the dumb, loud Hawaiian shirt under his torn windbreaker. She stroked the few remaining tufts of black hair on his exposed skull, trying to soothe herself more than anything.

He didn't deserve this. None of them deserved this.

She laid his head on the cold, cement floor and surveyed the piles of broken bodies. Without the protections of Death Raven created, creatures would soon find this place and feast on their bones.

Sam raised her arms, feeling the molecules of these people, she accelerated their decomposition. Flesh dropped away, the blood on her hands dried and flaked off in the wind sweeping through the room. Bones cracked and crumbled until only dust remained. Sam opened a high window and sent the particles flying farther and farther away to every corner of Sunset Cove.

She crossed the now-empty, cavernous room. A set of white double doors beckoned. At this point, she knew every door hid a trap, but that fucker Conal would burn by her hands or she'd be damned in the trying.

Sam yanked the doors open with bravado she didn't actually feel to reveal a twelve-foot-tall, snarling, snow white werewolf. Blood and ichor dribbled from his massive jaws onto his snowy chest.

"Awesome. Great. So, so fun."

*****

4:46 pm, Oct. 30, 2020, 32 days after The Fog

Dylan Efran Villalobos realized at 6:17 pm Saturday, Sept. 28 that he was going to be late for work.

The four-months-away-from-his-sixteenth-birthday-year-old, committed the cardinal sin of walking into his dad's bedroom to wake him up before midnight.

"Dad," he said from the doorway. His dad worked nights and was almost impossible to wake up without an air horn. "Dad." Dylan sat on the edge of the bed and shook his shoulder.

His dad peeled one eye open and murmured:

"Offspring."

"Dad..."

"Is someone on fire?" His dad muttered into the pillow.

"No, but Dad…"

"Then why am I awake?"

"I need a ride to work."

His dad fell into silent, resolute disappointment.

"What time does your shift start?"

"Seven."

"What time is it right now?"

"6:20," Dylan replied.

His dad sighed, did the mental calculations for how long it would take to drive down the mountain into Sunset Cove proper, sat up, swung his legs off the bed, put his robe on and began what Dylan secretly called his Epic Dad Lecture (trademark pending) about responsibility ("You said you were ready for a job.") and time management ("When did you know you were working tonight?").

Household chaos ensued.

His uncle, Miguel, wanted a ride too but couldn't find his jacket. His dad did what he always did, pulled on his combat boots and waited behind the wheel of his little, blue Honda until everyone sat in the car. Dylan couldn't find his phone for some reason. He wanted to get the new girl, Taylor's number. She was muy caliente. Her butt…

Sam interrupted him.

"I don't need to know how caliente Taylor is."

"I … you wanted to know how I got here," he growled in Werewolf.

"Yes, but what does Taylor's butt have to do with that?" Sam sipped her tea while the giant, teenage werewolf scarfed down the third rotisserie chicken she'd tossed his way.

At 6:32 pm, the little, blue Honda careened out of their driveway. Dylan's dad drove at breakneck speeds down the mountain.

"Where do you live anyway?"

"Rock Ridge, past the corner store."

"There is no way you were gonna be on time for work! That's an hour's drive."

A hour's drive down winding, redwood-lined vistas, deep in mountains that Sam swore, even before The Fog, were rife with beings that didn't like people living among them.

"Hey, can I have some of that?" Dylan gestured to the pint of ice cream Sam spooned into her face.

"No," she admonished him. "Absolutely not."

Every muscle in his body fell and he became the most crestfallen and hangdog of creatures.

"Why not?"

"Because it's chocolate and I'm pretty sure you're part dog."

"Oh," he brightened, "that makes sense. You're smart."

"Thank you, please continue."

They sat on the floor of Dylan's cramped cell. After she snapped the thread in his ear and the chain on his neck, the giant werewolf begged for food and Sam realized she'd picked up werewolf speech along the way. Also, she needed water and snacks before venturing any further into this hellhole.

Blood splatters and deep claw marks decorated the walls. A human femur lay two feet from her on the floor.

"Okay, fine." She pulled another chicken from her hoodie. "But please eat this one slowly. You're going to make yourself sick."

He bit the chicken in half, ignoring her advice completely, swallowing bones and all before continuing.

"Okay, so my dad drives like a psycho but I'm late because we got stuck behind the slowest car going down Copper Head."

"Tourists." Sam nodded.

He threw his hands in the air, which Sam suspected was a carbon copy of his dad's response to slow drivers.

"Tourists! Anyway, I'm soooo late for work."

Sam wiped chocolate ice cream from her lips with a napkin she pulled from her hoodie.

"Where do you work?"

"Pie-zaz," he replied, picking his teeth with a chicken bone.

"The second best pizza in Sunset Cove. The first is Rocket's next to the Red Stallion across from the Purple Pear."

"Too greasy."

Sam fought the impulse to argue with an almost sixteen year old who clearly never had the drunk hungries at 3 am on a Saturday and Rocket's was the only thing open. One of her favorite memories was giggling with Dre outside the hole-in-the-wall pizza joint, orange grease pooling on their paper plates as they huddled under the yellow streetlight against the damp, cold night. Rocket's never handed out enough napkins.

"Okay, you were soooo late," Sam prompted.

She pulled a water bottle from her hoodie, twisted off the cap and handed it to him. His giant paw dwarfed the bottle as he poured water down his gullet. Half of it missed his mouth.

"Oh, that's good."

Sam pulled out another water bottle for him and one for herself.

"You're dehydrated."

"Okay, so we're at the intersection off the highway and shi–stuff," he glanced at her, "gets so crazy. Like crazier than you can even imagine."

He used his back leg to scratch behind his left ear.

"The intersection by the pool supply store?"

"Yeah, like who owns a pool in Sunset Cove?"

"Tourists," Sam said.

"Tourists! Anyway, we're, like, at the intersection and this fog rolls in and shi–stuff goes crazy. Like so crazy, like ghosts, and stuff came outta nowhere and the car in front of us turned into a giant horse, but my dad. He just deals, ya know? He said he had to get to the cemetery. Right. Now."

"The one by the highway?"

"Yeah," Dylan said, wilting a bit in the telling of this part. "And my uncle got real quiet in the front seat but then it turned out he was humming."

"Like a song?"

"No, like a guitar."

"He was vibrating?"

The young wolf giggled and looked away.

Oh, good grief. The Holy Darkness save me from teenage boys.

"Anyway," Dylan said. "My dad got out of the car right in the middle of the highway."

Sam drank more water and contemplated the half of the human intestine in the corner of the medicinal-green room.

"And he ran to the cemetery?"

"But first…" Dylan's yellow wolf eyes got wide. "He got hit by a truck and the truck exploded."

"Like a semi or a regular truck?"

"Like a semi."

"Huh," Sam said. "Then what happened?"

Dylan howled softly.

"My uncle, he got out of the car too … and he turned into this giant ball of fire and shot into the sky."

Tears formed in the werewolf's eyes. He brushed them aside with the back of his paw.

That's a new one.

"So I ran after my dad, and he got to the cemetery. He was really far away but I could see him and all this crazy shit is going on, like giant butterflies and demons, and krakens and shit and my dad gets to the cemetery and he just…"

"He just fell over." Sam finished for him.

"Yeah." Dylan stared at the cement floor. It was caked with the dried bodily fluids of all the people he'd eaten.

"And you turned into this when he fell?"

"Yeah."

"And you haven't been able to change back since? And not too long after that red shirt guy found you and locked you up in here and he made you eat people even though you really didn't want to?"

The giant werewolf nodded.

"I'm sorry, kid." Sam leaned over and patted his massive shoulder. "If it makes you feel better, I'm going to let your dad kill the red shirt guy."

"You think my dad's alive? Really?" His big, yellow eyes looked at her with a child's hope

"I know he is." Sam pushed herself off the cold floor, hydrated enough to go kick some ass. "Because he's like me."

Dylan's head tilted, a dog not understanding.

"Okay, but like, you've been super nice and everything but who are you?"

She held out a hand.

"I'm Sam. I'm The Morrigan."

His head tilted in the opposite direction.

"I don't know what that is."

*****

5:36 pm, Oct. 30, 2020, 32 days after The Fog

Conal Estes Mayeaux was sweating and pacing. He'd created a dais in the back of the room – small and tasteful, only five-feet off the ground, forty-feet across. His footsteps rang hollow and deep on the floorboards. He'd been told she would come – warned even – reassured though that she 'wasn't anything special' and 'nothing to worry about.'

Dark patches appeared beneath his armpits. A sweat stain on the small of his back spread down into his khaki shorts.

He hated her. He never met her but he hated her. Hated all of them – staring at him – waiting for him to tell them to do stuff. Half the building smelled like piss because they'd just start peeing without warning. Conal told them to tell him but then it was constant lines. Easier to just make them clean up after each other. Right?

The Man in White had told him in holy dreams that she, like all women, needed to be led – that his words would guide her to righteous purpose.

The hair on his arms stood straight up for the past forty five minutes.

They were restless too. Shifting, muttering, trying to rebel.

He damn near opened the door himself to get it over with but the pageantry, the spectacle would be lost. He made them work so hard building this stage – they even covered it with fake grass for him. It was so important to set the scene.

When she finally walked through the werewolf's door, he laughed at how he'd got himself all riled up. She was nothing, like they all were nothing – just a woman in silly socks and a stupid hoodie. Real women dress to impress.

The hair on his arms did not lay back down.

He giggled at her. She was so small across the football field of his riches. The werewolf didn't follow her. He must be dead … Oh, well.

Her head on a swivel, she surveyed his kingdom like it was her own. Calculations in her eyes. The Man in White warned him that she thought she was crafty.

"Did you murder my wolfman?" he called out to her. His voice echoed in the huge cement room.

"Why would I kill an innocent kid?" she yelled back.

He had no idea what she was talking about. Maybe she didn't hear him.

"Is my wolfman dead?"

She stalked toward him, past the five-foot-tall pallets of grain, rice and oats.

He allowed it.

His sentinels in dirty clothes lined the walls. They were ready to attack at his word. She turned sideways to move between two, gray plastic tubs of fruit. She snagged a banana and chomped on it as she walked closer.

"The kid is fine, not that you give a shit about him."

Conal admitted to himself that he liked her voice – concise and raspy. He'd make her read to him – after he was done debasing her. She needed to understand her place. Not that he did that kind of thing often. But a divine decree was a divine decree.

He was a one woman man. He smiled at his beloved, Melissa from Accounting. Tears ran down her face. She must be so happy, he thought. When he turned back, she had traversed the football field of food stuffs and stood before the dais, chewing on a crisp pink apple.

The sweat stain on his back grew larger.

"He told me about you, you know." He smirked while looking down on her. He liked the view.

The sentinels stepped away from the concrete walls to close ranks.

She shifted the chunk of apple to her cheek to answer.

"Oh, yeah? What did he say about me?"

"That you think you're strong but you're not." Conal's grin took a turn. "That you think you're smart but you're not. That you think you're special but you're not."

Her eyes drifted past him. He could feel Melissa fight him. Her mouth formed words he didn't approve.

"Don't look at her! Look at me!"

She took a huge bite, chewed thoughtfully and her eyes didn't leave him. Bits of apple and spittle spread across her cheeks.

"You two must talk a lot, huh? You must be super important to him."

"Oh, yes!" Conal tucked in his red shirt and smoothed the front of his shorts. "The Man in White visits my dreams a few times a week. I am his divine messenger. I am blessed."

"Uh, huh," she tossed the apple core in an empty blue bin, "did he say when I was coming?"

Conal tapped his chin and glanced away. The show of it all thrilled him.

"Ya know. I don't think he did."

"Did he tell you *what* I am?"

She appeared before him on the dais, ten feet away. He recoiled.

"Don't do that! You scared me!"

The sentinels twittered, murmuring with his anger. Their hands twitched and grasped at their sides.

"No!" He yelled, boots crunching on fake grass as he stumbled back. "He barely mentioned you."

That was a lie. The old man was obsessed with her. He brought her up every time they talked. The woman in the black hood. *Enslave her and I will make you a god.*

She tracked him across the twenty-foot stage.

"Where is he? Did he tell you where he is?"

He reached the edge of the far side of the dais, and after a moments' pause, climbed down.

"Of course not," he said, backing into the safety of his sentinels. They edged closer at his thought, shuffling footsteps echoing around the building. "He's in heaven."

She stopped, open mouthed and stared down at him.

"You think he's God?" And she laughed. Full-throated, head thrown back, neck exposed, the hollow, column wrinkles and all, genuinely laughing. At him. He decided then that he would strangle her. Not enough to kill just enough so she passed out, limp and helpless, lying on the ground. Maybe he'd kick her too. Right in the ribs. Hard.

Her laughter trailed off. She wiped an errant tear from the corner of her eye.

"Oh, man, I needed that. Thank you."

He raised his right arm, about to cast her sentence.

"Enough!" he shouted. "Blasphemer! Whore! **I COMMAND THEE...”**

A thin, silver thread snaked out of his mouth, skittering across the gray, industrial floor, up the wood platform, and straight at her ear. He would say such things to her. Unspeakable things. Her brain would burn with what he would say to her.

She caught it. That bitch caught the thread between her thumb and pointer finger. A tiny twang in the air as she held it.

"I'm gonna do what now?" she asked, before sending a shock wave of black sparks back along the thread.

Nightmares swam in his vision – Sunset Cove gray, lifeless and endless, creatures of thirst, with corrupt and consuming teeth. He shrieked out his terror. Screams filled the air.

"Oh, fuck!" she exclaimed. She leapt from the stage with her hands up, dropping the thread. The pain stopped.

His sentinels, in fact every being in the room, fell to the floor.

"Oh, shit! Is everyone okay?"

Her voice came to him from a million years in the past. Conal realized he lay face up on the floor, staring at the steel gray triangles holding up the building. Thick cables ran along the beams bringing electricity to the swinging industrial lights.

A more self-aware man, in this moment, might have realized his hubris. Conal's blinding rage and self-assurance propelled him into a sitting position to find the woman crouched before him – close enough that he could see the threads of gray in her wild hair.

"Hi!" she said.

His mouth flopped open. She wrapped her hands around the mass of strings falling from his lips. She twisted and snapped them like breaking pasta.

Thoughts that were not his own inundated his mind. They drowned him. Fantasies about murdering him. Pain. Endless stabbing pain through his eyes. It licked around his ear lobes. Their pain. The stench of *their* rage at *him*. The scent of it burned through his nostrils, coiling around his brain stem.

She… he realized he didn't know her name, yanked his jaw. His eyes fluttered back into his skull as he heard it pop. The wet emptiness must be where she'd torn it away.

Cool air and colder iron hit his tongue. He met her eyes and she held the blade. She glanced down at it and cursed.

"Fuck."

The knife disappeared to be replaced by another. She glanced down again. This one seemed to satisfy her.

In the flashing glint of the blade, Conal remembered the night of The Fog. He was closing at the office supply store – the one across the parking lot from the weirdly, empty pool supply place. The Saint Augustus river slogged along twenty-feet away beyond the berm.

The key clicked the tumblers in place but he yanked the double doors like he always did to check. The Fog rolled in fast, casting impossible shapes in the parking lot lights. Conal licked his lips. He could taste it – cotton candy laced with endless power.

An earthquake of car alarms and screams went off as it hit the intersection by the highway. He stood still in the empty parking lot. Conal stared up at the soft, ephemeral blanket enclosing him. The chaos was of no concern to him. The stillness knew him. It would give him what he wanted. He just had to wait.

Sure enough, within minutes, a giant, white werewolf stood before him.

Conal tried to smile at the memory but Sam had ripped off the lower half of his face.

She wrapped his tongue in brown paper and tucked it into her hoodie. Then she traced a circle around the dying Silver Tongue and called forth Darkness to chain him to her.

"Carl!"

The bird appeared on top of a pile of apples.

"Yes, Your Loudness," he squawked.

The room began to fill with the shocked murmurs of beings who survived hell.

"Remind me to organize the knives."

The suffering in this room threatened to overwhelm her.

"Organize the knives," Carl said.

Sam glared at him in Disapproving Goddess.

"How many more body parts can I label, do you think?" She gestured wildly. "I see so many. You have claws, wings, legs, that thing on your chest that puffs out when you're mad at me, what is that called…?" her eyes narrowed menacingly, "… individual feathers."

Defeated, Carl bowed his narrow head.

"I'll remind you tomorrow," he sighed, "and it's called hackles."

"Excellent, thank you."

The beings in the room began the slow work of rousing themselves from the somnambulance of Conal's mental prison.

A middle-aged couple along the wall held each other. The woman, short and round with fiery red hair, seemed familiar to her. Those that could helped the person next to them. More than a hundred beings stood in this room and Sam didn't know how to help any of them. A giant sobbed in the corner. Three blue scaly creatures leaked water from their hands and feet while staring at the floor. Others milled.

Sam felt three no nonsense taps on her shoulder.

"Is he dead?" Melissa, the woman who signaled her from the stage, stood there, black mascara crusted onto her cheeks, hair in shambles but with clear, brown eyes and a straight back.

"Not yet."

"Will it be painful? Slow?"

"Yes," Sam said. She didn't see a reason to lie to her.

A lanky dude in a black t-shirt and jeans, flicked his fingers at the double loading dock doors. They rumbled open to reveal the long lines of people outside waiting for food.

"What are you going to do?" Melissa asked.

"About all these people? I dunno. I'm not a Healer. This is not my wheelhouse, man."

Melissa stepped back from her.

"So you're not going to take Conal's place? You're not going to try to rule Sunset Cove?"

Sam scrunched up her face in distaste.

"Why on earth would I do that? Do you have any idea how much work that would be? Absolutely not. Oh, fuck no. I'm just here to deal with this shit."

She gestured to Conal.

The denizens of Sunset Cove, waiting in line for food, gasped at the bounty the rising door revealed. Sam couldn't tell if it was manners or fear that kept them from rushing in.

One dude couldn't be bothered with either. He strolled through the open double doors in loose khaki pants, hands in his pockets, ugly orange and yellow Hawaiian shirt covering a belly that was two double cheeseburgers away from being called pot.

While Sam watched with a dropped jaw, he stepped on an unconscious man to get to a bin of apples.

"What the hell, dude?"

"What?"

He filled his pockets with apples, thin arms shoving them down his shirt front. A couple fell out and rolled across the floor. He stepped on the man again to walk back towards the double doors.

"Like you're gonna stop me," he tossed over his shoulder. Flames erupted from his hands and he turned back to her.

"Do you not see this?" Sam gestured to Conal, who tried to groan behind his gag of Darkness.

The flames grew larger in his hands.

"Whatever," he replied and spun back to the doorway.

A small creature, blue and shiny, standing by the door, set its jaw and water shimmered into existence soaking the man.

The flames went out. He stopped. Heat poured out of him in waves. His wet pants steamed and dried. Flames raced up his arms.

The room held its breath. Sam had almost formulated a plan when the gray-haired man who had been holding his wife earlier jumped forward. He smashed his fist into the apple thief's face. He crumpled to the ground. The gray-haired man's wife stepped forward and, with whispered gestures, the apple thief shrank, turning yellow and then brown until a large, bumpy toad remained among the ruins of burned apples and rumpled khakis.

She scooped up the amphibian and tucked him into the breast pocket of her over-sized, button-down shirt.

"That was so awesome!" Sam yelled. "Holy shit!" She raised a fist and jumped a little. The traumatized and injured people glared at her.

"I'm sorry," she dialed it down several decibels, "but that was so cool right?"

She glanced around for affirmation.

"No? Okay, but seriously that was awesome."

"Hello?"

Sam whirled to face the voice and instinctively took a step back. The woman speaking wore a red leather jacket. Her scarlet box braids with perfectly laid edges were draped over one shoulder. Large silver glasses framed her dark brown eyes and accentuated her deep terracotta skin.

"You're a Healer," Sam blurted.

"I'm a doctor," she said, her tone firm and commanding. "These people need medical treatment. I'd like to set up a triage."

Few people who chose to battle The Goddess of Death earned her admiration or respect. Healers were another matter entirely. Sam bowed with her hand over her heart.

"Of course, what do you need?"

The gray-haired man lifted a bin full of greens in each hand and made for the door.

The Healer pulled off her jacket revealing a black tank top and tattooed sleeves.

"Beds, light, a sanitizing station, running water, medicine, blankets, heaters… six more doctors and twenty nurses."

Sam waved the items into existence behind her.

"There ya go." Sam pointed. "We can ask the crowd outside if there are any more Healers. See if they'll help out for food."

"Are you a threat to me?" the doctor asked Sam. "You are activating my flight or fight response."

She held two fingers to the pulse in her neck.

"I am no threat to you, Healer. I am The Morrigan."

At her bewildered look, Sam explained.

"...The Goddess of Death.'

The Healer stepped back.

"What?"

"Goddess of Death," Sam said and noticed the room becoming more chaotic. People from the line outside had wandered into the room in search of food.

"Okay," Sam called out. "We need to move the food out of here and create a triage for the sick and injured."

In full Anand Mode, she ordered one door closed, the gray-haired man returned and hauled out more bins, taking them to the people in line, the small blue creature by the door turned out to be a siren. She began repeating Sam's orders loud enough for the people outside to hear.

A small melee ensued with people outside coming in, food going out and beds moving around.

The middle-aged couple were Constance and Edgar.

"Just Constance, please," she said. "Not Connie."

Edgar, obviously not Ed or Eddie, volunteered to search the rest of the building to disarm Conal's traps once the food bins had been moved.

"I'll be fine," he said and waved away Sam's concern. His wife shrugged.

Dylan came bounding in, following the noise. Half the room screamed. Sam reassured everyone that he was just a fifteen-year-old kid, Conal tortured him too and he was very, very sorry.

Dylan dropped his head to the floor, a-wooo-ed and wagged his tail in contrition.

"See," she yelled. "Apologetic Werewolf Child."

The room returned to mid-level melee, ignoring the giant werewolf.

"I'll take him," Edgar told Sam. "Hey kid, you want to help me look for traps?"

Dylan wagged his tail enthusiastically. Something in this man's demeanor and complete lack of bullshit made Sam trust him. Also, werewolves were pretty indestructible.

"Sure, but be careful, please."

After the Healer, whose name was Dr. Williams, found enough doctors, nurses and therapists to her liking, she set up a triage in the warehouse. Constance and Melissa decided that Dog was not up to the challenge and moved outside to organize the crowd.

Carl appeared by her side.

"So… how do we know we can trust these Healers, Boss?"

She folded her arms and eyed him.

"So… you've decided to be helpful?"

He bobbed side to side but didn't answer.

"I was just thinking the same thing," Sam said with a sigh.

"Should I bring the Unkindness in to keep an eye on them."

"Yeah," Sam said with a nod and surveyed the room. "Invite them."

"Those Healers don't like you at all."

Conal bobbed up and down five feet overhead, tethered to her like a blood-soaked, half-dead party balloon.

"Well, they have sworn oaths to spend their lives fighting me so," she shrugged, "makes sense."

A Healer in mauve scrubs and a thick, dirty blonde, side ponytail scurried up to Sam. She thrust a large bottle of water and a bundle of bananas into Sam's hands.

"You're dehydrated and malnourished," she muttered and scurried away.

Sam examined the items.

"You think they're poisoned?" she asked Carl.

"No bet," he squawked.

The Unkindness swooped in and settled among the rafters. Dr. Williams looked up from her patient and glared at Sam.

"Security," she told her. "Just making sure everyone's behaving."

The doctor straightened her spine and Sam felt the oncoming lecture from fifteen feet away.

"Go check on Dylan. Will you, Carl?"

"She's gonna rip you a new one," he cackled as he flew through the room.

"You're making my staff uncomfortable." Dr. Williams put her hands on her hips.

"As soon as the kid comes back and the building's clear, I'll leave." Sam tried not to smirk at the woman. She really did, but battle instincts were hard to lose.

"Animals don't belong in a hospital setting." The doctor gestured to the three-foot-tall ravens in the rafters.

Sam didn't bother to point out the female presenting centaur to her right or the mermaid to the left. The other Healers in the room gathered behind the doctor and glared daggers at Sam.

"Look, I get that you think I'm the villain here. You have sworn oaths to save people from, well, me. I respect that. Your over-zealousness concerns me but I am not your enemy."

"Did you do this? Did you? Did you do this to us?"

"What are you talking about…" Sam asked and then it hit her. "Are you asking if I brought The Fog? Are you asking if I changed everything?"

"Yes," Dr. Williams said as she assessed Sam.

"No, I didn't change Sunset Cove. That is beyond my power."

For long, uncomfortable moments, Sam felt Dr. Williams take pieces of her apart, scrutinize them and put her back together.

"The Fog changed me too." Sam offered out of nervousness. She wanted to make the examination stop. The Healer was winning this battle. "I used to be a bartender."

The doctor laughed – the tension eased with her disbelief. The dismantling ended.

"I did," Sam said and pointed. "Ask your nurse. He used to be one of my regulars. Hey, Inoke."

The heavyset man with curly hair waved back, pausing in the middle of bandaging the centaur.

"Hey, Sam," he said and went back to wrapping a forelock in white gauze.

"Weird times, huh, Inoke?"

He pushed a mass of curly hair from his face and went back to tending his patient.

"Fuckin' eh. Fuckin' eh."

The doctor raised an eyebrow at her.

"So you're just Death?"

"Whaddya mean 'just Death'?"

Dr. Williams turned back to her colleagues and waved them off.

"It's okay, everyone." She reassured the group of Healers who continued scowling at Sam. "She's just Death. We deal with her everyday. Let's get back to work."

The nurse with the thick blonde braid stuck her tongue out at Sam and flounced away.

"Hey! She stuck her tongue out at me! I'm helping! There's such a thing as professional courtesy here!"

Dr. Williams turned around but didn't bother to look up from the clipboard in her hands.

"Aracely, be nice please," the doctor muttered, a little too softly, in Sam's opinion. She glanced up from the clipboard. "We need meds. Can you do the wavy thing and get us meds?"

Sam clapped a hand over her mouth to muffle the outrage.

"The *wavy* thing?" She squeaked through her fingers.

Dr. Williams blinked and clicked her pen.

"Lab coats, we need lab coats."

How, the fuck, did I end up here? Being condescended to by a Healer? I defeat them. I trounce them. They swore an oath against ME. I didn't pick this fight. Also, where the FUCK did she get a clipboard?

For one brief, shining moment, Sam thought about it. She considered packing up her 'wavy thing' and storming out of that warehouse in a fit of Goddess Pique.

Sam closed her eyes, inhaled and remembered to be an adult.

She waved her arm, creating a cabinet that would last twenty-four hours and would dispense whatever drug was requested. Lab coats and new scrubs were handed out to all in need. Sam bit the inside of her cheek until it bled when Aracely crossed her eyes and puffed out her cheeks at her over Dr. William's shoulder.

Sam pushed her hair out of her eyes for the fifth time in ten minutes. For some reason, it felt like it was getting bigger.

Carl swooped over head.

"Your hackles are rising," he cawed.

Dylan careened back into the room, which, Sam had to admit, looked a lot like a hospital at the moment. Someone found a hose and sprayed down the floor. The giant picked up the stage and carried it outside. Dylan tried to come to a stop next to her but the wet floor conspired with high speeds and teenage gangliness causing him to spin on all four paws past her.

"Use your claws," she called out as he slid. "Dig your claws into the -"

The wall stopped his momentum as he bumped harmlessly off it.

"You should have seen him!" Dylan babbled at her. "It was so cool! The thing just went whoop out of the wall and cut him in HALF!"

"What!?"

Before Sam could complete her panic, Edgar walked over carrying the bottom edges of his black thermal vest.

"Damn," he said and threw the pieces in an empty bin. "That was my favorite."

"And then," Dylan continued as Sam stared at Edgar, not quite comprehending what she was seeing, "one half of him is over here and the other half was over there and the top half crawled over to the bottom half and he stuck himself back together."

Dylan howled at the coolness of it.

"Are you okay?" Sam asked Edgar.

"Yeah, I'm fine," Edgar said looked around the room. "Have you seen my wife?"

Sam pointed to the door.

"I think she's getting things organized outside."

"Great, I found everything I could," Edgar said. "I'm sure the bird and the kid can give you more info. I think there are vampires buried around here somewhere but that's all I could find."

Sam examined him. On the surface, he appeared to be an ordinary, middle-aged man with thick, choppy gray hair in need of a cut, average height, average build, average blue jeans. But death had been scrubbed from his cells. Sam tilted her head. No where. Death did not live in him. Then she saw it – the lone, black spark in his heart.

He stared out the door.

"Do you need anything else from me?"

"No."

"Great, then I'm off to find the redhead."

He walked through the warehouse door into the waning day.

"Carl…" Sam gazed after the man.

"You want me to follow him, Boss?"

"No, he's fine. Go get the vampires. Tell them to come collect their people."

She tapped her chin. Dylan licked blood and water off his paws.

"Okay, kid, let's go find your dad." Sam turned on her heel, making an Irish Goodbye to the room at large.

As she exited, giant werewolf at her side, Conal floated above and behind her. He banged into the metal tracking at the side of the door, bounced and hit the top of the door. A raven shat on Aracely's shoulder.

*****

6:25 pm Oct. 30, 2020, 32 days after The Fog

The human Raven stood at the edge of the Old Beeman Building parking lot. Behind her, the denizens of Sunset Cove were getting organized. Melissa and Constance barked orders – Melissa's in Spanish, Constance in English.

Food was handed out at an astonishing rate. The sick were directed to the warehouse. Plans were made to send Healers and supplies to the far reaches of Sunset Cove. Crafters repaired clothes. A jam band picked through a couple melodies at the far side of the parking lot.

The atmosphere bordered on convivial.

Raven bit another nail and chewed it.

She's going to be so mad.

She's not going to be mad. She was nice. Remember? Okay, but this is bad… just call her. You can't leave this here. She said to wait.

'This' was a thirty-foot-wide, one hundred-foot-high, twenty-mile-long Death Trap around Sunset Cove's food supply.

Just summon her.

"Okay, fine!"

Raven jumped up and down three times to burn off some fear. Her big boots cracked against pebbles in a satisfying way. She shook her arms to tamp down the nervousness, shut her eyes and made herself say it.

"I summon thee, The Morrigan, Goddess of Death," Raven intoned, head tilted back against the twilight.

"Hey," Sam said, right in her ear.

Raven's eyes popped open and she screamed. Sam stood two feet away. The Goddess of Death windmilled backwards, tripped over a rock and landed on her ass in a small pile of gravel.

"Oh, sorry," Raven said and bent over to help her stand. "I am so sorry, but you scared me. I am so sorry."

"You called me!"

She brushed dirt from her backside and raised her eyebrows at Raven.

"I know, I know," Raven said as her thoughts skittered around. Her gaze dropped to the ground. She heard Sam take a couple deep breaths.

"It's okay. What do you need?"

Raven kicked a rock. She wrapped her thin arms around her middle and regretted ditching the cloak as the sun set. She pointed.

"I need help with that."

She wouldn't look at Sam as she rubbed her arms and tried to pretend that she didn't just realize she was four inches taller than the Goddess of Death. Raven slouched in reflex.

"Here."

Sam pulled a jacket from her hoodie and handed it to her.

"Wait, what?"

"It's a coat. You look like you're freezing."

See, Raven decided, that was the problem. She looked scary. Then she'd say and do nice things in a grumpy way. So you never really knew if she was nice or not.

The coat was a taupey, yellow garment, lined with warm, soft fuzz. It had long, straight lines, multiple pockets and a huge, fake-fur-lined hood. It was the most beautiful thing Raven had ever seen.

"Is this mine? Can I keep this?"

Sam's face was right up against the edge of the Death Trap.

"Of course, you can keep it. That's why I gave it to you. Did you make this? Of course, you made it. That's a silly question. This is amazing."

Sam stood back from the trap. She assessed its height and width.

"You just do *not* fuck around, do you?"

She whistled. Raven stopped jumping up and down over her new coat.

"Do you like it? Conal made me build it. I didn't want to but he…"

Beyond the trap, running for miles and miles along the coast, was the source of the bounty in the barrels inside the warehouse. Bananas, corn, wheat, sugar cane, plants not native to Sunset Cove thrived and grew to dizzying heights, in bewildering proportions due to Dre's acolytes.

The Death Trap, though, interested Sam more than the labor of her brother's kingdom. Woven Death, built up upon itself. Thin strands of it, hung invisible in the air, crafted and wrapped together with love and care. It was inescapable, impenetrable and utterly beautiful – a cage of absolute ending. Sam marveled at the precision.

It hurt her heart knowing that it had to be taken down.

"It's exquisite. It's a work of art. I am so proud of you."

"Really? You aren't mad?" Raven stuck a booted toe in the dirt.

"Why on Earth would I be mad?" Sam ran her hand along the edge of the trap.

"Because I used death to help a tyrant and people got hurt and I'm so..."

"Raven, please stop."

"But."

"Stop."

Raven pulled the hood over her head and crouched on the ground.

"I know you say that I shouldn't feel guilty and that I didn't do anything wrong, but I built this." She stabbed the rocky ground with a stick. "I hurt people and I did it in your name with your power."

Several pops, snaps and groans preceded Sam sitting on the ground next to her.

"Would you like me to be mad at you? Would it be easier if I yelled at you for what you did to survive that mad man? Hmm?"

Raven kept poking the ground with the stick. Sam sat with both legs straight out. She leaned back on her hands and gazed at the stars. Long, silent moments passed between them. The music wafting in from the parking lot did little to lighten the mood.

"I guess," Raven said, *stab, stab*. "I dunno. But... what if I'm not a good person anymore...?"

Sam laughed.

"It's not funny."

Sam held up a hand.

"No, you're right. I'm not laughing at you. I'm laughing at the ridiculousness of the question. Look at this trash."

She gestured to Conal floating overhead. The Darkness wrapped around him muffling his cries.

"Do you think he ever spent one second wondering if he's a good person?"

Raven's lower lip stuck out and trembled. She swiped at the tears coming down her cheeks.

"No." She jabbed the ground.

Sam crossed her legs and leaned forward. She grabbed the stick to get Raven's attention.

"I know why you're a Death Bringer."

Raven stared at the trap.

"He was so little," she said and wiped away more tears. "They kept giving him drugs. Drugs to keep him from screaming. Drugs to keep him awake so Mom and Dad could pretend…"

"So they could pretend he wasn't dying."

Raven whirled to stand and paced

"They said it didn't hurt." Her blue eyes burned in the dark. "They said he wasn't in pain. But they lied. They lied. I could tell." She pushed the heels of her hands into her eyes to hold back the pain. "So I prayed."

"You prayed for him to die so he wouldn't be in pain anymore?"

Raven nodded. Her mouth open and heaving against the memories.

"And when he did…"

"And when he did you were relieved. You were happy."

Raven nodded.

"Permission to hug?"

Raven nodded again and Sam wrapped her arms around the crying girl. Her heaving eventually faded into hiccups and trembling.

"I did the same thing," she told Raven when she calmed. Sam handed her a bottle of water.

"What?"

"My grandmother," it was Sam's turn to stare at the ground, "she was more like my mother, really. My mother was not… nice. Anyway, cancer. It took a long time. I watched her die slow. Painful. I prayed everyday for years. She became a skeleton and everyone acted like it was fine."

"Fucking Healers!" Raven shouted at the sky. The ravens in the trees shrieked in agreement.

"Fucking Healers." Sam nodded and took a swig of her own water. "The thing is, they mean well."

Raven growled.

"Truly, they do," Sam said and spun the cap back onto her water. She inhaled the cold night air. "People get so wrapped up in their grief and fear that they can't see death for what it is. That's why you and I are like this. We know. We understand."

Raven nodded, using her coat sleeve to wipe off her face.

"Death is sacred."

"Death is holy."

"Death is kindness," Raven added.

"Death is kindness," Sam agreed.

She walked towards the trap.

"May I look closer?" she asked Raven out of professional courtesy.

"Of course."

Sam stepped into the Death Trap.

Now, this was the good stuff: A warm shower after a long workout. A delicious meal you didn't have to make when you're starving, not having to go outside on a rainy day. An old bookstore with creaky floors.

The sound of waves crashing against rocks. A monstrous cave facing the ocean. Desperate people with obsidian skin huddled together inside the rocky opening against the elements. A tiny hand reaching out from the Darkness, pulling her through. A woman's bewildered, desperate voice asking: **What are you doing? No, don't. What are you doing? Stop!**

Raven yanked Sam out of the trap. She fell to the ground, body still and mind blazing.

What the fuck was that?

"I'm so sorry!" Raven patted her back. "Are you okay? Please say you're okay. I shouldn't have let you go in there. This is all my fault."

Sam sat back on her heels.

"I'm fine, Raven. I just wasn't expecting… whatever that was."

"Whatever 'what' was?"

She was clearly as flummoxed as Sam.

"The cave? The woman? All those people?"

Raven's big eyes got even larger. She shrugged. Sam pushed herself off the ground. She breathed in the cool air to gain her equilibrium – ignoring the woman's voice echoing in her skull.

"Just another Tuesday in Sunset Cove, right?" Sam joked to cover the ravaged, hollow longing in her heart.

"Exactly," Raven said with a giggle. "But I think it's Sunday"

"Fucking hell, is it? Okay, whatever. So how do you take this down?"

"I dunno." She deflated again. "That's why I asked you here. I figured you would know."

Sam did know, but she came from the Auntie School of "help them figure it out" instead of "do it for them." Sam ran her left hand over the trap. Delicate, black tendrils appeared in the air.

"This is beautiful and so spectacular, but I did catch a flaw or two."

Instantly panicked, Raven engaged. She leapt to check out the lines.

"W-w-what? A flaw? No."

She pressed her nose close to the tendrils Sam exposed.

"Okay, if you want to take this thing down, you need to exploit the flaws, right? And it's good these flaws are here otherwise, even I might not be able to take this down – it's that well done."

Raven became all shoulders and ducked head modesty.

"You're just saying that."

"I don't just say things," Sam said and went back to the lines. "You see here. This point. It's just a tiny bit wobbly and it's connected to all these other key structural points? What happens if you snap it?"

Raven reached up, the Shadows of Death played along her cheeks. She snapped the knot with her fingers. The Death Trap fell in a cloud of glittering black sparks.

Sam held up her hand.

"Well done, high-five."

Raven slapped her hand. Sam contemplated her for a second.

"Yeah, okay. Let's do this. Kellyman!" Sam yelled into the night.

A giant raven landed on her outstretched forearm.

"Okay, this is your familiar," Sam told human Raven. "His name is Kellyman."

She leaned into Kellyman and whispered dark secrets into his ear. Sam met the bird's inky eye.

"Her will is my will, understand."

The bird shook, oily, black feathers rearranging themselves. She held her arm up to Raven and nodded. The girl held up a croaked arm and the animal hopped over to her.

Raven immediately cooed at him and scratched his ruff.

"Okay, so Raven." Sam attempted to pull her attention from the animal.

"Hello, is your name Kellyman?" Raven murmured. "Aren't you the sweetest?"

"Raven." Sam tried again. "He is not sweet."

She stroked the top of the bird's head.

"No, okay, Raven. Raven, please look at me."

The girl's eyes were a million miles away.

"Raven, he is not a good bird. The soul of a murderer is trapped in there. He's bound to the Darkness for his crimes. But not a good dude. He's not sweet."

"Is that what's going to happen to me?" Raven gasped.

"I feel like I gave you too much information without context, so let's take a step back. Kellyman here," the bird dug its beak into its feathers to eat a mite, "was a mid-level enforcer for the Irish mafia in the 1930s. He killed a *lot* of people."

Raven's eyes turned into saucers.

"How many people?"

"Three hundred and thirteen," Kellyman squawked.

"Holy shit!" Raven dropped her arm and fell on her ass. "He can talk!! He talked! Did he just talk?"

Kellyman flew to the tree above them.

"You can understand him." Sam put her hands on Raven's shoulders to get her attention and pull her up off the ground. "I need you to focus, okay? Because you need to know about Kellyman. He can talk. He can help you. He can be useful. You can trust him, but like, don't *trust* him, trust him. Okay?"

Raven's eyes did not get any smaller.

"And no, you won't become a bird when you die. You haven't done anything remotely that bad."

"But I murdered people." Raven's voice was a tiny whisper in the night.

"Conal murdered people," Sam reminded her. "You were his weapon of choice."

Confusion crossed the girl's freckled face.

"Yeah, I realize that makes it worse, in a way, and I'm sorry."

"Can Kellyman hurt me?" Raven squeaked.

"I don't hurt no dames," the bird said. "No kids neither, Boss."

"See," Sam said and glanced around. "Now, where the hell is my bird? Kellyman's got a code of conduct. It's why he's a Raven and not a Wraith… well, that and the mitigating factors of lead paint, fetal alcohol syndrome and a very fucked up childhood. Right, Kellyman?"

He nodded.

"But, still, at one time, he was single-handedly responsible for a third of the bodies fished out of Lake Michigan… Carl!!"

He appeared on a tree branch beyond the edge of the fallen trap.

"You rang," he intoned. A cool, ocean breeze blew in the scent of salt and rotting seaweed. To Sam's utter horror, a light fog was rolling in.

"It's okay," Raven said, seeing her freeze. Sam turned to find Kellyman back on her arm, being scritched to his heart's content. "It's the old, regular fog. No magic – well, no more magic than we've already got."

She shrugged and returned to her familiar.

"Were you raised in toxic masculinity and not given enough care as a child?" she asked Kellyman.

"I would take a bullet for this broad, Boss," the bird crooned.

Sam gave up.

"Where's Dylan?"

"Lifting heavy things to impress girls," Carl said. "Dog did not approve of being tossed twenty feet in the air and caught. Also, the vampires are here. It caused a kerfuffle."

He titled his head to the apprentice Death Bringer and her new familiar.

"How come you never scratch my head and call me a good bird?" The sticker on his beak glowed in the fog.

"You wanted to eat my eyes and intestines," Sam reminded him.

"Well," he ducked his head under his wing, somehow seeming abashed, "you were dying."

"And that was helping?" Sam truly wanted to know.

"You are rage-motivated."

Fair enough, you fucking bird.

"Go a week without threatening to eat my face and we'll discuss behavioral rewards."

"Caw," Carl replied.

*****

6:55 pm, Oct. 30, 2020, 32 days after The Fog

Constance was caught in the center of a maelstrom.

"Do we have anyone in the south?"

"Where's my list? Have you seen my list?"

"No, I didn't know we had a cobbler. Good. Then let's get shoes on people."

"Orphans. What are we gonna do with all the orphans?"

Somehow when she started barking at people to figure it out themselves and stop asking her, they did.

Colorful tents popped up around the parking lot. Magic users made signs.

"Clothes!"

"Shoes!"

"Alcohol!"

A jam band tried to set up next to where she and Melissa were making sense out of absolute chaos, but Melissa saw the look on her face and told them, in no uncertain terms, to head elsewhere. The skinny, blond lead guitarist held up his hands for mercy and backed away.

Word spread like wildfire in this town. The sick and injured wandered in from all corners of the county. It was going to be a long night. Edgar appeared at her side. He held out a canteen.

"Tea, my love?"

She accepted it with thanks.

"What do we do with all the orphans?" It was a rhetorical question. She'd forgotten that her husband didn't do rhetoric.

"Well, I assume child labor laws are no longer in place and the cobbler could use an apprentice or two."

He winked and wrapped his arms around her.

"You're not funny."

He kissed the top of her head.

"You think I'm a little funny."

She sipped her tea and sighed. Constance eyed the dread Old Beeman Building, all the sick injured people going in and out. She formulated a plan.

"Melissa," Constance patted her husband's chest as she stepped away from him, "see if you can find us teachers. We'll need beds and clothes."

Melissa stood guard over the fifteen or so children who wandered her way simply because she'd gotten a hold of a bullhorn and seemed in charge.

"Am I following you?" Edgar asked Constance.

"Yes."

Thirty minutes later, Dr. Williams added a children's orphanage wing to her impromptu hospital. Beds were set up, teachers and nurses were vetted and assigned shifts.

Constance followed a strange instinct and yelled at an idle raven in the rafters.

"You! Bird!"

The creature swiveled its massive shoulders to her and clicked.

"You're not doing anything. Watch over these children. Keep them safe."

The animal clicked and wheezed at her. To her unending surprise, it flew to the other side of the room to keep a better vantage on the children.

"I can't believe that worked," she said to Edgar.

He was in the middle of carrying a cot to the other side of the room.

"Me either."

The vampires arrived to collect their buried and starving brethren.

"We can help." The small girl, with thin limbs and too-vibrant eyes pleaded with Dr. Williams.

Constance had to admire her pluck.

"Absolutely not," the doctor replied, not looking up from her clipboard.

"She commanded us to help," the man next to her added.

"She can command you to help somewhere else," Dr. Williams drawled and clicked her pen.

A small meteor shot through the open door, barreling straight for the children. The female vampire, with a degree of casualness Constance would have found disconcerting in any situation, leapt up, tackled the fireball and placed it on the cement floor.

The ball unrolled into a stout kid in red basketball shorts and a black t-shirt.

"Hey, sorry, is this where you're supposed to go if you don't know if your parents are dead?" he asked.

The pen clicked again. Dr. Williams arched an eyebrow.

"What's your name?"

"I'm Nestor, ma'am."

"Please check in with the nurse in the pink scrubs over there." The pen pointed.

The burns on the vampire girl's arms sizzled and healed. She took a sip from a flask and grinned with bloody teeth at the doctor.

"Fine, you can stay and help. But don't lurk… or be … weird… or eat anybody."

Edgar appeared at Constance's shoulder.

"I managed to procure a way home."

Constance sagged in relief. Home – it had been a distant memory for so long. Melissa understood as Constance made her goodbyes. She needed to be back at their house in the woods that The Fog had transformed into a quaint cottage with chicken legs.

Constance and Edgar walked across the parking lot to find the ugly, orange bicycle that magically duplicated itself once it was moved from its spot.

The crowd gasped. Constance turned to see the giant, white werewolf running across the Old Beeman Building's roof. He was followed by two ravens, one of which dragged Conal's soon-to-be corpse behind her, making the shape of a sideways question mark.

A hushed silence blanketed the crowd. All movement paused to watch the strange group leave.

Deep within the crowd, a keening rose – a cry of loss and remembrance. The sound, caught between a song note and a scream, hung low over the parking lot. As it began to fade away, other voices rose in chorus. No words were sung. Just grief. The song bounced from singer to singer. The pitch went high to low. From nowhere and everywhere, a low drum beat in time. Then, just when the depth of misery became unbearable, another voice, high and razor thin, cut through – the long, clear note of hope.

Others joined in, the crowd clapped in time. Hope bounced around the parking lot. It gained strength and momentum from the crowd of misfits and malcontents.

And because, in Sunset Cove, magic was real – that song, that hope, spread to every being in the county. The sightless, floating monsters within the ocean's deep heard every note. The strange, twisted, deaf, creatures lurking deep in the mountain forests saw it. The fearsome angels of the sky felt it.

One and all, the residents of Sunset Cove faced the night with the tiniest spark of hope.

Within the cold, white house, perched high over the ocean, the gray-haired man's fingers twitched.

*****

7:28 pm, Oct. 30, 2020, 32 days after The Fog

"That was nice," Dylan said.

Sam reverted back to human form and dropped to the ground. She turned her ankle a bit on the landing and tried to walk it off.

They landed in a torn up ditch on the far southwest corner of the cemetery, the surrounding trees were blackened and stripped of bark. Glowing eyes loomed among the shadowed tombstones. Sam could smell the freshly overturned earth.

"The singing."

He placed a massive paw over his heart and sighed.

"Yeah," she sighed in agreement. "It was nice. Well said, kid."

They had traveled across the rooftops of Sunset Cove, Dylan leaping from building to building. Carl, Sam and her Conal corpse balloon followed close behind. The swath of town below them was a mix of old Victorian-style homes and flat, squat mid-century modern commercial buildings. Sam was happy to see the majority of the old, painted ladies had survived The Fog.

They reached the edge of the largest cemetery in town. It stretched for two miles along the bank of the Saint Augustus. Sam had spent her very muddy month less than a mile down river.

The cold and damp air seeped through Sam's hoodie, bringing a chill to her bones. She reached out to the resting dead of this place and found them to be neither. Dylan stepped forward but she stopped him.

"Wait."

She put her right hand over her heart and bowed. It felt even more ridiculous with someone watching.

"I am The Morrigan," she called to no one.

"What are you doing?" Dylan asked.

"I'm introducing myself, I think," she whispered out of the side of her mouth. "I am the Queen of Darkness."

Dylan paced back and forth.

"This is so embarrassing," he muttered in pure teenage angst.

"How do you think I feel?"

The looming trees stirred above silent, gray tombstones. A large, wooden gate, marked with white, Chinese letters, stood twenty feet to the left.

"Eh, hem. Anyway, I'm the Queen of the Darkness and I seek an audience with the Werewolf… uh, King, the one who stands guard at the entrance between worlds. I come bearing gifts – the return of the king's son and the man who harmed him… Plus, his tongue – the man's tongue, not his son's … in a bag…"

Dylan danced back and forth on his forepaws.

"I am embarrassed for you."

But the forest stilled, the dead beneath their feet became a little more restful. The glowing eyes around them retreated. Conal squealed and squirmed behind her.

"Okay, I think that worked. Let's find your dad."

A small coyote dotted with gray and white fur, eyes gleaming yellow in the night, appeared before them next to the aged grave marker of William Thomas Blackburn, born September 28, 1883, died June 30, 1904. It bowed.

Sam bowed in return. The animal whirled, then turned its head to make sure they were following.

"What the fuck?" Dylan muttered. "That's so crazy. Did you just see that? He wants us to follow."

"She," Sam said. "Dylan, you're a twelve-foot-tall werewolf. I don't know why you're amazed by this."

"It's just cool, is all I'm saying."

The coyote led them down the remains of a narrow, one-way asphalt road. Parts of the path stood uprooted with shards of half-rotted, wooden planks jutted outward – like cracked teeth in the gaping maw of the earth. The trees lurked here – hanging lower than the typical redwoods and pine of Sunset Cove.

Sam smelled the dank river to her right. Neat rows of monuments, buffered with low white retaining walls, rested along the upward slope to her left. The trees swayed and whispered to each other in a language Sam couldn't speak. Faded path lights flickered in and out of life. This part of the cemetery felt… still. Not the calm before a storm but the stillness of final rest. Sam tried to remember a time when this would bother her instead of thrill her, but she couldn't. The beauty of it all, the artistry behind the veil, always excited her blood.

"Yeah, kid," she finally replied, picking her way over an upended, moss-covered tombstone. "Your dad is pretty cool."

The coyote led them toward the newer section of the cemetery. Flat stones embedded in the earth marked the resting place of the recent dead instead of the upright markers. This part of the cemetery felt more alive. The frayed, waving flags and the garish, plastic flower offerings littering the homes of the dead offered the illusion of life.

The animal turned right on a footpath and stopped next to two, large willow trees.

Sam could see the tattered remnants of a homeless encampment's blue tents beyond the cemetery hedge.

Between the two trees, and just a few feet from a marker with vertical Chinese characters, fused shards of bone pierced the earth, forming a triangular coffin.

"Dad!"

Dylan ran toward it. Sam managed to catch his tail.

"Dylan, wait, please."

"But that's my dad," the boy said, pulling her along. "He's in there. I can smell him."

She dug in her heels and tried not to hurt him.

"Kid, I get that, but this place is super dangerous and the closer we get to him the worse it gets."

The giant wolf stopped in his tracks.

"My dad wouldn't hurt me."

Sam scrambled around to face him and offer reassurance.

"No, honey, of course he wouldn't." She held up both hands, pleading for patience. "But I'm overly-cautious and I need to make sure it's all okay."

The boy whined and scratched his face.

"He looks hurt. Is he dead?"

"He's not dead."

"Are you sure?"

The boy pawed the earth.

"He looks dead, Sam. He's not moving."

Dylan brought his nose low to the ground and whined, high and piercing. He yipped and rolled over.

Sam approached the structure. Her hands out in supplication. Thick, razor-sharp shards obscured the man's form.

"I was like this three days ago."

"With the bones and everything?" He flipped back onto his stomach then leapt to standing. "Whoa. That's crazy."

"Uh, no," Sam said, pointing downstream. "I was in the river. Right over there."

"You sure he's okay?"

Dylan circled the structure.

"Yes, kid, I'm sure."

Sam sat down at one end. Her left hand hovered a couple inches above the cage's thick femur bones.

"I need to touch him to talk to him," she told no one.

Dylan turned around three times and curled up at the other end of the coffin. He pushed his snout as close to the bones as he dared without touching them. The boy a-wooo-ed in sadness – eyes rolling back in his skull. The coyote approached and sniffed him. She laid her head on the back of his neck in sympathy.

"I don't like this," he muttered.

Beneath her hand the shards parted revealing a hairy calf and black combat boot.

"It'll be okay," Sam whispered. "Carl?"

"Right here, Boss."

The bird said from his perch within the willow tree to her left.

"If anything…"

"On it."

Sam took a deep breath and wrapped her left hand around the God Xolotl's leg.

*****

The Werewolf King's Domain, The Liminal Space

She found herself deep within a marshland. The moon hung low and monstrous overhead. The reeds wrapped themselves around her. They writhed and shimmered in the ghostly moonlight. Sam could almost make out the barest hint of color. Verdant greens and oranges faded into near black and white. Creatures howled and gnashed – the sound muted by the soft damp flora. Through the thick and treacherous brush, Sam saw a path. She stumbled and shoved her way forward but the marsh fought back. Mud and vines grabbed at her, slowing her progress. The humid night air made Sam's curls stick to her forehead and neck. She shoved it back, cursing the green surrounding her.

"Fine! You wanna dance?"

She summoned Death to her – perhaps a little too violently. Everything within a five-foot radius exploded. Wilted vines and the checkerboard tail of a snake dropped onto her head and shoulders.

"Oh, fuck! I'm sorry. So sorry!"

She shrunk the radius to a foot. Sam picked off the debris and tail.

"That's my bad," Sam said to the headless tail between her thumb and forefinger before flinging it away. "I should not have done that. Although, are you a real snake or the construct of a … never mind. Not important. I should not have done that. I apologize."

The marsh shrank from her. The vines that tripped her wilted and died. Sam twisted her hair into a bun on the top of her head as she sauntered to the clearing.

The claustrophobic reeds opened up into a plaza. A fifteen-foot-wide path led to a geometric pyramid that rose hundreds of feet from the marshland floor. It glowed. The full, perfect moon hung massive and white behind the structure. About twenty feet from Sam, between her and the stepped pyramid, a man lounged on a throne of human bones.

This place held ancient death. She smelled the distant metallic twang of blood in the air. The pyramid stones had been painted with it. The path she walked ran red with rivers of it hundreds of years ago.

The gravel beneath her feet crunched too loud with each step – almost as loud as her heartbeat in her ears. Predators hunted here.

She'd gotten ten feet closer to the man on the throne, who she assumed was Dylan's dad, when several thoughts bombarded her simultaneously. They were, in no particular order:

- He snored.
- Big dude. Well over six feet.
- In his haste to get his kid to work, he'd pulled on a fuzzy, pink bathrobe with a teddy bear hood over his pajamas
- Black boots on his feet
- He didn't wear pajamas to bed – or anything else.
- One leg was hiked over the armrest of the throne
- HE WASN'T WEARING ANYTHING ELSE!???

Sam held up a hand to shield her eyes.

"Hello!" she called, trying to walk toward him without looking *at him*. "Hi! Hello! Please wake up! I brought your son. Hello?"

The Werewolf King snorted once, went silent and then went back to snoring.

"Naked man! Please! Wake up!"

She circled around the throne until she stood within arms reach of the teddy bear's glittering, judgmental eyes. It gazed up at Sam with such accusation and reproach. The bear could clearly read her thoughts.

"How am I supposed to know he was naked?" she whispered to it. "I'm trying to do the right thing here. This is not my fault."

Sam grabbed his giant, pink, fur-clad shoulder and shook.

"Hello! Please wake up."

The snoring stopped with a snort and a cough. Silence. The air stilled with the imminent threat of violence.

"Hello?" The Goddess of Vengeance squeaked.

A man-paw rose up and pushed the hood back from his eyes. One of them popped open.

The other followed suit and a wide, slow grin spread across his face.

"Hello, Radiant Darkness," he growled, sharp canines visible.

Sam couldn't help it. He'd just given her the best compliment of her life. She twinkled down at him, charmed.

"Hello, Soul of the Wolf."

She cleared her throat, eyes darting to his waist and back up again.

"Ahem."

He glanced down.

"Ah."

With more grace and purpose than she'd ever done anything, he swung his leg down, pulled the robe together and stood.

"I wasn't expecting company," he said without a trace of embarrassment or discomfort.

"Fair enough," she replied, locking on to his gaze so her eyes wouldn't be tempted to wander. "I'm Sam."

She stuck out her hand. He took it in his massive paw.

"Manny," he replied, looming over her. "Who are you?" He arched a black eyebrow.

"Oh! right! I'm The Morrigan." She pointed at herself. "I brought your son. Goddess of Death, Queen of the Darkness…"

He bent over her hand, sniffing it.

"And other… stuff…"

He turned her arm over, palm up.

"May I?"

His face, at close range, was mostly covered by a thick, black and silver beard. Long, inky hair fell past his shoulders to his waist. Everything about him screamed 'intimidating,' yet his brown eyes were calm and merry. His manner was gentlemanly.

Sam sighed.

"Sure."

He sniffed the air a foot or so away from her – close enough to be bothersome but not intrusive. His nose hovered over her shoulder.

"What about my son?"

"So he's here or outside – whatever you want to call it." Sam rambled on in her nervousness. "There was a Silver Tongue. I cut out his tongue. He, like, kidnapped your kid and a bunch of other people. I brought the tongue and the dude for you… a peace offering, truce thing. Ya know, visiting someone, it's always nice to bring a gift or two… also please don't go on a blood-soaked rampage through the county looking for your kid or the man who took him because I brought them… here, to you."

"Would you try to stop me if I did?"

He interrupted her blathering. She couldn't tell if he was threatening or not so she bet on honesty and turned her head to him.

"Yes."

"Do you think you could?" He sounded amused with a smile on his face and a chuckle rumbling in his chest.

"I don't know," she shrugged, "probably."

He stood behind her and sniffed the top of her head. Sam's spine tingled.

"As long as you don't sniff my butt, we're fine."

"Okay, I won't … now." He barked out laughter. She could hear the sniffing on her other shoulder.

"Good, so yeah, anyway, the dude who took Dylan was answering to this other bigger, badder dude – he's like us, the bigger dude, I mean. If you'd like to help me take him out cool, if not we're all good."

"You're a generous queen," he said and patted her shoulder – distracted. "I like you."

"...Thank …you?"

He drifted farther away. The Werewolf King looked to the sky and the marshland, searching in each direction. He moved to the other side of the clearing, stopped, drew a lungful of air, threw back his head, thrust out his chest and howled. He howled to the night sky, to the four winds, to the souls of the dead and to the thrill of the hunt.

Wildness ripped through the night air, buffeting Sam with endless possibility, wonder, excitement, freedom. This was not the chaos at the opposite of her nature. This was feral.

A great, thunderous crash rushed through the other side of the marsh. Sam stepped back in apprehension until Dylan's giant, goofy, white head popped out of the trees.

The hair on Sam's neck rose and she turned to see Manny transform. He leapt over her – tall as a house, claws like machetes, black and silver fur glinting in the moonlight.

Then she remembered, remembered why this was so urgent. So important. She had seen him before.

They'd blinded him. Figuring his eyes would be the weakest point – trying to halt the rampage. His fur matted and streaked with blood. Buildings exploded as he tore through them like paper. Without eyes, he couldn't find his hope in the night sky but he could smell their blood. He would make them pay with it.

On her way to Dre's house, after leaving the Liminal Space, she'd flown over him – the giant wolfman howling like the damned. He decimated everything in his path.

The Werewolf King landed with the soft grace of a kitten and threw himself at his son. They crashed into trees. The smaller white wolf rolled into his back while the large black one licked his face.

The boy's massive paws batted his father's face. The black wolf leapt back and bowed on his front legs. The white wolf lolled over, stood and repeated the gesture.

The two then chased and tackled each other, knocking down trees, crashing into the pyramid. Pebbles tumbled down the structure in their wake. Sam had lived through earthquakes that made less noise.

Their chase edged near Sam. She skittered away.

"No! Nope! Absolutely not!"

The two halted before her. The haggard, white wolf, tongue falling out of his mouth in exhaustion, hung across the black wolf's shoulders. The two transformed before her eyes – Dylan, into a lanky, blonde kid, long, matted hair brushing his shoulders, all elbows and knees, clad in the khaki shorts and the blue Hawaiian shirt that was the uniform of Pie-zaz (the second best pizza joint in Sunset Cove).

Manny extended his hand.

"Can I have my gift, please?"

It took Sam a second to remember what he was talking about.

"Oh! Sure!"

She rooted around in her hoodie and found the paper-wrapped package.

"Here ya go."

He held the parcel in one hand as he peeled the paper back to reveal the bloody tongue. Manny grinned. He brought the mutilated muscle to his face and bit down. Blood dripped from his beard. It left bright red spots on the pink robe. Sam licked her lips.

"Here," he said and handed it over.

She sniffed it, smelling the lies and torture it carried. Her stomach rumbled. Sam sunk her teeth in and tore off a chunk.

"Thank you," she said around the mouthful. It tasted of fear and metal – slick bursts of cinnamon and flashes of terror. It intoxicated her. Blood dripped onto her chin. Sam handed it back to Manny.

"This is delicious," she said as she giggled and stumbled.

"Are you drunk?" Manny demanded, shaking her shoulder.

"I'm a little blood drunk," Sam said, wiping her mouth. She licked the blood from the back of her hand. "Are you blood drunk?"

Manny snorted, twirled, pink bathrobe ties flying as he fell on his ass. He pulled his beard up to his mouth to lick blood drips from it.

Dylan covered his face with his hands and pretended to not know them.

"No," Manny growled. "But this is bloody delicious."

Sam froze.

No.

She glared down at the prone Werewolf King, legs splayed before him.

"What?" He gazed up at her, innocent and knowing. "Don't you think I'm punny?"

By the Holy Darkness, NO.

His eyes widened and his mouth dropped open like some 50s game show host waiting for applause. Sam sucked in her lips to squash the rising scream of horror.

"No," she muttered and pointed. "Absolutely not."

"Don't tell me you're already regretting our pact?"

"Dad," Dylan joined in. "I think we should make her a member of the pack before she gives up and packs it in."

Sam's eyes rolled back in her skull.

"You are both awful."

"Yes," Manny blinked up at her. "We're so full – full of awe."

Dylan helped his father stand.

Sam plopped down onto the ground. The thick exhilaration of blood running down her throat evaporated in the face of bad puns and a very long day.

"Wait," she said, rewinding the conversation in her mind. "Pack?"

"Yup." Manny leaned over and offered her a hand. "You're in the pack."

"I am?" Sam panicked, not sure what to do with that information. "Since when? How? Are there dues? What does that mean?"

Manny brushed dust from his robe.

"I like you. You're in the pack and you have a pact."

"Nooooo, stoooooopppppp," Sam groaned and rolled her eyes.

"He doesn't like anybody," Dylan chimed in.

"I do not," Manny said and held up the last bite of tongue to the night sky. "For you, brother."

To Sam's astonishment, the bit of flesh turned blue and twirled as it rose out of Manny's hand. It disappeared into the dark.

The Morning Star flashed red and danced in the sky.

"The fuck...." Sam's mouth dropped open. "Is that...?"

"Sam, this is my brother, Miguel. Miguel, this is Sam."

The star twinkled.

"Nice to meet you," Sam said.

It spun in circles.

"Show off," Manny muttered, glaring at the sky. "He's a flirt. Don't mind him."

The star, Sam had trouble thinking of him as Miguel, shined brighter, zoomed closer and continued to dance.

Yup, I'm a little in love.

Manny raised an eyebrow at her dazzled expression.

"Every time, every fucking time."

Sam shook herself out of it and they agreed Dylan would stay in this space for a day or two and Sam would come back and escort him to Manny's girlfriend's house.

"I'm not trying to be an asshole or a downer here, but what if she's not alive?" Sam asked.

"She's alive," Manny said. "I talked to her before you got here. She's a Chaos Witch."

He grinned with pride.

"Oh, fuck," she breathed before she could help herself.

With that, Sam exited his kingdom. The bone coffin expanded to cover Dylan's prone and now very human form.

The Silver Tongue was nowhere to be found. A three-foot patch of freshly, overturned earth marred the ground where he had floated behind her. Sam grinned with sharp bloody teeth. She licked her lips. The taste of Conal's terror was still fresh.

She brushed the dirt from her backside. The cemetery seemed calmer now. The dead surrounding her actually rested now. She prepared to fly home when Carl landed on the bone coffin.

"Hey, Boss."

"What's up, Carl?"

He bopped up and down, examining his wing. The sticker on his beak had disappeared. She decided to give him the benefit of the doubt that it had just fallen off.

"Don't you think it's funny that the Healers didn't use magic?" he asked while casually grooming his wing.

Sam raised both arms overhead and stretched to the rhythm of the wind in the trees. She contemplated for a moment and reached the obvious conclusion.

"Well, fuck."

The moon hung high overhead. It must have been 2 am or so. Sam had just lived through the longest day of her life. She had enough gas to fly home and fall into bed.

"I need to sleep, Carl," Sam said with a yawn. "Can I deal with this tomorrow?"

He twisted and shrieked to the sky. The rage in his soul escaped unbidden. His feathers gleamed oil slick red and purple in the moonlight.

"Yeah, Boss. That should be fine, but it can't wait."

She arched her back, stretching, and found the Morning Star. Sam winked at Miguel and smiled.

"First thing."

She turned into a raven and flew home – too tired to even notice the distinct lack of screams from the world below.

When she reached the Leary's doorstep, the Wraiths shrieked about the Healers.

"Yeah, I know," Sam mumbled, grasping the door jamb to stay upright in her exhaustion.

One of their gummy mouths ripped wide open.

"The Celestial Mothers decree that you must help the Goddess of Healing." It screamed in her face at 2:30 in the morning.

Sam rubbed her forehead. Then rested her head against the pale yellow door jamb and studied the Leary's doormat that read, "GO AWAY!" The spiderweb to the right of her head glittered green and gold in the light. Bee corpses spun slowly within the web.

"Great. Fine. Sure. Where is she and what's the problem?"
Crickets.

"Fantastic," Sam said and wobbled. "Call me when the Celestial Mothers decide to be helpful. I'm going to bed. I will deal with this in the morning."

*****

4:15 am, Oct. 31, 2020, 33 days after The Fog

Conal awoke in his own grave. He knew because the bones whispered it.

That Bitch, as he'd come to call her, had passed out in the graveyard. He thought he could escape her but the dark bonds around him only let go when skeletal hands pulled him beneath the earth.

He had blacked out in terror and awoke to a darkness so absolute he could touch it.

Warped, splintering wood let in clumps of earth and insects a few inches from his face. His trembling hand rose to meet a long, slender, dense material. Conal pushed against it and realization set in as it pushed back.

The smell of cold, damp earth choked him. He vomited. It rolled down his cheek under his head, matting his hair.

He lay pinned on his side. Air reached him somehow.

It came to him in waves.

He wasn't going to suffocate. He wasn't going to choke on his own vomit. This was his grave.

If he had a tongue, he would have screamed out an empty apology.

Instead he laughed, a strangled chortle, blood bubbles rose and popped out of his throat.

Little critters, insects and new, slimy, Fog-created creatures without names crawled onto him to investigate, to feast.

He shook, flailing and tried to brush them off but skeletal hands pinned his wrists to the wood beneath him. The bones chittered and scratched to each other as he writhed in a futile attempt to escape.

Something with a thousand legs crawled onto his face. He squealed and banged his head into the wood to squash it, but the bug prevailed. It crawled over his nose, down his top lip, over his exposed teeth and into the bloody maw that was once his mouth.

Conal blacked out again.

He shifted in and out of consciousness. He dreamt of a silver and black werewolf, bigger than a house, stalking him through the night. Conal begged the wolf to leave him be. He tried to explain why he was innocent, to cry for help but no words came.

It took him thirty-two hours to die from a massive infection in what was left of his face.

Upon his death, Conal Estes Mayeaux found himself standing in the parking lot outside the office supply store where he once worked – the one by the weird swimming pool supply store. The glass doors to his former job were wide open and bright light blasted out from them.

Standing between Conal and those welcoming doors, stood the giant, gray and black werewolf. He snarled. Bloody saliva dripped from his jaws.

Conal knew this was the end of him. No more life. No more existence. This creature had the power to void him.

He said the only thought that popped into his mind.

"I didn't know he was your son."

The wolfman howled.

Rows of red-stained teeth were the last thing Conal Estes Mayeaux ever saw.

THE TOURIST FOR THE WIN

Yong Ji Hyon, father of Yong Zhu Yun, was lost at sea five days after his son's eighth birthday. Yong Zhu Yun's mother, Nam Ho-Yeon, arranged the funeral within three days of his father's death. The little boy knew he was supposed to cry before the picture of his late father surrounded by flowers on the tall, black dais, but he couldn't.

Three months after his father's funeral, they moved from the port city of Busan, South Korea, where his father had been a fisherman to San Jose, California. His mother became a dental hygienist. Yong Zhu Yun changed his name to Joon Yong and pretended that he didn't miss the clean symmetry of the rigging and bright boat hulls of home.

As a child and into adulthood, Joon met and exceeded the expectations placed on him. He went to school to become a computer programmer and landed a good job in South San Francisco. He tried not to think about the ocean too much. His apartment window faced another building and he kept his days full.

The morning of Sept. 28, 2020 he followed the same routine that he did every Saturday, with a few notable exceptions:

6:30 am - Wake up without an alarm, use the bathroom, wash his face, brush his teeth.

6:45 am - Take the elevator down five floors to the laundry room, throw in two loads (clothes separated by light and dark – obviously).

6:46 am - Smile like a fool when placing a blue-green hoodie in the washing machine

6:55 am - Run the stairs back to his apartment.

7:10 am - Drop and do a hundred push ups inside his front door.

7:20 am - Make a breakfast smoothie

7:45 am - Take the elevator back down to the laundry room, run two more loads (bedding and towels), throw the clothes in the dryer.

8 - 8:45 am - Scrub the toilet, bathroom sink, shower and bathroom floor, dust and vacuum

8:45 am - Run downstairs, get the dry clothes, put the clothes from the washing machine in the dryer. Take the elevator back upstairs.

9 am - Leave clothes on bed to deal with later, separate green hoodie from the pile and lay it flat so it doesn't wrinkle, wash kitchen counters, take out the trash, mop the floor.

9:45 am - Pretend the mop is both a microphone and dance partner while blasting 80s dance pop.

9:55 am - Drop the mop. Do the Running Man.

10 am - Run downstairs, get the bedding and towels out of the dryer.

10:15 am - Snack time! Trail mix.

10:25 am - Finish the last forty five minutes of Pretty in Pink on the laptop in his bedroom while putting away his clothes and towels, organized by color.

11:15 am - Start *Some Kind of Wonderful* while making the bed.

11:30 am - Sit on the freshly made bed and yell at Keith for not seeing that Watts is his One True Love.

11:45 am - Lunch! Ramyeon while watching Keith get detention on the big screen in his living room. Slurp noodles while muttering about Keith being a "damn fool."

12:30 pm - Wash dishes.

12:45 pm - Jog to the rock climbing gym. Try not to think about her.

Unbidden, he remembered the moody colors of the watercolor painting she'd given him. He taped the scene of a forest sunset to the white wall of his bedroom, right above his desk. Her hand curved just so as she layered oranges and pinks above the pine green tree line. His eyes traced the movement of her hand, up her delicate wrist to the brushed, pink cherry blossom tattoo on her forearm.

She kept up a steady stream of conversation as she painted – asking him about his work and hobbies.

Every Saturday night, Joon hopped in his blue-green Nissan 400z with a manual transmission and drove like the devil chased him. He hit the highways and byways of Northern California without a destination or schedule. Weaving in and out of traffic, zooming up hills and braking down valleys, he spent his Saturday nights driving. Sometimes, if he traveled too far, he'd find a hotel and crash overnight in some tiny, California shit town. Sundays were his only free day.

Last Saturday, Sept. 21, he'd taken Highway 1 down the coast. Joon couldn't have said why. He usually avoided this route but he was bored and looking for new vistas.

He traveled through the low buildings and rich exhaust smell of south San Francisco emerging to the bouji and carefully salt-bleached, coastal towns. Fog clung to the land and buildings.

Joon's soundtrack on this journey was a collection of 80s and 90s classics, including, but not limited to: Pat Benatar, Barenaked Ladies, Talk Talk and the Breakfast Club soundtrack.

He flicked his wrist to change gears. As the towns dissipated, the forests rose up – redwoods, pine and low chaparral scrubs hushed the purr of his car, which he had named Molly.

He spent thirty agonizing minutes stuck behind a burgundy minivan with Missouri plates that slammed their brakes to fifteen mph at the hint of a switchback. After Joon was finally able to pass the dread tourists, he rounded a corner and passed a little green sign proclaiming that he'd entered Sunset Cove County.

Molly took him past farms with crooked, hand-painted wooden signboards urging him to buy six avocados for a dollar and vans parked on turn outs that lead to the ocean cliff's end.

Wind blasted the car, making it wobble. Joon rolled down the window and laughed.

Salt water blew into the car, ruffling his short, straight, jet-black hair (that he never quite knew what to do with). It hit his lips as he belted out every word of "One Week."

A little town clung to both sides of the highway. Wine-drunk tourists stumbled across the busy road to stare at the ocean.

He kept driving down Highway 1 until he reached the Sunset Cove proper. Joon switched on his GPS and asked his car:

"Where am I?"

"Sunset Cove, Sunset Cove County, California," Molly said monotonously. "City population: fifty-five thousand. County estimated population: two-hundred, fifty-two thousand as of the last census. Sunset Cove is home to Cal State Sunset Cove. It is a popular tourist destination due to its Boardwalk and lively downtown. In the 1960s and 70s, Sunset Cove was the murder capital of the United States as it was home to three prolific serial killers."

She didn't even pause.

Highway 1 turned into a busy commercial road with low, dusty doughnut shops, suspicious-looking pizzerias, abandoned meth shacks and brightly lit palm readers. Joon found it charming.

"Molly, is this downtown?"

"No, this is Cedar Street, one of the main arteries. Would you like me to direct you toward downtown?"

"Yes, please, Molly. Thank you."

The sun was setting as the car told him to turn down a tree-lined street at the top of a hill. Every block had a different personality – hippie gardeners offering free food and skaters in black socks with scabbed knees flying across intersections. A giant dude in a pink bathrobe, sunglasses, black sweatpants and combat boots jaywalked across the road, waving in apology as he ran toward a ballpark. Homeless people in tattered, sun-bleached clothes congregated around an ice cream shop across the street.

In contrast to the low gray buildings and sullen wariness of South SF, this place teemed with carnival, confectionery life.

Molly told him to pull into a three-story parking garage. He drove straight to the top, parked and got out to stretch. The sound of music floated in the air. Joon touched his toes three times and took off at a light jog toward the sound. He ran down the cement stairs and headed to the music.

On a raised cement pad a half-block away from the parking garage, Joon found a thin man with a drawn, pale face, all in black, strumming a guitar. His voice echoed, hollow and strange, among the low, concrete buildings surrounding the square. The crowd around him stood still and rapt, attentive to the haunting melodies he offered.

Joon shook off the musical trance and jogged away. This was not his scene.

For the next thirty minutes, Joon wandered around downtown Sunset Cove. Like the drive through town, each block offered a different experience – the line of overdressed young people outside the hipster club, the crowd of punks and metalheads gathered in a cloud of smoke outside of a tiki bar. Buddhist monks and nuns in red and orange robes talked and laughed as they walked through the crowd – so many people, just walking around, talking to each other, looking at each other. They just existed here, ambling amongst one another – enjoying being among strangers.

Joon had not dressed for this town. The damp cold bit through his thin t-shirt and shorts. Shivering, rubbing the goosebumps on his arms, he turned back to his car and ran straight into the woman behind him. Her face stuck in her phone, she bumped into his shoulder.

"I am so sorry!" She looked up and reached out to check on him. "Are you okay?"

Her eyes were large and strange in her round face, as though she'd just emerged into this world from elsewhere. He liked her instantly. Growing up, Joon always had more female friends than male. She struck him as the kind of person he could stay up until 3 am watching Ghibli movies with.

"I'm okay," he said. She glanced down at her phone and tucked it into the pocket of her gray hoodie.

They stood beneath the glaring lights of a movie theater marquee. Foot traffic streamed around them. Seemingly every person wore more clothes than him - except the club girls in their tiny skirts and razor heels. Joon's breath floated up and away from his mouth up to the sign announcing a midnight showing of *Scott Pilgrim vs the World* and that their Halloween midnight showing of *Rocky Horror* was sold out.

"Okay, cool," she said, and turned to walk away. "Whew."

"Hey." He stopped her. "Do you live here?"

Her lips quirked. She knew what was coming.

"Yeah," she said, cocking her head a bit. Her wild hair fell over one eye. She pursed her lips and tried to blow it away. When that didn't work, she batted her hair like a cat. "I live here."

"Where can I get coffee? Or tea? Someplace warm?"

"Sure, that's easy."

She pointed at the half-naked, glittering mannequins in the sex shop across the street.

"Go to the other side of this street, head that direction until you can see the Clocktower. To your left there will be a brick building at the end of the block. There's a sandwich board and chairs outside. Ruby's coffee. Like six blocks"

He rubbed his arms again.

"They have good coffee?"

"Yeah." She smiled again – a real smile, not a 'get out of my face' tourist grimace. "But don't go to the hipster joint across the street."

"Why not?"

She glanced down at her phone.

"It's full of fucking hipsters."

He threw back his head and laughed. He wanted to ask if she liked *Ponyo* and if she had strong feelings about *Moonstruck* but he didn't. Making friends as an adult was so awkward.

"Thank you!" He took off at a jog as she pulled her hood over her head to block the cold.

"Welcome!" She waved and turned back to her phone.

He swore he heard her mutter: "Well, he was nice."

Joon ran across the two-lane street at a decent pace and passed a silver jewelry shop. The bored, blue-haired teenager out front tried to hand him a flier about their fifty-percent-off sale. He weaved in and out of the crowd, past shoe shops and a man dressed in head to toe, black glitter, including a face mask and top hat, playing an accordion while standing on a box, past a nurse in blue scrubs and long, brown ponytail with red eyes and a puffy face – her hands stuffed in her pockets. She refused to make eye contact with anyone.

Joon wondered for the thirtieth time today what was up with this town. Two young women clad in full-body, shimmering yellow, with slinky antennas on their heads, high-stepped arm in arm by him. An old woman bedecked in voluminous scarves asked everyone around her for money. A shocking number of people wore either hoodies or Hawaiian shirts.

He jogged past a poke shop and a man sitting on the sidewalk with a sign that read: 'money for the apocalypse' until, like the woman said, he reached a brick building with a sandwich board out front advertising bouji breakfast specials.

Before walking into Ruby's, he spared a glance at the coffee shop across the street. It was wall to wall gray scarves and beard oil.

Immediately, the scent of roasting coffee hit him. This long, narrow room with high, bronze ceilings felt ancient, like it was the most recent incarnation of a long line of spaces where people gathered together to study and work with an endless supply of WiFi, beverages and snacks.

The counter to his left was burnished wood. A dappled mirror behind it showed him his own shivering reflection. To the right, on the narrow walkway, milk jugs, sweetener and half and half rested on a counter top below a selection of vinyl records.

This place was so warm Joon wanted to run back and ask the woman for more recommendations.

A tall Black man in a purple Hawaiian shirt stood in line in front of him. He leaned down, face pressed into the pastry display case.

"Hello, my love," he crooned.

For a split second, Joon thought he meant the apple pie.

"Yes, we left early," the man said into the phone in his ear. "Sam got cold and I didn't want to drive too late. She sends her love by the way. I'm at Ruby's. I know you enjoy their pastries. Would you like a brownie? The butterscotch blondies look particularly delectable."

The man noticed Joon and waved him along with a half bow, covering his phone with his other hand.

"Please, go ahead. It's all so gorgeous, I can't decide."

The man reminded Joon of the woman in the hoodie in a way he couldn't quite place.

"Oh, yes," he continued into his phone, tapping his fingers to his lips. He hovered over the pastry case like he wanted to prevent its escape. "Their cover of Old Town Road was as zesty as ever."

Joon ordered black coffee and a slice of the coveted apple pie.

"Excellent choice," the man mouthed, giving him the thumbs up.

Joon balanced his pie in one hand and the scalding hot coffee in the other as he scoped out where to sit. Two-person tables littered the narrow room on the other side of the bar. Canvases of green and blue abstract art hung on the brick walls.

He heard only the tapping of computer keys and the bluesy horns whispered from the record player behind the counter.

He sat, shivering at an empty table, not paying too much attention. Joon wrapped his hands around the cup and shook.

A greenish-blue hoodie appeared in his peripheral vision.

"You can borrow this until you get warm – don't steal it."

"What?" Joon's head snapped in the direction of the low drawling voice and every cell in his body sang "Crazy for You" by Madonna.

THIS ONE.

"You're cold." She glanced up from the white paper, flicked the blue paintbrush and immediately returned her gaze to the paper. "You can wear it until you warm up. Just don't steal it."

Her enunciation was terrible. Joon fought the absolute, irresistible urge to rip his heart out of his chest and place it at her feet. He didn't know what was happening.

PROPOSE. NOW.

Despite being colder than he had ever been before in his life, (including that one February in Busan when their heater broke for a week) with a frigid numbness that gnawed on his bones, he broke out in a full body sweat.

"Here." She waved the hoodie at him.

Joon took the garment largely because he couldn't think of anything else to do. He put it on. His muscles relaxed with the warmth. The hoodie was too big for him. It must swim on her tiny frame.

He tried not to stare as he chewed pie and sipped his coffee. Her hoodie smelled like cinnamon.

"You visiting from over the hill?" she asked as her pale, thin hand swept across the paper. Joon couldn't see her. It was like looking at a forest. The reality was too much. He had to focus on the details – red hair, pale, visible tattoo. The hoodie carried warmth from her slender body.

"Huh?"

He really needed to step up his game.

"Are you visiting from over the hill? San Jose? You're dressed like you thought it would be warm."

Ask her to get up and dance. This is what those ballroom dance classes were for. THIS IS YOUR MOMENT!

Joon eyed the crowded room. He considered for a moment before dismissing it – too many chairs.

"Nope." He shrugged. "South SF. I didn't plan very well."

And then he uttered the phrase that would haunt him for the rest of his days.

"Do you come here often?"

His own mouth dropped open. *He* couldn't even believe that he'd said it.

Why are you so bad at this?

He'd dated before – nothing serious. He did okay – not great, not terrible. Okay. He'd gone out on a date last night, in fact. It was okay.

"I didn't… I don't…" He stuttered, trying to crawl out of the hole he'd dug for himself. "I mean…"

She giggled – not at him, not cruel, but cute, like she thought he was cute. Her eyes flashed up at him from behind her lashes.

"It's okay," she said, taking pity on him. "I'm here every week. I don't have a car. My shift ends at seven. My mom's shift ends at nine so I wait here."

A terrible thought struck him.

"How old are you?"

She rewarded him with a soft, sly smile.

"Twenty-six. How old are you?"

"I'm thirty-one," he said. He was so glad she cared enough to ask.

With the awkwardness out of the way, their conversation was off to the races. They spent the next hour talking. She loved *Ponyo. Of course!*

Neither understood this country's obsession with dairy.

"I'm lactose intolerant."

"So am I!"

And then, upon hearing that he was born in Korea, she did this:

"안녕하세요. 어떻게 지내세요. (annyeonghaseyo. eotteohge jinaeseyo) (Hello, how are you doing?)"

"한국어를 하세요? (hangug-eoleul haseyo) (Do you speak Korean?)" He answered - shock and awe radiating from his body.

She inclined her head, the delicate line of her chin and neck pointing toward him.

"적고 많지 않다, (jeoggo manhji anhda) (A little, not very well,)" she replied.

"Erin!" yelled an older woman from the entrance of the coffee shop. She had gray roots, wore a puffy, leopard-print coat and a black mini skirt. An unlit cigarette dangled from two fingers. She obviously had run out of fucks decades ago.

"Let's go."

Joon blinked and the woman next to him had her art supplies packed up in a canvas bag. She slid the finished painting across the table to him.

"Here," she said, standing, "this is for you."

Flummoxed, he stood with her.

"You're leaving?"

She twirled back to him and smiled in a way that destroyed his blood pressure. She bounced on her toes.

"See you next week," she said and winked.

He could absorb the totality of her now – the gray sweater, red jeans, hips for days, bright green eyes and blue combat boots. Joon somehow fell even more in love.

He understood her meaning.

"See you next week!"

Then Joon winked back. Before this moment, he'd never winked, ever, in his entire life. So this wink, for his first, turned out okay – not great, but okay.

"He's cute," her mother said as they turned to leave.

Maybe it was wishful thinking, but he swore he heard Erin mutter:

"I'm going to marry him."

He did not realize until he got back to his apartment at midnight that he was still wearing her hoodie.

Had Joon not arrived at Ruby's Coffee shop half frozen and desperate for a hot beverage, he might have noticed that the seating arrangement changed dramatically from when he first walked in to when he actually sat down.

What happened was this:

Erin Angelica Fern glanced up from working on her watercolor of the tree line of the Santa Muerte Mountain range as Joon entered the coffee shop.

THAT ONE.

She saw his thick, jet-black hair, jawline sharp enough to slice through an overripe tomato, broad shoulders, tiny waist, whipcord muscles and butt like a juicy, golden delicious apple she wanted to nibble on, and every fiber of her being resonated to the tune of "Friday I'm in Love" by The Cure, despite the fact that it was, indeed, Saturday.

Erin assessed the room, weighed her odds and formulated a plan. She turned to the lanky, fellow ginger sitting alone at the table behind her.

"Excuse me, would you mind switching seats with me?"

The girl looked at her with wild eyes.

"Uhh…" Her tone was perky even in doubt.

"I want the guy at the counter to sit next to me."

"Oh!" The girl's winged hair bounced as she understood and instantly began gathering up books and papers. "Is he a friend of yours?"

Erin decided on honesty.

"No, I just saw him and I'm in love with him."

"No way!" She glanced at the two men line. "The tall one's married. I can see the ring from here."

Erin leaned forward and shook her head.

"No," she whispered. "The other one."

"The tourist!" she blurted out at full volume, then covered her mouth in shame. Five or six people in the room looked up from their work to glare at her.

"Sorry," she mouthed to them.

Erin shrugged

"I know." She held her hand over her heart. "I don't care."

"Damn."

Her fellow ginger squared her narrow shoulders, stood and surveyed the ten, two-person, rectangular tables scattered around and the one, large, eight-person table in the corner. "Okay, then. Let's do this."

Erin's new best friend dumped her science textbooks on the large table with a thud – earning another glare from the room. Then she scuttled around, rearranging dark brown chairs and tables. Her antics caught the attention of everyone. What followed was a series of hand gestures, whispered explanations, hands held up as hearts and repeated exclamations of: "The Tourist?"

Yet, everyone played along. Much to Erin's astonishment, even the neck-tattooed skater in black knee socks offered a low fist bump with a whispered: "You got this."

When the quiet chaos settled, the only chair in the room was at the table next to Erin. A clear path led the way right to it as the tourist turned to look for a place to sit.

The tourist also failed to notice the entire room quietly eavesdropping on their conversation.

If Joon knew the true circumstances of how he met Erin, he might not have stood in his kitchen, wiping his sweaty palms on his freshly washed and ironed jeans, willing the minutes to tick by faster until finally grabbing his keys at 5:30 pm.

Joon crossed the Sunset Cove county line at 6:58 pm, Sept. 28, 2020. Emerging from the thick evergreen forest, Joon drove Molly down a steep incline, past the county line. To his left, a sandy cliff rose hundreds of feet above him. Cement barriers with expandable nets lined this side of the road to protect against landslides. To Joon's right, the emerald blue ocean glittered, rising and falling beneath the low-hanging sun. It sank slowly into the horizon line.

A sandy cove sat at the bottom of the hill. Bright red, green and blue wind surfers zipped across the waves. Joon made a mental note to look into learning to windsurf.

He glanced down from the clear road to skip past "Sad Songs" by Elton John. The Fog blasted in from the ocean on hurricane force winds. It drove Molly into one of the cement barriers. Airbags exploded around Joon. His head slammed into one. His nose broke. The impact ruptured his eardrums.

Stunned, he sat for several moments as The Fog seeped into the car. He thought he'd gone blind until he brought his hand in front of his eyes.

"빨리 나가 (ppalli naga) (Get out!)

Joon fumbled for the handle and pushed it. He tried to get out but the seatbelt held him back. Blood from his nose dripped down his chin. It took him five tries to click the seat belt lock. The car released him from its grip. Joon fell onto the concrete.

The thick ringing in his ears didn't stop. He forgot where he was.

가장자리로 이동 (gajangjalilo idong), (Go to the edge.)

He tried to stand but fell to his knees, scraping his palms. He stared at blood bubbling up from the meat of his hand. The world around him disappeared. Soft gray permeated everything. Only the road beneath him existed.

His head hurt and Joon was so, so tired. He curled up on the cold asphalt. It rippled beneath him but he didn't care. Joon closed his eyes, sinking into the road. He was suddenly eight years old again and in need of a nap.

아니! 일어나! 일어나! 일어나! (ani! il-eona! il-eona! il-eona!) (No! Get up! GET UP! GET UP!)

The voice chanted in Joon's mind. Relentless. Urgent. It would not let him sleep.

"No, Dad," Joon muttered, swiping the air in front of him. "Five more minutes, please. I'm so tired."

"I'm sorry, my beautiful son" The voice changed. It became kinder but still insistent. "You have to get up now."

"I don't wanna," Joon whined. "My head hurts."

"I know." The voice needled into his brain. "But if you get up, I'll give you medicine. It'll get rid of that headache."

Put upon, Joon pushed himself up into a sitting position and began to crawl.

"No!" His father scolded. "This way. Follow my voice. Please, son."

Joon swerved to the right. His eye lids were too heavy to open. Blind and deaf to the outside world, he crawled. His father's voice moved slightly from place to place so Joon had to course correct to find it.

"Please, Dad. I'm so tired. Can I stop now?"

"A few more steps, my son… this way."

Cool, saltwater wind blew across Joon's face, clarity descended.

"Wait."

He opened his eyes – too late.

Joon put his right hand down on empty air. He dropped like a rag doll into nothingness. Bouncing against boulders, he slammed into rocks that cut like razors. His body made unnatural shapes as it traveled down the cliff. His left thigh bone snapped. The femur protruded from his jeans. He idly cursed because these were his favorite pants. He had just washed them.

Then he passed out. Mercifully, he was not conscious when his body came to an uneasy rest ten feet from the ocean's edge.

Saltwater mixed with his blood and streamed into the algae-crusted tide pools. Tiny crabs scuttered across his hand. Joon's breath shuddered from his body – one of his lungs collapsed.

Water burbled and boiled. A massive orange body waved beneath the surface. Its inky, black eye, alien in knowledge, fixed on his prone form. Two immense tentacles, each a foot in circumference and twenty feet long rose out of the water and wrapped themselves around his broken body. They lifted him straight up as the creature moved away from the shore. It sank further and further down, pulling Joon beneath the surface of the swirling gray water.

*****

7:12 pm, Sept. 28, 2020, 11 minutes after The Fog

Twelve miles south along Highway 1, an older, bearded man, face creased and brown from a lifetime in the sun, ran out of the gleaming white and glass mansion on the cliff. Ripping the clothes from his body, he hopped down steep, slippery, stone steps to the ocean.

Naked, he dove into the rough sea and swam. The ocean called to him – as she did every day. He answered her, as he always did. Offering his body to her depths, arm over arm, he swam waiting for her to embrace him. The light glinted off the sun spots on his shoulders and arms. He thought of them as kisses.

A life-long surfer, he'd spent hours in this water. He thought he knew her moods. The whims she kept hidden beneath the salty waves.

He swam until his lungs burned and his legs gave out. Floating on his back, he stared at the endless gray around him. The call lessened the further he got from shore yet he refused to give up.

This water and all within it belonged to him.

The old swimmer with the long, white hair didn't even know which direction land was. He rocked with the low waves letting the water move him. Waiting to hear her voice, he didn't notice the gray fins fifteen feet away. Then ten. Then five.

Sandpaper brushed his hand. He jerked upright, choking on seawater.

It didn't make sense. He couldn't comprehend that his beloved had changed her mind as serrated teeth dragged him under.

*****

7:46 pm, Sept. 28, 2020, 35 minutes after The Fog

Yong Zhu Yun found himself on a red throne. Said throne sat on a seven-foot-tall dais in the most beautiful room he'd ever seen.

Scarlet pillars supported the ceiling rising thirty feet above his head. Stone-gray tiles dotted the floor. Blue cross beams, buttressed with wooden cloud carvings, ran the width of the room that was half the size of a football field. It seemed to be filled with the watery outlines of people dressed in the hanbok from the Joseon era. The thick, rich scent of sandalwood incense filled the air. Joon glanced up and found he couldn't look away from the ceiling. Pale, watery light streamed in from small, square windows at the second story of the pagoda. He knew the intricate red and blue tiles symbolized the heavens. He blinked and rubbed his eyes. His hand moved against a resistance that wasn't air.

Water.

Joon gasped. He tried to breathe. He clawed at his throat. Jerking away from the throne, he floated up to the ceiling as he frantically searched for air.

"Oh, calm down," a high, tired voice behind him sighed, "You're fine."

"I am not fine," Joon snapped, without thinking. "I am drowning."

He spun, bubbles churning around him to face a short, white-haired, bearded man. He had deep smile crevices, a red 곤룡포 (gonryongpo) (dragon robe) was draped over his stout frame.

"The Dragon King!" Joon yelped, unable to scramble away in the water. He wrapped himself into a ball and cowered. "The Dragon King! No! No! Get away!"

They had learned The Dragon King folktales in school – three weeks before his father drowned. Nightmares of the red-robed man transforming into a blue dragon, rising out of the sea and pulling his father under the cold waves haunted Joon for years.

The stories said The Dragon King was a wise and kind leader. Little Joon thought that was nonsense.

While the nightmares were long gone, and Adult Joon knew in his head that his father's death was nothing more than a dumb, human accident, his heart had other ideas entirely.

The man sighed.

Trapped in the fetal position of his own terror, he didn't notice the seawater ebbing out of the room. His body drifted to the floor as reality crackled and shifted. Joon felt The Dragon King's footsteps as he walked to him, first light and short, then heavier and longer.

"Is this better?"

The man's voice transformed, becoming deeper, more melodic – the steady ebb and flow of waves on the shore.

Joon peaked from behind his hands. He didn't swear often – not that he had anything against the practice. He liked to keep swearing in his pocket. Cursing all the time lessened the impact, in his opinion. So when he shouted at the man:

"Why the fuck do you look like a Hallyu star?" He meant it.

The man before him was much younger – not as young as Joon, closer to middle age. He had warm, glowing skin, thick, black hair, high cheekbones, broad lips, and a razor-sharp jawline. He looked like the kind of man who held doors open for women and then spent fifteen minutes wondering if it made him a bad feminist. This new king brushed the lapels of his blue and green Hawaiian shirt.

"Don't you like it? I'm so tall."

He turned to admire his long legs and the black and white slides on his feet. The Dragon King's clothes were somehow dry. He felt his smooth cheeks and gave him a dimpled smile.

"What the fuck?" Joon demanded from the floor.

The King knelt next to him.

"You don't fear this man, do you?" His handsome face was solemn. "Do you respect him? But you don't fear him? You've never had nightmares about him?"

Joon scrambled farther back. He realized that the water was gone.

"How did you know about that?" Joon asked, as he searched for an exit.

Massive wood sliding doors blocked an entrance large enough for an army. A heavy, iron u-shaped lock kept him from escaping. The man strode around the room like a model on a catwalk.

"I should have been tall in my past life. This is fantastic."

Then he turned on his heel and sauntered back across the room until he reached the throne steps – where he lounged dramatically.

Joon's next objective was the wood-carved windows. A strange, murky light shown through the thin, rice paper shades. He undid the iron latch and swung the fifteen-foot-tall panel inward.

The sea floor lay beyond the window. A dolphin darted by. It reminded him of the aquarium in Monterey – except there was no glass between him and the exhibit. Joon reached out a trembling hand and yanked it back when he touched the cool water. Icy panic spiked through his gut.

"I'm dead. I died."

A full-length, wrought iron mirror appeared in front of the lounging man. The Dragon King pulled hats from the air and tried them on. He sucked in his cheeks and tilted his head as he posed while he modeled a large, white, panama hat.

"You aren't dead," he replied, offhand – in the casual manner of water lapping against a rock. "You are The Dragon King."

Joon closed the window. He leaned against the wooden cross beams and sank to the floor. Resting his hands on his drawn up knees, he stared into the middle distance at the pagoda-shaped braziers.

"I'm dead."

"You're not dead," The Dragon King repeated while he tried on chunky, silver rings.

"I looked away to change the song…"

"Excellent choice, Elton was harshing your vibe. Nothing against the man, of course, but that was not the right song for the moment."

"And I swerved. I hit the retaining wall…" Joon continued, ignoring him.

"Magic fog."

"And bounced because I was going too fast, I flipped over off the cliff into the ocean…"

"You were only going thirty five," The Dragon King reminded him as he leaned back against the dais stairs. "But you do drive too fast. I've been meaning to talk to you about it. I think you're an adrenaline addict."

"I'm drowning and my brain is trying to make sense of it all," Joon said, rubbing his face.

"Still magic fog," The Dragon King repeated, for what felt like the thousandth time.

Joon had to admit that he looked like a king in his artistically-torn jeans, tailored-Hawaiian shirt and over-sized, silver sunglasses.

"There's no such thing as magic fog," he snapped from the cold stone floor.

"There is now." Joon's hallucination skipped down the red stairs. "By your logic, you should be dead any minute now."

The room shook like a bomb went off. The roof timbers rattled and cracked. Sawdust and splinters dropped to the floor. Water sloshed in from beneath the door.

"Oh!" The Dragon King's mouth made a perfect 'O.' His eyes darted around the ceiling. "The Kraken's here. Now, it's a party."

Joon had never, once, ever, raised a hand to anyone in his life. That being said, this guy needed a fist in his perfect face.

"There's no such thing as kraken!"

The Dragon King loomed over him, arms folded over his chest.

"Aren't you dead? Do you feel dead?"

It peeved Joon to admit that, no, he did not, in fact, feel dead. No bright lights, no souls of the departed, no tunnel. He didn't even feel a joyous sense of relief. He was just annoyed – at this man, at this room, that his clothes were wet, that his plans were ruined and that he was having *such* a stupid hallucination.

"So, you don't feel dead?"

Joon crossed his arms over his chest and considered throwing a tantrum. He chose to remain silent instead.

"So, no? That's a no? Is that a no?"

Joon titled his head back against the wood wall and glared at him.

The Dragon King held out his broad hand.

"Then get up. We have work to do."

Running out of options and with great begrudgement, Joon took The Dragon King's hand. At his touch, the pulse of the moon thrummed through his veins. Joon stumbled. The Dragon King caught his shoulder and steadied him. With closed eyes, Joon felt the vastness of his kingdom. Life in forms still undiscovered hid in the depths. The tumbling, teeming, tangled madness of it all – gardens of coral, schools of flashing silverfish taller than the empire state building. And sound. Human ears thought the ocean was quiet. Muffled thunks and swirls. The noise bombarded him. The squeals, sonic booms, and crashes overwhelmed Joon until he caught the low, haunting rumbles of whales. He followed their thread into dolphin chatter and onto rhythmic waving of jellyfish. Then Joon realized. It was music. Each piece on its own, while beautiful, made no sense. Together, this world made a raucous, glorious symphony – intertwined and perfect with the pull of the moon acting as the steady beat holding it all together.

Joon burst in happy laughter at the beauty of it.

"Can you hear this?" he asked The Dragon King – too loud, like a man wearing headphones, he couldn't hear his own voice.

"All the time." The man smiled, full of the same wistful love Joon felt. "This is your kingdom."

Joon wiped away tears and stepped away from The Dragon King.

"Look, dude. You seem… nice. I don't know what's going on but there's no way I'm The Dragon King. I'm just not. It's not possible."

Joon spun around.

"Besides, you look like The Dragon King to me. *You* be The Dragon King."

The man studied him and pulled off the sunglasses. His eyes glowed blue in the watery light.

"I am dead," he said, polishing the glasses on his shirt. "I died 2,500 years ago. I am the distant memory of who you used to be. You, Yong Zhu Yun, are very much alive and without you, this world will burn.

"This is the Liminal Space. This is where you will learn … or perhaps it is 'remember' how to be The Dragon King."

He seemed puzzled by that last part.

Joon was just done. He'd never been this done in his life.

"I need to get out of here."

"You can't. You're not ready. When you become The Dragon King, you can leave."

Ignoring him, Joon stalked to the window. He flung it open with a bang, climbed onto the ledge and dove into the water.

The Dragon King shrugged and walked to his throne. With the wave of his hand, a big screen TV appeared before him. The opening credits of *Some Kind of Wonderful* appeared.

A bowl of popcorn materialized in The Dragon King's hands. He threw a handful at the television.

"You idiot, Keith! You deserve better, Watts!"

Joon emerged in the icy waters of the Pacific. He kicked as hard as he could. A pod of dolphins passed him – slick backs arcing through the water.

I am not The Dragon King. I'm not. I can't be.

He rose for long moments, expecting his lungs to burn, waiting for the deep, visceral panic of not being able to breathe.

It never came.

This scared him more than anything.

Joon glanced down to see the palace below. The pavilions and walkways around the central palace stretched for miles. Long, wooden buildings would have been the offices of court officials and military barracks. Joon wondered idly if The Dragon King had any fish on his council and giggled at the thought. Air bubbles escaped his lips and he inhaled water, but he could breathe just fine.

Waving, towering, kelp forests surrounded the palace. Moody light streamed through them. Joon kicked and pulled at the water, rising higher and higher. Fish of various shapes and sizes floated out of his way.

The closer Joon got to the surface, the farther away it seemed. After endless minutes, Joon reached the end of the water. He brought his arm up but found that he couldn't break through. The surface tension had turned into an impenetrable membrane. Joon kicked as hard as he could but the ocean wouldn't release him. He could feel dim sunlight on his face but as soon as he stopped kicking he was pushed away.

Joon screamed. He swam back down and swam up to the surface with all his might only to bounce back. He lay floating in the water. His tears were lost in the ocean.

After about a thousand more tries, he gave up and swam back to the palace.

The Dragon King was halfway through *The Princess Bride*.

"How was your swim?" he asked, tossing Joon a towel.

"I am not The Dragon King," he replied. His face puffy and swollen, his eyes red. Rage like he'd never felt vibrated through his bones.

"Repeating a lie doesn't make it true."

He tossed popcorn into the air and caught it in his mouth.

"I know who I am!" Joon yelled as he stomped across the stone floor.

"It's fairly obvious that you don't."

"I am NOT The Dragon King," Joon said and got in his face because he needed to make him understand. "And I will NEVER be The Dragon King." He didn't think too hard about why his voice wavered on that last sentence. "It doesn't make any sense. It's not possible."

The Dragon King's eyes glowed blue. His soft smile didn't waver. The symphony of life that had been playing since he took Joon's hand ended with a whisper.

"I see," The Dragon King said as he stepped away and threw up his hands. "That's okay. It's fine. Well, as long as you're stuck here, I could use some help. Run a few errands for me and I'll find a way out for you. Okay?"

He held out a broad hand to shake. Joon took it, hoping the music would return. It didn't.

"Okay, but I'm not The Dragon King."

"Yup, I understood that the first eight times you said it."

He settled back on the stairs, popcorn bowl in hand.

"Do me a favor, please and check in on the Jangjamari?" he asked, running his fingers through his now icy blue hair. "This transition must have unsettled them. I'm sure they're looking for a friendly ear."

So Joon bowed to The Dragon King and swam off to listen to the Jangjamari gossip about the Kappa and complain about the cold as great white sharks hovered overhead. The odd little creatures, with bird bodies and high voices played him a lovely song on a 가야금 (Gayageum) to thank him for his time.

For the next month, Joon found himself picking starfish off the Kraken, helping selkies find their lost skins, arbitrating a bloody and protracted disagreement among the mermaids and picking up endless plastic pollution from the sea floor.

Joon wanted to ask The Dragon King if Erin was alive, but he was afraid of what the man would say. It felt easier not knowing.

Until one day, Joon sat on the floor in the center of the throne room, de-tangling a very irate Mo'o, currently in the shape of an eel, from a ghost net, when a loud knock rang out.

Joon, shocked, looked up from cutting through the net to meet the eyes of The Dragon King.

The knock came again – as insistent as the first. He heard muffled voices behind the large, double doors.

"You should answer it." The Dragon King was watching *Howl's Moving Castle.*

Joon stood, and walked to the door. As he reached out to open it, the hairs on the back of his arm stood up. He paused and closed his eyes. Behind this door stood three men, none of them from the sea. One man was dying, always, for eternity, over and over again. One man brought death with teeth and claws. The final man was life itself. Joon refused to think too hard about how he knew any of this.

"It's fine." The Dragon King waved his hand in dismissal. He must have seen Joon's trepidation. "They're friendly. Open it."

Joon unlatched the heavy, metal lock and cracked open the thirty-foot-tall door to reveal a large man in a pink bathrobe. Two other men – one all in black with a sallow face and the other in a purple Hawaiian shirt, stood behind him.

"Hey, bro," the robed man said, his hairy face brimming with excitement. "We're barbecuing. We got a roasted pig and some veggies. You wanna hang out? We have beer."

The man in black clacked a pair of tongs. The one in the Hawaiian shirt held up a six pack.

The Mo'o, freed from the net, slithered out the door, past the men and swam through the night sky. It leapt into the starry night's ocean with a plop.

Joon turned to The Dragon King. Loud blasts of cannon fire came from the television. The Emperor of the Seas waved in dismissal.

"Go ahead," he said. His eyes never left the screen. "Have fun."

So Joon, thinking this wasn't the weirdest thing he'd done in the past month, shrugged and joined three strangers for a feast.

He walked through the door into the forest at night. The low chirp of crickets greeted him. He emerged at the shore of a lake. Mountainous trees surrounded them – whispering impossible secrets to each other. The biggest moon Joon ever saw hung low over the mountains. Taking up half the sky, its light rivaled the sun.

"I'm Manny." The man in the cute robe held out his hand. Joon shook it. A jolt traveled up his arm at the man's touch. Joon jumped.

"Joon. I like your robe."

He grinned – all wolf.

"Thank you!" My mom gave it to me for Christmas."

The other men introduced themselves. Joon learned that the man in black was Jakob. The Hawaiian shirt guy was Dre.

Normally, Joon hated gatherings like this. His company held an annual summer picnic. His boss would drink gin and tonics as the sun turned him into a crispy red lobster while his co-workers gathered around him – pretending to care about his golf handicap. Joon begged off due to "food poisoning" and a "cold" the past two years. He was running out of excuses and his manager sent several pointed messages about how everyone was looking forward to seeing him at the picnic next year.

If he was honest with himself, he didn't like the air at those events. Even though it was outside, he could barely breathe. The oxygen settled into the dirt around the picnic tables and refused to rise up to where he could breathe it.

But these men…

They milled around the fire, warming themselves against the night air. Waves lapped gently against the shore twenty feet behind them. Their faces danced with black and red shadows in the fire light. The bright moon cast a spell turning the forest an eerie, midnight blue. Jakob turned the spit as a whole pig roasted over the flames.

Dre handed him a beer and welcomed him with a small bow. He then turned to face the fire. A small knife flashing in one hand.

"Just a nibble," Dre said, gesturing to the pig.

"Absolutely not," Jakob replied and clacked his tongs. "The juices will escape!"

Dre ran to the other side of the roasting animal. Fat sizzled as it dripped into the fire below.

"What about this side?" Dre asked with a maniacal grin. "A tiny slice. It smells divine."

Clack. Clack.

"Do you want dry pork? Do you?" Jakob waved him off. "Shouldn't you work on vegetables? Aren't you on vegetable duty?"

Dre sighed, shoulders slumping in defeat. Pumpkin and squash vines bloomed at his feet. Corn stalks burst forth from the earth behind him. He bent and collected his bounty, side-eyeing the pork. Jakob clacked in warning.

Joon watched the tableaux from a camp chair made of bones, draped with cowhide, and laughed.

Manny stood next to him and a skeletal camp chair grew up from the dirt. He gathered his robe around him and sat with a grunt. He raised his legs and two, upside-down leg bones – tarsals still attached, rose from the earth. He rested his booted feet on the flat bones.

"It's a footstool." Manny pointed, eyes wide with excitement. "Get it?"

Joon didn't flinch.

"Yeah, I got it."

Manny continued to point – needing a reaction, any reaction. Joon refused and the two became ensnared in a battle of wills until Joon relented, sighed and rolled his eyes.

Manny chuckled in triumph. Joon raised his beer in salute.

"How long have you all known each other?"

"A few hours, I think," Manny replied with a shrug. "Not that time means anything here."

"You're serious?" Joon couldn't believe it. "You act like you've known each other for years."

"Nope," Manny said with a shake of his head. "Whoosh, a door shows up in my kingdom. I walk through it. There's this dude." He pointed at Jakob. "Then another door pops up and this guy walks through it. We're all like, 'Are you hungry? I'm hungry. Oh hey, I'm the God of so and so' let's eat. And then this super rad door shows up and there you are. Now here we are."

Joon had almost finished processing that story when the world around them shivered. It rippled like a pebble was dropped into the water of reality.

Dre looked up from cutting up pumpkin.

"Sam?"

An ordinary, white-paneled door – identical to the one in Joon's apartment bedroom appeared. Behind this door was Death itself, the fabric and texture of the final gasp and all the need it held, crafted onto the blood and bones of a person.

The door swung outward. Joon rolled off his chair in anticipation.

An old woman crept through the opening. Her back hunched, face haggard with the weight of the years of her life, dark hair shot through with white. She grasped the door jamb for support and threw up a peace sign.

"'Sup," she croaked.

The three men exchanged looks and sprang into action. Manny reached her first.

"You need a chair," he said and extended an arm.

"Thanks." Sam's voice came out in the hoarse, raspy gasp of a lifelong smoker. "It was the longest day ever."

Manny produced a chair for her next to Joon. Jakob piled cow and bear hides on for cushioning. Then he threw a heavy bear hide over her after she sat down.

"It's cold," he muttered before running back to the pig.

"Thank you."

The hide reeked of grease and game but warmth settled into Sam's bones for the first time that day. She made a face and pushed it away from her nose.

Dre appeared at her side carrying a bowling-ball-sized coconut with a bamboo straw sticking out of it.

"Is there rum in this?"

"No rum for you." He patted her shoulder. "Drink it. You'll feel better."

She thanked him and he returned to the fire.

Manny built a 'footstool' (trademark pending) for her and examined her feet. It was then, and only then, that Sam realized she was still missing her shoes. He knelt before her.

"May I?"

"Sure."

Sam shrugged, unsure what he was about. He lifted up her foot and examined it.

"Your footwear was insufficient," he said with barely contained disgust.

"I'll find myself new shoes when I've recovered from the Longest Day of My Life."

She drank the coconut juice and a tiny bit of her exhaustion fell away.

"Hey, is there a dude sitting next me I don't know or am I hallucinating?"

"That's Joon." Manny turned her foot to the left and then the right. "What do you look for in shoes?"

"That they're comfortable," Sam replied. Her eyes went to Jakob and pointed at Joon, voice tense. "Is he…?"

Jakob handed Dre a clay plate of glistening pork. Dre's eyes lit up.

"Gorgeous," he said and picked up the morsels with his fingers. He closed his eyes as he chewed. "I will never doubt you again."

"It's good?" Jakob's brows furrowed.

Dre's eyes rolled back in his head. He gave Jakob a thumbs up.

"Naw," Jakob answered Sam. "He's cool. He came through that door. Their door's over there."

Sam twisted as much as she could with a fifty-pound bear pelt draped across her lap, to see the outline of Joon's red, wood and wrought iron door nestled among the trees. On her other side, a few hundred feet up the mountain, Sam could just make out the white, Grecian marble outlines of *their* door.

She twisted back to Joon.

"Hi, I'm Sam."

She reached out her hand to shake but Manny wouldn't relinquish her foot. Joon stood and closed the distance between them. They shook hands and Sam pretended this was normal. That they were two normal people meeting at a random normal barbecue and that she hadn't felt the cosmic wave of life and death within the briny deep at his touch.

Joon stared at his hand.

"Yeah, I'm not used to it either."

Dre appeared between them and shoved a bamboo cup into her open hand.

"Drink this"

Sam tried to sniff the contents over the stench of bear. She titled the cup to get a better look.

"Is this green?" she asked and arched an eyebrow at her brother in accusation. He knew how she felt about green juice.

"Avocado," he replied, refusing to meet her gaze. His eyes darted to the glimmering lake and beyond. "You like avocado."

Sam pursed her lips and sipped with all the suspicion she felt. The concoction was surprisingly tart and sweet.

"It's pretty good."

"And kale," he said. "You told me you're trying to eat more leafy greens."

"The betrayal." She gasped. Yet, she continued sipping the thick liquid. "Et tu, Dre? Et tu?"

He nodded and went back to vegetable duty.

Jakob stood next to her with a plate piled high with pulled pork.

"Manny, she needs a tray."

The Werewolf King didn't even glance up from his work at her feet.

"Lift up your hands."

Bones slid horizontally from the left armrest and connected to the right. Jakob set the plate on the bones in front of her. The smell of the roasted pork overpowered the rancid bear stench. Her mouth watered.

"He's measuring your feet," Joon said. Sam was thankful that the newcomer seemed delighted by the mayhem and not freaked out.

"Yup."

Manny, had indeed, gotten a measuring tape, from goddess-only-knows-where, and was taking precise measurements of her foot, ankle and calf.

"Why?"

"No idea," Sam replied before biting into a luscious pork shoulder.

"You need footwear." He held up her shoeless foot in judgment. "And socks. This does not befit a member of my pack."

Dre paused over the makeshift table he'd built out of driftwood, knife poised mid-air. "Pack?"

He arched an eyebrow. Sam shrugged.

"Pack," she mouthed.

"Huh."

He went back to alternating between chopping vegetables and gleefully sampling bits of pork from the plate to his left.

Joon continued standing awkwardly. He saw Sam's shadow in the firelight. It was so dark it looked like a deep hole in the ground. He stared at his hands, flipping them over, palm to back over and over.

"I'm not dead."

"You are not dead, Yong Zhu Yun," Sam said.

"She would know," Dre said. He did not look up from chopping. "You are very much alive, Yong Zhu Yun."

"He would know," Sam said around a mouthful of pork.

"I'm not being punished?" Joon asked and they all answered him with quiet noes, worried noes. He squeezed his eyes shut as tears leaked down his cheeks. Sobbing, he crouched onto the balls of his feet, wrapped his arms around himself and rocked back and forth.

Sam struggled to push the pelt off so she could go to him. But she didn't need to.

Manny was there. He knelt next to Joon and patted his back. Sam couldn't hear the whispered words of comfort but she understood the sounds of loss Joon made. They all knew.

They stopped what they were doing. Knives were put down. Drinks and tasks halted. At that moment, they all mourned. The impossible weight of loss. The grief of lives they could no longer live. Like autumn leaves fluttering from the sky, this sadness drifted slowly among them, brushing their hands, arms, faces and hair until it settled and stilled on the cold ground.

Joon stood up and shook out his hands.

"I-I don't…"

"I cry every day," Dre said.

The others nodded.

"It doesn't make any sense," Joon said. "I can't be…"

"You can't be what?" Manny asked. "A God? We're all gods here, man."

"Goddess," Sam interjected. "Joon, you wouldn't be here if you weren't like us."

He ran his hands through his hair.

"Well, I don't want to be. No offense, but I don't want to be … this."

He gestured to himself and the moonlit night.

"We didn't choose this," Dre said.

"This is who we are," Jakob said. "It's who we have always been."

Joon stood there, bare, exposed shivering. His sadness shifted to an impotent rage that he fought to bury. Jakob appeared before him and offered a plate full of roasted meat and veggies.

"You hungry?"

He wanted to flip the plate over and run screaming from this place never to return, but that would be rude.

So, instead he said: "I could eat,"

They ate in silence. Dre put a plate full of roasted pumpkin, squash and corn in front of Sam.

Joon heard her mutter: "Seriously?" before tucking in with gusto.

Perhaps it was a trick of the moonlight or his overburdened brain, but Joon swore the gray in her hair receded. Her cheeks filled out, became rounder and flush with life. A sparkle twinkled in her strange eyes.

The atmosphere of the impromptu barbecue remained thick and tense. Joon shoveled food in his mouth and tried to pretend everything was fine until he couldn't take it anymore. He rubbed his hands together.

"I lost my mood ring the other day." He registered their confused looks and said:

"I'm not sure how I feel about it."

Sam groaned from the depths of her soul.

"Nooooo."

Manny looked up at them.

"I'm good friends with twenty five letters of the alphabet," he said. "I just don't know Y."

Sam rolled her eyes so hard she thought she might have a seizure.

"Who invented King Arthur's round table?" Joon asked. "Sir Cumference."

Sam hid under the bear hide and yelled her incoherent disapproval – only to be met with snorts of laughter. The convivial atmosphere restored, they cracked jokes and told stories. It was a light affair. No one mentioned The Fog.

The conversation lulled.

Sam stared into the fire. Her eyes burned from the smoke. The soft lapping of waves on the shore made her nostalgic for a simpler time – when slitting the throat of a self-righteous, arrogant man solved most of her problems. Half asleep, warm and happier than she'd been a month, she knew she needed to broach the subject sooner than later.

"Hey, I hate to bring this up, but I could use some help." She scanned their faces. They each nodded, their stomachs full and relaxed. "The Goddess of Healing is in trouble. Are there any more doors around here, Jakob?"

He yawned and patted his belly.

"I sense a few more, but they're far away – not including the big one. None of them want to be found and none of them are Healers."

"Well, fuck."

"What about her physical form?" Dre stretched, his long arms reaching into the night. "You could find her body out there."

"Yeah, but where? I don't know where to look."

Joon's eyes shot open.

"You're out there? You can go out there?"

"You could find Erin." Awakened from his food coma, he stood up and paced. "Red hair, about this tall." He gestured to his shoulder. "She has a cherry blossom tattoo on her forearm. I think she lives in the mountains. Loves to draw. She's beautiful. Her front tooth is a little crooked. Is she okay? I need to know. Please."

Rant over, Joon collapsed back into his chair.

"Please."

"I…" Sam began, unsure of where to begin.

"Erin's fine." Manny belched. "I talked to her yesterday."

"You talked to her?"

They were all wide awake now and staring at Manny.

"She's my girlfriend's daughter." He shrugged, then took a swig of his beer. "You're the guy she met at Ruby's."

Joon's eyes were saucers. His lips formed a perfect 'o.' He nodded. Manny's eyes twinkled.

Dre fell off his chair in delight.

"No way!" Sam exclaimed.

"It *is* a small county," Jakob said and raised a beer in salute.

Dre giggled and chortled from his spot on the ground. Joon's mouth hung wide open.

"You're gonna catch flies," Jakob warned him. His mouth snapped shut. "Okay, let's think about this goddess. Where would her body be?"

Jakob clapped his hands together. Dre stood, wiping tears from his eyes.

"There's Five Rivers," he said, suggesting the local metaphysical healing school, popular for acupuncturists and reiki practitioners.

"Maybe," Sam said. She made a mental note and looked around the fire. "Any other suggestions? I gotta find her."

"She could be anywhere," Manny growled. "The rehab center in Ridge Point. The Buddhist monastery outside of Seacrest."

"The Healing Waters Tea House on 27th," Jakob added.

Sam sighed, about to give up. You couldn't swing a dead cat in Sunset Cove without hitting a massage therapist, energy worker, addiction counselor, nutritionist, acupuncturist or faith healer.

"Fuck," Sam muttered. "She could be anywhere."

Hopelessness sunk in. She was going to fail. Sunset Cove would be lost. They'd all die. "Fuck."

"Why don't you go to the hospital?" Joon asked.

Four bewildered pairs of eyes turned to him in the moonlight.

"What?" Sam needed to hear it again to make sure she got it right.

"She's probably at the hospital," Joon repeated, wondering for the eightieth time why he liked these lunatics so much.

Four pairs of shocked eyes turned to each other in the moonlight, each feeling incredibly stupid for not having thought of that.

"She's at the hospital," Sam said.

"Good job, Joon," Manny said. Joon beamed.

Sam closed her eyes and leaned back in her chair. She opened them only to be confronted with the upside down face of a five year old mere inches from her own.

Sam yelped.

"Morning, Auntie!" Malak chirped at 5,000 decibels. "Mommy's going to work today. Daddy made waffles!"

Her niece's hair brushed Sam's nose and eyes. She batted it away but Malak thought that was hilarious and kept swinging her head until she sneezed.

"Okay, I'm up. Please give me some space, Malak."

Sam sat up to see Malak standing before the blow-up mattress in a pastel pink and purple unicorn onesie, black combat boots five sizes too big on her feet and black socks wrapped like a scarf around her unicorn neck. She put a hand on her hip and posed.

"Very adorable." Sam gestured. "Can I have my boots and socks please?"

Malak's shoulders drooped. She hemmed and hawed until Sam raised an eyebrow.

She handed over Sam's new socks. They appeared obsidian until the light hit them just so. Then an oil slick pattern of red, blue and purple on them. They were light, warm and soft.

"Oh, well done, Manny," Sam muttered.

"Who's Manny?" Malak piped up. She had a boot balanced on her head.

"You're so goofy," Sam said. Malak giggled.

"Such a goof." Sam plucked the boot from her head. "He's a friend. He made these for me."

"Oooo, pretty."

"Right?"

She pulled on the black combat boot with thick soles and noticed the little pouch attached to the side.

"No way! Pockets! My boots have POCKETS!"

Malak twirled in commiseration, one foot stuck in the other boot. "Oh, my gosh! Pockets!"

Chiba appeared at the open door.

"Hey, I'm about to head out."

"Mommy, Auntie's boots have POCKETS."

"No way! Pockets?"

"I know!" Malak said before falling over in excitement.

"Wait, seriously?" Chiba checked out the boots, eyes wide. "These are so cool. Where'd you get them?"

"A friend made them for me."

"That's a good friend. Okay, I have to go pick up my fare."

She wrapped her arms around Malak and kissed the top of her head.

"I love you, wriggly bug," she said.

Sam stood, balancing on one foot. Chiba wrapped her arms around her and kissed her head.

"And I love you, other wriggly bug."

"Be safe," Sam ordered.

"I will." She blew a kiss to Malak and walked out the door.

Sam pulled on her other boot, not bothering to lace them up. She held out her hand.

"Okay, wriggly bug. Let's go get some waffles."

TALKING RACCOONS AND TWO VERY TIRED WOMEN

9:46 am, Oct. 31, 2020, 33 days after The Fog

Raquel Ani Poochigian checked the back of the beeping alarm clipped to the lanyard around her neck. She used to write little phrases to remind her why each one was going off. Then the words blurred and swam in her vision. So she wrote symbols. Then she couldn't remember what the symbols meant so she wrote out a key in large, block letters and tucked that into a clipboard attached to the end of the lanyard.

This alarm had three droplets, a circle with a slash through it and a four. Raquel checked the sheet: 'Change Mr. Kodua's catheter bag.'

She dropped the clipboard. It clattered in slow motion at her feet. Three more alarms beeped in her ears as she bent to pick it up. Raquel turned to hurry through the hallway back to her patients but the floor became a deep pool of molasses. The faster she hurried, the further away everything became. She lost the reason why she'd stepped away from the nurse's desk.

Alarms beeped and beeped. Synchronizing, they became a single scream inside her skull.

Reality slipped away and she found herself standing at the edge of a battlefield. People, *her* people, lay around her begging for help – pleading to be saved.

Raquel shook it off. Exhaustion threatened to send her to her knees again.

Too much. She couldn't do this.

Raquel closed her eyes. Just a little more. Just one more time. Just a tiny, tiny shred. The luminescent threads lived deep within her mind. Just a little more and she could get all this done – change the catheter bag, administer the meds, change Mrs. Guiseppi's bandages, remember why she left the haven of yellow walls and white curtains. A little more and the incessant beeping would stop. Raquel tapped her forehead and pulled. A fraction of the fabric tore. It exploded within her. The flames propelled her into action.

She didn't even need the clipboard.

The tearing left her with the usual scarlet throbbing in her skull and dull feeling of her muscles and organs hanging from her bones.

The chill was new. The hair on the back of Raquel's neck stood up. Goosebumps rippled along her forearms.

Clang

The makeshift alarm she'd jury-rigged after the first night went off. She'd tied suture thread to stacks of pots and pans from the cafeteria and ran it across the hallway.

"The fuck?"

Raquel chucked her clipboard at the shadowy figure.

"Ow!" A woman's voice echoed out of the corridor.

No one and no *thing* had come near her since that night. Creatures would sniff about the place and wander off. Raquel felt them at a distance. This one was different. This one had purpose.

She hurled the half-eaten apple from her pocket at the woman.

"Oh, come on!"

Still, she kept coming. Ducking her head behind her arm, she emerged from the shadows.

"Go away!" Raquel yelped. "You can't have them! I won't let you have them!"

"For fuck's sake," the woman roared. "Have who? What are you talking…"

Her strange eyes settled on the four beds around the circular desk. Crowded behind a dozen plastic and metal machines, tubes and wires trapped these people in an artificial nest of life. Though her patients slumbered, heart monitors went wild.

"Oh, no." The woman said and her posture changed from defensive to seeking. She reached out to Raquel's patients. "I am so sorry."

She planted herself between the woman and her charges.

"Stay away from them!"

She grabbed the item closest to her without looking and held it high.

"WHOA! Whoa! No!" The stranger held up her hands. "Do NOT throw that at me. That's against the Geneva Convention or something. There are *laws* against biological warfare. Chill! Just fucking chill."

The woman stepped back. The heart monitors calmed. Raquel looked up and realized she was about to heft a bedpan at a complete stranger.

"Whatever," Raquel said. "It's empty."

Well, she was pretty sure it was empty.

"It's still a BEDPAN!!"

Cold liquid ran down Raquel's arm. The acrid scent of urine hit her nose.

"It's not empty," she admitted.

The woman closed her eyes, going green around the gills.

"The shit I do, I swear by the Holy Darkness," she muttered. "Is it worth it? I could just go home. I don't need this shit. This literal fucking shit. But they'll die. They'll all die. It's worth it. It's worth it. Remember Ridley. Do it for Ridley."

"Are you talking to yourself?"

The woman sighed, wrapped her arms around herself, lowered her gaze and glared at her.

For a fleeting moment, Raquel felt the clash of swords, the tang of fresh blood in her nostrils and heard the cries of the dying. The strange woman shook off her pique and held up her hands.

"Can we talk, please?" she asked.

She pulled up a wheelie, black office chair across the cracked, yellow linoleum floor and settled on it.

Raquel considered her offer. She hadn't had a real conversation since that night. She spoke to Mr. Kodua a lot, but he couldn't answer her through the ventilator. The last out-loud conversation she had was when her head nurse briefed her on the night's work. Five minutes into her shift, a thick fog crept through the walls. Her very no-nonsense, straight-backed, tight-bun at the exact top of her head, boss transformed into an eight-foot-tall chimera in front of her shocked eyes. The animal chuffed, like it was catching its breath and blasted out a guttural roar. It snuffled the air around Raquel, chuffed again and flew off down the hall.

A conversation with someone who could talk back? She was willing to risk it.

"You'll stay away from them?"

"I'll stay away from them until you give me permission to go to them, how about that?"

"Give me your word," Raquel said.

The glare returned. She knew, somehow, that her word was important to this woman. She paused and chewed her lips. Raquel raised the bed pan again.

"Fine," she gritted out through clenched teeth. "You have my word."

She crossed her leg, resting her foot on one knee. Raquel caught sight of the woman's black boots.

"Great shoes."

"Thank you! They're new. A friend made them for me. They have pockets."

She leaned over and extended a hand.

"I'm Sam."

Such a normal gesture. Such a human thing to do. But who was even human anymore? Raquel knew this woman was dangerous yet she wanted to pretend, for a moment, that there wasn't a snarling chimera in front of her. She reached out and shook her hand.

"I'm Raquel."

Pain. Soul-searing, heart-destroying agony. The shredding of a mind, split between a past without meaning and a future of nothingness. She stood in the middle of a vast cavern of darkness. Within her grew something beyond Raquel's comprehension.

She snatched her hand back.

"The fuck?" The two women muttered unison, staring at their hands.

"What happened to you?" Raquel asked. She would have cried but she was too dehydrated.

"You didn't go under," Sam said to her hand. "How did you not go under? That's not possible."

"How are you still standing?"

"How are *you*?"

The two women stood and circled each other. The monitors went wild as Sam edged closer to the beds. She hiked up the bedpan in warning. They both sat back down.

The energy Raquel pulled from within ran out. She slumped onto the chair. Sitting was dangerous. It led to sleeping. She picked at her black scrubs with yellow and white daisies. She couldn't remember the last time she changed them. It was probably that night. Her eyes burned. Her skin sagged.

"You're dying," Sam said and pulled a bottle of water from her hoodie. She untwisted the cap and handed it to her.

"Is it poisoned?" Raquel asked, taking a swig.

Sam snorted.

"You know what I am then?"

Raquel nodded, closing her eyes in bliss as her thirsty cells finally received sips of hydration. Cracks and canyons had formed inside Raquel's mind the night of The Fog. Whispers crept out of them telling her things – like her old name, when Mr. Ramirez was about to code and the truth of the being sitting before her.

"Do you know what you are?"

Raquel stared at the floor. The dead lying beneath it stared back in accusation, demanding to know why she hadn't saved them.

"They don't have their names," she said. "They're all lying there. Death took their names. They want to know why I failed."

Sam pulled out a banana, peeled it and handed it to her.

"You didn't fail. How are you still awake? I didn't take their names. I remember them. I remember all of them. Their names are sacred."

Raquel munched on the banana.

"Holy fuck, this is the best thing I've ever put in my mouth." She wiped her lips with the back of her hand. Sam flinched and Raquel realized this was the hand with pee on it. She shrugged and licked banana off the back of it. "I bound my eternal soul to Life itself to fight you. I can't let you win, can I?"

"If you die here, I win," Sam said, trying to use logic against an exhausted mind and heart. "Anahit, please let me take what's mine. You can go to the Liminal Space and rest."

This conversation reminded Sam of trying to get Malak to go to sleep.

"No, I'm not going to die and I'm not letting you take them, *Anand*," she said. Two could play the ancient name game.

The caverns in Raquel's mind widened. Her old self stood on the edge, staring down at the infinite darkness, beyond that was a woman she couldn't see, didn't know and couldn't understand. At least this slow dying, the pulling at the threads of her soul until it unraveled into a heap of nonsense, was familiar.

"What's your plan here? Run yourself ragged keeping these people on the precipice forever?"

"Nemain with her fucking plans and her fucking logic," Raquel said, bits of banana and spittle flying from her mouth.

"You said that out loud."

"Did I?"

Sam handed her another banana. She sighed and gazed around the space. Raquel looked too, really looked for the first time in a month. The putrescent yellow walls were dotted with green goo and fur. Long claw marks slashed through the ceiling tiles. Raquel had pulled the privacy curtains from the eight beds around the circular nurse's desk. She couldn't remember why. Paint on the other side of the room peeled off. There were scorch marks from the heat. Raquel knew the state of the rest of the building but couldn't bear to think about it.

Sam stood. She brushed her hands off on her shorts.

"I was told you were in danger," she said. "I can't make you do anything you don't want to, but you should know that your Healers can't use their power when you're like this. Sixty-two thousand, three hundred and forty-one people have died in this county since The Fog. Two thousand, five hundred and sixty-two more are at the crossroads this *very* moment. You want to hand them over to me? You want to sacrifice their lives for four people who are no longer in your realm? Fine," Sam smirked and shrugged, "You have abandoned your sacred duty. You are giving up. You are letting me win."

Raquel leapt from her chair. Pulling a curved bronze sword from nowhere, she struck at Sam, only to be stopped by a sinister black blade. The force of their meeting made Raquel's ragged bones shake. Yet, Sam refused to counter strike.

Steady, unyielding, she met Raquel's gaze over their weapons.

"Please," she whispered. "Please sleep. Please let them rest. They'll die. Everyone in Sunset Cove will die. They'll all die and I'll be stuck here all alone with that bitch for eternity. Please don't do this. Please."

Sam's sword clattered onto the linoleum floor like a death knell.

"Please," she begged. "Please save them. I can't. It's not my realm. Without you, a paper cut will kill. Please. Please go to sleep."

Raquel held her weapon to The Morrigan's throat and imagined it – never again watching the life flare out of a person's eyes. All the burned out parts of her soul ground together and broke apart. Sam's pleas reminded her of all her patient's loved ones begging her to save them. Their faces, clothes and circumstances were all as varied as clouds in the sky. Yet, each one stood before her – clutching the life before this moment in their teeth, not opening their mouth too wide out of fear that precious life would escape. Their hands grabbed the air in fists, their own arms and or the sides of chairs. Their world was so unstable. She prided herself on being a rock for them.

Reality swam before Raquel's eyes. The accusing dead fell silent and as much as she wanted to be the woman who conquered death, Sam needed a rock.

Her bronze sword wavered. A thin line of black blood appeared on Sam's neck. Her eyes never left Raquel's.

"Excuse me, please?" Mr. Ramirez appeared between them. "Hello, I must to speak to her."

His mouth rolled English words around like it wanted to add the decorative purrs and snaps of Spanish but these words, these strange, functional words, flatly refused to comply.

He grasped the back edge of Raquel's sword between his thumb and forefinger and pulled it away from Sam.

Raquel knew she was witnessing the impossible. Stage IV lung cancer, in a medically-induced coma so he could be intubated – impossible. Yet, there he stood, grizzled, snow white beard on his sunken cheeks. His kind, amber eyes laser focused on Sam.

"Hola, Señor Ramirez." Sam bowed her head in greeting.

His hand, knuckles thick and crooked, patted her cheek.

"Mi amiga la muerta." He grasped her hand in both of his. "¿Español?"

"Si, I can understand."

His breath came in sporadic bursts. He swayed. A black office chair flew into place behind him. He picked up Sam's hand as she sat next to him. He stared at her for a long moment.

"¿Dónde has estado? (Where have you been?)" His rheumy eyes filled with tears. "He estado esperando y esperando. (I have been waiting and waiting.)"

"I know." Sam bowed again. "I am so sorry. I got here as soon as I could. I shouldn't have kept you waiting."

He patted her hand.

"It's okay," he said. "Quiero descansar al lado de mi esposa. (I want to rest next to my wife.) ¿Te encargarás de esto? (You take care of this?)"

"Of course."

"¿Puedes vestirme con mi traje gris? (Can you put me in my gray suit?)" He smiled, deep creases around his lips forming into dimples. "Muy guapo."

In speaking of his beloved, time turned backwards and Raquel glimpsed the young man he once was.

"Y flores. (And flowers)," he gasped. "Debo tener flores para ella. Lirios para mi hermosa flor. Ella se va a enojar si me olvido. (I must have flowers for her. Lilies for my beautiful flower. She will be mad if I forget, no?)"

"Then we won't forget lilies." Sam grinned at him. "Does she like chocolate or is that too much?"

"Le encanta el chocolate, (She loves chocolate,)" he said and threw his hands in the air in excitement. Mr. Ramirez tapped the side of his head. "Tu mente todavía es ágil. Muy bien. (Your mind is still nimble. Good, good.)"

He hung his head, rubbing his hands across his bearded face. Tears fell down his cheeks.

"Estoy tan cansado. (I'm so tired)," he sobbed. "La extraño tanto. (I miss her so much.)"

Sam patted his back and put her arm around him.

"You'll see her soon," she soothed him. "You have my word. Are you ready?"

He nodded, grasping her hand in both of his. His feet planted on the floor, eyes alight, leaning forward as eager as a child on Christmas morning.

Sam pressed her hand against his weathered cheek. He leaned into it with a sigh. The last, small breath escaped his body and he stilled. Sam wrapped her hand around the back of his neck and touched her forehead to his. Then she stood and kissed the top of his head. With a wave of her hand, he was clothed in a dark gray suit, with black piping, and a large, silver, belt buckle. The scraggly beard disappeared. Another wave and a bouquet of fresh white lilies appeared in his folded hands. Their sweet scent cut through the stink of medicinal death in the room. A box of chocolate tucked under his arm.

Sam stepped back and admired her handiwork. She spun Darkness around him.

"Carl."

"Yeah, Boss?"

The bird appeared on the edge of the five-foot hole in the wall behind the nurse's desk.

"Please take Mr. Ramirez to Manny. Mrs. Ramirez is buried in the lower southeast corner. He'll find her."

The bird bopped and bobbed.

"Sure, Boss."

Black tendrils wrapped around Mr. Ramirez's body. He floated gently in the air. The bird took one of the tendrils in his beak and flew out of the hole where he first appeared. Mr. Ramirez followed close behind.

Sam turned to find Raquel slumped cross-legged on the dusty floor, holding her sword across her lap. She looked up at Sam. Tear tracks ran down her grimy cheeks.

"I can't do this anymore," she said.

She held out her hand and helped Raquel up.

"So don't," Sam replied. A hospital bed appeared and Raquel sat down hard on it. The wheels squealed in protest.

"Am I the asshole?" Raquel asked.

Sam pulled a package of wet wipes from her hoodie and handed her a few. She scrubbed her face.

"I mean, sometimes," Sam said with a shrug. "But sometimes, I'm the asshole."

"I mean now." Raquel gazed at the three beds. The soft beeps and sighs of machinery that let her know her world was stable. "Am I the asshole now?"

"You missed your nose." Sam gestured with a fresh wipe. Raquel tilted her head back and Sam got the smudge.

"No, you are not the asshole now. You did your best under crazy circumstances. Shoes?"

Raquel nodded. Sam pried off her scuffed, white Crocs and winced at the smell. She chucked the plastic shoes through the hole in the wall.

"I can't hear them." Raquel undid her braid with absent fingers. "I used to hear them. Mr. Kodua would tell me about dancing. He misses it. Take him dancing."

Sam wrapped a yellow hospital blanket around her shoulders, pulled the lanyard over her head and tossed it into the hole after the shoes.

"I will."

"You can take them now," Raquel said. The weight of these endless days pushed her further into the cot. She rolled onto her side.

"Thank you." Sam's shoulders dropped in relief.

"It's not really about winning," Raquel said. "You know that, don't you?"

Sam fluffed up a pillow and tucked it under her head.

"Yeah, I know. I think your job is harder than mine. When they get to me, they're decided. With you, they're fighting and need you to fight with them. I'm fine with being your enemy if it makes it easier for you."

Raquel exhaled long and slow.

"Yeeessss." Her eyes fluttered closed. "Easier. Stay with me until I'm under. Please."

She pulled her hand out from the blanket and held it out to Sam. She took it.

"Of course." She gestured and the machines fell silent.

Raquel didn't have to open her eyes to feel the magic racing around the room. She knew the other patients were being wrapped in Darkness and their bodies taken away.

She sighed again. The Accusing Dead stepped back as she walked among them until she reached a small woman with a khaki complexion. Clad in a white robe held closed with gold cords, long hair woven in an intricate crown, hands on her hips, lips pursed, she glared up at Raquel. She tapped one delicate, sandaled foot. Raquel had never felt so grubby, tall or chastened in her entire life.

"It's about damn time," she said. "Do you know how far behind schedule this puts us?"

Raquel's hand went slack in Sam's. A faint iridescence appeared on her skin. Sam rubbed her eyes, thinking it must be a trick of the light. The glow brightened. She stepped back.

Carl appeared at the hole in the wall.

"Boss!" he shrieked. "You gotta get out of there!"

"What?" Sam grimaced. The pure, white light got brighter and brighter.

"No, we're fine now. She's cool."

Carl screamed. The sound pierced her skull.

"Get out! Get out! Run!"

The light swirled and expanded, blinding Sam. She turned and ran for the hole in the wall. Leaping through it, she transformed into a raven thirty feet above the ground.

The glaring white light swirled and expanded beyond the broken confines of the hospital. Only the third floor corner, where

Raquel had set up her triage, remained. The rest lay scattered in piles of rebar, electrical wires and rubble. Sam flapped like mad, feeling herself at the edge of danger – a rabid wolf nipping at the tips of her tail feathers.

She flew and flew but the light, terrible and bleak, overtook her. Sam returned to her human form and tumbled through the air. She landed with a dirty thud on the tarmac of a parking lot that, until a month ago, was home to Sunset Cove's weekly flea market.

Sam tasted asphalt, blinked at Carl harassing her from a eucalyptus tree at the edge of the lot and passed out.

*****

10:11 am, Oct. 31, 2020, 33 days after *The Fog*

High above the low chaos of Sunset Cove's towns and forests, an eagle flew, glinting gold in the sunlight.

With a wingspan larger than most men are tall, this unfamiliar bird stalked not mice or vermin as its sharp narrow beak suggested. This bird hunted for one very special person.

Ignoring the white light spreading across the county, the eagle noticed a massive wall of greenery at the southern edge of Sunset Cove.

The sleek bird honed in on this location. It soared and swooped within the ocean breezes.

The menagerie below was confirmation enough but as he dipped closer, he caught sight of a little girl with a halo of curly, dark hair.

The bird cried out – high and piercing – a rhythmic ratatat that curdled the blood of its prey. It circled once and flew back to the white mansion on the side of the cliff above the ocean.

*****

The Cave

She sat on a low outcropping facing the ocean. It was her favorite kind of day. The sky and sea colored the same endless gray. The waves chased each other to the shore with a reassuring, endless roar, cresting with a flash of green before exploding into white foam. Each one flowed into the other like a distant memory. A light, ocean spray cooled her. Thirty feet behind her stood the cave's opening. She knew she needed to face what lurked inside it, but she didn't want to and she couldn't yet make herself.

Sam sighed and shielded her eyes from the sun. The lull of the waves soothed the abject fear of what lay behind her.

*****

10:21 am, Oct. 31, 2020, 33 days after The Fog

Dr. Jeddah Castle Williams rested her forearms against the rib cage of the stabbing victim whose heart she'd been massaging for the past five minutes. Sweat dripped from her brow onto her nose. A month ago, a nurse would have dabbed it away with a soft cloth.

None of this made sense. Patients coded for minor injuries with standard care. Five patients went into anaphylaxis while getting sutured for minor lacerations. Someone carried Bigfoot in on a stretcher with an open ankle fracture with luxation. At her touch, the bone retracted beneath the skin, snapped back into place and the wound closed. It was one of her few wins of the past day.

She sighed and tried to wipe her nose on her shoulder – without letting go of the heart. Jeddah wanted more than anything to give up, go take a nap and get a hot shower. Then she wanted to curl up somewhere with a good mystery novel and a strawberry margarita. She hadn't slept more than twenty minutes in three days.

Through the thin office partitions of her makeshift surgery, she heard them – sniffling and sobbing – the low hum of misery.

As her auntie in medical school used to say: "A good work ethic makes a soft pillow."

So Jeddah held onto the heart, forcing it to pump blood through the damaged body beneath her hands. Tears leaked from her eyes and she tried to wipe those off on her shoulder too. Just five more minutes, she told herself. Five minutes more and Jeddah could say she'd done her best. Five more minutes so she could sleep.

It took less than four minutes for the light circling the skeletal remains of the hospital on the Eastside of Sunset Cove to reach the Old Beeman Building.

Jeddah heard it before she felt it. The triage behind her quieted and her gut went: *What now*?

A soft glow lit up the room, blinding Jeddah for a moment. It was the antithesis of The Fog. It filled her cells. It was a warm bath, a good strawberry margarita and the high of saving a patient times a thousand.

Joy erupted within her.

Her hands holding the precious heart glowed, and she knew in a place she could not name, yet was ancient and alive, that she could let go now. So she did. The red muscle rippled and jumped, then expanded and contracted over and over again. A different type of tears blurred Jeddah's vision. She wiped her eyes on the back of her forearm and pulled her glowing hands with slow care out of the chest cavity. Jeddah clicked back the metal retractor and held her hands over the gaping wound. The white bones of the rib cage moved back into place. The torn lining of the chest wall knit back together. Even the skin, swollen and broken, looking more like rubber than real human anatomy, put itself back together beneath her hands. The patient's breath skipped. Her brilliant green eyes fluttered and opened.

Jeddah threw back her head and yelled. She danced and thanked every ancestor for this moment.

All pretense of professionalism gone, she turned, yanked open the curtain to her triage and bellowed:

"Let's do this!"

She didn't need to.

Her staff, nurses and doctors, iridescent against the open bay doors of the Old Beeman Building, healed every injury and ailment in the room – to accompanying screams, snaps and a few patients passing out from pain.

Jeddah clapped her hands at the sight.

"Great work, everyone!" She addressed her stunned and chagrined staff. "I'm so proud of you. But let's follow a policy of anesthetization before big healing next time. Anyway... fantastic work! Let's bring in the next round!"

With no small amount of grumbling, gratitude and some "What the fuck was that?" the current patients wandered out and a new group wandered in.

*****

12:14 pm, Nov. 2, 2020, 35 days after The Fog

Sam awoke to the gentle rattle of shopping cart wheels. The back of her head bumped against a wire grid.

"Ow."

Not remembering what she'd done to deserve a hangover of this magnitude, she peeled her eyes open. Her tongue had been replaced by a dead, furry thing and her feet dangled over the wiry edge of the cart, bouncing as it bopped along.

Sam squinted at the overhead sun. It must be about noon. She was being pushed along in the vast empty lot that once was home to Sunset Cove's wildly popular weekly flea market. Sam had attended *once* and promptly gave up on the idea of cheap belt buckles after wandering for hours among sweaty, cranky humans.

"You're awake! Goodness! I am so humbly and graciously pleased."

A young man's face appeared at the side of the cart. A red hood, tied too tight beneath his chin, squashed his angular features. His ochre skin gleamed with sweat. He smiled – all teeth and delight. His entire being screamed, too loudly, in Sam's opinion, considering the headache roaring through her skull, of someone who had been born in the wrong place at the wrong time.

"My most sincere apologies," he said. "I had to pick you up. I realize you did not consent to that but she was most adamant. Your resonant frequencies do not align – extremely dangerous for you, she said. So unfortunate. She assured me you'd revive once we exited the light, and you did so. It's exciting. I am excited. I'm also Henry. Please call me Henry. Are you in pain?"

Henry returned to the handles and wheeled her across acres of empty, black tarmac ringed by peeling eucalyptus trees to the street entrance. A lone RV, turned to solid glass, stood at the far side of the lot.

"Nope," Sam croaked. She glanced behind them. A swirling column of pure white light enveloped the hospital.

Oh, that's why my brain is on fire.

He clapped his hands in perfect rhythm.

"I am supremely pleased to hear this. Were you in distress during your time in the light?"

"Not really," Sam said and considered having the frog that had replaced her voice forcibly removed. "You're her heir. That was fast."

"Oh, not at all," Henry said, words quick and scattershot. "She called me in a dream two nights ago and I only just found you. You were held within the light for two days."

"WHAT!?" Sam tried to eject herself from the cart. "Two days!?"

She flailed, unable to extricate her limbs from the cursed wire prison. The entire apparatus tipped over sideways.

"I beg you desist," Henry said and wrestled the cart back to level. "You could receive an injury. She said you may experience some weakness for a day or two."

"Chiba is going to lose her mind." Sam flopped, trying to get out of the cart in a more balanced way.

"Stop, please," Henry begged. "I fought two talking raccoons to obtain this transport. I don't know where to find another."

Sam stilled.

"Raccoons talk now?"

"Yes," Henry said, keeping a firm hand on the cart. "It's most upsetting."

Sam shivered, picturing it.

"I am so sorry."

"Thank you."

"Are their voices really high or really low? What do they sound like?"

Henry stopped the cart and faced her.

"Regular voices," he replied. "Like people you'd overhear in line at the grocery store."

"Oh, that's so much worse." Sam clawed at her ears in disgust.

"It is awful," Henry said. "And they rub their little hands together maniacally. They toss out insults and … other things."

"No!"

Henry planted a foot on the bottom of the shopping cart and held out a gloved hand.

"Yes!"

Sam took the offered hand and leveraged her way out of the cursed cart.

"How did you fight them off?" She had to know. Henry's face fell with guilt.

"In truth, I fought no animal. I waited until they tired of mocking me and left."

Finally free, Sam brushed bits of rock and asphalt from the front of her hoodie and bowed to her rescuer.

"Jamison Henry Montgomery," Sam said, putting her hand over her heart. "I am in your debt. If there is anything I can do for you now or in the future, please don't hesitate to ask."

His eyes dropped and his thin hands twisted themselves together.

"Um."

Sam could have dropped a blue whale into the vast puddle of silence coming from this previously loquacious young man.

"Is there something you need now, Henry?"

He pulled a yellow cord draped that ran cross ways across his thin chest. A black instrument case appeared. Henry placed the case on the ground, knelt before it and pulled off his gloves. Sam joined him on the ground. He popped open the latches. His long fingers were quick and competent – as if this were an action he'd done a thousand times. He lifted the lid and spun the case to face her.

Sam gasped. Nestled within the red, silk lining, lay a burnished and broken violin. Sam's hands hovered over the snapped neck and dismembered strings. Deep cracks ran through the body in three places.

She could feel his love for this instrument through her fingertips. The hours they'd spent together. The safety and sense of belonging he'd found within its musical confines. This was the most tragic corpse Sam had ever seen.

"Oh, Henry," Sam breathed. "I am so sorry."

He wrapped his arms around his legs and rested his chin on his knees.

"The Fog," he muttered. "My sister…"

He turned his face from her, staring across the empty black parking lot.

"I am so sorry."

Henry remained silent and he looked back down at his broken heart.

"I can repair it," she said.

Sam balanced on the balls of her feet, lingering over the remains. Sharpened splinters brushed the tips of her fingers, embedding microscopic fragments in her skin.

"It won't be the same. It won't feel the same or play the same. I cannot reverse what has been done. That is not my magic. I can only move forward with what is."

Henry brushed a tear from his eye and nodded.

She took a deep breath. Thin ribbons of darkness snaked from her hands. They weaved themselves into the molecules of the wood, with the tiniest of snaps the cracks in the body meshed together. Only thin, jagged lines betrayed the instrument's violent past. The neck settled back into one slender line. The strings healed with a twang.

Sam stood. She worried her lower lip with her teeth, hoping her magic was enough to heal this holy object.

Henry cradled the neck and body. He rose swiftly – a grace in his sudden movements that hadn't been there before. He tucked the instrument beneath his chin, closed his eyes and set the bow.

Henry began with a high, piercing note. The sound flew around the parking lot. The eucalyptus trees shivered and shed their bark. Sam wrapped her arms around her torso to protect herself from what was coming. His emotions, pent up and taut, burst through the sound. The high of discovering his abilities and wondering if he might fit better this new world mixed with the guilt over those he could not help and sadness over those who would never see him for what he was.

Sam stood in this empty space. She stared at the sky because looking at him at this moment was too close. She closed her eyes and let the sound wash over her.

The music stopped and Sam was both relieved and disappointed to be released from the spell.

"You can go now," he said.

Sam, understanding, perhaps better than he realized, bowed with her hand over her heart.

"Of course, should you need anything, Jamison Henry Montgomery, please summon me. A crow or raven will find me."

His sharp chin nodded above the violin.

Sam turned into a raven and flew home.

*****

12:43 pm, Nov. 2, 2020, 35 days after The Fog

Jimmy couldn't say how long he'd been wandering around these damn tunnels. His blood flask kept refilling. Time disappeared down here. He couldn't tell if it was day or night and these party sounds didn't get any closer. It coulda been days. Hell, it coulda been weeks. He wasn't sure why he kept chasing them. He sat with his back against the tunnel wall, long legs sprawled across the tracks. He sipped from his flask and recited quarterback stats.

*****

12:58 pm, Nov. 2, 2020, 35 days after The Fog

Sam transformed at the edge of the driveway and strode to the door. The shower curtains stared straight ahead. She rolled her eyes and walked into a wall of stress and tension.

The girls sat curled up on the couch, one each tucked beneath Danny's arms. Malak sucked her thumb.

"Auntie!" Zara flew from the couch to her arms. "Where's mommy? Is she with you?"

"What?"

Danny stood, not letting go of Malak. Her head nestled under his chin. Sam hadn't seen her look this small since she was a baby.

"Chiba never came home," he said. "Is she with you?"

THE TSUNAMI AND THE BEGINNING OF ALL THE THINGS

Oct. 31, 2020, 33 days after The Fog

Chiba Leary loved her dog. And her husband. And her kids. And her best friend. Glorious happiness consumed her for loving her dog. Her husband, her kids and her best friend. Okay, the insanity of this new world hadn't gone away but Sam was fine, her pantry was stocked and her family was safe.

With a belly full of waffles, she hugged her dog, her husband, her kids and her best friend and took off to pick up her mysterious bird fare from the rain forest in Redwood Valley.

The sun shone bright and cheerful. It was one of those crisp, moody fall mornings where the warm sunlight fought against the residual night's chill. Chiba set off on the Orange Monstrosity through the broken streets and alleyways of Sunset Cove.

When she made this journey three days ago, the creatures she passed stared down at the sidewalk. They would look away with a huff or a growl. Today, her neighbors nodded, offered little, half waves and gave her that polite half-grimace, half-smile that was the common greeting Pre-Fog.

Chiba turned on Stone Creek. The houses sat further away from each other and farther back from the road. The forest held this part of town in check. The road dipped down into a stone bridge.

The wind picked up and leaves scattered across the road. It brought back one of her few good childhood memories. One of her foster families, it must have been one of the nice ones but she couldn't remember who exactly, had a large yard full of maple trees. They raked the big orange and yellow leaves into a pile on the front lawn. She spent hours throwing herself into the heap pretending that she was exploring the Pyramids of Giza. They even gave her hot chocolate with marshmallows when she ran inside covered in leaves and twigs. Chiba couldn't recall their names. She thought the woman was blonde, but didn't trust her memory.

A beautiful, white horse trotted out of one the driveways, breaking her reverie. Chiba's eyes must be deceiving her but as the animal drew closer she swore its coat glittered in the subdued morning light. Then she realized a single, ivory horn grew out of the top of its head. Chiba stopped the bike out of pure self-preservation and stared, slack jawed as the unicorn passed her. It nodded as it passed, mouth stretched into a polite half-grimace, half-smile.

"No way," she breathed. "The girls are going to lose their minds."

Then Chiba did something that would have been unheard of for her only a week ago. She threw back her head and yelled:

"It's such a nice day!"

"Sí, it is lovely," a soft voice replied.

Chiba whipped her head back and discovered a small, bearded man dressed in leaves and twigs standing five feet from her – a large, wooden flute strapped to his back.

She recovered from the shock, and for lack of anything better to say, blurted:

"Not too cold for fall."

"No, it's very pleasant," he said. "But I do hope it rains soon. The forest is very dry."

"Yes, very dry."

"Well, that barn isn't going to fix itself." He tipped his leaf cap and headed down the road in the opposite direction. "I hope you have a nice day,

"Thank you, you too!"

What a nice man, she thought as she started back up the mountain on the Orange Monstrosity.

As she rode through the rolling hills, she began to entertain thoughts of the future.

What if I can go back to my dance class? What if the girls can go back to school? What if we can get some normalcy back? What if I don't have to be terrified every day?

The sun won its battle against the morning chill as she biked up the mountain and her mood lightened even further. She fantasized about all the ways she could go back to living her old life in this new world.

Chiba reached the top of the hill right before the descent into Redwood Valley. The suburban town stretched out below her. Beyond Redwood Valley, the trees of the mountain forests seemed to grow taller as she watched.

Chiba turned around and got the tiniest glint of the gray ocean. She loved this place. Sunset Cove became her home twenty years ago. She'd bounced around the Bay Area from one foster home to another. When her last foster father split her lip for eating a can of tuna, she ran away with her boyfriend at the time (a greasy punk with a purple Mohawk and access to fantastic weed) to the mythical land of Sunset Cove.

She lived on its streets and beneath its bridges. She shed blood here, nearly died here – a few times, once from a kick to the head of a jealous boyfriend (not the greasy punk). Yet, somehow, in her quest for oblivion something shifted. Chiba couldn't pinpoint the exact moment. Maybe it was the night she lay with a bleeding skull under the Saint Augustus bridge, spitting rage, that she decided she was well truly done with this bullshit.

So Chiba changed. She found friends – crazy, cool, weird friends who didn't want her for her body or drug connections. Friends who fed her and housed her. She got a job at the Boardwalk selling tickets to loud tourists. Then the weirdest things happened. She got her GED and went to college. She graduated with honors, met her husband and got a job at a brewery. She gave birth to two beautiful daughters. She found a best friend.

Chiba couldn't be certain – she could never be certain of anything. It was her nature and a consequence of her abuse. Deep in her suspicious heart, she suspected that this town saved her. It swallowed up so many of the lost, wrapping them into the confines of addiction until they disappeared beneath the weight of it. But Sunset Cove gave Chiba door after door. She kicked, scratched and clawed a few of them open, bruised, bloody and raw, but still, she pried them open.

Whatever battles she won to build her life here, they were tiny in comparison to the wars raging inside her own mind. As she rode up to the remnants of the coffee shop, without a distraction the ever-present tsunami of depression and fear threatened to pull her under.

Chiba hit the brakes and climbed off the Orange Monstrosity in front of the brown, brick, chain coffee shop she used to meet Sam at before going to the movies. Roots larger than her house crushed the building beneath them. She set the kickstand when an eagle dropped out of the sky and landed on broken and upturned remnants of the sidewalk next to her.

"The hell?" Chiba yelped.

An owl fell onto the bird, its brown and white feathers tiny in comparison to the eagle's giant wings. The owl wrapped its claws around the eagle's torso. The larger bird's shocked yellow eyes met hers as it squalled.

Chiba's fare appeared behind her. They dumped two large bags of rice into the cart and climbed in. Chiba didn't know what to do.

"Are you seeing this?" she asked and stepped to the side, gesturing to the large bird flailing in its death throes. Her fare shrugged and nodded in the direction back down the mountain.

Chiba stood, mouth open, wanting to help the distressed animal but unsure of how or whether she should interfere. A low scratching came from within her fare's quilt. A tattered piece of newspaper popped out.

Leave it. Owl friend.

Chiba blinked at the paper. Her fare waved at her from inside the cart. Chiba sighed for the thousandth time at this new world, hopped on the Orange Monstrosity, put the kickstand back and ignored the beautiful animal dying in front of her. She stopped, unable to ignore how the sight hurt her heart.

"Okay, but are you *sure*?"

More scribbling.

YES! Eagle BAD.

Chiba sighed again.

"Okay, then," she said and snapped the kickstand into place.

As she made the wide turn back down the mountain, her bird friend screeched at the owl. Chiba didn't bother to turn around as the owl hooted back. She wiped away a tear and pedaled hard back down the mountain.

*****

The Beginning

It is said that the god Ama appeared from a tear within the fabric of space itself. He emerged from this tear as his primordial self in the form of an egg. As this egg spun and broke open in the emptiness of space, the blinding pieces of the shell swirled and became the galaxies. Ama threw clay from his hands and formed the sun, the moon and the earth. He then had relations with the Earth and she gave birth to twins. These were the Nommo. They created and held much thirst. These twins spread across the Earth endangering Ama's second children – man. When confronted with the harm they caused, one twin was defiant, the other sad and repentant. He sacrificed his earthly body to trap and cast out his violent brother into the Darkness.

*****

3:16 pm, Oct. 31, 2020, 33 days after The Fog

Chiba found herself in the five square block of space in Sunset Cove called "Midtown." No one had ever been able to explain to her why it was called that, as it was only vaguely in the geographic center of Sunset Cove proper. If one stood three feet to the left of a map of Sunset Cove, closed their right eye and squinted real hard, Midtown would be in the middle. As it was, with two main arteries, and nothing truly special about it, Chiba suspected it was called Midtown because it was, by Sunset Cove standards, spectacularly bland.

This part of town always made her think of burnt yellow. Her own neighborhood, suburban as it was, had a Stepford Wives quality to it that Chiba not-so-secretly enjoyed. But Midtown? It was too far from downtown for homeless people to wander. It had one bar, a bunch of strip malls, some forgettable, mid-century modern-style homes and a large parking lot where the Midtown Farmers market was held every Saturday morning from 7 am to 1:30 pm.

Chiba dropped her bird fare off at the Clocktower and a tiny, delicate wing-creature with perfect, golden skin landed on her nose. In a voice more like a squeak, the creature pleaded in Chiba's ear, the buzzing of its shimmering, lacy wings almost louder than its voice, to please take these crates to Midtown.

"Sure." Chiba couldn't help herself. The girls would go nuts when they heard this. "I'll help out a fairy."

"I'm not a fairy," he squeaked in high dudgeon, "I'm a Peri. P as in Peter. E as in Edward. R as in Ronald. I as in Indigo."

Chiba blinked.

"Never mind," he said and sighed. "Here's the address."

So she brought the man, who was no bigger than her thumb, and his incredibly heavy crates to the big, burnt mustard, box store that was once a toy store and had bloomed through The Fog's power into a two-story-tall golden flower.

"What do you think it is?" The Peri squeaked in her ear, musing at the incongruous plant before them.

Chiba tilted her head at the underside of the flower. She'd never given this grandmother's plant much thought before, but standing in the shade of silky petals the size of her car, light glinting through the yellow petals, she decided it was her new favorite.

It reminded her of the moment in her foster family's yard. She sat, small, arms wrapped around her knees gazing up at the sharp autumn light glinting through the leaves. They surrounded her – a dry cage, a warning system, above, below, everywhere, in her hair warding off the autumn chill. Their dusty, crinkly scent filled her nostrils, tickling her nose but she refused to sneeze. No one could touch her without their snap and crunch giving her warning. Rough twigs poked her scalp and knotted into her hair.

But the light, the light enchanted her, the world beyond the leaves felt soft and out of focus so unreal and far away. She could make out the minuscule drifting of a fluffy cloud, the dark, broken arm of a tree branch waving in the breeze. This was the first moment that she truly felt safe. This was the moment she suspected, for the first time in her little life, that there was something good and sacred in this world after all.

"It's a marigold," she mused. "It's so majestic. It's beautiful."

The Peri paused, then clapped his hands.

"Well, time to unload," he said.

If Chiba were less distracted by the flower swaying above them, she might have felt suspicion at the glee in his tiny tone.

The three crates weighed at least a ton each. She was certain she pulled a back muscle hauling them into her cart in the first place, but the tiny man had seemed so desperate. Chiba bent her knees and remembered to lift with her legs, like her chiropractor scolded her the last time she'd visited him a week before The Fog.

I wonder if he's still alive, she thought as she heaved the wooden crate up and out of the cart.

"What have you got in these things? Rocks?"

With that, the little man doubled over in laughter – arms wrapped around his chest. He choked and tears ran down his tiny visage. He floated down to the crate and yanked off the lid in a surprising feat of strength to reveal… rocks.

"What the fuck?"

The Peri's face turned bright red from lack of oxygen. His minuscule chest heaved.

"It's rocks! You carried rocks!" He collapsed on said rocks, unable to fly in his glee. "The look on your face! It's so good!"

"The fuck…?"

"I got you so good! You dragged rocks up here! Get it? It's a joke!"

"You asked me to carry rocks all the way over here for a joke?"

Chiba couldn't entirely comprehend what had happened but she could feel anger rising. She felt safe for a second and now he mocked her after she helped him.

"You're an asshole."

The Peri sat up and sighed.

"It's just a joke. Laugh a little. It'll help your resting bitch face."

"Hey, asshole! Get your rocks the fuck out of my cart."

She pulled the baseball bat from the cart, closed her eyes and swung. The little man thwapted against wood as it caught him square on, flinging him thirty feet away. No one was more surprised by this than Chiba.

She gasped, covering her mouth with her free hand.

"Oh, I'm so…"

She stopped as the tiny man barreled toward her in the air. He reached her protective bubble and bounced with a tiny *sproingggggg*. He shrieked an incomprehensible blue streak as he tumbled through the air. When the momentum let him, he righted himself, wings jittering in an erratic dance.

"Fuck you!"

He flew off, indignantly muttering as he went. Chiba realized that two, million-pound crates still sat in her cart.

"You get back here!"

His tiny fist was too far away to make out the details, but Chiba knew the little shit was flipping her the bird. In a futile grasp at closure and justice, and in the name of every "bitchy" woman everywhere, she flung the wooden bat at his minuscule back. The sleek, shiny, wooden implement, leftover from Danny's attempts to join the neighborhood league, flipped end over end, suspended in the air. Staying aloft longer than mere physics dictated, fueled by her righteous pique, the top part of the bat dropped onto the tiny man, shoving him into the asphalt with a diminutive, "Oof."

Chiba stalked across the parking lot. She rolled up her sleeves and plucked her despondent foe from the tarred earth. With her bat in her other hand, she stalked back to her cart and tossed him into it.

"Deal with your shit," she said and grasped the bat with both hands and pointed it at his grape-shaped skull.

Grumbling like she'd kicked his dog, he jerked the two boxes out of the cart and slammed them onto the asphalt. Refusing to meet her gaze, harrumphing, he gestured to the finished chore.

"You can go," Chiba said and stepped back. "But don't cross my path again."

The little man zipped off, hurling curses as he flew.

Chiba's knees shook and she sank onto the asphalt. All the violence she ever experienced flooded into her mind. Her body trembled. She felt the hands touching her, pawing at her clothes, punching her nose, the sick crack it made as it broke, the bruises on her shins as they kicked her, their sickening breath in her nose and mouth.

In these moments, she imagined the present and all she'd accomplished as a tiny, battered dingy riding the wave of a massive tsunami. The little boat swamped beneath the thousand-foot wave of depression and shame. No matter how hard she tried to let the tsunami pass through her, leaving her a little intact, it never did. It swallowed her happiness, her love, her accomplishments over and over again. Chiba, stranded in the writhing waters that wanted to drown her, would grab the closest floating plank, hoist herself up onto it and build her little dingy from scratch over and over again.

What the fuck was wrong with that guy?

Maybe I shouldn't have reacted?

It was a joke.

It was a dumb joke.

Is it me? Is there something about me that made him think it was okay to do this to me?

Sunlight shone through the petals and Chiba felt the warmth of it on her face. She brushed the angry tears away and stood up. The tsunami still at its peak, the detritus of her past swirling in the murky waters, she found a plank – her kids needed her and she had beer at home.

She pulled herself up, put herself on her bike and started home.

*****

The Cave

The Great God Zeus, Father of the Pantheon, God to all the Gods, is said to have feared one being.

Passing a cave in the seawall, he warned his followers to keep silent.

"Do not awaken her," he shushed them. "She must not know we are here. This is her domain."

Among all the Gods and Goddesses, she alone held the power he feared – the power of Darkness.

*****

4:42 pm, Oct. 31, 2020, 33 days after The Fog

In Chiba's distracted state and in an unfamiliar place, she turned left instead of right at the artisanal cheese shop next to the breakfast place that let you eat scrambled eggs in an open lemon yellow van parked out front.

Fucking hipsters, Chiba mused, as she passed the buildings. But she did miss the breakfast place. They made amazing crepes.

As she rode along the bland, tree-lined streets, the way back dimmed in her mind. Chiba turned again. Unsure of where she was and how she got there, she performed an awkward u-turn with the Orange Monstrosity. She just kept turning and turning, getting more and more lost, without a single soul to ask for directions, the mediocre streets of Midtown swallowed her up.

Hours passed, the late afternoon sun cast long shadows on the asphalt. Chiba's panic descended into madness. She could not escape. Every turn led her down an identical, empty, beige street. Landmarks blurred into boxes and roads wound in and around themselves. Nothing resembling a human lived here. Not even a spastic squirrel crossed her path as the autumn wind tossed leaves across the empty road.

The tsunami rose again in her mind, toppling the two planks she lashed together with busted twine and futile hope. She floated those hostile waters, circling the mundane streets of Midtown until the faint aroma of sativa reached her nostrils. The familiar citrus scent with notes of mango and sour cherry called to her. Chiba's mind cleared. The tsunami ebbed and she found an ancient plank of rotted wood to hold onto – her oldest and dearest frenemy — pot.

She followed the scent to a park she used to sleep in back in the day and turned right at a cul-de-sac. Here the scent concentrated and Chiba never thought she'd be so ecstatic to see her old dealer – a scarecrow of a man, stick-straight, straw-colored hair past his shoulders. A brown and yellow Hawaiian shirt hung from his wide shoulders and a thick, scraggly beard sprouted from his chin. Davey McAllister's narrow chest contracted as he exhaled. The lighter in his hand snicked. She could hear the water burble. His chest doubled in size as he took a hit from a foot-long, orange, yellow and blue glass bong.

"Davey!"

Chiba stood on the pedals of the Orange Monstrosity, but the bike protested. Its gears ground against her as she struggled to pedal to her old friend.

"Davey! It's Chiba!" She yelled from twenty feet away.

"Chibs!"

He jumped up, toppling the lawn chair.

"Get over here! Come here! Hurry up! Let's go!"

Abandoning the Orange Monstrosity to the streets, she climbed off the bike and ran to him.

"Davey!"

She tried to hug him but he looped one long arm around her shoulders and hustled her up the driveway.

"Come on inside, Chibs. Come on. Come on. Get inside. Get inside. It's bad out here. Hurry. Hurry up. Get inside."

They passed through the wooden door with three small window panes across the top and Davey placed a joint between his lips, lit it, inhaled and passed it to her.

"Take this. It'll clear your head."

Without thinking, Chiba took it and inhaled sharply. An explosive cough erupted from her lungs. Davey patted her back

"Rookie move, Chibs" he said and turned the lock on the door and tested it.

Chiba's lungs struggled for air. Her eyes burned but the tsunami retreated another one hundred feet.

"It's... *blech*... been... *hack*... a while," she said and slumped back against the door jamb.

Davey patted her arm with a fond smile but his bleary, bloodshot eyes wouldn't meet hers.

"Good to see you," he muttered. "Welcome. Chiba, these are… people. People meet Chiba."

Sprawled out across the room, she could make out the figures of about five or six people in the dying light. These were the same people she'd found in rooms like this decades ago. Their names and faces changed, but there was always one guy sitting on the couch staring at his hands, another passed out in a corner while some girl with braids and questionable fashion sense danced in the middle of the room to music that wasn't there. Two or three people communed with the house plants.

Chiba waved.

"Hey."

The people, though, weren't what interested her about this room. Six couches were stacked upright against the walls. A dozen coffee tables in a mish mash of shapes and sizes, some ratty, old, second hand finds, others new, sleek and expensive stood sentinel next to the couches. As many as two dozen mattresses littered the floor. Books were shoved into the spaces between the puzzle-piece furniture. There were thousands of them.

This room must have been large – particularly by Sunset Cove standards – where real estate was the most expensive in the nation and college students rented closets for a thousand or more a month, but with all the furniture and bodies, the air felt muggy and stale. Maybe it was the sativa, but the ceiling sat too close to the top of Chiba's skull.

She stepped onto the mattress and clambered over to the low, black, leather couch.

The dancing girl paused, skin shimmering green and gold in the fading sky light. She smiled with serrated teeth at Chiba.

"Welcome to the meat locker," she said.

"Ignore her," Davey murmured. "Sit. Sit. Sit down."

Chiba blinked. Maybe she was full up on people fucking with her today, or maybe she just was so used to stoners making overblown pronouncements, but Chiba did ignore her.

Davey had worked in shipping at the Sunset Cove Brewery with Chiba, Dre, Sam and Jimmy. He quit years ago, once cannabis became legal. Chiba heard he found some angel investor and went legit. He opened his third dispensary last month. She passed the sleek green and white building on her way to the grocery store. She'd always meant to stop by and see if he was around to say hi, but never did.

The dimensions of the room stretched and snapped around her. Chiba plopped down on the couch next to the dude with his hands on his knees. He was blonde, lanky and had a bit of a pot belly beneath his flannel shirt.

"Hey." Chiba nodded as her head disconnected from her body, traveling to the past and future at the same time. "You look really familiar. Have we met?"

It was a common Sunset Cove conversation – left over from before The Fog. Even with a population of a quarter of a million, stretched across 607 square miles, the same people ran into each other over and over again.

The man ignored her.

"Lost him," he muttered under his breath. "I lost him. This is because I lost him. Lost him. I lost him. Stupid. So stupid. Shouldn't have left. Stupid. Stupid."

Chiba blinked and the room disintegrated then built itself back together in a new configuration. She stared up at the sky light. The moon and stars shone through the clear glass. They danced and sang to her with songs of light, joy and warning.

The Queen of the Darkness.

Such a pompous title. Chiba smirked at the idea of Sam, of all people, carrying such a thing around – the woman who sent her twenty texts, including pictures, agonizing over whether to buy Zara the pink stuffed unicorn with the gold horn or the purple stuffed unicorn with the silver horn for Christmas,

"Okay, the pink is cuter but the purple is sassier, don't you think?"

"It doesn't matter. She'll love it either way."

"I'm going with the purple. She said we wanted sassy. This one looks sassy.

...But

...is it sassy enough?"

The Queen of Darkness? No. Just no.

Buried a million feet below the high decimating her judgment and the tsunami of rage and trauma, Chiba wished, as one of those singing stars shot across the sky, that Sam were with her now. It would be better, Chiba knew, if she sat beside her in this lonely room.

*****

1:08 pm, Nov. 2, 2020, 35 days after The Fog

Sam knelt on the dirty, taupe carpet of the Leary's entryway and lived every nightmare she'd ever had.

Zara's round little face, splotchy and red with tears, snot dripping from her little nose – as though all the emotions were too large for her body and were leaking out of her face, snuffled inches from her own. Danny and Malak stared down at them. They were giants against the backdrop of grief. Sam's breath caught. Her chest felt small and tight. Her lungs threatened to seize out of habit.

"Promise you'll find mommy, please," Zara heaved.

She remembered the day she met Zara. A few days out of the hospital, a preemie and improbably tiny, Sam couldn't believe anything so small could survive on its own.

Sam pulled her sleeve over her hand and wiped the tears away.

"I don't make promises, baby," she said. Sam knew what she was about to say might be lost on her but the delicate magic of this moment required truth. "You know that. I keep my word. Promises are made to be broken. Words are made to be kept. I will find your mom. You have my word."

Zara tried to inhale all the snot and tears back in. She nodded. Sam pulled a black handkerchief from her hoodie and gave it to her. Then she stood and kissed the top of her head.

"I will find your mom," she repeated.

"What if she's dead?" Danny blurted out.

Sam closed her eyes against the need to murder him. The girls wailed in earnest. Their cries bounced off the inside of her skull and tore at her very tenuous grip on sanity.

"She's not dead," Sam snapped, head down, glaring at the floor instead of Danny.

Malak and Zara stopped shrieking in surprise. She took a breath, raised her head and glared at Danny anyway, because fuck, that was a dumb thing to say.

"She's not dead. *I* would know."

"Oh, right because you're…"

"Stop talking, Danny." Sam could barely contain her fury. She felt it spreading across the room, reaching for his throat. "Just stop talking about me. And stop talking about Chiba. *Period*. I will handle this." She bit through the words.

He stepped back from her and held up a hand – self-preservation instincts finally kicking in.

"I'm just…"

"Don't. Don't. Just." She made her voice soften and turn conciliatory and placating. "I'll take care of it. Don't worry about it."

Malak stared at her with wide, bloodshot eyes while sucking on her thumb.

"What are you, Auntie?" Zara asked, worrying her bottom lip. "What do you mean, Daddy?"

"It's nothing, honey," Sam said. "I'm just someone who knows a lot of things."

"Because you're smart?" Malak asked.

Sam, ignoring Danny, kissed the top of Malak's head too.

"Yes, baby, because I'm smart. I will find your mom, okay?"

She turned to leave but paused before Ridley's crate. The dog raised his head and looked at her with one disinterested eye.

"Make sure he doesn't do anything stupid, please," she said in a whisper only dogs could hear. He blinked, snuffled once and laid his head back down.

Sam stormed out, ignoring the Wraiths flanking her.

Fat lot of fucking good they were.

From his perch in the tree across the street, Carl could tell something was very, very wrong.

She stormed down the cul-du-sac to the park. With her every step, afternoon shadows stretched and strained to follow. The creatures trapped within them begged with silent eyes for release.

"Boss?"

She ignored him.

"BOSS!"

She scaled the thirty-foot wire fence surrounding the baseball diamond and perched there. The Darkness, such as it was in this daylight suburb, crawled from the shadows, grasping at the ground, and yanked itself towards her. It cleaved a red hatchback in two to get near.

Carl, as a rule, was not prone to panic. The fluttery tension rising in his chest was wholly unfamiliar.

"Boss, whatcha doing?"

The power she called was far beyond her capacity to control. He knew it – even if she didn't. She was still too broken, too human. The summoning of such a mass of Darkness would kill her and leave Sunset Cove in ruins.

He did not relish the idea of what would happen to him if she died before… He squawked in terror. His feathers shook reflexively from his tail to the top of his head. Out of desperation, Carl flew to her. He meant to land on the fence beside her but she turned and raised her arm at the last second. He landed on her forearm – talons sinking into her flesh.

"Where is she?" The Morrigan demanded. "Where is my sister?"

"I don't know," he chirped. Her dead, sunken eyes bore into his.

"How many soldiers do we have in the air?"

"Three hundred," he replied.

"Not enough," she snarled.

Before this moment, she'd always been Sam to him – constantly in motion, a cool, refreshing breeze lifting and shifting scattered orange, red and brown leaves on an empty road. A soul younger than she ought to be – considering the circumstances.

The empty stillness of her in this moment took him aback. She had made herself a void of seething, helpless rage to bring them closer. Distant screams grew louder. She was summoning them. Calling his siblings to do her will. Carl knew the effort of bringing forth millions of thirsting, wretched souls in search of her lost sister would kill her. Her lips went white and trembled. She sucked them between her teeth and bit hard. Black blood seeped from her lips. Yet, her will did not falter.

"Stop!" Carl shrieked. Her empty eyes swiveled in his direction. "Give me thirty minutes. We will find something."

She went back to staring at nothing, ignoring him.

"What would Nemain say?"

"Fuck Nemain," she muttered, but at least he had her attention.

"It's a shit plan," he squawked. "You summon the lost souls of the Darkness and they kill you. Then what? If Chiba's in danger, you can't help her when you're a corpse. Millions of the Damned roaming free around this town. It's stupid and shortsighted, Boss. Gimme thirty minutes. I'll find something."

"Give me your word," she said. Inky liquid poured from her mouth. The air around her reeked of decay.

They were so close. Carl felt their breath on his neck. Their forms solidified and clamoured against a reality that was now alien to them.

"What?"

He jerked back. This was ancient magic – older than her by millennia. She should not have known about it.

"Your word," she repeated. Her eyes scanned the manifesting Darkness and a smile played around her lips. Though it was afternoon, the sky was almost pitch black and screams filled the air as an ill wind whipped her wild hair about and ruffled his feathers. The Morrigan seemed pleased with her work.

"I want it. Give me your word that you will have a lead on her location within thirty minutes."

Razor thin nails emerged from the gathering Darkness and stroked the back of Carl's head.

"You have my word," he blurted. "You have my word."

"Good."

The Darkness retreated back into the shadows of this world. Sam's eyes rolled back in her head. She swayed on her perch. Carl flew off her arm – knowing what was coming.

"Wake me in thirty minutes," she slurred.

Her hand let go of the aluminum bar and she flopped backward, thirty feet onto the overgrown grass of the Huey P. Cowell Baseball Park. Carl rolled his eyes. He floated down to where she lay, sprawled out and already snoring. Her breath hitched and caught. He sighed and head butted her shoulder until she rolled over onto her side.

"Jerk," she muttered in her sleep.

This impudent, thankless child was going to be the end of him. A thin line of black blood mixed with drool dribbled out of her mouth. He cleaned his feathers, standing guard so she didn't roll over and aspirate. Carl counted the passing of thirty minutes the old way – watching the angle of shadows grow ever longer in the fading sunlight.

*****

1:12 am, Nov. 1, 2020, 34 days after The Fog

Chiba awoke to the strumming of acoustic guitar. She snorted. Her head jerked up from the couch and she earned herself an instant neck cramp.

"Oww," she muttered.

The blonde man hadn't moved from his seat next to her, hands still on his knees, tapping in an unknowable rhythm.

Davey sat cross-legged on the mattress at her feet, noodling away. The lizard girl slept in the fetal position in the far corner of the room. Her head rested on the sideways arm of a couch, her legs on a random mattress.

"Where are the others?" Chiba muttered. Her mouth felt full of cotton balls.

"Gone," Davey said. He took a hit off the joint in the ceramic ashtray to his left. "Hey, Chibs, you remember this?"

He struck three slow minor chords.

"'My Lady Farts on Tuesday," she croaked. "A Davey McAllister classic."

"Sing it for me," he said.

"Ah, Davey, I can't. My throat's on fire. I need water. I'm not warmed up…"

"Here." His lanky legs shifted as he turned to pull a bottle of water from somewhere behind him. He handed it to her and went back to the guitar.

As she sipped, she studied him. The wide streaks of gray in his beard and hair were new. His eyes were always a little sunken and bloodshot but the dark circles must have appeared in the past decade.

"Has it been ten years?" she asked.

"Hmm," he said and set the guitar aside. He stretched out his legs and leaned back to look through the skylight. "Yeah, sounds right."

Davey picked up the guitar and strummed – not meeting her eyes. He seemed so sad. That's when Chiba realized the man before her was nothing like the hyper, clumsy, goofy dude who let her crash on his couch when she crawled out from under that bridge, soaking wet and covered in blood. He told her butterflies held the world together that night.

"That's why the monarchs come here, Chibs. This is where they recharge on the magic that holds everything together. No place else. Isn't that beautiful?"

She could tell he believed it.

"What happened to you, Davey? What's going on?"

He strummed a heavy G chord and laughed, showing his big, straight teeth.

"I sold my soul at the company store," he sang with his vibrato baritone.

"What do you mean?" Panic hit Chiba. She clutched her knees with white knuckles. "What are you talking about?

He inhaled from the joint deeply then he turned and blew smoke in her face. The glittering cloud – full of razor blades and lies hit her brain like a bat.

"Go back to sleep," he ordered, voice raspy with smoke.

So she did.

*****

1:45 pm, Nov. 2, 2020, 35 days after The Fog

Sam awoke to something thunking her forehead.

"Owww," she muttered and flailed at the thunking.

"Wake up," Carl screeched in her ear. "It's time."

"Fuck's sake, Carl."

Sam rolled onto her back – narrowly avoiding another headbutt. He hopped onto her stomach, marched over her boobs and got in her face.

"Boundaries!"

Sam shot up. He fluttered to the ground.

"You told me to wake you in thirty minutes. It's been thirty minutes."

Sam used her hoodie to wipe crusted blood mixed with drool from her cheek.

"What did you find out?"

"There's one of your kind living in a vineyard near Bonne Chance in the northwest mountains."

"What?" Sam stilled. "What do you mean 'my kind'?"

"The slovenly, ungrateful, asking stupid questions kind," he said, flapping his wings at her. "God Kind, you reckless child. God Kind."

Carl had spent the past thirty minutes imagining all the terrible things that would have happened if she'd succeeded in calling forth his siblings and he was in NO mood.

"Hey!"

"They will know how to find your sister."

His stick legs marched back and forth in the tall grass – his dudgeon at its highest. The feathers on his chest puffed out to triple their normal size. He reminded Sam of a short, self-important general inspecting his troops.

"They are not your ally but they can be bargained with," he said.

Without another word, he flew off, too upset to help her any further.

"What the hell, Carl?" Sam didn't have the will to compel him back so she stomped her foot and settled for yelling. "I don't need your passive aggressiveness right now, bird! A cryptic harbinger is not a good look! It's a little on the BEAK, Carl!"

Sam stopped when she realized that she looked like a complete idiot.

Ignoring her heart pounding in her ears and the coiled vipers in the pit of her stomach at the thought of confronting a member of 'her kind' in the real world, she pulled her form in until she became a raven and took to the air. She put all the tangled thoughts of Chiba in a plastic box in the corner of her mind. They could not be allowed to roam free. Sam needed a clear head and a steely heart to find her.

Sam hadn't spent a lot of time in Bonne Chance, which was not really a town, in the western mountains of Sunset Cove. It was just what people called that part of the county. Before The Fog, the area was sparsely populated by a few houses clustered together here and there with the occasional winery and ice cream shop thrown in for maximum Sunset Cove-ness.

As she flew over the area looking for signs of 'her kind,' Sam realized that:

This once desolate forest, picked over by decades of wildfire and human occupation, had disappeared.

In its place were dozens of magical landscapes, including an endless desert to the east, shimmering lochs and meadows to the west, in the south – lush wetlands and towering frozen tundra to the north. A large volcanic island had emerged just off the coast. These landscapes seemed both infinite and crammed together. Between these polar opposites were lands of enchantment where every imaginable creature roamed.

Sam spotted a beautiful, raven-haired woman with the legs of a horse wearing a tattered, Black Flag t-shirt. Lizards the size of pickup trucks stalked over sand dunes. Rabbits with unicorn horns jumped over trees and bushes. A purple dragon scampered across a dirt road.

Between the edge of the desert and the wetlands in the south, Sam found what she was looking for – a Greek temple, white columns shining like gold in the setting autumn sunlight, surrounded by a verdant vineyard.

Sam landed among a cluster of olive trees next to the vineyard about thirty feet from the temple. She pulled her human body back together. The sounds of a raucous party greeted her. A woman shrieked in delight. Incoherent conversations and the skunky stench of pot wafted out from the temple.

Sam rolled her eyes. She sighed, pulled her hoodie over her head, straightened her spine and went to join the party.

They sensed her when she was within ten miles as the crow flies – pun intended. They stood on the path waiting to welcome their guest. It was only good manners after all.

She stepped out of the trees and they couldn't help their surprise. They thought she'd be taller, more willowy, not so… average. A less perceptive being would ignore the terror playing around the base of their skull and assume she was a normal, bookish woman. But they understood this was camouflage, of course, and admired the efficiency of it. She could walk on any street, into any party, any room unnoticed and unremarked upon. The beings she walked past would attribute the chills she induced to an errant draft or an iced drink.

But if they noticed the details – the strange eyes that glowed in the right light, or the sighs of the forest as the trees dropped their leaves with anticipation at her nearness, or the grapes that withered under the weight of her gaze, they would understand the horrifying truth of her that lived in the quiet places people pretended not to see.

So they stood with an unopened beer in one hand and inhaled from their vape with the other, hoping this was a social call even though they knew it wasn't, damn their father's eyes. They tucked the vape back into their black fanny pack. When she noticed them, they exhaled long and slow into the mid-afternoon air.

"Hello!" they greeted The Goddess of Death, bowing a bit with their hand over their heart. "Welcome! Welcome! I'm Dyn." They handed her the bottle. "You're just in time for beer pong. I've been expecting you for thirty minutes now. I'm so glad you got here in time. Have we met? You seem familiar."

"Maybe?" Sam asked and tried to remember them. "Probably at some party somewhere."

She stared at the gold chain around their neck with the words "THEY/THEM" emblazoned in six-inch, gold letters.

"Do you like my necklace? I had it made. Isn't it brilliant?"

She took them all in – from their cloven hooves to furry legs with the red t-shirt long enough to be a dress over their prodigious beer belly, thick beard and two baby horns sticking out of their greasy, curly, brown hair.

"It's awesome," she said, lips quirking in amusement.

On a whim, they pulled a pink lighter from their fanny pack, took her beer, popped it open and handed it back.

"I'm not going to help you kill my father," Dyn said. This was the Most Serious Thing they had said in a very long time and they wanted to get it over with as quickly as possible. "I mean he's a bastard… but…."

"I won't ask you to give up the Man in White. I'm just looking for my friend. I was told you could help me."

Dyn threw up their arms in relief.

"Holy fuck! Is that all?"

They ushered her down the path.

"Of course, welcome. They're probably here. What's your friend's name? I love your boots by the way. Very revolutionary."

"Thank you," Sam replied and glanced down at her feet. "They have pockets."

"Shut the fuck up."

"Seriously," she said. Sam tilted her legs to show the outside of her boots better. "Pockets."

"I need me some of those," Dyn said." So cute."

They arrived at the temple

"Holy shit," Sam breathed.

It had not looked so impressive from the air.

The rising edifice dwarfed her. Flaming torches illuminated gleaming, white Corinthian columns, ten feet in circumference, as they supported the triangular entablature more than fifty-feet overhead. There was no doubt this place was holy. Sam, once upon a time, would have worshiped here, had she not found her own path.

"I gotta get me one of these."

"Aww," Dyn blushed. "You're so sweet. It's pretty great, isn't it? I love it."

They paused at the entrance and turned to Sam.

"Welcome to the Temple of Dionysus," they said with a bow.

Sam nodded and bowed.

"Let me give you the rundown - drinks are on the red table, regular drugs are on the blue one, magical drugs on the black. The vomitorium is past the kitchenette to the right. You know where the orgy pit is. Condoms and dental dams are along edges. Consent is required. NO exceptions. Any injuries, the Healers will fix you right up. I heard that was you – thanks for that. Another quick note about the orgy pit – politeness never hurt anyone. You know a little please and thank you while you're fucking goes a long way. Oh no, they started beer pong without us. Well, we'll get in on the next game. Any questions?"

Sam blinked. While the outside was pure Greek Classical, the inside was pure Greek Week. Half a dozen mismatched thrift store sofas, of questionable cleanliness, dotted the tile floor. Flimsy card tables sagged under the weight of kegs and suspicious substances. The 'kitchenette' was a crusty microwave on a rolling cart next to a mini fridge, a burning trash can and a seven-foot-long stone altar. The orgy pit took up most of the floor space in the center of the temple.

She blinked again and batted at what felt like a spider web across her face. The screams of pleasure from the orgy pit increased.

"Someone's having a good night." Dyn grinned with uneven goat teeth.

Sam shook her head but the feeling of the spiderwebs wouldn't go away. She brushed her arms and legs.

"My friend?" She reminded Dyn.

"Oh, right!" They spun around. "Callie! Could you come over here please?"

A slender brunette in Sunset Cove hippie gear – faux-fur vest, sparkly leggings and dozens of leather corded necklaces with no fewer than seven different religious symbols on them – peeled herself from a couch and sauntered over.

"Dyn, darling." Callie snaked an arm around Dyn's waist and handed them a red, plastic cup.

"Callie, my dear." Dyn stumbled, either from Callie's resting weight or the effect of the drink she handed them. "This delightful creature is looking for her friend. Could you help her please?"

"Oh, of course." Callie blinked and swayed. "What's your friend's name?"

Sam could not rid herself of the webs. Invisible hairs tickled her skin, stuck in her hair, buzzing against her ears. No matter how she twitched and brushed, they vexed her.

"Chiba," Sam said, shivering at the feeling of stickiness brushing against her skin. The musty scent of desire from the orgy pit distracted her.

Callie nodded.

"Chiba," she repeated, then closed her eyes and held her hands out before her. She spun in a slow circle.

"Callie's a telepath," Dyn whispered loudly. "She can read minds."

Callie stopped when she faced Sam again.

"I'm sorry, sweetie," she said. "There's no one named Chiba here."

Sam was in the process of scratching her neck raw. The screams and moans of pleasure from the pit rose to cacophonous heights.

"What about Naomi? Naomi. Or..." Sam paused, hesitant to say this name out loud, and in front of strangers even, but it was an emergency: "Kalima."

Callie nodded with big eyes and a seriousness that was suspicious from someone so obviously fucked up. But she did two more slow turns.

"No, honey, I'm sorry." She patted Sam's shoulder. "There's no one here with those names."

The screams reached a fever pitch. Even Dyn seemed surprised by it. The caterwauling of pleasure bounced around the sandstone columns. The incessant spider webs – in her hair, her eyes, in her mouth, threatened the integrity of the plastic box in Sam's mind.

"Would you all just shut up?"

She shut her eyes, trying to shore up her fragile composure. Sam closed her left hand into a fist. To her shock, both the orgasmic shrieks and the itchiness ceased. The silence was a relief. Her shoulders dropped. One hundred suddenly sober, turned off, disappointed and instantly hungover eyes swiveled to glare at her from the depths of the temple.

"What did you do?" Dyn demanded, their eyes wild.

Sam slowly brought her left hand before her face and opened her fist. Hundreds of tiny, shining, black threads criss-crossed her palm.

The fuck is this?

She stared for several long, puzzled moments before realizing what she held.

"What did you just do?" Dyn repeated.

"Why do you have the Consolations of Death?" Sam asked them.

The threads formed a thick web through the temple, tracing back and forth from body to body connecting everyone to Dyn. Humans had learned long ago to exploit the Consolations of Death – the intense pleasure released before the body expired. They mimicked it through slow poison with drink or drugs or the mechanics of touch to recreate the cascading loop of ecstasy called the Little Death. With this power, anyone near Dyn would experience endless, ecstatic pleasure.

"Whoa, whoa, whoa!" Dyn raised their arms and backed away. "I don't *have* anything. I borrow – with *permission*."

"How are you *borrowing* the Consolations of Death?" .

"It was a gift, or maybe it was payment. I dunno. Doesn't matter. Whatever it was, you can't have it. It's mine. Give it back."

"Help me find my friend and I'll give it back."

Dyn's face turned wild and red. The stench of alcohol poured from them. They stepped back another foot. All traces of the genial host disappeared. They pawed at the ground.

"Give it baaaack!"

They bent over and charged.

Sam spun out of the way like a toreador dodging a bull. Dyn stumbled, bleating. They picked themselves back up and pawed the ground again.

"Dyn, knock it off! Get it together. Help me find Chiba and you'll get it back."

The god snarled and snorted as an answer.

"Fine."

Sam pulled down the neck of her hoodie and slapped her hand against her chest. The Consolations, jagged, black, crosshatches, nestled across her collar and rib cage. They fizzled like warm soda against her skin. Dyn pushed her into a corner against one of the massive columns. Sam pulled her sword from her hoodie and wrapped herself in Death.

"You wanna fuck around? Help me find her – she's got brown hair and hazel eyes. She was wearing a lemon-yellow jacket and a green scarf that I got her for Christmas."

The plastic box cracked but didn't disintegrate.

"She's got a pointy chin and resting bitch face. She was riding an ugly orange bike. Help me find her and you get this back. You want to try and take it? Go ahead! Try!"

Sam thrust her chin in the air and dared every being in the temple to cross her. They stared back – lips parted with desperation – eyes feral in the firelight. These creatures needed an escape, not with the finality of death but a temporary, joyful reprieve from the endless weight of physical existence.

"Give it back!" Defeated, Dyn sat on the temple floor and resorted to whining. "Please. Please give it back. You shouldn't mess with her stuff anyway. She might get mad."

Sam straightened from a fighting stance. She felt the world tilt at an odd angle as déjà vu swept over her. Her voice felt a million years and another reality away when she asked: "Who might get mad?"

"Who do you think?" Dyn pouted.

They said a word. It was small, as words go – three letters, one syllable – but it made Sam's eyes roll back. She dropped to the ground, shaking and foaming at the mouth.

The last thing she saw before passing out was Dyn lunging toward her.

"Oh, shit! Are you okay?"

*****

2:05 am, Nov. 2, 2020, 35 days after The Fog

Chiba lay, half in and out of consciousness, drifting among the flotsam. The alarms in her mind were too far away and too muffled. It was too hard to pull herself out of the muddy water to silence them. From the distant shore – a million miles away from where her body lay suspended on the surface of the sea, Chiba caught bits and pieces of an argument.

"I'm not eating that."

Collective sighs.

"It's fine. We'll put a little barbecue sauce on it. You liked the last one with barbecue sauce."

"Oh, shit."

"What?"

"This one has a band."

"No, fucking way. It's not a kid."

More sighs.

"Just smoke it. It's fine. You like it smoked. Remember the last one? Meat so tender it fell off the bone."

"Let's put the werewolf back."

The peanut gallery did not agree.

"This again?"

"Nooooooo."

Chiba could discern three different voices – two masculine, one feminine.

"They're so stringy," one of the masculine voices whined. "The meat's so tough. I've still got gas from that lizard." The voice belched, low and wet. "See? Let's leave it. We'll get it later, okay?"

"Lizard tastes like chicken."

"No, lizard tastes like alligator."

"Barbecue sauce."

"Barbecue sauce isn't the answer for everything."

"Yes, it is. Barbecue sauce. Barbecue sauce. Barbecue sauce."

"Does chicken taste like alligator? Or does alligator taste like chicken?"

"Nooooooo."

"Let's just take these two and leave the werewolf, puh-leeezeee."

"This one has red eyes," the feminine voice said. "I want to eat them."

"I'm putting the werewolf on the curb. If we need to, we'll pick it up tomorrow. Okay?

More sighs.

"I'll barbecue it myself – if I have too. Okay?"

"Fine."

The water got choppy. Waves tossed her gently up and down. The awake and screaming part of Chiba's brain knew she was in a cart, that her head hurt like hell and something heavy and lifeless pinned down her left arm.

She tried to claw her way back to consciousness but the rocking lulled her back to sleep.

I miss my girls, was her last thought before going back under.

*****

8:24 pm, Nov. 2, 2020, 35 days after The Fog

Sam regained consciousness to find herself lying on her side on a couch that appeared dirty from a distance but was truly filthy up close. She blinked as the stale body odor embedded in the fibers of its gray and brown block pattern attacked her nostrils. She ran her fingers through her hair and idly brought her hand to her chest wondering why it hurt, tracing the edges of the open and bleeding cuts there, she tried to remember what happened.

"What's your name?" A voice she'd never heard before asked from beyond the edge of the couch. Sam tried to focus.

"Sam."

She swallowed and tried to sit up.

"Okay, maybe hold off on that for a minute." The voice was kind and steady – exactly the kind of voice you want to hear when you don't know what the fuck is going on. "Do you know your full name?"

"Yes, I want to sit up. This couch stinks."

"Okay." The voice was masculine. "Let me help you then."

Hands grasped her shoulders and held her steady as she flopped into sitting. Her eyes focused onto a shirtless ginger with masses of freckles across his face and shoulders.

"Is that better?" he asked.

"I don't know."

"Hi, Sam." Another person appeared behind the ginger. "Do you remember what happened?"

Sam licked her lips. The memory felt raw and dangerous. It was littered with warning signs. It oozed pus that might explode – spreading an infection through her thoughts. But that was too much to say at the moment, so she settled on: "Nope."

"Just heal her already, would you?" Dyn said – she remembered that voice. Sam struggled to focus on them but they were a yard away and nothing about that distance made sense.

"We can't," the ginger snapped. "How many times do we have to tell you? It doesn't work on her."

He held a white, glowing hand to Sam's chest. Its presence made her queasy.

"Oh, please stop that. That's terrible."

"See." The ginger pointed to her still bleeding chest.

Dyn came into muddy focus.

"I don't think you're trying hard enough," they replied, arms crossed over their expansive beer belly.

The other, the more authoritative tone, belonged to a pert blonde, who at the moment was clad only in a dirty bed sheet. She rolled her eyes. Without a word, she snatched a corkscrew from the card table and slammed it into Dyn's bicep. Blood spurted into the air.

"The FUCK!?"

She grabbed their arm. The woman's hands glowed pale white. The blood gushing down Dyn's arm slowed then stopped.

"Okay, fine." They gave up. "I believe you but why her?"

The room swam into focus. All the people were still there – huddled beneath blankets. The overwhelming, gut-punch reek of puke made Sam's stomach churn. Someone hadn't made it to the vomitorium. She desperately wanted to stab all of them with that corkscrew so she tilted her head back to look up at the ceiling instead. It was painted in delightful, garnish colors depicting scenes from Greek literature.

"Oh, this is nice," she muttered.

The blonde shrugged.

"She's The Morrigan."

"The Morrigan," Dyn sputtered. "What does that even mean? What kind of name is The Morrigan anyway?"

Sam realized she was staring at a very graphic rendering of an orgy.

"It's not her name," the ginger said. "I took a semester of Irish Mythology. It's her title – Queen of the Darkness."

"What did you say?" Dyn sounded like they were standing up now.

"Her title – Queen of the Darkness. You didn't know?

"FUCK!"

Sam glanced away from the fresco orgy to watch Dyn's meltdown.

"Fuck off!"

They spun around the temple and back kicked the flaming trash can. Sparks skittered across the stone floor.

"I knew it was too good to be true. I *knew* there was a catch. I *knew* it! I am SOBER for the first time in eight thousand years. This is *bullshit*."

Dyn paused, yanking on their greasy hair by the roots.

"I have to help her," they said. Then addressed the sad room at large. "We have to help her."

"Your dad won't like it," a tiny voice piped up from beyond the orgy pit.

"Fuck my dad! I want my gift back. Help or fucking leave and never come back."

What, in Sam's mind, appeared to be an over-sized dragonfly zipped toward her. A tiny, golden, naked man with sparkly wings hung in the air between her and Dyn.

"I brought her to Midtown two days ago," he squeaked.

Dyn dropped backward onto a shabby recliner at the news.

"Oh, fuck," they muttered, mouth slack.

Sam's brain fog cleared. She stood and confronted the little man with razor focus.

"Why? What's in Midtown?"

The room went silent. Sam spun in a circle, looking for someone to answer for the dread rising in her belly.

"What is in Midtown?"

Callie, sitting with her knees against her chest on the stone floor, didn't bother looking up from her thousand yard stare.

"It's the Meat Locker," she replied.

Sam snatched the little man out of the air.

"What is the Meat Locker? Is she still there?"

"Hey!" he yelled, high voice piercing the air. "Knock it off."

"He gets people to take him to Midtown," Dyn said. "There's a spell on it so no one can get out. This other guy lures them to a house, drugs them and these," they swallowed, these … cannibals take them to a cave where they eat them in my father's name. It gives him power."

The shadows in the room screamed. Sam let go of the little man clenched in her fist.

"Where is the cave?" Her voice sounded calm, but a thread of violence ran through every syllable.

The little man glanced at Dyn.

"You know the Grotto at Walker Ranch?" they said.

"Yeah."

"There ya go."

The little man got in her face.

"Look, just leave her," he said. "No one even likes her. She was a raging bi…"

The winged man exploded mid-air – blood and guts splattered to the floor. A tiny arm landed in Callie's hair.

Ignoring the shrieks and cries, she tore a gaping fissure in reality leading to the cave in the ocean cliff face. Dyn grabbed her arm.

"Give it back."

She pulled the cobwebs from her chest and slapped them onto Dyn's hand. The room sighed with relief as pleasure flowed through them again.

She stepped through the tear onto the sand, roaring black ocean at her back, and fell, vomiting, onto her face.

That word Dyn said was louder in this place. The noise of it bounced off the gray, striated cliffs. It lived in each grain of loose sand she tried to grasp. That word, that terrible word blew in on the rough ocean winds and splashed onto her face with each cresting wave. Yet, Sam couldn't hear it, see it or touch it, didn't even know what it was. Hell, she couldn't even spell it, but the word was inside of her – a seething hollow that split apart her soul. That word knew things about her.

She puked again. Her body emptying itself to make room for the expanding, nameless emptiness. The plastic container snapped under the weight of the word. One thought fought back against the rising emptiness in her mind.

Chiba. I need my Chiba back.

*****

7:45 pm, Nov. 2, 2020, 35 days after The Fog

Chiba awoke to muffled grunts of pain and the electric zing of a huge bug zapper. One of the grunts broke through and became wet hysterical cries.

"No. No more. Stop. Please stop."

She opened her eyes and couldn't comprehend what they saw. A man with jet-black hair, golden skin and one red eye sat with his legs hanging over the side of a stone altar. The stench of the place rolled over her. Chiba dry heaved only to discover a piece of cloth tied too tight across her mouth. Her eyes went wild and rolled back in her head. She was no longer in that cave. She was a five-year-old girl in her first day of foster care. They'd taken her pretty, yellow dress and given her a man's dirty t-shirt. Her foster 'brothers' shoved her to the floor, put their hands over her mouth and

…Chiba snapped back to this moment, to the crying man with one eye. She tried to breathe through the panic, but the gag wouldn't let her. Chiba jerked and realized her hands were bound over her head with a thick chain. She lay on the damp, rocky ground and convulsed, mewling in terror.

"Tomorrow's breakfast is awake." The woman's voice from earlier noted – dry as a bone. Her blonde hair in a ponytail, she wore a long, rubber apron over tight jeans and a black sweater. She looked like a yoga instructor slumming it for deals at the second hand shop after her mimosa brunch on the Westside.

"I got it." This was the voice whining about werewolves earlier. A lanky tech bro with russet hair, a neatly trimmed beard and thick, black 'statement' glasses stalked over to Chiba. He bent over her with a long stick. The huge bug zapper she heard earlier turned out to be a cattle prod. Her skin jumped. The pain, so quick and shocking, stopped her every thought. Her heart skipped several beats. He grabbed her chin.

"Shut the fuck up. Or you get this again. You understand?_

She nodded.

"Good."

He stalked back to the altar.

Tears rolled out of her eyes. She lay on that cold damp floor. Chiba knew this feeling so well. No one would believe her. No one would come for her. No one would save her.

*****

8:50 pm, Nov. 2, 2020, 35 days after The Fog

Sam clawed her way on her hands and knees through the sand to the cave thirty feet away. Walker Ranch State Park was owned by the Walker family one hundred years prior. The farmland, barn and Victorian-style houses sat less than a mile from the fifty-foot-tall, jagged, ocean cliffs. A series of paths led people to the edge of the Pacific Ocean. The Grotto was the only cave in that part of town. Rumor had it bootleggers used it during Prohibition. The opening was only tall enough for someone to crouch down to enter but once inside, it opened up into a fifteen-foot-tall cavern – long enough to park a Mac truck.

Sand flies flew into her face but she didn't have the strength to stand.

"What is wrong with you?"

She stood next to the dining room table, hands crossed over her fuzzy, pale blue sweater, blonde hair a halo in the overhead light.

As usual, when Sam was at her lowest, this special guest star appeared in her thoughts to make it all that much worse.

"Nuffin," she slurred, and then sputtered, trying to spit out the flies crawling into her mouth.

Screams emanated from the cave. She told herself they didn't sound like Chiba as her hands sunk into unruly sand. Sam tried to make her rebellious mind and body obey, to move faster, to walk but the word had devastated her so much she could only crawl.

"You're so angry. Why are you so angry?"

"Yer, visssouss bitch."

"No really, why are you so angry? What's wrong with you?"

"I ...Morrigan. Isss fine."

They had decorated the outside of the cave with trophies of their kills. Three heads on spikes and various bones – rib cages and swollen, rotting limbs proclaimed louder than screams what went on in this cave.

Sam rolled her eyes. So gauche. One does not adorn one's lair with the corpses of a teacher, a janitor and a pharmacist. One uses the bodies of one's mortal enemies slain in battle to show pride of victory – like Manny, whose throne was made of the bones of Spanish Conquistadors.

That laugh. Olga's frigid laugh. She wasn't trying to be cruel when she did it. She genuinely thought it was funny.

"You think you're special?"

Sam didn't have a snarky comeback for that. Her stomach empty, she paused to dry heave. Sensing an opening, her mother's spectre, the one that haunted the deepest corners of her mind, went in for the kill.

"Why can't you be perfect? I just want you to be perfect."

She asked Sam that question for years – usually at the dinner table. When forced into some semblance of familiarity, her mother would ask how her day was. It was a trap. It was *always* a trap.

"No one's going to love you if you're not perfect."

Her palms and knees rubbed raw in the sand. Her eyes rolled back in her head as she fought the need to pass out. This was her mother's response when Sam acted out – when she yelled, or ate too much, or got good grades or breathed. And Olga said it over and over and over again until a tiny part of Sam believed her.

"Chiba lo-o-o-ves me."

Sam had reached the entrance of the Grotto.

"Look where that got her. You think you're a goddess. You can't even keep your friends alive. What's wrong with you?"

"Chiba loves me," Sam whispered as she crawled into the mouth of hell.

*****

8:57 pm, Nov. 2, 2020, 35 days after The Fog

They cut off the man's leg at the thigh joint – twisting and snapping as he shrieked. Then they cauterized the wound with a torch. During the process, they discovered that the red-eyed man was a shape shifter. The yoga instructor tortured him with the prod, making him turn into animal after animal while the other two roasted his leg on a fire.

The smell of cooking flesh made Chiba's stomach roil. Vomit rose up in her but she realized the gag in her mouth could make her aspirate so she pushed it down – panicked, breathing through her nose. Her extended arms shook and cramped but she couldn't make herself move. Any sound might draw attention, she learned to be quiet a long time ago.

Chiba stared at the mouth of the cave – counting her breaths, and fought to be grateful for each one. She tried to pretend Danny was watching a shitty horror movie while she stared off into space during the gory parts.

Thirty-five

The shadows moved. She blinked.

Thirty-seven

It had to be her imagination. The need for help was so dire she was hallucinating.

Forty

But the shadow kept moving, small and steady, crawling across the floor, accompanied by the shuffle of sand. Chiba skipped a breath. The shadow paused. Sam's pale, round face appeared as she looked up, searching the cave. She found Chiba in the muted torchlight and swayed.

Chiba couldn't comprehend what she was seeing. Sam was there but this was not her Sam. Her Sam would have strolled into this cave with bravado and rage. Panic filled Chiba.

Maybe she'd been drugged too.

Sam crawled to Chiba. She leaned against the cave wall for support. Chiba caught a whiff of vomit. Sam held her finger to her lips. Her eyes rolled back into her head and Chiba squeaked. Sam squeezed her eyes shut. With a deep breath, she opened them. Then she reached out with a wobbly hand and snapped the chains on Chiba's wrists. She clawed the gag off her mouth.

"What is…" Chiba mouthed, but before she could finish Sam gathered the back of her coat in her hand, whispered "Carl" and flung Chiba at the cave's entrance.

She heard the flutter of wings and the shriek of a raven before being swallowed up into blackness. The howls of the damned assaulted her ears. Their hands tore at her. Chiba couldn't breathe. She flailed at the nothingness. She scratched at her useless throat and then, suddenly, another presence was there – not warm, not exactly kind, but as steady as gravity. A soft, papery hand held her own. It whispered incomprehensible words in her ear and Chiba found that she could breathe. The howls abated.

Chiba blinked. She was kneeling in the small circle of light outside the gray, cement bathrooms of Walker Ranch State Park. It felt like hours had passed. She'd taken the girls here a week before The Fog. The Orange Monstrosity was parked between the bike rack and the recycling bin. Danny's trusty baseball bat sat in the cart. A large raven, who Chiba assumed was Carl, stood on the top of the green, metal recycling bin. He cawed at her. Sam was nowhere to be found.

"Is this Walker Ranch?" she asked the bird.

He ignored her, staring out into the night.

"I know you understand me."

Blinking scratched her eyes. Her throat felt like a desert, she was so dehydrated.

The bird nodded.

"Were we at the Grotto?"

He nodded.

"Is Sam still there? Is she in danger?"

Did Timmy fall down the well, boy?

Again, he nodded.

Chiba shivered against the cold. Her adrenaline spiked. She stared down the parking lot that led to the highway back to her house. She wanted her bed, to hold her girls, to eat something. For a split second, she thought about it – getting on that bike and going home.

But rage grew in her heart.

"Oh, fuck that noise."

Chiba set her shoulders, hopped on the bike and turned in the opposite direction – to the dirt trails back to the Grotto.

They think they can take and take and no one will stop them? They took that poor man's leg. What else have they taken? Who else have they done this to?

The sun was starting to rise. The black night sky faded into a dark, purple bruise. The temperature dropped. Chiba made a sharp right onto the trail that was barely wide enough for the cart. The Orange Monstrosity was not built for this kind of terrain. The bumps and starts made her teeth rattle.

They always want something from me. My body. My innocence. My childhood. Hell, my own fucking name.

Chiba turned the electric motor to twenty mph as the Orange Monstrosity careened up the hill and over the washed out divots in the trail. The empty cart on the back jumped, swinging wildly. The light illuminated a raccoon ambling across the path. She rang the cheerful silver bell in warning. The raccoon flipped her off as it sauntered off the trail.

You don't get my best friend! You hear me! She's mine! And you aren't taking her away from me! You hear me, cannibal assholes!

Ten years ago, the new girl at work sat down across from her at the picnic table without asking. She introduced herself and started eating her sandwich while Chiba threw her The Most Disdainful Look. The new girl, ignoring the glare that had shriveled a lesser woman's soul, kept eating and said:

"You seem cool. Do you wanna be friends?"

Chiba wouldn't believe it at first, but she kept showing up everyday at that picnic table – being nice. Chiba tried to half-heartedly push her away. Her trauma wouldn't let her trust that this woman really wanted to be her friend, but Sam would just smile through her bullshit and ask if she wanted to go out drinking later.

Six years later, Sam was joking about an article she read on how if you're friends with someone for seven years then you're probably going to be friends forever.

"You have about a year to get out before you're stuck with me."

Chiba looked up from her phone, legs tucked beneath her on the red couch.

"You've shown me kindness. I'm not going anywhere."

The cart stabilized. Chiba spared a glance behind her and saw Carl sitting on the back rail.

Two more sharp turns, a near miss that almost sent her over the cliff and Chiba arrived at the brown marker pointing to the trail leading down to the Grotto. She hopped off and pulled the bat from the cart. Carl shrieked at her.

"What?"

His chest broadened and he made a low hacking noise from deep within his body.

"Don't you dare puke on me. I don't have time for that."

Chiba backed away as Carl vomited up a large object. It clunked as it dropped into the cart. She pulled the headlight off the front of the bike and leaned over to see what it was. Lying on the particle board floor was an obsidian, flint dagger. The rifling along the blade was perfectly symmetrical. A simple, brown, leather cord was wrapped around the handle. Something about the weapon made Chiba pause.

"Is this for me?"

He nodded.

She picked the dagger up with two fingers and went to wipe the bird bile off on her sleeve. Carl screamed in protest.

"Don't do that?"

He nodded emphatically.

"Can I put it in my pocket?"

Carl thought for a second and nodded. She slid the weapon into her pocket, zipped it shut and with the flashlight in her left hand and the bat slung over her right shoulder, headed down the steep trail to the Grotto.

As the sky lightened to dark blue, Chiba hoped that whatever Sam was, it made her less likely to be eaten. It wasn't until she reached the beach that Chiba noticed the black shapes soaring overhead. Ravens and crows – hundreds of them swooped and dived in the ocean breezes.

Without warning, Carl landed on her shoulder.

"The fuck, bird?"

She tried to shake him off but he wouldn't budge.

"Fine."

Chiba clicked off the headlight, unzipped her pocket and pulled the dagger out. She bent double and walked into the low cave entrance. Carl scrunched down low, becoming half his size.

"I am not eating *this*."

"Barbecue sauce."

"Barbecue sauce will not fix this, Andrew," the tech bro said. "Look at her. There is something wrong with her. She's covered in vomit. She's drooling and she smells weird. And! And, she appeared out of nowhere. What's that about? Fuck, no. Absolutely not."

"Barbecue sauce," Andrew repeated.

"Fuck you and fuck your barbecue sauce."

"I think she smells amazing."

Chiba emerged from the low entrance to see Sam sitting next to the shape shifter. Her arms were chained overhead. The blonde sniffed Sam's hair. She sliced into Sam's forearm with a paring knife and licked the black blood streaming down.

"Let's eat her," she said, eyes gleaming wild in the torchlight.

"Her blood is *black*?" The tech bro stepped back. "*Hell* na and if you say barbecue sauce one more time, I'm going to eat *you*."

He addressed the third person that Chiba hadn't noticed before – a balding, middle-aged, middle-management, so bland as to be utterly nondescript, man.

"Whatever, Kyle," Andrew said.

The yoga lady stumbled back – her skin ashen.

"I don't feel so good," she said, before projectile vomiting black bile.

"See!" Kyle said, pointing at Sam. "I was right!"

The room exploded. Hundreds of birds raced into the cavern. Their shrieks echoed off the rock walls into a deafening crescendo. They knocked Chiba over. She landed hard on one knee. It cracked as it hit a rock. The knife flew from her hand. A flurry of ravens harassed the cannibals. They landed on the yoga lady's back, pushing her to the ground. Three crows chittered to each other as they picked the gristle from a thigh bone lying in the corner.

Kyle flailed and ran for the exit. Chiba tossed the bat at his gangly legs. He tripped and fell. A half-dozen ravens settled onto his back.

Carl snatched up the obsidian knife in his beak. He flew through the chaos, dodging and weaving as his brethren fluttered in the confines of the cave, straight to Sam. Feathers shimmering in the torchlight, the raven landed on Sam's lap. Her eyes were rolled back. Frothy spit gathered at the corners of her lips. Chiba yelled at him to stop. She tried to stand but her knee gave way. In a motion strangely human, the bird aimed the dagger and plunged it into Sam's chest – close to her heart.

"No!" Chiba yelled.

The dagger sliced through Sam's hoodie and Carl flew from her lap. The knife hung there, the leather handle protruding from her body like an obscenity. The blade transformed into black smoke. Its leather binding fell onto Sam's lap. She inhaled the smoke deep into her lungs. The gaping wound in her chest knit itself back together.

Sam wailed. A sharp, guttural keening rose from her belly, out of her mouth and filled the cave with unimaginable loss. The birds froze and swiveled their heads in her direction as one.

Part of Chiba wanted her to stop. The pain of it hurt her soul, but she knew that same agony and it was nice, in its way, to hear this sorrow come out of someone else's mouth.

As abruptly as it started, the keening stopped. Sam moved so fast it made Chiba dizzy. With a crack, the chains were empty, broken and swinging. A black, human-sized tear appeared in the center of the cave.

"Leave," Sam bellowed.

The birds, quiet, and with a contrite air, flew out of the cave. Chiba blinked and the three cannibals lay piled in a circle in the corner next to the altar. Sam knelt over a bunch of body parts toward the entrance of the cave murmuring. She gathered them carefully up in her arms. Cradling them, she walked to the tear. Chiba gasped when she saw the lizard girl from Davey's house. One half of her face was gone, jawbone and teeth exposed. The girl blinked at Chiba before Sam walked with her through the tear in reality. After many long moments in the cave, with only the sound of the yoga lady's gagging to keep her company, she reappeared.

She stood before the shape shifter. He sat balanced on the stone altar in the form of a walrus. His lower half was gone and his eyes were closed. She grasped the top edge of one of his flippers.

"Nukilik Qappik, please look at me."

The walrus's one remaining red eye fluttered open.

"Have you come to take me, Death?" he asked in a wholly human voice.

"Do you wish to die?"

"No." His answer was immediate. Definite.

"Then I'm here to take you to the hospital. But your current form is unwieldy. I know it's difficult, but can you change back please?"

The walrus grunted.

"You calling me fat?"

Sam threw back her head and giggled.

"I'm calling you beautiful but getting you onto a gurney in that form is going to be impossible."

Nukilik inhaled and exhaled, tusks rising with the effort.

"Okay."

He slowly, painfully, inch by inch returned to human form. Sam held his hand through all of it.

"Well done."

She picked him up, carried him through the tear and after too many long moments for Chiba to count, returned. The rip healed.

Sam knelt on the ground before her.

"Hey, Chibs, long time no see."

"I didn't think you would come," Chiba said as she threw her arms around Sam's neck.

Sam wanted to squeeze her as hard as she could so she would feel how terrified she'd been, how glad she was to see her safe and how much she meant to her. Sam willed all her love for her friend to flow through her arm muscles. She buried her head in Chiba's shoulder and sobbed.

"Thank you for saving me. My crows and ravens can't go inside where people are present without an escort or invitation."

"Oh, ya know." Chiba pulled away from her. "I didn't do much. Thank you for saving me too."

Sam laughed at that and wiped away her own tears.

"Oh, ya know, I didn't do much."

"I can't cry. I'm too dehydrated."

"Oh, shit." Sam pulled a water bottle from her hoodie. "Here."

"I need to get out of here."

The cannibals were banging against some kind of invisible force field that kept them in place. Chiba needed to be as far away as possible. She tried to stand but her knee gave way. Sam caught her. With one arm around her friend, she assessed the situation and pulled a bright, orange sled from her hoodie.

"What? Am I ten years old?"

"Yes, Snarkypants McGee, you are, and we're going sledding."

Chiba maneuvered herself onto the sled and Sam pulled her out of the cave. Some of the ravens still soared overhead — catching the ocean thermals. It was an impossibly cold morning. The wet chill settled into Chiba's bones. Sam parked the sled a few feet from the cave. The rising sun transformed the bruised night sky to blazing orange, pinks and yellows.

Sam pulled a camp chair from her hoodie.

"Are you okay with sitting here for a minute? I need to deal with them."

She cocked her head toward the Grotto.

"Is it gonna take long?"

Chiba had already spent too much time away from her girls and felt the terrible need to see them again.

"Like five, ten minutes. Maybe fifteen."

"Okay," Chiba said and settled onto the camp chair and tried to relax, but the freezing cold wouldn't let her. Her teeth chattered. Her bones ached.

Sam gnawed at her lip.

"I'm fine. Just go do what you need to do."

Ignoring her, Sam pulled out a thick, puffy, quilt, along with gloves and a hat. She plopped the knitted cap on Chiba's head but kept gnawing on her lip.

"This is fine. Thank you."

"Your body temperature is too low. You're incredibly dehydrated. You haven't eaten in days and I can't make fire."

At Chiba's look, she shrugged, vaguely ashamed.

"Fire isn't in my nature."

She tapped her forehead and snapped her fingers. A banana, another bottle of water, an energy drink and several packets of hand warmers were pulled from her hoodie.

"You're ridiculous."

"Thank you," Sam said, with a proud smile. "Carl, keep an eye on her please. I'll be right back."

The bird cawed in response from a rock near the cliff face.

"Not today, Carl!" Sam yelled back, shoulders rising to her ears in annoyance. "Not, fucking, today!"

Then she stormed up the sand to the Grotto.

She opened the thermos and peered inside – half afraid it was blood. Floating at the top were tiny marshmallows.

"Hey," she yelled at Sam. "This is hot chocolate. How'd you know I like hot chocolate?"

She turned back.

"You totally thought it was blood, didn't you?"

"Okay… yeah… I did."

"At Christmas, probably. That seems like something you'd mention at Christmas, right?"

Chiba sipped the cocoa as Sam walked to the cave.

"Yeah, Christmas."

She leaned her head back against the chair and closed her eyes –
feeling warm for the first time in days.

"Okay, I'm done. Let's go."

"What? So fast?"

Chiba was certain she'd only shut her eyes for a moment.

"Well," Sam gestured broadly, "you were waiting."

"Did you kill them?"

"No, I didn't kill them. Let's go."

"But you can't let them go."

"I didn't let them go."

"But you punished them?"

"Yes, I did terrible things to them. Let's get you to the
hospital."

Chiba stood up on one leg. The sand made her wobble.

"I need to see. I need to know they can't hurt me or my kids."

Sam rubbed her eyes and shoved her hair back from her face.

"It's not nice, Chibs." Sam didn't feel ashamed of what she was
and yet the thought of Chiba seeing the results of her work made
her uncomfortable. "It might give you nightmares – what I did to
them."

"I don't care," she said, hopping toward the cave without
making any progress against the sand dunes. "I need to see."

Sam sighed, pulling at her hair.

"Fine."

She got out the sled and dragged Chiba back into the cave. The
morning sun cast bright light through the entrance illuminating
most of the cave but Sam pulled a flashlight from her hoodie and
handed it to Chiba anyway.

She couldn't believe this was the same place. It felt clean – as
pristine as a dank cavern could be. The bones and rotting flesh
were gone. The sickening, sweet stench of decay had been replaced
by damp earthiness. The altar at the far end was smashed to gray
bits of rubble.

"What happened to the dead bodies?" Chiba asked Sam as she helped her out of the sled.

"Disposed of per their owners wishes."

"Seriously? That fast?"

"Goddess," Sam said and pointed to her own face.

"Fair," Chiba said as she looked around the cave, remembering how her girls were running around it trying to scare each other a few weeks ago. "Where are they?"

"Chibs, it's gross, okay? What I did to them is gross. You may not want to see…"

"Show me so I can sleep at night."

"Fine," Sam said and waved her arm. "Show yourselves."

Three puddles of cave water resolved into human… scratch that, Chiba thought, *human-like* forms.

"Holy shit, Sam," Chiba breathed. "What did you do?"

The yoga lady lay on her side, mouth sewn shut with thick black cord. Dark ichor dripped from her ears, out of her nose and her empty eye socket. Her swollen limbs were contorted at impossible angles.

"I broke," Sam thought about it for a second, "most of their bones."

Chiba shined the light on the yoga lady's ashen face. In response, desperate mewling noises came from her throat.

"But they'll die soon." Chiba could not have said why that upset her.

"See," Sam replied with no small amount of pride. "They won't."

She knelt to face the yoga lady. The woman reached for Sam with backward fingers and a crooked hand.

"I have closed the Gates of Death to you all."

Sam grabbed the woman's chin.

"None of you will die. You will live. You will feel every agonizing second as your body decays and rots, your soul achingly ripped to shreds as it follows your atoms into new forms while you, inch by excruciating inch, go mad. Death is kindness and I have none for you."

Sam stood and faced Chiba. She froze at the dumbfounded look on her friend's face. It dawned on her that Chiba had never seen this side of her before and echoes of Olga's judgment and rejection made her stomach fill with lead.

"That was so badass," Chiba said.

"You're not creeped out?"

Chiba held up her arm.

"I got goosebumps, that was so cool."

Sam grinned from ear to ear.

"Yay."

They exited the cave and began negotiations on how to get Chiba up the slope.

"I'll hop," Chiba said.

"Absolutely not. How about I carry you? Piggyback?"

"I'm way too heavy. It's too far."

"Am strong like bull," Sam said in a terrible Russian accent. "Is no trouble."

"No, I'm fine."

"Your knee cap is cracked." Sam held up a hand and counted. "You're dehydrated. You haven't eaten in days. Your body temp is too low. You need stitches for the cut on your face. I'm pretty sure you have a concussion. I don't know what the hell that guy drugged you with. I can keep going or you can hop on. Unless you want to travel by tear?"

"Ugh, no," Chiba said, relenting. She hopped onto Sam's back. "That was awful. I can't believe you do that all the time."

"Meh, doesn't bother me."

"But the screaming, and they try to grab you."

"Oh, yeah, no, they don't get anywhere near me."

"Huh," Chiba said, as Sam started up the narrow, winding path. Thick scrub edged each side of the trail. A small stream criss-crossed the trail at various points making the ground slick.

"Why were you like that?" They'd gone more than fifteen feet and Sam wasn't wheezing so she relaxed a bit. "Did Davey drug you too?"

"Davey drugged you?" Sam could hardly believe it. She stepped over a rocky patch. "Wait. Which Davey? Sanchez, Hawley or McAllister?"

"McAllister."

"That fucker."

"Right?"

"I was gonna say, I can't imagine Davey Hawley doing such a thing," Sam said, skirting sideways to avoid hitting Chiba's leg on a rock.

"Oh, same, he's way too nice."

She noticed that Sam had changed the subject but she couldn't let it go.

"So… are you going to tell me what happened?"

"I mean it's not a big deal. It's just sort of weird. I asked the god Dionysus where you were and they told me, but first they said a word and it fucked me up."

"Until a bird stabbed you?"

"Oh, right, Carl says that was medicine – like an adrenaline shot."

It was quiet between them. The creatures around them stirred and trilled, searching for breakfast or sunlight to warm them against the night's chill.

"Sam…"

She paused on the trail, bracing herself in case she passed out.

"Nyx. The word was 'Nyx' and I don't know why."

They both heard it in Sam's voice – the tension, the fear, all the things she refused to face. Sam felt Chiba nod against her back.

"Okay, well, you'll figure it out. I know you will."

"Thanks, yeah, I hope so because that was bullshit."

They reached the top of the small trail where it joined with the larger dirt road paralleling the cliff edge. The Orange Monstrosity was right where Chiba left it.

As Sam helped Chiba into the cart, piling up pillows underneath her, a trim woman in white spandex shorts and sports bra jogged by, brown ponytail swinging as she ran.

They exchanged glances.

"Is she kidding?"

"Is this a joke?"

"She can't be serious… It's the APOCALYPSE!" Sam yelled after her. "In fact, it's probably not a good idea! There are monsters! …she's not listening."

She turned to Chiba.

"Maybe she doesn't know? No, she has to know."

"She has to know. Right?"

Chiba shrugged and sunk further into the cart. The tsunami was back – pulling her limbs and eyelids further into the raging sea. It hauled her deeper and deeper under. Spinning, she sunk farther down than she'd been in years. Past the broken planks of her lifeboat and into the nightmares she grew up with. The rational part of her mind could only sigh at how long it would take her to pull herself out again.

"Chiba!"

"What?"

"Honey, you can't fall asleep."

Chiba rubbed her eyes.

"So tired."

"Concussion, Chiba," Sam yelped. "Concussion."

Then Sam proceeded to break out into the World's Worst Rendition of "The Rocky Road to Dublin," while demanding Chiba sing along. As she sped toward the Old Beeman Building,

Sam thanked the Holy Darkness that Walker Ranch was only a twenty-minute bike ride away as she belted out "Hunt the Hare and turn her down the rocky road" for the third time.

"You're still tone deaf?" Chiba whined, in the same voice Malak used to try to get out of bedtime. Sam skidded to a halt in the parking lot. "How? You're a goddess. How can a goddess be tone deaf?"

Chiba normally lied to Sam's face out of kindness, telling her that her singing was "fine." So Sam knew Chiba was in a bad way as she helped her out of the cart. If Sam had been less worried about her best friend, she might have noticed how much the Old Beeman Building had changed in the past three days. There were no lines of desperate people. The tables had disappeared. Someone planted roses and Mexican sage at the entrance and there was a sign that flashed 'Emergency Room/Hospital' in English, Spanish, Tagalog and then said it out loud in each of those languages.

Across the bay doors, someone spray painted in thick, red letters: I WANT TO GO BACK.

"Well, that's Brigid's realm, honey."

"Who's Brigid? Where are we?"

"We're at the hospital."

"I don't want to go to the hospital." Chiba's whole demeanor changed – became smaller, her movements wild.

"Honey, you have to go to the hospital. You're hurt."

"I don't want to!" Chiba shoved at the arm Sam had wrapped around her waist. "Leave me alone."

She did not relinquish her hold.

A security guard, with a white uniform shirt, black pants and far too many buttons and pins, walked out of the door.

"Is everything okay here?" He hiked up his sagging pants with his own sense of self importance.

"Everything's fine. She needs to be seen. She's injured."

"No!" Chiba wedged her arms into Sam's side and pushed. "Everything is NOT fine. I'm FINE. I don't need to go to the hospital. They can't help me. They never help me. I want to *go home*."

"Ma'am, I need you to calm down."

In Chiba's mind, he was every cop who talked down to her when she told them, in detail, what was done to her. Their blank, uninterested faces over the notebook. She needed his help and to him she was just another homeless person, a street annoyance, more paperwork he had to do before he got to go home, anything but a human being.

"Uh, huh. He punched you in the head? Then what?"

"I will not calm down!" Chiba shouted in his face.

He grabbed her shoulder and yelled back.

"Ma'am!"

"Do not touch me!" Chiba screamed and shoved him – the fear and rage of the past three days pushing her past the edge.

He stood close enough that Sam could smell the sweetness of his cheap cologne and the stench of fear he tried so desperately to cover up. She grabbed his forearm and yanked his hand from Chiba's shoulder.

"Wanna keep this life?" Her voice was low and steady – as if the answer were completely unimportant because, to her, it was.

"Wha-a-aa-at?" His eyes darted back and forth between her and Chiba.

"I asked you if you want to keep this life of yours."

She twisted his ham hock of a forearm at an absurd angle. He danced on his toes in pain and in a futile effort to pull his body from her grip. The deadly calm of her stilled his bouncing movements. Yet, he could not answer.

"I understand this is confusing for you. You have been conditioned to think of people like us as weak, helpless – even. Yet, your animal brain is screaming that you are in mortal danger." She paused to let it sink in. "Be smart enough to listen to your animal brain."

He backed away and nodded. She released his arm.

"Do not ever manhandle or yell at a trauma victim," Sam spat at him.

"S-ss-sorry."

"Don't say sorry to me. Apologize to her."

"Sorry," he said to Chiba, who was crying into Sam's shoulder. He stood, awkward, unsure of what to do with his hands.

"Is Dr. Williams here?" Sam asked.

"I – yes."

"Get her."

Still he stood, shuffling his feet against his cognitive dissonance.

"Now!" Sam barked. "Go!"

She tilted her head back and prayed to the Holy Darkness that he would be fleet footed. The wind kicked up, ruffling the branches of the eucalyptus trees. The sun was warm and the breeze was just cool enough. Under different circumstances, it might have been a pleasant day.

"They won't believe me," Chiba cried into her shoulder. "They won't help me. They never help me. They never believe me. They're going to call me a liar. They're going to make me jump through hoops. They don't believe me. They never help me. They never believe me. I want to go home. Just take me home."

Sam patted her back with her free hand. Helpless rage boiled in her veins as morning clouds drifted across the sky.

"They're going to help you this time," Sam said, as she glared resolutely at the trees. Chiba was too far gone to hear the threat in her voice.

Dr. Williams jogged out of the double doors of the Old Beeman Building like every emergency room doctor in every TV show ever – white coat trailing dramatically, stethoscope askew. Two nurses with a gurney were hot on her heels.

Sam closed her eyes in relief.

"Thank the Holy fucking Darkness," she breathed. "An adult."

Sam moved slightly so Chiba could see Dr. Williams.

"The doctor's here, Chiba," she said. Sam met the doctor's eyes. "She's going to believe you and she's going to help you, okay?"

The doctor nodded and her total comprehension made Sam's shoulders relax.

"Hello, Chiba. I'm Dr. Williams. I'm going to do everything I can to help you, okay? And I believe you."

Then the doctor tapped the back of Chiba's head. White light flashed. She collapsed in Sam's arms.

"The hell," Sam said.

"It's easier for everyone – especially her," Dr. Williams replied. "Put her on the stretcher."

Sam did as she was told and followed the doctor and nurses as they wheeled Chiba's lank body through the glass double doors.

The interior, of what was a cement receiving bay, had been transformed into a gleaming, white waiting room, with soothing light, bright greenery, comfy chairs and a round desk in the center of the room.

Sam paused for a moment to absorb the change. She spun around to take it all in.

"Holy shit."

The doctor had already rolled Chiba down the hallway at the far end of the room. Sam hurried to follow them. A large, uniformed, but polite troll stood in her way.

"I'm sorry," he said and held up his hand. "This is a restricted area. Doctors and patients only."

Sam rolled her eyes, put her hand on his chest and moved him out of the way. She yanked open the door marked 'Emergency' to find a Dr. Williams and a crew of nurses bustling back and forth around Chiba. They all stopped when she walked in.

"Show me your hands," Sam demanded of the room at large.

Dr. Williams picked up a clipboard.

"You need to leave. We'll take care of her from here. Thank you for your concern."

Sam's fists shook at her sides – all adrenaline gone.

"I am not gonna repeat myself." Her voice quavered. She tried to remember who she was, but her best friend was lying, small and fragile, in a room full of strangers because Sam couldn't protect her.

"No one gets near her who is not a Sworn Acolyte. Show me your hands or get the fuck out of this room."

Dr. Williams, sensing she wasn't going to win this one, nodded and held up her hands. They glowed – a soft light that made Sam's head hurt. One by one, two nurses and an orderly held up their hands. The collective brightness made Sam's stomach roil. A nurse on the other side of Chiba's stretcher stepped back, tucking her hands into the pockets of her scrubs.

"I don't have to show you anything," she spat. "I have rights."

Without a sound, Sam leapt over the stretcher to stand between the pinch-faced, dark-haired woman and Chiba.

"Do you know what I am, Pamela Cherie Giancarlo?" Sam asked, tilting her chin like a bird searching its prey.

"You?" She backed further away, her shoulder bumping into the wall. "You're nothing. You're a shadow." Her voice was high and twangy. Sweat dripped from her milquetoast skin.

"Show me your hands," Sam whispered.

"Pam, show her your hands and we can get back to work, please," Dr. Williams said. "This is not a big deal at all, okay? I know her presence is … grating. Just show her that you've sworn the oath."

The nurse pulled a scalpel from her pocket and pointed it at Sam. A nurse in red scrubs gasped and covered his mouth.

"He will triumph over you," Pamela said. "You're nothing to him."

"I killed him once, you know," Sam said, stepping toward her.

"Lies! You are The Shadow Liar. He will bring the White Light of Truth. He will destroy you. He is the light of all goodness in the world. He will bring us back to what we were before. He will cleanse the world of your filth."

She held the scalpel to her own throat.

"Through him, I will escape you."

No one saw Sam move.

She grabbed the nurse's hand and squeezed. The small bones popped and broke through her skin. Blood burst through their clasped hands. The nurse screamed.

"No one escapes me," Sam whispered. "I see you, Pamela Cherie Giancarlo and the three lives you took under this roof – in his name. Again, I ask, do you know what I am?"

The nurse responded with another scream, but it died as it became the shriek of a raven with a broken wing. Sam tore a small hole in reality, snatched the raven up by the neck and tossed the bird through the hole. She turned back to the room at large. The nurses and Dr. Williams gaped at her.

"What?" Sam asked, with a shrug. "She's not dead. She's in the parking lot. You can see for yourself."

"Come with me," Dr. Williams snapped. "Now."

Feeling a little like she had just been called to the principal's office, Sam yelled for Carl.

The raven appeared, too tall, and absurdly out of place, on the metal instrument table next to the stretcher.

"Absolutely not," Dr. Williams said.

"Either I go and he stays or I stay and he goes. Pick one."

The doctor, realizing this was another battle she wasn't going to win, sighed and rubbed her forehead.

"Fine," she muttered.

Sam followed Dr. Williams through a maze of makeshift corridors. Thin, opaque walls were propped up with bamboo rods. Sam thought they were wedged into the ceiling until she saw the broken concrete around each shoot.

"What are the walls made of?"

"Plastic, I think. Here."

She stopped before a dusty, glass and wood office door with crooked, plastic blinds. The glass read: 'PLANT FOREMAN' in black, block letters. The cramped office, with its dark, particle board 'wood' desk and shelves reminded Sam of some 70s nightmare. Dust caked the tops of brown file boxes. A low cot with a red sleeping bag and a few toiletries were the only new items in the room. Dr. Williams' leather jacket hung from the wooden coat rack in the corner.

"Sit," she said, gesturing to the wide, mid-century modern chair before the desk. She pulled a small black bag, an ancient bottle of whiskey and two glasses from one of the desk drawers.

"You're injured."

"Huh? What? No, I'm not."

Sam had no idea what she was talking about.

"Roll up your sleeve," Dr. Williams said, with a nod.

Realizing the sleeve of her hoodie felt heavy and damp, Sam pulled it up to reveal the three-inch slice the cannibal gouged into her forearm.

"Shit, forgot about that."

Inky blood burbled and oozed too fast from the wound and ran down Sam's arm.

"Fuck."

She pulled the hoodie back down and clutched her wrist. Dr. Williams poured five fingers of whiskey into each glass.

"That," Dr. Williams gestured with the glass before knocking back the alcohol, "Should have killed you about thirty minutes ago."

"Well, Dr. Williams, I'm kind of already dead."

"Call me Jeddah," the doctor belched, "and no, technically, you're not. Your entire existence is super annoying, but dead? No. Just no. And don't worry about this." She waved at the empty glass. "I'll have one of my nurses detox me before I go back on duty."

Jeddah wobbled before grabbing the chair behind the desk with both hands and, using it as a crutch, rolled over next to Sam. It took her two tries to actually sit on the chair without pushing it away. She unzipped the black bag to reveal a suture kit.

"We are going to have to do this the old fashioned way," she said, pulling on black plastic gloves with a snap.

"Jeddah, my blood is dangerous. I don't think…"

"Is fine," the doctor slurred. "Is so fine. Raquel said it's fine. I'm safe as long as I don't drink your blood? Resonance-y frequencysss and all that. Why would I drink it, anyway? So gross."

The doctor snapped open an iodine swab and cleaned out the area around the cut. The liquid bubbled and hissed when it made contact with Sam's blood. An acrid stench filled the air.

"Thass not supposed to happen," Jeddah said, staring at the wound.

"It's fine."

"I need to sterilize the area."

"Do you really think anything can live on my skin?"

"Fair point," Jeddah replied. She held up the bottle of anesthetic and weighed her odds.

"Don't bother. It's not worth the risk."

The doctor shrugged and put it down.

Sitting so close, Sam could see the deep circles beneath her eyes, the fine lines of exhaustion around Jeddah's mouth and the gray pallor of her skin.

"When was the last time you slept?"

"Sleep? Pssshhhh. Tossshhhh. Sleep. I'm a doctor. We don't sleep. Roll up the thingy."

"You always a light weight?"

"Dunno," the doctor replied. "Don't drink much."

She held up five fingers.

"Four? Four times?"

"And you want to operate on me?" Sam asked.

"Suturing?" Jeddah laughed. "She'll be right. I can suture blindfolded. I did once, you know."

Eyes crossed, tongue tucked into the corner of her mouth, she took four – no, five tries to pluck the needle out of the plastic packet with her forceps. Sam pulled her arm away.

"It was in medical school. On a bet. I won. Of course. Didn't peek or nothing. Gimme."

Sam sighed. Not seeing any other option, she picked up the glass and tossed back the ancient, tasteless whiskey. With a grimace, she put her arm back on the table and reminded herself that she'd done much dumber shit and survived – mostly.

She waved her hand over the suture needle and thread, changing its nature so it wouldn't disintegrate inside her body.

Jeddah leaned over her arm and dabbed at it with cotton pads. When Sam's black blood was cleared from the wound, she sunk the needle into the layers of her skin. She exhaled through the pain. True to her word, the doctor spun the thread around the forceps, tying it even and tight.

"I thought this would end, you know?" Jeddah said, as she snipped the thread. "That we could go back to how it was. Build another hospital, help people. Wally? The security guard. He used to manage a restaurant. His daughter died here."

The needle pierced another layer. Jeddah fell into a slow rhythm as the words poured out. Bury the needle. Twirl the thread. Connect the lines. Snip.

"Conal made the werewolf boy kill her as an example. She was thirteen."

Bury the needle.

"He says he feels close to her here. So I told him he could stay. We need help."

Twirl the thread.

"I've known Pam for years," Jeddah confessed. "She was a good nurse. Took care of her patients. Listened to orders but didn't take anyone's shit. I vouched for her, ya know? It feels like my fault."

Connect the lines.

"It's not. You're doing your best under impossible circumstances. There's no way you could have known."

"Yeah, well, still feels like it is my fault, ya know? And those people … those people you brought in…"

She paused and raised her head, tears in her eyes.

"This job doesn't get to me. It doesn't get to me. I leave it here. I go home. But I can't stop thinking about it. Someone did that to them – for power. It's all narra, isn't it?"

She wiped her eyes on her sleeve.

"Raquel's not like that. She just helps. She wants to help."

Sam continued to study the wall behind the desk – filled with yellowing paper, machine parts and dust.

Snip.

Jeddah put the needle and thread down. She stood, swaying

"Can't go back can we? They won't let us. They never let us. I miss my home, ya know? I miss the land. It's so beautiful. It's my heart. My heart. My heart is broken."

Sam put her hand on Jeddah's forearm.

"You should sit. I think the exhaustion is getting to you."

"I'm fine," Jeddah said. "I'm a doctor, aren't I? People look to me to help. I have people to help. So many hurt people. I'm going to help them."

"Raquel," Sam prayed to the Goddess of this Temple, "her blood pressure and heart rate are too high. Way too high. You need to do something. Your acolyte is in danger."

"No," Jeddah said. "It's fine. I'm fine."

The blood drained from her face. White light flashed around her and she collapsed. Sam barely caught her before she hit the filthy cement floor. She checked Jeddah's pulse. It was slowing.

"For fuck's sake, Raquel. Warn me next time."

*****

9:43 am, Nov. 3, 2020, 36 days after The Fog

Paul David McAllister lounged on a dirty mattress on the floor of his living room. His feet were propped up on the couch next to the muttering werewolf. His back rested on several pillows as he munched on a bowl of carrots while he read *Zen and the Art of Motorcycle Maintenance*.

The sound of Led Zeppelin blasting from the record player in the corner covered the mutterings and mewlings around him.

Davey paused for a moment and sipped his beer. Something felt off. He looked around the room. All the meat was where it was supposed to be. He shrugged and went back to the thick paperback.

The room shook as the front door flew backward into the street. A dark figure appeared in the gaping hole. Davey rolled backward, holding out his beer bottle as a weapon. The figure strode nearer, pulled back its black hood and coughed from the cloud of smoke blanketing the room.

Davey stood.

"Sam?" He couldn't believe his eyes.

"Hey, Davey," she said, voice full of sweet venom. "It's been a minute."

"You?" He pointed with the bottle, beer spilling onto the mattress at his feet unnoticed. "You're the one the old man's afraid of?"

His thin frame bent over double with laughter.

Ronnie swiveled on the couch to face her.

"I lost Jimmy," he told Sam.

"Well, fuck," she breathed.

This moment of vengeful badassery was not going how she imagined it.

"I think he's dead." Ronnie covered his eyes with his hand. "I think my best friend is dead."

"He's not dead, Ronnie," Sam said, not looking away from Davey.

"How do you know?"

"Because I'm Death and I haven't taken him."

Davey's laughter got louder and meaner. Sam closed her eyes and counted to ten as he laughed his guts out.

"Do you remember how you got hammered after Brix dumped you so you went to his house to beg him to take you back and you puked on his lawn?"

She tilted her head and the room went silent. Sam stepped over the pillows as his eyes searched for help, thin hands at his throat but no sound came out. He banged the side of the couch but the room stayed quiet.

She plucked the bottle from his hand and examined it.

"Belgian sour," Sam said before taking a sip. "Not bad. Hey Davey, do you remember when you kidnapped and drugged Chiba? Then you handed her over to some cannibals and I killed you?"

Paul David McAllister ran as fast as he could. His angular limbs churned hard as he tried to escape.

He didn't even make it to the end of his driveway.

*****

11:13 am, Nov. 3, 2020, 36 days after The Fog

Chiba awoke on a hospital bed in a small, white room with odd, translucent walls. The room felt haunted – empty except for all the ghosts. An IV dripped fluids into her arm.

Panic hit her. She couldn't remember how she got there.

"How you feeling?"

Sam sat on a deep, blue chair next to the bed thumbing through a magazine.

Chiba swallowed. Her whole body felt like she had to move through a sky full of clouds to get to her arm or her thoughts. She debated that question for a moment.

"Like shit," she said. Chiba touched her head to make sure it was still attached. "My girls…"

"Know that you're safe and are so excited to see you."

"What are you reading?"

"Bubble Gum Manufacturing Quarterly from June 1988," Sam replied. "It's weirdly riveting. A lot of strong opinions on spearmint in the bubble gum world."

Chiba rolled over onto her side and held out her hand.

"Who knew spearmint was so controversial?"

Sam put her hand in Chiba's and squeezed.

"I certainly didn't."

Chiba's eyes drifted closed.

"I didn't think anyone was going to come," she said, half awake, her thoughts drifting away. "I didn't think anyone cared enough to find me."

"Yeah, I know, but you were wrong. You'll always be wrong about that."

"I shouldn't have doubted you." Chiba smiled with her eyes closed. "My badass bestie."

Sam held her hand until it went slack in sleep, refusing to move as her arm cramped and her palm got sweaty.

Then she placed Chiba's hand back onto the bed. Ignoring the band around her arm that had done nothing to protect her, she grabbed the throw pillow on the chair behind her.

"You were right to doubt me," Sam whispered. "I failed you. I'm such a fuck up. I'm failing all of you. I almost lost you. I'm sorry. I'm so sorry. I should have known. I should have seen it coming."

Then Sam walked to the farthest corner of the flimsy room, pulled her knees into her chest and sobbed her heart out into the gray, cotton pillow while Chiba slept.

ICE CREAM DAY

11:15 am, Nov. 3, 2020, 36 days after The Fog

The white haired man on the toilet could feel his body now. His cold toes. His frozen limbs. He blinked. His wrinkled hand skittered across the sink.

It wouldn't be long now.

*****

Life Itself

The great god Ama was very, very, very, very inebriated. As he stumbled through mountain passes, the wine jug clutched in his fist spilled a red trail behind him.

He had created his first children, the Nommo. Ama cut their mewling, jaundiced bodies from the womb of the earth. In celebration of his accomplishment, he drank himself into oblivion.

As he drunkenly slumbered in the bosom of the mountains, Ama's second eldest son crept to his resting place. The Nommo poured a concoction made from the Sleeping Flowers into his father's slack mouth. With the same obsidian blade Ama used to cut his children from the womb of the earth, he sliced a tiny opening in his father's forehead and carved out a sliver of his soul.

It burned in the Nommo's palm as he skulked far, far away to hide it in a cave.

*****

8:17 am, Nov. 10, 2020, 43 days after The Fog

Zara Agnes Leary worried about everything.

After the night of The Fog, she and her sister weren't allowed out of the house. Ever. Which was fine with Zara because the outside world didn't just worry her, it terrified her. Car accidents, people, explosions, knives, those weird little jacket hooks in walls – all those things happened outside their house and frankly, Zara would rather not. And that was before The Fog made monsters real. Her daddy tried to tell her it was fine, but she'd heard them that night – the liquid screams outside her door that her mommy ran toward. Zara asked her mommy why she'd done that, chased away the monsters. She'd kissed the top of her head and said:

"I had to, my sweet girl."

So Zara pulled her panic inside and pretended like she wasn't chewing away at the insides of her cheeks. Her mommy said it was safe outside as long as she or auntie was there, but the world was so different. People carried knives in their claws. Their teeth had become sharp. Explosions lived in their eyes and accidents were everywhere. So many buildings were broken or just gone. Her school didn't have a roof.

"Your auntie and her friends are working on it, Zara," Daddy said. "We wouldn't let you go out if it wasn't safe."

She and Malak came downstairs to find their Auntie Sam sprawled out on the couch. One arm flung over her eyes and Ridley tucked into her side, gray head resting on the crook of her elbow. She snored like a delicate chainsaw. They were dressed in their thickest pajamas and trailing blankets.

Their mommy had come back to them a week ago but she barely went outside. Instead, their auntie took them downtown, or what was left of it, for ice cream every other day.

"Ew," Zara plugged her nose and whispered to her sister, "she stinks."

"She punched a fox man and he puked on her shoes," Malak whisper-yelled back and pointed to the crusty, green goo caking their auntie's boots.

"You don't know that, Malak," Zara said, grabbing her sister's hand. "Don't be ridiculous."

"Auntie Bad Bird told me," she replied, yanking her hand back.

"Auntie Bad Bird isn't real," Zara said, putting her hands on her hips. "You made her up. She's your imaginary friend."

"DID NOT," Malak yelled. She stomped her foot and shoved Zara. "She not my 'majary friend."

Their auntie snorted and the girls stilled. Zara put her hands over Malak's mouth and shushed her. Malak yanked it aside.

"Shhhh," they shushed each other far too loudly.

The snoring stopped. Their auntie groaned and rolled over onto her side. Deep shadows ringed her eyes. Ridley snuffled once in protest and leapt off the couch.

"Is that puke, Auntie?" Malak asked. Zara clamped her hand over her sister's mouth and an epic slap fight ensued.

The sleeping goddess on the couch, swung her legs over the side and sat, slumped over her knees, cradling her head in one hand.

Neither girl breathed.

"No fighting," she muttered as she stood, bleary eyed and exhausted, ignoring the slight magical snap in the air.

"Okay, Pepperoni?" she said as she patted Malak's head then moved onto Zara's head. "Okay, Cheese? Gimme a few hours and we'll get ice cream, cool?"

Zara blinked. She felt a strong wind. Her ears popped and the next thing she knew, she was staring up at her own screaming face. Her arms were too short and every part of her felt stretched and compressed like she'd been yanked through a straw and put in too small a glass. Tears rolled down her cheeks and footsteps thundered down the stairs.

"What's wrong?"

Her mommy was there. She checked every limb, finger, toe and skull but could find nothing.

"What the hell?" their auntie asked.

"What is it? What's going on?" Mommy demanded.

Zara lifted a shaky hand with chubby, almost baby fingers, nothing like her own.

"That's Malak," she said. "I'm Zara."

Their mommy, kneeling on the floor, glared up at their auntie, whose guilt dawned on her like the sun.

"Oh, shit, sorry. Sorry. I am so sorry."

Zara's toes tingled, her hair felt too tight and her stomach lived both near her heart and her ankles. She gulped, trying to fill lungs that didn't belong to her with air.

"Take it back, please, Auntie," Zara sobbed while Malak kept screaming with her mouth.

"Did you just Freaky Friday my kids?"

"Not on purpose!"

"That's not better."

"I'm aware, okay," Auntie said. "I'm sorry, girls. I'm so sorry. I'll fix this."

She closed her eyes and became very still. The room got darker, Ridley whined and cowered in his crate. She pointed at each of them and snapped her wrists. The wind pulled Zara along, her ears popped again and her lungs breathed her own air. She looked down at her own hands.

Auntie leaned over to meet her gaze. Her strange eyes were full of cosmic storms.

"I am so sorry. That was an accident. It won't happen again."

It was everything Zara hated. Her world changed in an instant. She couldn't control it, didn't understand it and no one could explain any of it to her in a way that made sense. These emotions roiled around in her belly and she bit her cheeks, inhaling. Then she exercised the only power she had:

"It's fine, Auntie. I'm okay, but that was scary."

"I can't imagine. I am truly sorry, sweetie. That shouldn't have happened and I'm so sorry."

She turned to Malak and repeated herself. Malak hid behind Mommy's leg and kicked Auntie Sam in the shin.

"Malak, use your words, please," Mommy said. "No kicking."

They both smiled though.

"You kinda deserved that," Mommy muttered to Auntie.

"Oh, yeah, totally and worse probably."

Zara never understood why adults did that – say things quietly like she and Zara weren't paying attention or didn't care. Of course, they were paying attention! When they talked quiet-like was when they said all the interesting stuff.

Auntie stood in the middle of the living room, eyes unfocused and swaying.

"Sam?" Mommy put her hand on Auntie's shoulder and she startled into focus.

"Huh? What?"

"How late were you out last night?"

"She got home at sunrise," Malak piped up from the floor.

After the apology, she sat on the floor and chiseled green goo from Auntie's boots with a plastic takeout knife.

"I dunno. Sunrise sounds about right. There was this kitsune. Needed persuading." She rubbed her hands over her face and grunted. "I'm gonna catch a few more hours of sleep and then ice cream. Okay, girls?"

Malak freed a bit of dried gunk from Auntie's boot and triumphantly tucked it into her sparkly ladybug purse. Mommy pulled Auntie into the kitchen and spoke to her in a low voice again. Zara sat on the red couch and pretended not to hear every word while she and Malak pushed toys around in an effort to look innocent and busy.

"We talked about this," Mommy whispered, too loudly. "When was the last time you got a full night's sleep? Or took a break?"

"Ice Cream Day is my break," Auntie muttered.

Zara could see their heads above the short wall between the kitchen and the living room. Auntie rested her head against the cabinets and looked at Mommy with one eye closed.

"Taking my kids out to do anything is not a break. I'm worried about you. When was the last time you really slept?"

"Chiba, I'm fine. I'm a goddess, remember?"

"Yeah, I'll believe that when you didn't just Jamie Lee Curtis my kids."

"Wouldn't Jamie Lee Curtis be a slasher flick? Isn't that what she's more well-known for?"

Zara could feel her mommy's glare through the wall.

"Stop trying to distract me." Mommy paused. "I know you blame yourself for what happened to me. You are not responsible. You don't have to do this."

Auntie opened both eyes and met Zara's gaze from across the room. She quickly looked back down at the plastic unicorn in her hand.

"I am responsible. I am responsible for taking care of my people. What's the point of these powers if I can't be of benefit to you, huh? I should have known. I should have planned better and I'm so sorry you went through that because of my fuck up."

Her auntie wouldn't look at her mommy.

"Stop it," she whispered. "I don't blame you."

Auntie shook her head and wouldn't look up.

"You should," she whispered. "I deserve it."

Shocked, Zara could hear the tears in her voice. Malak slipped her hand into Zara's and leaned into her side. She wrapped her arm around her little sister and squeezed.

She'd never really thought much about what the woman who showed up for birthdays and holidays did when she wasn't making goofy faces at her annoying sister or taking a "Which Princess Are

You?" quiz with her. Zara couldn't comprehend the heartbreak in
her voice.

"I'm going to hug you now and you're going to stop this."

Auntie nodded and Mommy hugged her.

"Okay?"

"Okay, but…"

"No buts," Mommy said sternly.

"But listen," Auntie said, pulling away from her. "This place
has to be as stable as possible before he gets here. He will exploit
any weakness. I can't afford to give him any openings. I don't
know what his plan is but I know it's going to be bad, okay? I need
to do this right now. I need to make this place as safe as I can for…
I just need to do this right now, okay?"

Mommy sighed from deep within her belly.

"Take a break tonight, please?" Mommy begged her. "After I
get back from therapy?"

"Okay, I promise. I'll be home early tonight."

"Make her give her word," Malak piped up from her place next
to her on the couch. "It's magic."

Auntie cringed as Zara tried to shush her but she pulled away.
Ignoring her sister, Malak ran over to the kitchen

"What's that now, girls?"

Malak jumped up and down on her bare feet so Mommy picked
her up. Suddenly shy, she whispered too loudly while gauging
Auntie's reaction.

"Give the word, Auntie."

Zara pulled on Mommy's arm.

"She told us that 'promises are made to be broken but words are
made to be kept,'" Zara said. "That's how she found you. It was
magic."

Mommy's eyes lit up as Auntie bit her cheeks and regretted
several of her life choices.

"Give me your word then."

Auntie grinned at the girls while her eyes said bad words.

"You have my word. I'll be home early tonight."

"By eight," Zara said. "You can read us a bedtime story."

Auntie gritted her teeth.

"You have my word that I'll be home by eight tonight and I will read you a bedtime story."

"Yay!"

Mommy put Malak down and the three of them did a happy dance in the kitchen while Auntie rolled her eyes and stared at the ceiling.

"How's it feel to be defeated by a five year old?"

"So great. Really, it's the best ever. I need to sleep now."

"Go to bed."

As she was halfway up the stairs, Mommy yelled after her:

"I'm going to remember the word thing."

"I figured you would."

"I can't wait to use it again."

"Awesome, I'm excited. Stoked. Super stoked."

"Wait," Zara yelled. "Did she just call us Pepperoni and Cheese?"

"Yes, I did!"

*****

10:17 am, Nov. 10, 2020, 43 days after The Fog

When Jimmy saw the eerie, blue light during his endless march through darkness he thought he'd lost his mind. He blinked. Then he blinked again. He shook his head with all his might but the glow didn't disappear. So he ran for miles and miles. In his haste, he didn't notice the stone walls change to dirt and rock.

Jimmy found himself in a miles wide cavern. Tide pools along the floor glittered with bioluminescent life. Stalagmites and stalactites met throughout the room, forming giant hourglasses of limestone.

A tall woman with russet-brown skin, long, black hair wearing a rabbit fur headband, in a simple brown dress, turned to him. Her dark eyes twinkled in the blue lights of the pools. Three, thin black lines ran from the bottom of her lip down to her jaw.

She rushed to him and grabbed his hand.

"Hello, hola, hey, hi, good afternoon," she said and held his hand too tightly as she shook it very enthusiastically. "My name is Kito. How are you? Are you okay? How can I help you?"

*****

12:35 pm Nov. 10, 2020, 43 days after The Fog

As Zara walked down the street with her sister and her auntie, returning from their ice cream date, she noticed something peculiar.

They were a few blocks away from Priti's ice cream stand the first time it happened. Auntie had a deal with Priti where she pulled plastic jugs of cream, sugar and flavors out of her hoodie and in return she got salted caramel ice cream with toasted marshmallow fluff. Malak, as usual, got chocolate ice cream in a cone with chocolate sauce and sprinkles. She usually ended up with sauce up her nose.

Zara had just spooned up the perfect ratio of strawberry ice cream to brownie bite when an old woman, covered in hundreds of colorful scarves, saw them walking toward her. The woman picked up her skirts to expose sparkly, blue sneakers and jogged the other way. The bent street light behind her was plastered with posters that read: "The Shadow Liar Lies." Zara paused, spoonful of deliciousness forgotten as she realized this same thing happened last week. Just then, a small, hairy creature with wide-set eyes rounded the corner, got sight of the three of them and ran shrieking in the opposite direction.

"Auntie?" Zara asked, spoon hanging empty from her fingertips.

"Yes, sweetie?"

Her auntie had got cross-eyed she was so intent on consuming every last bite of toasted fluff.

"Why are people crossing the street to get away from us?"

"Are they?" Auntie Sam replied, furiously scraping the walls of the paper cup with her plastic spoon. "I hadn't noticed."

"'Cause they're scaredy cats, right Auntie?" Malak asked, as chocolate ice cream melted down her arms onto her shirt and shoes.

"Yes, Malak," Auntie Sam said, her eyes following the small, hairy creature as it ran over the crest of the hill. "It's because they're afraid."

"Is it me? Are they afraid of me?"

"No, baby," Auntie Sam said with a sigh. "They're afraid of me."

"You?" Zara giggled. "That's so silly. Why are they afraid of you?"

"They don't wanna die," Malak said, cone tilting at a precarious angle in her left hand as she opened her sparkly ladybug purse with her right.

Her auntie's eyes went wide and her mouth dropped open.

Zara got in her sister's face.

"Stop being ridiculous," she whispered. "That's our auntie, Malak. She's not going to kill anyone. That's just ridiculous. Why are you so ridiculous?"

'Ridiculous' was her new favorite new word.

Malak tried to whisper back, but instead muttered at regular volume.

"Auntie Bad Bird says she kills bad people."

"Does Mommy know?"

Malak nodded so hard she got dizzy and had to grab Zara's arm for support.

"But only bad people?"

"Uh, huh."

Her sister pulled a plastic take-out knife from her ladybug purse and tucked it into the waistband of her blue and green striped leggings.

"Malak! Where did you get that?"

Her sister held up her palms and shrugged.

"I dunno."

"Girls," Auntie Sam said, nodding in the direction of home, "let's go."

With that, she was gone, her body flying hundreds of feet in the air, sailing over the tops of the low brick buildings. A tall, dark-haired man with bare arms and a precise beard stood in her place. He grabbed Zara too hard by the shoulders and tucked her under his arm. Then he leaned down to snatch up Malak but she dodged his meaty hand. Malak scrambled up his back with the grace of a spider monkey. Wrapping her arm around his head, she plunged the white, plastic knife deep into his eye. He dropped Zara with a shriek.

He yanked Malak off him, tossing her like a football into the sky.

Zara stood in a frozen scream on the sidewalk. Her little hands balled into fists. The man, swearing, pulled the knife from his eye, and flung it aside. Blood oozed from the wound as he bent to grab her again but his knees buckled. He dropped, face first, onto the sidewalk. Auntie clung to his back. Her thick, black nails embedded deep into his neck. Inky veins pulsed across his face. His tongue lolled from his mouth as his dying, mutilated eye glared at Zara. She screamed.

Zara couldn't understand what was happening. This was a R-rated movie and she was only allowed to watch PG. This needed to stop.

"Stop it! Stop it, Auntie. Stop it now."

Malak ran up and kicked the prone man's leg with her white and pink sneaker.

"Stay away from my sister!" she yelled.

Her auntie ignored her demands. Her black hood covered her features while her obsidian nails pumped poison into Zara's kidnapper.

She stamped her foot.

"You're being a bad role model!"

Zara didn't know why she said it. Never ever in her life had she ever spoken to an adult like that, but something inside her recoiled and snapped.

This is wrong. This is wrong. This is wrong.

Auntie snickered.

"Are you laughing at me?" Tears spilled down Zara's cheeks. "Don't laugh at me. Malak, stop kicking him and hit Auntie."

"No laughing!" Malak pulled back her open fist and whacked their auntie on the arm and back. "No laughing at sister."

"Malak, stop hitting," Auntie snapped out of reflex.

Zara pulled her little sister away and held her. Malak felt so small, like a trembling little bird.

"Auntie."

She wouldn't look up and in a voice Zara had never heard before – a voice tight with rage, she said:

"This is a bad man. This is a very, very bad man. He was going to hurt you."

"It's wrong," Zara whispered.

"He is War. If I kill him, I could save …"

She met Zara's pleading eyes and stopped. Shaking, Sam yanked her nails out of his neck.

Zara's world tilted. Something old and hungry glared at her across time. She felt the mass of it turn, heavy and worn, in her direction. Her skin burned like she'd been outside too long. Malak stifled a squeak.

Zara blinked.

Auntie flipped the man over. She knelt on his chest – a knife, slick and deadly, at his throat. Her muscles stood out taut and ropey in her neck and hands as she pressed the blade into his skin.

"What was that? What did you do to them?"

He put his hands behind his head and grinned. The man's teeth were bright white and perfectly square.

"I like you," he said, standing. Auntie rolled away from the hulking mass of him and pulled Zara and Malak into her side.

"You're adorable," he said. "You thought you could hurt me? Cute."

"What was that? It was aimed at both of them. What did you do?"

Zara was too stunned to be afraid at the sound of her desperation. The monstrous thing hunting her paused.

"Me?" His chest puffed up to an obscene degree. "Almost nothing."

The world around them darkened. Shadows turned weird, stretching out to touch him. An ill wind howled through the black trees. The man shrank several inches.

"I told you – almost nothing. They did most of it."

The howling turned to shrieks. The sunlight faded to a dull, orange pulse barely able to penetrate the gloom. Auntie clutched her shoulder too hard but Zara was afraid to say something. She peeked up to see her aunt's features had become a mask of sunken eyes and hollow cheeks. The man got even smaller. Zara hid her face in her auntie's hoodie.

"Answer me."

"Well, that one saved my life."

"What does that have…" Her auntie rolled her eyes and let out a strangled scream.

"And that one," his voice got closer as he knelt, "that one took my eye in combat. She'll be a fine heir. I don't know why you never thought of that."

"She is five years old and I am not a psychopath."

The wind whipped their hair about.

"Auntie," Malak whined. "I'm scared."

The maelstrom calmed a bit.

"I'm sorry, baby. It's okay. I'll take care of it."

Zara looked up at the adults – her auntie's wild hair swirled in the wind, and the man grinned at her.

"I owe you my life, little girl."

"Auntie." Zara didn't know what he meant but that thing got closer as it stared into her soul.

"He has to do what you say, Zara," Auntie said. She closed her eyes against the sick reality of the situation. "He owes you a life debt. You are connected to him now and if he dies Malak becomes War in his place. So you will live, Smyth Delano Sylvanus. I curse you with life. The Door to Death will remain closed to you."

"Yes!"

He pumped his fist, turned and shook his hips in joy.

It sounded good to Zara, to not ever die, but her auntie called it a curse and she didn't have the same look on her face as she did when she handed out Christmas presents.

"Zara, baby," she said and squeezed her shoulder too hard again. "Please tell him that you renounce him. Say: I renounce your life, Smyth Delano Sylvanus."

"What does 'renounce' mean?" Zara asked.

"It means 'let go' or 'push away.'"

"Why?"

"Why does it mean that? I-I don't know, honey. I think it's an old word. We'll look it up when we get home. Please tell him you renounce him."

"No, I mean why should I renounce him?"

"What?" Her auntie stared down at her like she'd just turned into a duck.

"Why?"

"Yeah, Auntie, why?" The big man snickered.

"Be quiet," Zara ordered. His mouth snapped shut.

"Sit." He gracelessly plopped onto the sidewalk.

They were at eye level now and she could see the bloody, gaping wound in his pupil.

"Shut your gross eye."

Zara loved this. Her fear melted away. This big, scary man had to do whatever she said. He could explain exactly what was going on instead of vague hand waving. He could protect her and her sister. This was amazing.

Her auntie knelt before her and reached out her hands.

"Zara, honey, please, you don't understand. This trash," she nodded to the God of War, "shouldn't be anywhere near you. He will hurt you."

"How can he hurt me?" Zara was giddier than she'd ever been. She ignored the thing closing in on her.

"I dunno, honey," her auntie pleaded with her. "I don't know how he'll hurt you. I just know that he is evil and shouldn't be anywhere near little girls."

"I'm not a little girl." Zara stamped her foot. "I'm practically an adult. Why won't you tell me anything? I hate that you never tell me anything, like I'm some kind of baby."

"I am trying to protect you," she said, so desperate and sad. "I am trying to keep you safe."

"I don't feel safe!" Zara exploded. "I'm scared. I don't even know what I'm scared of. I want to know. I want to know what I should be scared of and no one tells me anything!"

The big man with big teeth and broad shoulders waved frantically from his spot on the ground.

"What?" Auntie snapped at him.

"He can't talk. I told him not to."

"Zara," her auntie used that voice that used to make her snap to attention, "this is not a game or a toy. This man is beyond dangerous. You need to be away from him."

"Talk!" Zara yelled.

"I'll help you, little girl," he said. "I'll protect you. I'll tell you what you want to know."

Auntie stifled a scream. Her hands balled themselves into fists. Thick, black nails jammed into her palms as inky liquid spilled from the wounds. It sizzled when it landed on the sidewalk. Auntie wiped the fluid on her hoodie. Before Zara could speak, she picked her and Malak up – one in each arm and ran so fast it made her dizzy. They were headed back to the house.

"You can move now," she yelled to the man, and although he was very far away she knew he heard her.

When they got to the front door, they stopped. Auntie hesitated before opening it. She shut her eyes and took several deep breaths. Zara knew this from a show she watched when she was little: "deep breath and count to ten keeps the anger from starting all over again."

"Shut it, you demonic drapery," she muttered.

"Auntie," Malak said, clinging to her neck. "I don't like them. They smell bad."

"I know, honey. I'm sorry. I just need a minute."

"What smells?" Zara asked.

"Them." Malak pointed to either side of the door.

"She can't see them and you shouldn't be able to either."

"Huh," she said and stuck her fist in her mouth.

Auntie exhaled, hiked Malak up on her hip and opened the door. She didn't put them down until the door shut behind her.

"How was ice cream?" Their mommy sat in her chair with a book in one hand. Their auntie wouldn't look at her. "What happened? Oh, my god."

She rushed to them and checked Zara and Malak for wounds.

"What is going on? I'm going to have a heart attack."

"They're fine physically. But we were attacked and…"

Mommy clutched them to her.

"And what?"

So Auntie told her what happened with thin words while she leaned, propped up against the wall.

"She stabbed him with a plastic knife?"

"Well, it was a magic knife. It looked like plastic but it was… not."

"Who gave my daughter a knife?"

"I'm pretty sure I did."

"You're pretty sure???"

"Who's Auntie Bad Bird, Malak?"

"Her imaginary friend?"

"You are," Malak whispered. Her eyes twinkled like this was the funniest story. "You're Auntie Bad Bird."

Sam sank to the floor.

"I think a subconscious aspect of myself has been visiting her dreams and teaching her to fight."

"What? How?"

She shrugged.

"Goddess."

Sam could see the war in Chiba. The helplessness at not being able to protect her children, the pride that they took care of themselves, the anger at Sam for overstepping, the relief that they weren't physically hurt and the sorrow that they were still in danger.

"Zara saved his life?"

Sam shrugged again.

"I was gonna kill him."

"In front of my children?"

"I'm not saying it was right. He tried to kidnap them and I kinda lost my shit."

Chiba remained silent. She would have done the same.

"But he has to do what she says?"

"She has a hurricane on a leash." Sam banged her head against the wall. "He's going to hurt her. I don't know how but this feels very, very wrong. She needs to renounce him right now."

"Zara, baby." Chiba put her hands on her daughter's shoulders. "You need to listen to your auntie now. Please do as she says."

"But, Mommy." Zara put her hands on her mother's cheeks. "I can help. I can be like you and auntie. I want to help you. I can make him not hurt people. It's okay. I got this."

"No, you don't, Zara," Sam said. "You don't understand what this man is. You are going to get hurt."

"No, you don't understand," Zara snapped. "I can do this. I know I can."

"Zara…" Chiba's voice became sharp.

"You can't make me!"

Zara felt her mommy and auntie talking to each other without words over her shoulder.

"Girls, could you please go upstairs and play? I would like to talk to your auntie for a minute."

Knowing a thousand really interesting things were about to be said, Zara started to protest, but Malak grabbed her arm and chirped:

"Okay, Mommy."

"What are you doing?" Zara whispered.

Malak shook her head and dragged her upstairs. A few steps past the landing, where a wall separated the living room from the stairs so the adults couldn't see them but close enough to hear everything, Malak stopped and pulled Zara to sit on the taupe-carpeted stairs. She shushed Zara with one emphatic finger over her lips and drew complicated symbols in the air. To Zara's shock, she heard footsteps in the hallway behind them. She almost blurted out 'What the hell?' but her sister's intent look stopped her.

"Are they gone?" Mommy asked.

"I heard footsteps."

Malak waved her hand and the door to their room slammed shut.

"There ya go," Auntie said.

"Give it a minute. They might be hiding in the hallway."

Zara was aghast. She and Malak lurked in the hallway all the time but it never occurred to her that their mommy knew about it.

"All quiet," Auntie said.

"Good."

They had seen their mommy cry but what they heard from the other side of that white wall were sobs – deep, earth-shattering sobs. Malak stuffed her hand into her mouth and mewled. Zara put her arm around her and hugged her little sister close. They stared at the blank wall with the small, shuttered window and the burnt out houses across the street. The thing with teeth glared at her through the window. Zara stuck her tongue out at it.

"I wanted better for them," their mommy cried. "I swore it would be different for them. I was going to protect them."

"I know," their auntie said. "I know. I'm so sorry."

She could hear her auntie patting their mommy's back, trying to soothe her. It went on like that for so long that Zara's arm hurt from holding Malak. Zara understood that she and her sister were the cause of this pain and she wanted only to help make it stop – to protect these women the way they worked so hard to protect them.

Zara could hear her mommy sniffling and wiping her nose, her voice became clearer.

"Sister?"

"Yes," Auntie replied.

The room became so silent. Zara could only hear Malak's deep, shallow gasps of fear and sadness.

"I want your word that man will burn."

The magic was suddenly a thick layer all around them. Her stomach clenched and dropped in anticipation. The tiny hairs on Zara's arms stood up and wavered.

"You have my word, sister. You have my word."

*****

4:42 pm Nov. 10, 2020, 43 days after The Fog

Sam walked out of the house with absolute defeat soaking through her flesh into her soul.

The Wraiths blabbered about the Celestial Mothers again. She ignored them as she wandered to the park down the street.

She was about to do the hardest thing she'd ever done in her life. The swing set was broken. The bar across its top had snapped in half so there were only two swings instead of four. Sam slumped down onto one and hated herself for a solid ten minutes before gathering up her will and announcing:

"I command the Celestial Mothers to manifest before me."

"How dare you?" Badb was there – as fierce and unrelenting as a wounded animal.

"Shut up," Sam said.

"Your strategy is too emotional," bland Nemain said.

"I didn't ask."

"Now, dear," Anand said, with all her bloviating.

"Cut the bullshit."

And she looked at them. Really, looked at them – these women who had advised her and cared for her. Who had motivated her during the worst times of her life, and she saw that each of them wore her face. It confirmed what she long suspected.

"I know what you are and I know who you are. I knew something was wrong when Ama didn't look like Dre."

"Daughter," Badb beseeched.

"I am not your daughter. You know that as well as I do."

She hated this – what she was about to do, but it was the only thing she could think of to protect the girls.

"I owe you my life and I owe you my sanity, but you do not get to dictate who I am or what I become. Do you understand?"

The women nodded as one.

"I have grown beyond you," Sam said. "I need you to do for Malak and Zara what you did for me. I command you to keep their minds, bodies and hearts safe and whole the way you did mine."

They nodded again.

"I don't care what you have to do to make that happen. Do you understand?"

The women agreed.

"When they have grown beyond you, you have to leave. If you don't, I will make you, Badb."

"I…" she said. "I'm sorry."

"I don't care. This conversation is over."

The three women vanished.

*****

8:32 pm Nov. 10, 2020, 43 days after The Fog

That night, true to her word, their auntie read them a story before their daddy tucked them in.

Zara pretended that the old, angry thing wasn't circling her the entire time their auntie told them the story of a courageous, red-haired girl who traveled across the universe saving her father and brother. When she left, Malak clung to Zara and tried to keep her from sleeping.

"I want a 'nother story. Not tired."

"Malak, leave me alone. Go to bed."

"Love you, sister."

"I love you, too."

Zara shut her eyes.

The ancient, toothy thing found her.

*****

2:42 pm, Nov. 10, 723 B.C.E., 2,742 years before The Fog

So long ago, when she was a child, before Kito ran from him, before the strangers came, before her people were scattered to the winds, she played among the rocks as her mother foraged for crab, kelp and octopus in the tide pools. The fog, misty and cool, rolled in. Her friends were trapped within it. She sang and played with them.

When her mother filled her woven basket with the creatures who would keep them alive, she sang the fog away. Her voice rang out steady and true. Kito's friends retreated back to the sea.

"Why do you always do that?" Kito asked. "Send them back?"

"How would you feel if you went to visit them and they wouldn't let you go home?" her mother replied.

"I'd be mad. I'd be real mad."

Her mother nodded, made the gesture of 'of course, you would' and hefted her basket onto her shoulder.

Many years later, they traveled far from the misty green sea, over the mountains to a place that was flat and foreign. Kito didn't like any of it. She didn't like the way the sun pierced the clouds and shined too bright in her eyes. There were no tall trees here and the grass smelled different. She didn't like being this far from her friends and she certainly did not like the purpose of this trip.

"Mother, I don't want to get married," she said for the thousandth time.

"Oh, hush," her mother said. "It will be good for you. You'll have something to do besides gallivanting on the beach all day."

Kito had plenty to do, including gathering sea creatures for food, weaving reeds for baskets and making sure her younger siblings didn't kill each other, facts her mother seemed to have forgotten.

"What if his hair is unkempt and he stinks like a skunk?"

Her mother sighed.

"I'm told he's a fine man who washes regularly."

They crested a small hill and Kito could see them all – the strangers who would become her family. The man in the center who would become her husband. He seemed nice enough. She had yet to meet any man who could hold her attention. Everyone, from a distance, seemed nice enough, but this wasn't her home and this wasn't the life she wanted.

So Kito turned and ran.

She pulled the deer skin closer over her shoulders and ran back up the mountain, through the tall redwood trees, over the freshwater streams, past the beach scrubs and rocky outcrops. This man who would be her husband chased her. She could feel his heat on her back. Kito ran faster and faster until she reached the water's edge. Breathless, she stomped into the sea and sang the song to bring the fog. She begged her friends to help her escape him.

Something was wrong. As soon as the song ended, she knew. The murky fog enveloped her. It pressed her down, down to the sea floor. Her limbs shrank. Water engulfed her but her lungs continued to work.

Kito gazed up from beneath the waves to see the face of the man who would have been her husband. He looked down at her, nodded and left.

She had become a shrimp.

Kito felt her people on the land and in the fog above her. She heard them, but she could not see or touch them. She told herself she was happy as the waves crashed over her. Kito cried often.

Sand covered her and the water receded.

An eternity later, men came. She welcomed them as new friends but they did terrible things. They starved her people, raped them, gave them terrible diseases, made them cut their hair and forget their names. The strangers beat Kito's people for singing to the fog. She screamed. The earth shook. Cracks formed for miles and miles in its crust.

These men used those cracks to draw a line around the land she loved. They called it Sunset Cove. They sent her people away, so far she could barely feel them.

She tried to send the strangers away, but she was so alone. Just the sound of their voices offered her some comfort. She banished as many of the vile ones as she could but always welcomed the lost and the lonely.

As the screams erupted from the streets above, and blood dripped through the cracks in the concrete, she made a choice. She needed to protect her people – scattered as they were.

So Kito sang. The Fog refused to go back to the sea, but it stopped at the cracks in the earth.

*****

The God of War's Domain, The Liminal Space

Zara didn't understand where she was. Explosions rocked the earth. In silent moments, fast clips of sound moved through the air – screams and fire. She stood on a rock as people died around her. The man who was supposed to obey her, preened at her side.

"You wanted to know, little girl?" he asked. "You wanted to see what they were hiding from you? This is it! This is war! It's the best."

It surrounded her – flames engulfing bodies, men hacked to pieces, naked corpses stacked like kindling. Blood rain fell from a roiling sky.

"Make it stop!" she yelled. "Make it stop."

His belly and shoulders shook with laughter.

"This isn't the real world, little girl. I don't have to do what you say."

She wrapped her arms around herself and screwed her eyes shut. She covered her ears against the assault but the burning, putrid stench of death wouldn't stop. The earth shook. She couldn't move. Her skin crawled. She just wanted it to be over.

"Mommy, help me, mommy, mommy, mommy."

He laughed again, perfect teeth, shining red with blood.

"Your mommy can't…" he trailed off as something caught his eye. "That dumb fucking cunt."

A small, black-clad figure sprinted across the battlefields straight at them.

He bellowed words Zara didn't understand and the weapons turned toward the person. Tanks unloaded shell after shell. Bombs fell from the sky. Men with blank faces and guns at the ready marched to face it. The figure didn't pause. It vaulted over the soldiers and ignored the explosions.

The big man yowled. The veins in his neck popped out – purple and obscene against his skin.

"You can't be here! This is my realm. This is my place! It's mine."

"Sure looks like a battlefield full of dead people to me, asshole!" The figure shouted back.

He charged the figure. It jumped high into the air over him and landed on the rock next to Zara.

"Hey, Cheese."

The woman looked like her auntie but much, much cooler – an angry scar ran down her cheek. Thick, coal-like makeup was smudged around her eyes. Wild braids kept her hair out of her face.

She yanked the long, black cloak off her shoulders and flung it around Zara.

"I'm Auntie Bad Bird," she said, pulling the hood over Zara's face. The world went dark and quiet.

"Mommy," Zara cried to the nothingness.

"Nemain, dear, if you wouldn't mind hurrying it up." This was her auntie's voice but dripping with saccharin. "We don't need to traumatize her any further."

"I am working as quickly as I can." This was also her auntie, but somehow flat and lifeless. "You clearly don't understand how difficult it is to both build a portal and construct a stable reality when the mind is in shock."

"I don't, dear, but I'm sure you appreciate that we haven't much time. Badb cannot hold that monstrosity off forever."

"I appreciate many things, Anand, such as excellent craftsmanship under intense pressure."

The eerie, black, emptiness snapped into focus and Zara found herself sitting on the wood floor of a log cabin.

"Well done, Nemain"

The woman, who looked like an older, more comfortable version of her auntie clapped. Her unruly hair was held up in a tidy bun. Her features were a bit worn and soft.

"You get two cookies." She knelt down to face Zara. "Hello, dear. I'm Auntie Bless. I'm making cookies. You must have one."

She led Zara to a small dinner table. She sat across from another woman who looked like a very dull and lifeless replica of her auntie. Her hair hung lank and straight past her narrow shoulders.

"I'm Auntie Bland. Do you want to play checkers?"

"I want my mommy," Zara replied.

"She's on her way," Auntie Bland said and moved a black checker one space.

"She is? Really? Truly?"

"Yes. Would you like to play or not?"

Auntie Bless opened the small oven with a flourish. The scent of fresh-baked cookies wafted through the air. Something banged against the outside of the cabin with a loud thud. Zara jumped.

"Ignore that, dear," Auntie Bless said. "It's fine."

"I want my mommy."

Auntie Bland leaned forward over the table.

"You should play checkers with me. It will distract you until your mom comes while giving your mind something to focus on so you can calm down."

Auntie Bless set the plate of warm cookies on the table.

"Have one, dear."

"I recommend that you have one," Auntie Bland said. "Even though it's not real, the placebo effect of the sugar along with the serotonin induced by the chocolate will help you process this experience and come out of the shock."

Zara picked up the cookie and gnawed on it thoughtfully. She decided that she really liked Auntie Bland. She moved a white checker on the board.

"Where am I? What's going on?"

The sallow woman moved a piece.

"Your body is still asleep. The God of War took your soul to the Liminal Space – to punish you, I suspect. This is a construct I made to give you a safe place to hide until your mom and auntie come and get you out."

"Oh." Zara pretended to understand and moved another piece. "You're not my auntie?"

"Yes and no. We are parts of her. When she was in a bad place, we showed up and helped her. She commands us to do the same for you."

"How did you help her?"

"I help her plan ahead and stay calm. I analyze and predict behavior and circumstances. That one makes people happy and is cheerful no matter what. The one outside…"

"Auntie Bad Bird?"

"Yes, Auntie Bad Bird is a fighter who is never afraid and will do anything to survive."

"What does "predict" mean?"

Auntie Bland studied the board.

"It's like looking at what's happening in the world around you and trying to tell the future."

"Oh."

A glass of milk appeared next to the cookies.

"King me," Zara said.

Auntie Bland raised one eyebrow ever so slightly.

"What's taking so long?"

"Your auntie needs help getting your mommy here," she said and jumped over four pieces until she reached Zara's side of the board. "King me."

Zara raised one eyebrow ever so slightly.

"I am not going to insult you by letting you win."

"Why does she need help?"

"Because your mommy is alive and your auntie would like to keep it that way."

Zara raised her other eyebrow.

"Living is not exactly her specialty, dear," Auntie Bless interjected from where she hovered over the stove.

"She is the Goddess of Death. If your mother were dead, it would not be a problem. Keeping someone alive and bringing them to this realm without some kind of tether is a problem unless you are the God of Life."

"Why can't Auntie just bring me back herself?"

"Because you don't trust her."

Zara's hand paused over the checker she was about to move.

"It is okay that you don't trust her, but getting you out of here is too dangerous without it."

Zara'd never thought about it until this moment.

"If she talked to me like you do, I would trust her."

Auntie Bland's lips twitched ever so slightly. She nodded.

"I will tell her that."

The house shook. Someone knocked three times on the door. Auntie Bless rushed to open it.

"Thank goodness you're here."

Her mommy, auntie and a tall man with kind eyes and a purple Hawaiian shirt burst in.

"Zara!" Mommy said. She rushed to the table and tried to yank her up, but the tall man held tight to her left hand.

"Chibs," he said, his voice low and rumbly in warning.

"Mommy!"

Zara stood on the chair and wrapped her arms around her mommy's neck.

"Oh, my precious girl." Chiba breathed into her shoulder.

"You should go now," Auntie Bland said.

Chiba paused, taking in the three different versions of her best friend.

"What the hell?"

"Chiba, Dre," Sam said. "I'd like to introduce you to my trauma responses – that's anxiety and depression. By the oven, you have fawning and toxic positivity. Outside is the will to survive and rage."

"Delightful to meet you, dear," Auntie Bless extended a hand.

"An honor to meet you." Dre bowed and shook Auntie Bless' hand.

The scream of a thousand crows pierced the air. The simple plank walls shook and rattled.

"That's the signal," Auntie Bless said, gazing at the ceiling.

"Go," Sam said.

She opened the back door and ushered them outside.

"But…" Chiba paused at the threshold.

"I'll be fine. Dre, please get them out now."

He pressed Chiba's shoulders until she went through the door. Sam slammed it shut behind them.

Smyth pulled the hoodie back in triumph. Sam found herself on the blood-soaked battlefield. He squealed in fury. Realizing that he lost, he raised both fists over his head to strike her down. Badb lay slumped over the side of the rock. Her face was a puffy mask of blood and fresh bruises. Even in her elevated position, Sam felt tiny and insignificant facing this raving behemoth. She blinked. He sank a foot into the ground.

"What the fuck?"

He tried to pull himself up, but he was buried up to his knees. Sam climbed off the rock.

"Have you ever thought about how many people have died in war?" He swung on her – beefy arms flailing like a helicopter. She stepped beyond his reach. "No, really. You ever thought about it? How many human beings you've slaughtered?"

The shelling stopped. The screams silenced. Even the fires died. In their place, was the steady march of relentless footsteps.

"Bitch, when I get my hands on you."

"Oh, you're not going to – ever. Don't worry about that."

He dropped up to his massive thighs into the earth.

"It's about one point six billion. One point six billion dead – all because of you. All because rich men expect poor men to die so they can get richer… and what you do to little girls."

She threw her head back and screamed, screamed for all the little girls. The air quivered. What was a steady march, accelerated into a run – an earthquake, an avalanche of bodies hurtling toward him. Sam backed away as the dead threw themselves upon the God of War. The nameless, faceless, forgotten dead pulled his legs further beneath the earth.

Sam picked up Badb and slung her over one shoulder.

He batted the dead away. His meaty fists pounded at their torsos and arms. Their blood and guts exploded onto his flashing muscles. He tossed them aside like so much trash, but soon the sheer numbers overwhelmed him. They held him down, pushing him farther and farther under the mud. Smyth grunted and squealed. Their boney fingers reached into his mouth, holding down his tongue. They tore at his ears and eyelids with rotted teeth. He couldn't escape the fetid crush.

Sam carried Badb to the edge of the battlefield. She put her down on the ground next to a Humvee, her back resting against the giant tire.

"Is the child safe?" Badb asked.

Sam knelt before her, pulling a bottle of water and washcloth from her hoodie. She wet the cloth and gently cleaned Badb's face.

"She's out. You did amazing."

"I did what needed to be done."

She did not meet Sam's eyes. Impulsively, Sam hugged her.

"I know. It's what you always do."

She felt Badb's dislocated shoulder grind beneath her hand. Badb's arm and nose were shattered. A few teeth were missing.

"I love you," Sam said. "I appreciate you so much."

Badb leaned over and spat out a mouthful of blood.

"I overstepped before. I'm sorry."

"You were just trying to keep me alive. I get that. But I can't act like her. I refuse to do to myself what she did to me."

"I know. It won't happen again."

She squeezed Sam's hand with her good arm.

"I love you too, you know," Badb said.

*****

3:44 am Nov. 11, 2020 44 days after The Fog

Zara awoke in her own bed with the purple rainbow comforter, in her own room with the rainbow unicorn pictures on the walls and she hated everything. She hated the loud overhead light. She hated the terrified faces of all the adults around her, but mostly she hated the way she felt – like she'd seen things too big for her brain so it had just given up and stopped. She hated the tears running down her mommy's cheeks and the way she clung to Zara's arms.

"It's okay, Mommy," Zara said. "I'm fine. It's okay."

The adults did that thing where they looked at each other over her head, like she wouldn't notice.

"It's okay," she repeated. "I'm ridiculously fine."

*****

4:23 am Nov. 11, 2020, 44 days after The Fog

Raven Rainbow Renquist, a name she gave herself, by the way, had many duties as Death's Apprentice in Sunset Cove. She wasn't sure what any of them were at the moment, but she knew everything would be explained in due time.

Sam told her to 'go to therapy, kid' so Raven went to therapy and took long walks every night to sort out her feelings. She met some lovely vampires and a few talkative werewolves along the way. News traveled fast in a small town, so the more unsavory element of Sunset Cove gave her a wide berth and the Life Bringers would give her food whenever she asked. The internet was down. She was pretty sure all her friends were either dead or mutated into forms that she couldn't talk to. Classes had been canceled the second The Fog rolled in so she couldn't even work on her degree.

Raven was probably the only person in the whole of Sunset Cove who was bored… and lonely. Kellyman sat on her shoulder while she vented, picking her way through the ruins of the Southside beach.

"It's not like I miss Organic Chemistry," Raven said.

"Uh, huh," he said.

She knew he didn't have a clue what she was talking about, but it was sweet of him to play along.

This part of the county had been a thriving alternative to Sunset Cove's downtown. Quaint restaurants and shops were squashed together next to a low sea wall. Tourists in the know would flock to this area, clogging up the streets and crowding out the locals. Raven used to sing bad karaoke at the British-style pub less than a block from the ocean. She wanted to visit the smoking crater it had become out of pure nostalgia.

"I mean," she said and thought about the late nights at Sunset Cove Diner where she and her classmates would study and cry over milkshakes until 4 am. "Maybe I do miss Organic Chemistry."

"I'm sure you'll meet Organic Chemistry again, Rave."

"No, Kellyman, Organic Chemistry isn't a person."

Lead paint, she reminded herself for the thousandth time. *Lead paint. It's not his fault.*

She hopped over the stone wall separating the road from the beach, not noticing the rows of hourglass posters plastered to it, and spotted her. The woman's long, blonde hair haloed in the one streetlight that still worked. She stood with her back to Raven before the wreckage of the Lonely Starfish, Raven's favorite pre-Fog hangout, in white stilettos, a crisp, black skirt and flowing, white shirt.

"Rave, I got a bad feeling about that sheba," Kellyman whistled.

"It's fine. She looks harmless. Maybe she's lost."

Raven couldn't take her eyes off her. *Maybe she misses the Lonely Starfish too.* She moved toward the woman without feeling her boots on the ground. The intoxicating scent of vanilla, vinegar, fish and chips and stale beer drew Raven closer. She hadn't smelled it since before The Fog.

Kellyman flew away with a squawk of disapproval. If Raven had her wits about her, she would have realized this woman was lit exactly like the stairwell in the *Exorcist* poster.

"Hey," Raven called to her. "Are you lost? It's totally not safe out here. I can walk you home."

The woman turned to face Raven, revealing almond-shaped, blue eyes, pale, silky skin, a pert, up-turned nose and plush lips.

"Aren't you the sweetest?" she asked Raven in a voice so husky it made her spine tingle. "But I'm right where I want to be, darling."

She hung on the woman's every word, leaning too close. Her eyes rolled back in her head at that intoxicating scent.

"Why, why here?"

"It's right where you are, baby," she whispered. The woman ran her manicured nail along Raven's cheek. She shivered.

The sound of Kellyman's screams penetrated Raven's brain fog. The woman tilted her head and lifted her chin for a kiss.

"Quiet that animal for me, would you, beautiful?"

"Yes, anything." Raven angled her head, snuck her tongue out to lick her lips and closed her eyes. "Kellyman…"

She opened her eyes to a free fall through yowling darkness.

"What in the tarnation?"

Raven landed hard on her ass next to a crooked tree overhanging a sea cliff on a moonlight night.

"Sorry," Kellyman said as he swooped down to land on one of the low, twisted branches. "Boss's orders."

He dropped into a fair imitation of Sam's irritated tones:

"'Bring her here if she's ever in danger. I'm serious, bird. If it's even a question, just bring her here, okay? Understand?' I don't know much, but I know a sheba on the make when I see one."

"Bring me back! Take me back to her! I need to see her. Please! You don't understand. I need her."

Raven wanted that woman. A gaping hole lived inside her head and she wanted that woman to fill it with her tongue, her scent and those impossibly perfect eyes. She wanted to peel away her own skin and crawl, bloody and honest, into her loving arms.

"What happened?" Sam emerged from the darkness. Her eyes searched the area. "Is Raven okay?"

"I dunno, Boss," Kellyman crooked. "Shit's weird."

"I'm fine." Raven pirouetted in her black, combat boots. "I'm better than fine. I'm amazing."

She grabbed the front of Sam's hoodie. "I'm in love. I'm in love at first sight. Please send me back to her. I need to see her. I need to sit in the warm sunshine of her presence."

"Oh, fuck." Sam rubbed at the tension headache forming between her eyebrows and prayed to the Holy Darkness that the sinking fear in her belly was misplaced. "Who? Who is this sunshine?"

"The most wonderful human that has ever or will ever exist."

"Great, and does this paragon have a name?"

"Yes! Of course, she has a name and it's the most brilliant and beautiful name in history."

"Kellyman?" Sam massaged her forehead as hard as she could but the headache refused to leave.

"A real sheba, Boss".

"What's a sheba?"

"A real sexy dame, Boss. Gams for days, blonde, an ass you could bounce a quarter off. Breasts like…."

"Okay," Sam interrupted. "How did she smell? Did she smell good?"

Raven spread her arms and leaned back to worship the invisible woman.

"She smelled amazing! Like fireworks on the Fourth of July, like homemade bread, like a hug from your grandma, like rain, like the best sex of your life," Raven said and fell backward for emphasis.

Sam set aside that horrifying barrage of imagery.

"Fuck me," she muttered. "That's Fiona."

"You know her?" Raven said. She popped up into a sitting position. "Of course, you know her! Isn't she amazing? Isn't she the best?"

"Technically, she's my ex-wife."

"What? How?"

Sam pulled two lawn chairs and a six pack out of her hoodie. She settled into the chair and invited Raven to use the other one.

Sam wanted to tell her all the ways she'd debased herself for that woman. In her vision of the future, after Dre died Sam thought she was all alone in the barren wasteland. Love, it seemed, had survived within Sam's heart, and therefore, so did Aphrodite, the Goddess of 'Love.' Sam had been so relieved when the most beautiful woman she'd ever seen crossed over the sterile dunes trailing the scent of everything she'd just lost. She wouldn't have to spend eternity by herself. In retrospect, being burned alive for thousands of years would have been preferable.

She blinked at Sam.

"Never mind," Raven said. "I don't care. I need to see her. Let me out of this place. Let me see her. I need to see her. I need to be with her."

"Raven, I think you need to hear this. She's not who you think she is. She's not a good person."

"You're lying! You don't know her like I do. You don't understand. She loves me. She's amazing and I love her."

"Please, Raven, just listen. Fiona is evil. She's one of the worst people I've ever met."

"Take me to her! Take me to her!" Raven chanted over and over again as she yanked out clumps of her own hair. "I need her!"

Then Raven sank her nails into her cheeks and clawed.

"Stop it, Raven," she said, grabbing her wrists. But Sam understood. She'd cut off her left breast, sauteed it and served it to Fiona on a platter because she had, with damp eyes, whispered how much she missed fresh meat.

Raven yanked her arms away with all her might. The bones snapped with the movement.

"Jesus, Boss."

Kellyman had lost his marbles over a dame or two in his day, but this was beyond mental. Hell, he'd even sent a few made men to sleep with the fishes over looking cross-eyed at his moll, but this?

"Okay, okay," Sam said. "I'll take you to her. I'll take you to her. Calm down. Please just calm down."

Raven wept, not from the pain in her wrists, cheeks or skull but in relief that she was about to be reunited with her most precious one.

"Thank you!" Raven dropped to her knees in gratitude "Thank you! Thank you!"

"Don't thank me for this. I might vomit."

So Sam, with every fiber of her being screaming in self-hatred, tore open the fabric of reality, gently took Raven's elbow in her hand and escorted her to Mulberry Square downtown.

In theory, Mulberry Square was cool. The county of Sunset Cove, in its infinite wisdom, converted an old loading dock outside of the only art museum into a mini town square. It was chock full of weird, cafeteria-style bars and restaurants. People would order, then eat outside on a patio near a little stage.

In reality, it was an overpriced, hipster mecca that committed, in Sam's opinion, The Greatest Sin of Hipster Architecture – exposed concrete. Sound bounced around the semi-enclosed area, gaining speed and volume like a meth addict at a Chuck E. Cheese.

She and Dre saw a local hillbilly cover band at Mulberry Square the Saturday before The Fog. Sam told Dre she wanted to leave early because of the cold. In truth, it was because the acoustics made her want to stab her eardrums with knitting needles.

Fiona loved the place.

When they discovered the cement pad and brick buildings around it were largely intact, Fiona was overjoyed.

"Look at my new stage," she crooned. "Isn't it perfect?"

"Yes, darling," Sam said. "It suits you."

Fiona whirled on her.

"Don't call me 'darling,'" she snapped. Her eyes flashed with venom.

"Okay." She was hurt by this but knew better than to say it out loud. Her shoulders slumped. "Why not?"

Fiona grabbed Sam's chin.

"I just hate the way that word sounds coming out of your mouth." She patted Sam's cheek. "Okay? Don't say it."

Deep within her, a tiny part of Sam thought Fiona was being ridiculous but she squashed it.

"Yes, of course, da-dear."

"Much better!" Then she twirled in the empty space and belted out a high c that pierced Sam's eardrums. Her blonde hair whirling around her. Sam hid a flinch.

"Beautiful, dear. Perfect!"

Sam knew that Fiona would likely gather her entourage there, and sure enough, as soon as they emerged, there she was – Hitler in heels, perched on a makeshift throne of stacked aluminum tables and chairs.

Raven pushed through the rapt crowd and rushed to her side, broken radial bones grinding together.

"My love, I found you," Raven called.

Sam followed several steps behind. Raven tried to climb up the rickety edifice before Fiona ordered her to stop. The Goddess of Love held out her delicate hand and an eight-foot-tall troll steadied her as she descended the six-foot-tall erection with the cosmic grace of a swan.

"My darling," Fiona crooned and embraced Raven who looked like she was about to perish from unbridled ecstasy.

"Beloveds," Fiona addressed the crowd. "This is the Heir of The Shadow Liar. She has so bravely decided to renounce that vile woman and join us. Let us welcome her! May her joy become our own."

Memories flooded Sam as Fiona's stench engulfed her senses. Even though it had only been a vision, it felt so real. She remembered her screams over the slightest misstep.

"You took too long to get me water. Are you even trying?"

The blame:

"It's your fault I'm stuck here. Do you hear me? Say that you hear me. Say it. Say that you're sorry. Again. Say it again. Say it five hundred times and then five hundred more."

The ridiculous statues she demanded Sam construct in her honor. She spent a thousand years carving Fiona's naked likeness into a mile long stretch of ocean cliff face and when Fiona saw it her response was: "This makes me look fat. Why did you make me look fat?"

"I want to get married," Fiona burst out one day after a ten thousand years of torture.

Sam was attempting to read on their beige couch.

"Okay," Sam said and put the book down.

Maybe this is the moment, she thought. Maybe it will be better after this. Maybe this is it.

After months of creating thousands of white plastic roses, decorating every square inch of rubble downtown with them, building an altar of whale bones in front of the Clocktower and selecting the perfect show tunes to sing, Fiona, in her tasteful yet sexy, ice white dress, declared them married while Sam, in an ivory tux she secretly hated, nodded hopefully. Then Fiona blinked and said: "Okay, we're divorced now."

The demands escalated. The screams got louder and the insults more pointed.

"Your mother was right!"

The moments of calm got shorter and fewer until one day Fiona asked for her heart.

"I want to eat it. I deserve that much, at least."

"What?" Sam asked.

They sat in the towering monument she had constructed to Fiona's beauty. Rising ten stories into the air, Sam pulled steel girders from old buildings and bent them by hand into shape. They were sitting in the breakfast nook inside the statue's eye overlooking the dead ocean.

"Cut out your heart and feed it to me."

She hated Fiona's voice - the pins and needles embedded in it, the whining accusations in the rollercoaster pitch and tone. Unexploded bombs rode through the highs and lows of her syllables.

Sam looked around the twenty-foot square room searching for a will to resist and couldn't find it in the hand-distressed, shiplap-covered walls, light hardwood floors, the shabby chic white table or the "Live, Laugh, Love" sign directly opposite her.

With a nod, not meeting Fiona's eyes, Sam dug the nails of the two fingers she still had on her left hand (Fiona bit the rest off during a tantrum, over what Sam couldn't remember) into her chest and with a twist yanked out the still-beating muscle.

Sam held this part of herself, wondering idly how she was still alive and clarity descended.

It will never be enough.

For so long, Sam kept hoping that if she just gave enough, if she turned herself into bloody knots, if she found some secret key, some perfect set of events, Fiona would love her back, the abuse would end and they could be happy together.

No.

It wasn't a thought, really, or even a feeling. Sam knew.

"No," she said.

"Excuse me?"

Sam looked up and met the eyes of the worst person she'd ever known.

"This is mine and I don't want to give it to you."

She awoke from her vision.

"Oh, look." Fiona pointed at Sam. "The Shadow Liar herself is here. Perhaps she has come to repent."

The crowd, made up of those poor souls unfortunate enough to catch a whiff, booed and hissed. Raven fell to her knees.

"Hello, Fiona," Sam said.

"Have we met?" The glowing swan goddess was confused. Her lovely eyes turned down at the corners and those exquisite lips pouted.

"Only in my nightmares."

Fiona's pout deepened. No one in her entire life had ever been unhappy to see her.

"Raven needs medical attention. Her arms are broken."

Fiona snatched Raven up from this ground and wrapped her arms around her.

"Oh, my poor darling, what did that evil monster do to you?"

Raven nestled her head into Fiona's shoulder.

"She tried to keep me from you, but I feel no pain as long as I'm near you."

Sam rolled her eyes so hard she almost gave herself a seizure.

"Right," she said. "Just get her medical attention and I'll go."

Fiona snapped her fingers and the crowd surged forward, surrounding Sam. She felt the hot breath of dozens of people on her neck and fought the impulse to kill them all.

"Raven, my darling," Fiona said – absolute malice gleaming in her eyes. "Crawl for me, dear."

Sam had never wanted to rip someone's face off and feed it to them before.

"Death Bringer?" Fiona raised her arms. "I am love. As long as there's love, I cannot die."

The crowd pressed against Sam's back. The concrete buildings loomed over her with silent accusations. Her heart pounded loud in her ears. One of the kindest people she'd ever met had tears running down her cheeks and her bones pressed outward against her skin because no one had ever hugged this fucking asshole as a child.

Sam was just done. She cloaked herself in a fraction of Death. Five rows of the mob directly behind her passed out. The rest gasped, trying to catch the falling bodies. Sam crossed the distance between them. She wrapped her hand in Fiona's hair at the base of her skull, exposing that swan-like neck.

Sam brought her mouth within centimeters of those plump lips. Bile rose and she fought the need to vomit as she stared deep into Fiona's icy, soulless eyes.

"Maybe I can't kill you,' Sam said. "But I can make you wish you were dead."

She brought her left hand up and tapped the center of Fiona's forehead. The Goddess of Love dropped to her knees screaming in ecstasy. Her delicate bosom heaved. A thin sheen of sweat glistened across her countenance.

"This?" She laughed a full throated laugh of exhilaration. "You think this is punishment, Shadow Liar?"

Sam turned away as Fiona's stench increased. She swallowed down the nausea clawing its way up her chest. It tasted like self-loathing and regret.

"Is there a Healer in the house?" Sam called.

"Hey, Sam!"

"Inoke!"

The heavy-set man with long, shaggy, black hair ambled through the mob in his knee-length basketball shorts and blue Hawaiian shirt.

"What are you doing here? Did you get trapped in this asshole's scent?"

"I mean," Inoke stared down at Fiona's writhing figure, "she's hot, Sam. She's really hot. She's like the hottest woman I've ever seen."

Sam dry heaved.

"Okay, man, she's absolute trash, but whatever. Raven needs your help."

"Don't you dare!" Fiona seethed from the concrete.

Inoke's shoulders hunched even further and his soft, light brown eyes twitched.

"I dunno, Sam."

"Who did you swear an oath to?" Sam snapped, totally unsurprised. "Was it this garbage scow excuse for a human being or was it the Goddess of Healing?"

He shrugged and shuffled. Fiona cackled.

"Oh, for fuck's sake," Sam said. "Show me your hands."

He pulled his hands from his pockets and they gave off the tell-tale glow. Sam yanked Raven off the ground and set her arms in Inoke's glowing hands. Her bones snapped back together as she yelled.

Fiona spewed curses at her, Inoke, Raven, every person in attendance and their distant ancestors. Sam turned to Raven.

"If you ever come back to your senses, you know how to find me. You are always welcome in my realm, young Death Bringer."

Sam walked through the mob. Not one of them looked at her, even though she recognized a couple people from the Old Beeman Building. She paused across the street from Mulberry Square right in front of a minimalist, bougie sex shop. The storefront was plastered over with posters of an exaggeratedly pointy woman's face with wild hair and the words: *The Shadow Liar Lies.*

Kellyman landed on the top of the trash can next to her.

"What about me, Boss?" he asked. "What do you want me to do now?"

"The same thing you did before," Sam said. "If she's in danger, get her out of there. Otherwise, hang back, try not to get noticed and ignore everything she says to you."

"Got it, Boss," he croaked. "I'm gonna miss that kid, ya know?"

"Yeah," Sam said with a sigh. "I know."

Kellyman nodded and flew to the top of one of the adjacent buildings.

Fiona's screams increased in speed and volume as Sam turned into a raven and flew away.

*****

10:19 am, Nov. 10, 2020, 43 days after The Fog

"How is your grandmother?" Kito asked. "Is she well?"

"What?" Jimmy asked. He paused in the middle of a slow turn, checking out the low cave with iridescent walls.

"Your grandmother?" she repeated. "How is she? The last I heard, she was having problems with her hip. Poor dear. I hope she's doing well… she seems… nice."

Kito trailed off as Jimmy stared at her.

"Why do you know about my grandma's hip? Do you know her?"

She thought long and hard about what it meant to know someone in this world. She could tell he was afraid. His voice had risen to become toothy and pointed.

"I hear things," she said and pointed at the cave's ceiling. She hoped that would reassure him. As she moved, the iridescent light from the pools caught the abalone dust on her skin, making her shimmer.

Jimmy's expression cleared.

"Oh, you're magic, too."

"Me?"

Kito has always liked Jimmy. He would run around downtown with his parents as a child. When he was eight, he tried to go swimming in the pool beneath the Clocktower on a hot July day. She tried to keep an eye on him during his teenage years, while he drank and did drugs on the streets until the early hours of the morning. He'd grown up as well as she hoped he would. It was the kindest thing anyone had said to her in thousands of years.

"Yes," she said, looking at her arms. "I, too, am sacred."

"That's cool," Jimmy said. "So what's your deal? Do you like, read minds? Turn into a bird?"

"I sing and make art," Kito said. "Would you like to see?"

She pointed to the cave wall behind him. It was covered with abalone shells. Subtle patterns appeared. Each shell was carefully chosen for its slightly different color and sheen. Faces emerged – the half smiling face of an older man, his eyes crinkling with laughter, people, so many people – a woman kneeling in the surf, a group of hunters crouching in a meadow, women in long grass skirts and animal skin capes. These images were interwoven into a backdrop of massive trees rising up behind a swelling ocean. It felt alive - the people caught just in the act of looking at you. The waves were about to crest on the beach. The trees swayed in the breeze.

"Whoa," Jimmy breathed.

"Do you like it?" Kito hopped a bit in her excitement. "I'm undecided on this part right here."

She gestured to a small portion of the mosaic in the lower right entrance of the cave. Instead of shells these were fossilized creatures, immortalized in soft gray rock. They congregated near the corner but as he stared, he realized they were interspersed through the rest of the artwork.

"Is that The Fog?"

"Yes!" Kito clapped and spun around. "You understand. What do you think of it? Do you like it?"

Jimmy loved it in places he didn't understand but he wasn't an art guy. The last time he'd had a brush with the art world was the Thanksgiving turkey he drew in the shape of his hand in kindergarten. It still had a place of honor on his grandmother's fridge. She'd had it laminated.

"It's cool," he said, for lack of anything better popping into his mind.

Kito's whole being drooped.

"Oh."

He felt like an ass. This was the most beautiful thing he'd ever seen – better even than YouTube videos of The Miracle on Ice. But he didn't know how to say that so he went with what he did know.

"It's, umm." Jimmy cleared his throat and subconsciously put on his best sports announcer voice. "This section of trees creates a direct path to this figure here and that hits, um, this part."

She looked like she was gonna cry. Al Michaels would be so ashamed.

"It's so pretty it makes my stomach hurt," he said, deciding on honesty.

Kito lit back up.

"Really? Are you sure? You like it?"

He nodded.

"Yeah, yeah, I am."

The silence stretched between them into agonizing awkwardness.

Jimmy finally broke down.

"Hey, so you live here, right?"

"Yeah," Kito said.

She wanted to tell him about the oceans of minutes she'd spent here. How, when the sand covered her, pushing her further and further down until Kito thought the pressure would kill her, part of her was glad of it. But it was too many words, too soon – they got tangled up in her mouth.

"Okay, cool," he said. "How do I get out of here?"

"You want to leave?"

Kito liked the way his voice rose when he greeted his friends, the way he got so excited to see them. She imagined him greeting her that way – happy, familiar, at ease. When she heard him in the caverns nearby, she'd sung a song hoping and praying he would find his way to her and now that warmth was going away. Her heart shattered.

"Yeah, if that's cool. I don't even know how long I've been down here. My grandma's gotta be worried."

Kito wouldn't meet his eyes. She nodded.

"I think I can send you home," she said, grabbing his rough hands in hers. The time underground had not been kind to them. She sang to him as tears streamed down her face.

"Hey, are you okay?" Jimmy asked – too late.

He was gone.

*****

2:43 pm Nov. 12, 2020, 45 days after The Fog

Fiona couldn't understand why all these terrible things kept happening to her.

First of all, her daddy insisted that she drive all the way from Carmel to this backwater hellhole on a Saturday when he knew she had a perfectly amazing party at Gustav's to attend.

He said he had some surprise announcement about a boat or something. She absolutely had not been paying attention. Then her driver was some local day laborer of her uncle's who smelled like fish and insisted on talking the entire car ride.

When they arrived at Daddy's house, cringe of all cringe, her gross husband was already there. Daddy made her marry him like a thousand years ago, he said he was some kind of tech genius who could build a bath bomb out of legos or something. So she took pity on him and they got married in Ibiza, despite the fact that he was the 'c' word. She even fucked him. Ew. Her generosity was endless.

Whatever, anyway. Daddy had this lame party and she was forced to attend and in the middle of it, when she was in a compromising position with either her husband or her brother, honestly, she couldn't remember – not that it mattered – this crazy magic shit rolled in and she was like, in a coma for two months with her cooch out for everyone to see. Then she was the Goddess of Love, but that wasn't really The Fog. That was something Daddy gave to her ages ago.

Anyway, being a goddess wasn't so terrible except all these people kept showing up, expecting her to be nice and then Daddy told her to go find that girl because she was Death's Hair or something.

And then that woman showed up. That absolute bitch. It was fun for a while. Fiona couldn't lie. Like endless screaming orgasms? Yes, please! Sign me up for that shit.

But the pressure built and built and the satisfaction was more fleeting. She couldn't, like, eat anything because she kept screaming and these people were looking at her.

Fiona thought about ordering all of them to claw their own eyes out so they couldn't see her except that would make them more useless than they already were and she didn't need any more 'c' words in her life. So pathetic.

Fiona held onto her thoughts long enough to form a plan. "You."

She snapped her fingers and pointed. She lay where that bitch left her. Fiona couldn't walk and no fucking way was she letting these grubby monsters carry her. The thought of their hands on her body almost made her miss an orgasm. They all crouched with their heads down on the concrete. She'd ordered them not to look at her.

The pressure built. Her toes curled and breath came in deep pants.

"Hair Girl." She snapped when she could think for a half second. "Death Minion, come here."

"Yes, my love."

A lanky goth with rainbow, glitter eyeshadow crawled over.

"Right, you're the one who looks like Morrisey fucked a Care bear."

"You're so funny, my darling," Raven said, still not looking at her.

The waves built again. Fiona wanted to rip her clit off.

"Call her," she moaned. "Bring your cunt ass of a boss here. NOW."

"I don't know if I can." Raven bit her lip in uncertainty. "Kellyman left. I'm all yours now."

"Call her, you dumb bitch!" Fiona screeched. "Do it now! Get her here! Get her here!"

So Raven, taken aback, called out Sam's name as loud as she could over Fiona's cries of ecstasy.

A long tear appeared in reality and The Shadow Liar emerged from it.

"Hello, Fiona. Long time no see. I thought you said this wasn't any big deal? It's been an hour."

An hour? It was decades of torture. How dare she? This bitch looked down on her, Fiona could tell. She looked at her like she hated her, like she was worthless. No one hated her. Daddy made sure of that.

"Care bear Goth," Fiona snapped at Raven. "K-k-k-kill her."

"I can't."

Raven hung her head in shame.

"You brought me all the way over here for this? She can't kill me, Fiona. She tried once. It was adorable."

Fiona ground her teeth together so hard the top front two snapped and flew out of her mouth.

"Kill him then, little Death Bringer." She swung her finger to where Inoke knelt on the concrete.

"What?" He glanced between all of them. "Me? Why me?"

"Oh, you know what you did. Kill him. Kill all of them until that bitch makes it stop."

And Raven knew. This woman didn't love her. This woman didn't love anybody. She couldn't.

"No, I don't want to. That man made me hurt people. I didn't want to then and I don't want to now. If you were really the goddess of love, you wouldn't hurt anybody."

Sam gazed up at the sky and thanked the Holy Darkness.

"That's my girl," she breathed. "I am so proud of you."

Raven's emptiness consumed her. Somehow, she was more bereft than she was before she met Fiona.

"I want to leave now," she told Sam.

"Okay."

Sam opened a tear in reality.

"I think you should stay with us for a while. Is that okay?"

Raven's shoulders were the narrowest Sam had ever seen. The young woman shrank into herself.

"Yeah, that would be nice."

"What about me?" Fiona writhed on the ground. The back of her shirt was shredded and blood from the scratches soaked into the concrete.

Sam glared down at her.

"What about you?"

Fiona flopped onto her stomach and crawled towards them.

"Make it stop," she begged.

"Why?"

Fiona didn't know what to do with that.

"Because I told you to."

Sam crouched down to meet her eyes.

"No." Then she stood and walked toward the tear.

"Please! I'll give you whatever you want."

"What could you possibly have that I want?"

"Them." She nodded to the mob, who sat without moving during this entire exchange with their heads bowed. "You can have them. You can do whatever you want with them. I'll just tell them to listen to you. They'll do it. They do anything I say. Get up and hop on one foot."

As one, the mob rose and hopped.

"I don't need slaves. I am the Goddess of Justice."

Fiona was genuinely confused.

"Isn't that the thing all those icky protesters have on their signs?"

"For fuck's sake, I do not have the time for you to figure this out. Let them go. If you can't, you're stuck this way. Okay? Understand?"

"Don't talk to me like that. I am perfect! I am the Goddess of Love. You don't get to talk to me like that."

Sam's eyes narrowed and the pressure increased. The waves wouldn't stop. Blood flowed from between Fiona's legs.

"Shit, you're really hurting her," Raven said.

"She's got it coming."

"Pun intended?"

"Maybe."

She bent over Fiona, and with her hands under both arms, hiked her up onto The Second Most Egregious Sin of Hipster Architecture – uncomfortable aluminum chairs.

"You want it to stop?" Sam asked.

Fiona's mind was gone. Her eyes darted, unfocused across the skyline. Sam eased back on the curse a little.

"Do you want it to stop?"

"Yes," Fiona gasped.

"Can you free them?"

"Yes."

"Great, do it and I'll make it stop."

"Make it stop first."

"Bye," Sam said and turned her back to that wretched excuse for a human being.

"Wait!"

Sam paused.

Fiona spat on her palm, spread her legs and wiped her hand across her vulva.

"Ew," Sam said.

The people around them rose in fits and starts. Muscles had cramped and legs gone numb. No one met the eyes of anyone around them.

Sam snapped her fingers and the waves inside Fiona's body quieted and then stopped, but the Goddess of Death was not done with her yet. She leaned over her with those strange eyes and a threat in her voice when she said:

"I can bring it back with a thought. If you ever do this to anyone again, I will put you back on the ground like the useless, fucking insect you are. Understand?"

Fiona nodded and plotted her revenge.

"My daddy's going to kill you."

"Your daddy's gonna try," Sam tossed back as she led Raven through the tear.

"No," Fiona muttered after she'd gone. "My daddy is going to kill you and every trash townie in this hellhole."

NO. WHO ARE YOU? REALLY?

2:09 pm Sept. 28, 2020, 5 hours before The Fog

When a bland man in a good suit headhunted Dr. Matthew Lanier Cowart the week before graduation, he couldn't believe his luck.

The pay was outstanding. They wanted him to live in Sunset Cove – a cool little town he'd spent too much time getting stoned in when he should have been studying. Amazing!

Then the bland man told him that the job would be searching for Hawking Radiation in the Pacific Ocean and Matt laughed so hard he fell off his chair.

"Did Gin put you up to this? She thinks shit like this is hilarious. How much is she paying you?"

The man pulled a sheaf of papers from his sleek, black, briefcase.

"Dr. Chandra has already turned us down," he said and handed Matt the papers. "She asked if you were paying me as well. I told her that you were not."

Matt glanced through the papers – no NDA in sight.

"My employer strongly believes that a primordial black hole exists off the coast of Sunset Cove. He would like to pay you handsomely to find it."

1)   There were so many things wrong with that sentence Matt didn't know where to start. Primordial black holes or micro black holes, a theoretical type of black hole formed after the Big Bang,

had a lifespan much shorter than the existence of the Universe and therefore, could not exist in the present.

2) A primordial black hole, especially one large enough to emit detectable radiation, during its very short lifespan would obliterate … Matt did a quick calculation, Earth.

3) The amount of heat generated by such a thing would cause the entire Pacific Ocean to boil.

4) Why the hell did some Silicon Valley billionaire care about theoretical physics?

"The list of candidates for this position is short, Dr. Cowart," the Bland Man said. For the life of him, Matt could not remember his name. Although, he'd introduced himself twice. "I am authorized to double your salary, provide you with a lovely beach house and a company car as part of the incentive package."

Shit, it was almost too weird not to.

"It is a year-long contract. The only requirement is that you do not publish your findings. However, as you know, my employer has a relationship with CERN and would be happy to provide you with a glowing letter of recommendation and several references once your time with us is complete."

A year with no record and that kind of cash? He could fund his own research on dark matter for a few years and tell people some aunt had died and left him enough money to go on an extended bender. His friends would believe that.

"You did it, didn't you?" Gin texted him that night. "You took that weird-ass job."

"I can neither confirm nor deny."

She responded with the eye-rolling emoji.

So he found himself in the afternoon of Sept. 28, 2020 on the deck of a gleaming, white, double deck, luxury yacht, retrofitted into a research vessel trolling Monterey Bay for extreme water temperature changes.

It was shockingly dull. He spent most of the time day-drinking.

The whole thing would have been a very decent waste of a year if it hadn't been for the witch. He wasn't being derogatory – that's what she called herself. Bedecked in silver charms from head to toe and dripping in multi-hued, silk scarves, Persephone Liadan Morpheus Aradia liked to chat – about everything from her cat familiar, Athena, who she mostly referred to as 'her sweet Sniffle Whiffles,' to the moon water she collected last night, or how Matt's astrological chart said he was meant for great things among the stars.

"I'm serious, man," she said for the eighty-five millionth time in the past six months. "You should see the readings. Big things, man. Big things in your future."

"Uh, huh," he said for the eighty-five millionth and one time. "I'm going to go check the instruments."

"Good idea!" Her face brightened beneath the thick eyeliner she wore everyday. "I'm going to cast some runes. I've got a good feeling about today."

She said that every day.

Matt popped open another beer as he escaped to the instrument room, which had once been a luxury bedroom. The laptop in the corner next to the bed collected readings and the gray panels with lights flashed and beeped. Matt flopped face first onto the bed, spilling not a single drop and began his daily, three-hour-long, afternoon nap.

Beep.

He reached over and hit the return key.

Beep. Beep. Beep. BEEP.

He smacked the keyboard. It may have been his imagination but the beeping became hurt and accusatory. Matt sighed, rolled over and pulled the injured laptop closer.

The numbers he was reading didn't make any sense. He restarted the computer and realized he was sweating… on a boat… in the Pacific Ocean… in the fall. He scrambled to the deck and saw the sea around them gently boiling. Dead fish bubbled up to the surface.

Matt ran to the helm.

Thank god this thing is made of fiberglass. An aluminum hull would have cooked us alive. He stopped dead in front of the door. *He **knew**. That's why he gave them this boat.*

"Stop the engines!" Matt yelled as he pounded on the door. The engine sounds sputtered and ground into silence.

The ship's captain, Xavier Mendoza, a short man with a trim mustache, who hid all the crazy shit he'd seen behind weary professionalism and a smart hat, opened the door.

"The engines overheated, sir," Capt. Mendoza said. "We are stalled for now. I radioed the shore for support. If the situation doesn't resolve by nightfall, they will send a rescue vessel."

Persephone rushed down the stairs in a flurry of whirling fabric and jingling silver.

"Cast the nets!" she said. "It's here. We've found it. It's here."

Captain Mendoza met his eyes. Matt shrugged. She asked them to cast the nets once or twice a day.

"I mean the readings are good," he said. "I think we should."

They used to cast the nets everyday until Matt found out that bottom trawling, where weighted nets are dragged across the ocean floor, destroys habitats and leaves scars that never heal so he put his foot down. They only cast nets when he gave the go-ahead.

So the crew loaded up the nets and dropped the concrete blocks that would hold the fifty-foot net onto the ocean floor. Without the engines, it was unlikely they would catch anything.

Persephone stood on the railing of the hull. She stared, unblinking, at the murky, gray water. The boiling stopped.

"That's it," she said. "We got it. Bring up the nets."

"Persephone," Matt said. "I think we should wait. There's no need."

She glared at him and with a commanding presence he had no idea she possessed, turned to the deckhands:

"Gentlemen, bring them up, *now*," Persephone barked.

The wind tossed her stringy black hair around as she helped them. With madness in her eyes, she clawed at the net, using her body to pull the weight of it back.

"Persephone, maybe you should…"

"Shut up, Matt," she growled. Sweat made her eyeliner smear across her nose and temples. "I am so sick of your condescending bullshit."

"I…" He didn't have a defense for that. Honestly, he didn't think she noticed.

She got down on her knees and crawled across the net, tossing starfish, kelp and other detritus aside she went.

"I can feel you," she chanted. "Where are you? I can feel you. Where are you? Show yourself please."

Matt felt it too, like a whisper, like a memory of something so important he couldn't believe he'd forgotten. It crawled up the back up his neck, through his thinning hair. It made him want – what it was he wanted, he could not have said, but he longed for it desperately.

Beneath a bit of bleached and dead coral, there 'it' was. Small for the impact it made – a gray, stone box. Perfectly square, he estimated it was about five inches across. Inky black marks decorated each side. No barnacles clung to it. The box looked both eerily new and incredibly ancient. One corner of the lid had chipped away. The whole thing practically gleamed.

Persephone gasped at the sight of it. Matt reached out to grab the little receptacle.

"Don't touch it!" she yelled. "No one touch it."

The few crew members and Captain Mendoza gathered around the box. They were as transfixed as Matt was. Everyone coiled like a broken spring. Matt needed to open it.

"I'm sorry," Persephone said to the cloudless sky. "I didn't know. I didn't know what this was. I thought it would bring me closer to you. I am so sorry, great lady."

"What is it?" Matt breathed. He needed to rush past her and lift the simple stone lid with no latch, no hinge – the one that should have opened on its own ages ago.

"It is grief," she said, and wrapped her arms around herself. "This is unimaginable loss and blind revenge in the face of that loss. It has no place in this world of men. It has to go back."

She gathered the netting around the object, careful not to touch it.

Matt rushed past her. He shoved her and snatched the box from the deck. He had to know. He had to see. His logical brain disappeared and all that remained was the truth of him – the insatiable curiosity, the desperate need to know what made this world the way it was.

It felt warm in his hands. He cradled the box like a baby.

"Matt!" Persephone yelled. "Stop! Don't do this!"

He could barely hear her over the rumbling in his ears. It was the sound of tectonic plates moving in the earth. It was the impossible wind sweeping across the desolate moon.

He could not have stopped even if his hands were shattered. Matt lifted the lid. A black dot the size of a quarter appeared above the box. Thick, gray fog cascaded out of the dot, giving off an eerie glow. Time halted its inevitable march. He could not move as the atoms of his body stretched and narrowed.

The woman appeared. In less than a blink of the eye, the sky became an endless, starless black. She moved in waves and particles. His brain struggled to make sense of the proportions of her – the immense height that shifted to normal as she walked toward him in a simple black shirt and pants with bare feet. Her face chiseled from stone with burning eyes.

The world leaned toward her. His analytical brain saw the way the lines of the boat fractured in her direction. He concluded that the sheer gravity of her bent light.

She assessed them with a clinical gaze and plucked the box from Matt's hands. He ached for its return.

"Your master does you no favors," the woman said in low, clear tones – so normal for such a creature. She turned to Captain Mendoza. He was frozen in the act of reaching for the box.

"He gave you a missive for me," she said. "May I?"

The woman held out her hand. The captain blinked and pulled a folded piece of paper from his breast pocket. Without meeting her eyes, he gave it over. She glanced at it and laughed. The paper evaporated. Matt still could not move.

"Arrogant, Nommo." She rolled her eyes and paced across the gleaming wooden deck. He could see black markings on her left hand and foot.

"But if he is here…" She paused and looked directly at Matt. He wished she wouldn't. That gaze stripped him down to his blubbering, needy essence without compassion or care. "So must she. These things must end as they began."

She tilted her head and peered further into the dark recesses of his soul.

"Are you the confluence? Are you the point of connection?"

To his immense relief, Matt realized he could move, breathe and think again. He rubbed the back of his neck.

"Is that a rhetorical question?"

A smile flashed across her lips so quickly he thought he hallucinated it.

"No. Do you know a woman with wild hair and disquieting eyes?"

Sam.

"Um," he replied.

"Think well before you answer, your life and the lives of everyone on this boat depend upon it."

She said it with absolute certainty and zero emotion.

"What happens if I don't?" He had to know.

That fleeting smile again.

"I put that," she nodded to the dot, "back in the box, kill all of you and destroy this boat in a way that looks like an accident. Then

I place this box somewhere it will take a dozen lifetimes for your master to find."

"He's not our master," Captain Mendoza said.

"You swore an oath to him," she said. An ornate black chair appeared behind her. She reclined upon it. "Profoundly stupid of you, in my opinion."

"What happens if I do know a woman like that?"

She leaned forward, elbows on her knees, ready to deal.

"I grant your heart's desire. I send these people beyond the boundaries of this county before the doorway closes. They are all handsomely rewarded for their service to me and I let that," she nodded to the dot, "go."

He trembled under the weight of it.

"People will die."

"Not all of them. If that woman is here, she'll protect many of them. You, Dr. Cowart will survive and receive everything you desire."

He wiped a tear from his cheek.

"You'd kill all those people just to find one person?"

"I enjoy your company, Doctor," she said. Those eyes burned in ways he couldn't understand. "You keep your wits about you in moments of terror. It is a rare gift. So, I'm going to be honest. There is no crime, no sin, no atrocity I would not commit to get to her. Do you understand?"

He nodded. In the end, he bent to her will. Perhaps, he thought, this is better than the alternative of letting this monstrous being run rampant.

"Sam," he said as his voice quaked. "I think you're looking for Sam. I don't know her last name."

The woman stood in a flash, knocking over the chair. She grabbed the front of his Hawaiian shirt. He became aware of the fearful stillness around him — the constant engine noise, the lapping of waves against the side of the boat and the chuff of wind against his ears were gone.

When Matt was a kid, he was obsessed with sharks. He spent hours poring over books and pictures. His public library ordered twelve shark documentaries because he pestered them about it. He always imagined what it would feel like to be one – swimming up to a smaller animal, their scent taking over your reason, and chomping down, knowing nothing could stop you.

With her breath in his face, he knew what the shark's prey felt – that split second of knowing you're fucked before the jaws close in

"Tell me everything," she demanded. "Everything."

He babbled. Information poured from him in fits and starts:

"She's a bartender at this brewery I go to a lot. She's nice enough, kinda funny, but weird. Likes to read. When I told her what I do for a living she asked me these random questions about dark matter, like: Is it alive? Does it think? Is it interconnected to regular matter, like a web that regular matter lays over? Is that where the souls of the damned go when they die? Are crows and ravens black because they're descended from dinosaurs that absorbed the dark matter from the mini black hole when the meteorite struck and killed them all? Weird shit like that. Doesn't drive a car, I don't think. Umm, somehow her and the brewmaster are related. I haven't figured that out yet but they act like brother and sister. There's another woman who works there, she's friends with her too. They're close. She looks mean but she's nice, too. I dunno. I dunno what you wanna hear."

"Enough." She raised her arm and Matt got the distinct impression that this stone woman was absolutely gleeful.

"CARL!" she yelled into the darkness.

The biggest fucking raven he'd ever seen appeared on the deck railing. It clicked at her.

"Did you hear that?"

The bird nodded sharply and croaked as its throat rose and fell.

"It is what it is, but she's here, Carl. She's here."

The corvid squalled and flapped in response.

"Stay by her side through what's coming. She lives, Carl. If she dies before she can face me, you are a cooked Nommo. Understand? I do not care what it takes."

The bird snapped its razor sharp beak twice and flew off into the darkness.

One by one, she released the crew from the event horizon and with a wave of her arm they disappeared.

Persephone did not rise. She knelt with a bowed head.

"Great Queen, please," she said. "I beg of you, spare this place. I saw what was lost to you. I saw what happened. I see what will happen. I'm so sorry but there has to be a better way. Please don't do this. Please take our lives instead."

Matt felt certain she would kill the witch for her insolence – snap her neck there and then with a twist of her wrists and flashing eyes. Instead, she placed her hand on the kneeling woman's head and crouched to meet her eyes.

"My sweet sister, your heart is too good for this world. This is the way I have chosen. Will it ease your conscience to know you will not remember this? And that I will reward those who die handsomely in their next life."

"No," Persephone said, tears streamed down her face. "It won't. I helped make this happen. I didn't know. I grew up here. This is my home."

"I am in your debt." The woman nodded and kissed Persephone's forehead. "I am grateful for your help. You will be rewarded. Blessings of Darkness upon you, sister."

She waved her arm and Persephone disappeared. Matt stood alone, in infinite cold blackness with the most terrifying being imaginable, and all he had were questions.

The woman eyed him – like she knew something about him he didn't.

"I suppose I should be thankful that you are a descendant of Nommo. That thirst of yours is more predictable than the sunrise on this world."

He didn't know what to say so he shrugged and felt vaguely ashamed.

"What do you want, Dr. Matthew Lanier Cowart?" she asked as she sat back down. "It's not blood. I don't think it's money or power. Your incessant inquiries and chosen occupation lead me to believe it's knowledge you seek. Correct?"

Matt exploded with questions.

"How did you suspend a primordial black hole in a box? How did my boss know it was here? What's it made of? Is this Hawking Radiation? But it doesn't have the right properties. What's going to happen now? How did you stop time? How did you free human beings from an event horizon? None of this should be possible. Am I dead? I'm dead, aren't I? This is a hallucination? The edibles were way too good last night. Does Persephone know you?"

The woman suddenly became very weary. An ornate footstool appeared. She rested her bare feet on it.

"You want a chair? Do you have beer? You look like you have beer."

"Yeah, it's downstairs in the cooler," he said. "I'll go get it."

"Don't bother," she said and his cooler appeared beside her. She waved and a seat appeared for him. Then she pulled a bottle out of the chest and handed it to him. He opened it with the lighter in his pocket and handed it back to her. The stone woman leaned back as she took a long swig, exposing the black symbols running along the left side of her neck. He waited on the edge of his seat for answers. She stared at the bottle.

"This is from where she works, isn't it?"

"Yes," he replied.

"Huh," she said and then stared through the blackness toward shore. "Very well, Little Nommo. The answer to most of your questions is: I built it."

"The box?"

"The universe," she replied. She held the box in her hands and traced the markings with one elegant finger.

"Oh."

"I used the black hole to capture a part of the magic in this world. The box is just rock, but I held all that power in place with my grief."

She paused but no tears came. To Matt, it seemed she had reached a place beyond sadness, beyond rage.

"Your boss found it because it's been leaking for thousands of years." She smiled long enough for him to see it held no joy. "Grief so rarely stays put. Can you imagine losing the thing most precious to you? Most holy in all creation, only for it to fall into the hands of those that would treat it like such garbage because they're too angry, too broken to know what they have? And despite the immense power you hold, you can do almost nothing to stop them?"

She took a long swig, finished the bottle and pulled another from the cooler. Nyx snapped the cap off with the tip of her fingernail.

"So I took from this world. I took part of the magic of this world. I made it imperfect and broken. I took it so you would all spend your lives longing for something – not even knowing what it was. Then I etched her name on it with my tears and my blood."

She traced markings again – starting from the top and moving through each side over and over again as she spoke.

"The woman you call Sam? This is her true name. She has something that belongs to me."

She paused, unable to tear her eyes from shore.

"Now the magic in this box will escape." The stone woman finished her second beer and gestured for him to hand her another. "It will cause incalculable violence and chaos.

"You are not dead. You are not stoned. The edibles last night were good. Persephone does not know me. She knows of me. I am one of the goddesses she worships."

"Oh."

Matt didn't know what else to ask. He hoped these answers were not the reward she mentioned. Yet, the woman remained quiet as she sipped her beer and gazed into the black.

"So, Little Nommo." She broke her reverie. "The real question is whether you would like me to give you the answers you seek or if you would like to discover them yourself."

"I can pick? I can … how would I seek them myself?"

"Travel across my creation. See it. Do the math. That kind of thing."

"But that's impossible…"

She stared at him over the lip of the bottle and he realized he needed to reassess his definition of that word.

"You would need to leave your body behind," the stone woman said. "But it can be easily done."

"Do I have to give up my body forever?" Worth it, he thought. So worth it to travel through space and time.

She shrugged.

"I can put it in storage. You can get it back when you're done."

"Are you joking? No way!"

"I will take this as your answer, Little Nommo."

She stood and tapped his forehead with her left index finger.

Matt's body fell away. True to her word, his consciousness was free to explore the mysteries of creation. He heard the impossible roar of the Big Bang. He lived inside the sun, feeling atoms break apart and explode. He knew it all.

But before she let him experience the joy of creation, she made him watch. As his physical body fell away, his mind would not leave Sunset Cove. He could not tear his gaze from the consequences of his choice. Every drop of blood, every lost child, every heartbreak was his to cherish. He knew it all. She would not let him turn away.

As he traveled the vast emptiness of space, Matt remembered every word Persephone told him – the endless lectures about the goddesses she worshiped. The witch spoke glowingly of most of them, of the lyricism of Brigid, the mystery of Bast, the mercy of Guan Yin, but she spoke two names in hushed tones.

"There's Nyx, the Primordial Goddess," she said, barely loud enough for him to hear. "She had other names, of course, but we don't know what they were. Nyx was the first and then there's The Morrigan."

He must have been bored so the change caught his attention.

"What's so special about them?"

"The Darkness," she said in a whisper that could have been mistaken for a prayer. "They live in the Darkness."

*****

3:06 pm, Nov. 13, 2020, 46 days after The Fog

Sam, as drunk as she'd been since before The Fog … three beers? No, four beers deep, sat reclined on a terrible aluminum chair, her feet propped up on another equally terrible aluminum chair, and booed the middle-aged man making proclamations on stage.

"This is bullshit, Frank!" she yelled. "Objection!"

It was definitely five beers.

Raven giggled in the chair beside Sam and did her very best to stay upright. She was only two beers in – lightweight.

This was the third, no fourth, city council meeting since the wreckage of Sunset Cove began to coalesce a few weeks back. Excessive day drinking was the only way Sam could get through it without murdering anyone.

About fifty people, most of whom appeared human, sat baking in row after row of aluminum torture devices beneath the unrelenting sun. Behind them, more creatures lurked in the shadows next to the store fronts. No one was happy to be there.

"This isn't a courtroom, Sam!" Frank yelled back. "You can't object."

Beneath the black, walrus mustache, bald spot, late Gen X slouch and spreading beer gut, Frank had a distinct honey badger energy that made Sam think he might be a little less human than he appeared. He ran these meetings like a rabid weasel looking for a fight.

"Fine," she said. "I don't object, but it's still bullshit."

The meetings were held at 3 pm every Thursday at the Clocktower downtown. The decision on the day and time took the better part of four hours during the first 'new' Sunset Cove City Council meeting. Sam spent that meeting resisting the urge to stab her own eyes out.

That day, like all the other days of the past few weeks, was too hot. The leaves of plants and branches of trees stretched their edges to the sky only to shrivel and burn in the relentless sunshine. The thick, coastal fog that used to roll in at night had disappeared. Fresh water was in increasingly short supply and no one could sleep because of the heat. It hadn't rained in Sunset Cove since well before The Fog.

Sam, as a creature of darkness, was particularly testy. She wiped sweat from her forehead and cursed the soul of the sadistic bastard who invented meetings.

"You can't just get rid of money," Frank shouted from the makeshift stage twenty feet from the Clocktower. The audience sat kitty-corner with their backs to the gray, triangular building that housed the hipster coffee shop.

"Why not?" Sam yelled back. "It's not like we have banks any more. Or jobs. Or a way to get out of this county. Why do we need money? Or rent?"

The problem was twofold: an inordinate number of tourists were visiting the weekend of The Fog because of some basketball game and, according to Sam's research, forty percent of all structures in the county had been destroyed. The ones that remained no longer had running water, lights, or adequate sanitation.

By Sam's estimation, a quarter of the population of Sunset Cove had died in The Fog and resulting catastrophes. Roughly seventy percent of that surviving population had magically transformed.

Without shelter, more and more people were visiting the hospital with heat stroke or some kind of infection. Without clean places to eat, they were getting sick. Without potable running water, they were turning to fouled lakes and stagnant rivers.

Many refused to go to the hospital. Rumors of people losing their souls to Anahit for payment were muttered in every homeless camp.

Death was on the rise again in Sunset Cove but this was not screaming, violent death. This was shitting, cursing, feverish death – foul, preventable death.

"The Shadow Liar is wrong, again," Dena Marchetti stood and announced. "We need to go back to the way things were."

The Marchettis owned half the land in Sunset Cove. They had settled in the county during the mid 1800s. Several streets, buildings, overpasses and dog parks were named after them. The Fog left the dynasty suspiciously untouched – only a couple of them died and even fewer had transformed.

"The Shadow Liar has already taken so much from us all." Dena bowed her head mournfully. "Good jobs disappeared because of her nonsense."

"Call me The Shadow Liar one more time, Dena," Sam dared her, "one more fucking time."

As propaganda went, Sam thought it was subpar, but that didn't mean it wasn't getting on her nerves.

"Stop it!" Melissa stood. "All of you. There is a compromise here somewhere."

The air weighed down on them, pregnant with unanswered questions, intimate rage and seething potential.

Before The Fog, Sam called this Earthquake Weather.

"I don't care about your stupid land," a man stood up and yelled. "I need water."

"Here." Sam pulled a bottle of water from her hoodie and tossed it at him. "Take it."

The bottle dropped into the crowd. No one touched it.

"I am the Goddess of Death, if I wanted you dead I wouldn't have to go to the trouble of poisoning you."

She had announced this many times, at several meetings, and yet, no one was reassured.

"I'm working on the water thing, okay? The water guy is just…"

Sam gestured vaguely to her brain, trying to convey Joon's state of mind, which, at best, could be described as denial and, at worst, careened into a fugue state.

"The Shadow Liar has taken not only good jobs, but now she's poisoning our water." Dena addressed the crowd. "To be a Healer, you must swear an oath to do no harm. To be a Life Bringer, you must swear an oath to grow food. Swear an oath to whom, I ask? Who are these gods we never see?"

"And goddesses," Sam muttered under her breath.

"Why don't they want money? What do they want instead? Is it your soul?"

"I'm done with you," Sam said. She waved her hand and Dena, with a graceless squawk, transformed into a crow. "Anybody else wanna call me The Shadow Liar?"

She turned to the crowd behind her and wobbled in drunkenness. Raven held out a hand to steady her.

"Anybody else wanna to fuck around and find out, huh? Anyone?"

Raven giggled again.

"You can't turn people into birds when they piss you off, Sam," Frank yelled from the stage.

"Can't I, Frank? Can't I? Anyway, she's fine. She'll turn back at sunset. I established a boundary – which she ignored. There's consequences for that!"

Melissa hadn't sat down.

"Wait, so you're saying there's a water god?" She stared at Sam, dumbfounded. "And he's the same as you?"

Sam glared at Melissa. Her soul felt like a melting two dollar Popsicle and Melissa glistened … slightly.

"Yeah, he's like me. Well, not exactly like me but his job is water."

"Where is he?" Melissa asked. "Is he punishing us?"

"No, of course not. He's a good guy. He's just…"

Not coping at all, grieving, refusing to acknowledge reality for reasons I'm certain are good but I don't know or understand.

Jakob kept telling her to be patient with Joon, that he needed time. So while fruit shriveled and rotted on the vine beneath a cloudless sky, she sat as stoically as she could in these meetings surrounded by the feckless, impotent and fearful.

"It's complicated," Sam finished.

The dude from earlier leaned back in his chair.

"Bullshit," he said. "If there's a water god, what's his name? What god is he?"

"The Dragon King," Sam said.

"The Dragon King's a myth," someone in the crowd yelled back.

Dozens of eyes swiveled in his direction. Sam felt several witches in the crowd gather the energy for a hex.

"Nope, you're right." He raised his hand. "I heard it as soon as I said it. My bad."

The mob's rage subsided a little.

The sky above them darkened. Clouds roiled in, oily and wretched, promising consequences but no water.

"Are you doing this?" Raven slurred.

Cold terror rippled along Sam's skin.

This was the moment she'd been preparing for.

She wanted, with every fiber of her being, to not be standing there. She wanted to hide behind someone bigger and stronger like a terrified child and let them face what was coming because she knew she wasn't enough. Sam knew that she couldn't fix or change what was about to happen. Then, like always, she gathered the loneliness and terror around her shoulders and stapled it to her spine to keep her upright.

"Kellyman!" Sam yelled. "You're up."

She grabbed Raven beneath her arms and tossed her into the sky.

"I'm gonna puke," she said as she disappeared into the blanket of dark wings.

Sam willed herself to sober up and remember that she knew this was coming.

"Carl!"

The bird did not respond.

"For fuck's sake, you goddamn bird. Answer me!" She scanned the charcoal sky.

"I'm here, Boss." He landed next to her.

"It's time. Get out of here."

He nodded and flew off.

The sky cracked apart.

Better her than anyone else.

A lighting strike, more massive than any skyscraper, pierced the heavens. It split the world into before and after. Sam covered her head with her arms. The circle she cast around the meeting warped but held as it absorbed the shock wave, heat and current. The concentrated light blinded her through closed eyelids.

The thunder that followed swallowed up the screams and curses of the crowd. It shook the world and made Sam's organs ache. The ground heaved. She fell hard onto the toppling chairs.

Where the lightning struck, a man with slicked-back, snowy white hair, in a pristine three-piece ivory suit, stood a few feet outside of her circle.

Fucking propaganda.

His arms were spread wide as if to embrace the entire town. The wet sheen of unpromised tears lived in his eyes.

"My beloved Sunset Cove," he proclaimed. "I have come to save you. What has she done to you? Why have you let her bring you so low?"

He had the voice of a Sunday morning TV preacher – sonorous, reassuring and covered in slime.

"I didn't do this," Sam called out to him. "This was you. This was all you."

Ignoring her, he reached the edge of her circle. With a perfectly manicured fingernail, he popped it. The Man in White swept through the crowd, tossing aside chairs and the people in them on his way to the stage. Sam pulled her sword from her hoodie and hacked away at aluminum chairs in her drunken struggle to follow him.

"You don't have to do this! We don't have to repeat history. Just go home to your family and leave everyone alone. They've been through enough."

He paused at the foot of the stage stairs to face her. His features did odd things to Sam's mind. They muddled together and gave the impression of a face – attractive, reasonable, strong but for the life of her she couldn't have described them. They were a word jumble of a nose, mouth and eyes meant to portray 'human.' His teeth were crooked. His lips were redder than blood.

"I do not repeat history, Shadow Liar," the Man in White said. "I learn from it."

The world disappeared into blank stillness. The hollow center of white flame threatened to steal her soul. Sam's mind went fuzzy and weak.

Vision returned first – black outlines suddenly focused into shapes, color and details. Hearing came next – a clamorous ringing drowned out thought. Smell – that unmistakable, acrid stench of fire and burning flesh assailed her nostrils. She brought her hand up but jerked it back from the heat. Flame leapt from a deep hole in her chest.

My heart is burning.

Across the county, every black arm band disappeared.

Massive wings flapped behind her head. The wind pushed her hair into her face as she fell backward into endless darkness.

*****

1:43 pm, Nov. 13, 2020, 46 days after The Fog

Constance Alexandra Forster puttered around her garden. Deep within the Santa Muerte mountains she and Edgar owned two point five acres of hilly, tree-lined property that was constantly under vague threat of landslides, downed trees or power outages. The previous owners used it as a vineyard and then a dumping ground for old construction materials.

She spent the better part of two decades picking broken bottles, old shoes, bricks, car parts, and rotting two by fours out of the ground and planting as she went. As a result, her garden, while perfect in her mind, was not intricately designed and regimented for aesthetic appeal. Volunteer pumpkins sprouted next to the compost pile two years ago and she ran with it. Seven plum trees bloomed in her yard and she wasn't exactly sure how that happened. One year, she'd gotten a mad hare and planted 300 daffodils because they were on sale and so very pretty. Life happened in riotous color, luscious textures, rich scents and delicious tastes wherever she made room for it. In the terrible weeks after The Fog, this garden was her refuge. This time of year, it was largely resting but splashes of life remained.

She sipped her coffee. Her cat, Jeff, clung to her chest as she tried to harvest persimmons to bring to the meeting.

Jeff, not appreciating her efforts at all, yowled as she bent over.

"Yes, I know." She patted his back.

Jeff did not believe her. He blinked his soulful amber eyes, and yowled, mournfully, again.

"Well, you are the prettiest cat in the world. Of course, you are. I don't know why you would ever doubt that."

The toads and frogs in her little pond croaked in agreement as they hopped and swam.

"See?"

Mollified, for the moment, Jeff leapt out of her arms and tucked his white and gray paws beneath him as he settled into the dirt at her feet.

Bees darted back and forth in a velvety, tenuous, rising hum. Constance inhaled the perfume of warm dust, the overripe red plums on the garden floor and the faint, bitter itch of leaf mold. The leaves crinkled softly in the dry breeze. Constance felt the abated life around her – the way each cell connected to another, and all the ways she could trade and move them to help or hinder as she chose. Beneath it all ran the deep thread of need – need for water, sunlight, food, care and growth – life's insatiable thirst to survive.

Edgar strode toward her with an unwieldy, green tool box and a shovel. They lived close enough to the Saint Augustus river that they just treated the water and pumped it directly through their taps, but the water level was so low the water pump kept burning out.

Constance, in desperation, tried her hand at dowsing with a cut plum branch and found a small aquifer beneath their driveway. Edgar's plan for the day was to run a line from the aquifer to the water pump. She wanted to explain what she had done at the meeting and offer her help to those needing water.

He put the shovel and tool box down. Jeff meowed so Edgar scooped him up.

"For the meeting?" He nodded to the growing pile of persimmons in a cardboard box.

"Mmm."

"Would you like me to put these onto the cart?"

"That would be lovely."

He picked up the box and put it inside the cart of the Orange Monstrosity. Everyone in the county had one these days. When he returned, they wrapped their arms around each other for long dreamy moments as the sun rose higher above them. Jeff was scandalized. He protested that he was obviously dying between them, before leaping huffily away.

Edgar went off to work on the water situation and Constance breathed in the life of her garden before walking the Orange Monstrosity down her driveway to the road.

The bees, so peaceful moments ago, swarmed her. Thousands upon thousands of them darted in the air, blocking her path. The sound of them overwhelmed everything else. Constance had never seen them so upset. She sang to them. Low notes of reassurance to let them know she was coming back later on this afternoon. They persisted, flying thickly about her face and bothering her hair.

"What is this? What is going on here?"

In response, the bees massed in front of her and flew toward her. Constance realized they were herding her. She stepped back and the swarm abated. Intrigued, she moved forward and the swarm increased. Bees landed on her face and shoulders. They buzzed loud and insistent in her ears. She realized what this meant.

Bad Omen.

Terrible Omen.

The worst fucking omen.

*****

3:33 pm, Nov. 13, 2020, 46 days after The Fog

The Man in White ascended the three wooden steps up to the stage. He turned to the cowering, flummoxed audience. Frank had fled from the stage when the lightning struck.

"My beautiful, beloved Sunset Cove," he said. His voice boomed through the crowd. "You've been through so much, haven't you?"

The Man in White nodded as he paced. Several audience members murmured in approval.

"The Shadow Liar has taken your food, your water, your homes, your safety." He wiped a tear from the corner of his eye. "She brought this great county to its knees. I have seen it. I have seen you suffer. I have been right there with you."

He gazed off into the distance. His profile to the audience was strong and majestic.

"Perhaps no one has suffered as much as me," the Man in White said. "She has attacked my family."

With a gesture, Fiona and Smyth walked up the stairs to stand behind him.

"My beautiful daughter," he grasped Fiona's chin, making her look at the audience, "look at her." He stroked her cheek with the back of his knuckles. "Who could want to hurt her? Hmm? What kind of monster would do that?"

Several audience members glanced at each other. Their eyes asked 'What the hell?' Others stared in absolute rapture at the stage.

"It's not right," he said mournfully. "It's just not right, what she's done. Is it?" The Man in White gestured to the magical creatures on the outskirts of the crowd. "I mean look at these poor bastards. Look at what she's done to them."

Frank stood up from where he'd been cowering on the ground at the edge of the stage.

"Hey, man," he yelled up at him. "Sam and I have our issues but she says she had nothing to do with The Fog. I believe her."

The Man in White flicked his hand in Frank's direction. The lightning flash blinded the audience and made their hair stand on end. Where the honey badger of a man once stood, was a smoking black crater in the concrete. When they could see what he had done, several people in the crowd screamed. Others clapped. Their response thrilled him. He soaked it in and for one beautiful fraction of a second, he felt their fear, their approval and then, like The Fog, it disappeared into nothingness.

The absence enraged him. He squashed it with a carefully paternal smile.

"I can save them," the Man in White announced. "I can save all of you. I can turn back time to the days before The Fog. I will return you to what you used to be."

With the flick of his wrist, the Clocktower behind him split. It leaned like a drunken sailor. Where the plain, concrete fountain once was, raged a pale fire. It was only a few feet tall but its presence felt like a desecration, a vile and heart-rending abomination.

He grinned down at his enthralled audience.

"Of course, there must be sacrifices," the Man in White said. "But only small ones."

They were already running. Half the crowd scrambled over fallen chairs to get away. The creatures at the back collected their young and raced into buildings. The rest, faithfully gazed up at him, hanging on his every breath.

"Don't run from me!" he screamed. Fury erupted from him. "How dare you? You should be grateful! I am here to save you!"

Lightning exploded from the heavens, vaporizing those who ran. The Man in White bellowed as they escaped.

"Worship me. You will worship me. You will worship me. You will love me or you will BURN!!"

*****

2:16 pm, Nov. 13, 2020, 46 days after The Fog

Constance scrapped her plan for the day, parked the Orange Monstrosity and went off to find her husband.

True to his word, he crouched on a patch of dirt by the river, swearing at the water pump.

"This fucking thing," he said, as he wiped his brow. "You forget somethin'?"

Edgar's Southern accent only made an appearance when he was truly annoyed.

Constance paced. Her hands fluttered around her and she tried to explain what happened.

"What do you want to do?" Edgar asked.

"I don't think we should leave, but we should be prepared."

"Okay, how can I help?"

"I don't know yet," she replied. Too many possibilities for disaster existed in this new world. Thick panic squirmed inside her veins. "I don't know."

Constance stared down at the earth as she tried to find a path. The bees seemed to be trying to tell her not to leave but other than that, they weren't screaming out instructions.

"I don't know." She shuffled and fought the terrible thought that something worse than The Fog was coming. "Prepare. I need to prepare."

The lackadaisical morning, full of gentle pats and soothing tea, was replaced by a manic afternoon.

Edgar dropped the water project and gathered bundles of rosemary. She bundled them, along with sprigs of garlic, and hung them over every doorway. She drew sigils on piles of thick artist's paper and burned them, then spread the ashes across the doorway and throughout the cardinal points of the garden. A red ribbon was plaited into a small braid in her hair.

The most difficult part, the Zagovory, she saved for last. Constance couldn't relax. She and Edgar said very little as they hurried from one chore to another. He would complete each task and come to her for another. Her mind wandered. Terror dwelled there. The Old Beeman Building and all the horrors she'd seen and committed sat like poison in her mind.

Edgar found her standing in the center of their simple kitchen. She couldn't move, but blinking, rocked with Jeff in her arms. He took her hand and led her to their short blue couch. Edgar sat next to her, with his arms around her. He kissed the top of her head and murmured words without meaning that told her everything she needed. How long they sat there, she could not have said. Until it was time. They both stood and she whispered the precise words of protection.

"I am rising for my blessed day, striding through the entrances to the East, to clean fields, to the rising ocean, to God's holy island where lies the stone Alatyr..."

It took hours to recite all the words. Any mistake would ruin the spell and she would have to start over.

Nearing the end, the sky outside their sliding glass doors darkened, not from the night but from something insidious and vile. Constance nodded and Edgar covered her head with his hands. It was almost here.

She inhaled, pulled every scrap of magic she could find to her and said: "May my words and thoughts be cohesive and unyielding."

The sky broke open. Light blinded her. Reverberations shook the floorboards.

An awful stillness enveloped the world. Minutes ticked by like a hooded executioner sharpening his blade.

In the moment Constance thought she could take a deep breath, lightning inundated the forest around them. Edgar yelled. She ducked as it flashed inside the house, striking the corner by the chimney as it arced straight down into the floor. A thick, black, scorch line was left in its wake.

"I didn't install a lightning rod," he said. "Did you?"

She shook her head.

They ventured to the glass patio doors. While the house was prone to all sorts of forest terrors, including ants, rats, bats, flood and fire, Constance had always loved this view. Half the valley spread out before them. The lightning made arching pinpoints across the sky, racing from cloud to cloud, branching out and reaching for the ground. Then the inevitable rumble of thunder, but no rain. She held her breath for the gray plume that would billow up and signal the beginning of another nightmare.

She and Edgar stared for long, tense moments as strike after strike rattled the bone dry forest, and yet, the smoke never came. Each time the lighting tried to touch the earth it hit a point well above ground.

"They're everywhere," she murmured. Constance couldn't imagine the time it took to put thousands of metal rods across every part of the county. Yet, she'd never noticed a single one.

"They must be invisible," Edgar said.

But who would do such a thing? Lightning was extraordinarily rare in Sunset Cove. Before The Fog, she'd only seen two, maybe three, lightning storms in the county.

As the onslaught failed to provoke fire, hope bloomed in her chest.

She grabbed Edgar's hand too hard. She prayed to the earth and to every goddess that was listening for a stay of execution, for a miracle she knew would never come.

Still she gasped when the inevitable smoke cloud rose up through the trees. Edgar turned on his heel and without a word yanked open the patio door, leapt over the balcony railing and began ripping trees and shrubs from the earth and tossing them aside.

Her numb mind went blank. Of the thousands of things she could do at that moment, a single one refused to coalesce into action. Constance wanted to crawl into bed, pull the covers over her head and pretend none of this was happening. Jeff sat at her feet and meowed up at her. She pulled him into her arms, buried her face into his fur and went to put his cat carrier by the door. A few moments later, while she was in the middle of making a burlap sack fireproof, a disembodied voice – as lyrical as it was foreboding – announced that six acres were burning near the intersection of Love Creek and Paseo – about five miles south of them.

The lightning stopped.

For the next two days, she and Edgar pretended everything was fine. Constance went back to planting garlic and consoling Jeff. Edgar continued perfecting his rosemary-artichoke sourdough.

They stubbornly avoided talking about the fire until the fear became too much. Then they would meet in the living room as they told each other 'it was so far away,' 'the wind looks good,' and 'I'm sure it'll burn itself out.'

Every hour, the disembodied voice announced the fire's progress. There were rumors in the valley that werewolves were fighting to extinguish it. The air became toxic. Her lungs felt heavy and thick inside her own house.

Then, at around noon on the second day, ash fell like snowflakes in the garden. They gazed through their patio doors at the ridge line where burnt leaves, blackened twigs, paper and bits of houses swirled in the sky above the fire.

Without a hint of rain in sight, there was no hope.

In this moment, as the air shimmered with heat, they knew they needed to run. Now. Edgar turned off the oven and abandoned the loaf of bread beginning to rise within it. Constance poured Jeff into his cat carrier. As she gathered her valuables along with some food and water, they took a moment to say goodbye to their little home on chicken legs with the perfectly creaky floorboards that smelled like old books.

You have been such a wonderful house. Thank you.

Then she thanked the bees for warning her and for all their hard work. They swirled away from her in the hot wind, seeking a safe place.

She and Edgar shoved everything into the back of their two Orange Monstrosities and sped down the mountain.

Constance was too numb to cry.

*****

10:11 am, Nov. 15, 2020, 48 days after The Fog

Joon thought he was going mad.

For weeks, his skin itched like it wanted to peel away from his body. His joints felt too hot and too tight. His hands, feet and the top of his head felt icy and loose. Electrical storms ran up and down his limbs.

He tried to talk to The Dragon King about it but he had switched to reading and would only nod with his nose stuck in a book at every one of Joon's rants without comment.

The itch had gotten a thousand times worse in the past two days. Joon sat in the corner with his knees pulled into his chest and tried not to climb the walls. Scorching hot fire ants paraded through his nerve endings. He scratched his neck and back until crusty, brown, blood appeared beneath his fingernails. His mind darted from insensate rage to manic laughter at the absurdity of it all and back down to soul-crushing depression. He hadn't slept in weeks.

Fed up, he marched to The Dragon King who sat in the usual place on the stairs and snatched the copy of *Kim Ji Young, Born 1982* out of his hands.

"What the hell is wrong with me?" Joon demanded.

"Psychologically, physically or spiritually?" He arched a brow over those dragon eyes.

"Thank you for the sarcasm," Joon snapped and clawed at his forearms. "My skin. What is wrong with my skin?"

The Dragon King retrieved his book from the floor and elegantly dusted it off.

"The balance exists within and without you. If there is an imbalance, it affects your body. Also, you are molting. You are trying to shed your past self but your mind is fighting the transformation. It must be excruciating."

The King settled gracefully onto his place on the stairs, sighed and found his page in the book.

"The drought…" Joon said.

"Has sparked a fire," The Dragon King replied. He didn't look up as he turned a page. "It has become an inferno. Thousands will die. Their forests will be decimated within a few weeks. The ash will run down the land and poison this ocean a month later."

Erin lived in the forest. She loved it. She thought the trees sang to each other.

"Do something!" Joon broke. His soul cracked open and seeped out. "Help them. Help me. Why don't you do something? Don't you care? You're supposed to be good."

In every myth, every story, The Dragon King was kind and just. He set down the book.

"Believe it or not, I am limited in how I can help, but… there is one thing I can do."

Joon's insides were frozen solid. He wrapped his arms around himself.

"Do it."

"You won't like it," The Dragon King said, his legs coiled beneath him like a spring. "But it will help."

"I said 'do it!'" Joon screamed. "Help us!"

He collapsed as his legs shook too hard to sustain him.

The Dragon King sighed and rushed down the steps. He pulled Joon into a sitting position and set his back against the wall. Then he took off his Hawaiian shirt and put it around Joon's shoulders. A cup of barley tea appeared in his hand. He urged Joon to drink it.

"Blegh," he replied. He remembered his mom giving it to him as a kid when he was sick. So gross.

"It will help with the itching," The Dragon King said.

Joon snatched the cup from his hand and chugged the nutty, bitter brew. It tasted much better than he remembered. The tea settled warm and comforting into his belly. It spread along his anguished nerves, assuaging the fires within them. Even the Hawaiian shirt helped. Its presence soothed his tattered mind.

The Dragon King waited for him to finish. Then he sat, cross-legged in front of Joon.

"Is that it?" he demanded. "Is that all you can do?"

"There is one more thing," he replied. He took Joon's hands in his own. "I can tell you a story."

"You are fucking kidding me?" He banged his head against the wall.

"It's a very powerful story," The Dragon King said. "It will either cure or kill you."

"Whatever." Joon rolled his eyes.

"I need your permission to tell this story. Otherwise, it won't work."

"Fine."

"Once I have begun, I cannot stop until the story is told."

"Okay."

Joon did not believe a word of this bullshit, but his skin didn't hurt at the moment. His entire body sagged with relief, and truthfully, he would rather die than feel the itching again.

"May I tell the story?" The Dragon King asked.

"Sure." Joon waved an uncaring hand. With the excruciating pain gone, his body wanted sleep. His mind drifted idly away from consciousness. His eyelids felt so, so heavy. They fluttered closed. "You may tell the story."

The Dragon King took several deep breaths. He held onto Joon's hand and began the tale.

"Many years ago, a little boy was excited for his birthday," The Dragon King intoned.

A thought, too terrible to be real, niggled at the back of Joon's mind, but the King's voice was low and hypnotizing, so he ignored it.

"His father, who he didn't see very much, because he worked so very hard, promised the little boy he would take him to the amusement park for his eighth birthday."

Joon's eyes snapped open.

"On the day of the little boy's birthday, his father broke his promise." Joon tried to yank his hand away from The Dragon King but he held fast. *"You see, he was a simple fisherman and he was*

called to work on that day. He needed the money and he needed to keep his job for his family. So he hugged his crying son and went to work instead of taking him to the park."

"What do you think you're doing? Stop it. Stop talking. Let me go."

The words drilled holes into Joon's skull. He tried to shake it off. He stood. The Dragon King rose with him, refusing to relinquish his hand.

"The little boy went to the park with his mother but he wasn't happy. He was angry with his father. In his mind, he called his father all the bad names he wasn't allowed to say. He drew a picture in red crayon of his father falling from the boat. He refused to say a word to his father when he got home. For the next five days, the little boy didn't speak to him."

"씨발새끼야 (Shibal-saekki-ya) (You fucking asshole)," Joon yelled and swung on him with his free hand. The Dragon King ducked.

"On the fifth day, when the father went to work…"

Joon tried to cover his ears, but The Dragon King grabbed his other hand.

"He fell off the boat and he drowned. His body was never recovered."

The story seeped into Joon's brain. It made him blind. Suddenly, he was falling, until with a splash, he wasn't in the palace anymore.

He was eight years old again, sitting at his father's funeral while his mother keened. Her face was red and blotchy with tears. Joon was so ashamed. He didn't want to be there. He didn't deserve to be there. He tore the drawing into a thousand pieces and ate it. One by one, he placed the bits of paper on his tongue and swallowed them. It made him sick, but he wouldn't allow himself to throw up. Joon never told a soul what he did.

"You blamed The Dragon King. You told yourself he was responsible. It was so much easier to pour your guilt and shame into a story than admit the truth."

"Shut up," Joon screamed.

The ocean stilled and went absolutely quiet.

"It was an accident. You are not responsible for your father's death."

Joon knew it wasn't his fault. He knew he hadn't killed his father with a childish wish. But his heart wouldn't believe it. He felt like he had murdered him – that his rage would burn everyone around him, so he pushed any feeling of anger or sadness deep, deep down and he got very good at pretending, at ignoring, and most of all, at distracting himself.

"You got so used to carrying this guilt and shame that it became part of you. Until you were terrified of who you would be without it."

Bile rose up in his throat. An impossible thing sat like a brick in his stomach. He heaved and retched. Sweat broke out across his forehead.

"You are The Dragon King because you are a good man. You are a kind man. Your father does not want you to torture yourself like this. He loves you. He is so proud of who you have become."

Joon sat back and let loose his grief. Torn bits of paper flew from his mouth into the air. They caught fire and turned to ash. Thick tears poured down his face as he sobbed.

The Dragon King patted his back. He murmured soothing nonsense.

As the grief ebbed out of him, music slowly flowed in to replace it – the thrum of the moon, the low rumble of whales and the chittering of dolphins. Then he heard the dissonance of the land. It creaked like a violin strung too tight.

Without a word, Joon stood. He opened the large doors and dove in. The second he hit the water, his skin shattered. It rearranged itself as he swam higher and higher. He broke through the surface and flew toward the battered land – a massive, shimmering blue and green dragon with glowing eyes.

*****

12:12 pm, Nov. 15, 2020, 48 days after The Fog

Constance and Edgar had only been pedaling down the mountain for fifteen minutes when Jeff lost his mind. The sky hung low – a deep, foreboding crimson. They wrapped scarves over their faces to keep out the smoke and ash raining down on them. Constance could barely see the road. In the far distance, she heard the fire roar – too close.

Jeff yowled and clawed. She had put him in the soft carrier and slung the strap over her shoulder. Constance hoped that being close to her would help keep him calm.

His nails poked through the material and into her side.

She tried to keep up a steady stream of reassuring murmurs as they traveled down the winding mountain road but the smoke took her breath. Jeff threw himself back and forth inside the carrier until Constance couldn't keep her balance.

They paused at a curve in the road next to what was once a creek. The trees lining the road were a threat. She tried to pet Jeff through the carrier. She didn't dare open it but he managed to hook his nails through the zipper and yanked it partially open. He shoved his head through the opening – eyes wild and unseeing. Before Constance could stop him, he bolted.

"Oh, no, please, no!"

Edgar grabbed a fireproof sack from the cart.

"Meet me at the Clocktower," he said, grabbing her arms. He squeezed them before running off to find Jeff.

Constance wavered. She desperately wanted to follow Edgar.

Poor Jeff must be so scared.

Hot wind roared around her. The forest shivered. The ash now carried sparks. She had never felt so alone.

Please find him.

Panic threatened to consume her mind but then she remembered that she had to stay alive. Death was not on the table. She stood up on the pedals of the Orange Monstrosity. It was hard to remember that this forest was her home. As she got further down the mountain and closer to Loch Lomond, the flames drew closer. The ominous red glow peaked through the trees. It chased her as she traveled. It stalked her as she pedaled and struggled to breathe. The trees snapped and groaned against the crackling flames. The fire hunted her, drawing closer and closer until it licked the edges of the asphalt.

The sound of thunder, too loud and imminent to be Constance's imagination, shook the world. She gasped.

Widowmaker.

Falling trees or even their broken limbs could kill the poor unfortunate soul who happened to be in the wrong place at the wrong time.

Constance searched frantically through the forest – hoping the widowmaker was farther ahead or behind, too late she caught sight of the massive eucalyptus smashing through the branches above her.

She shouted and cowered, throwing her arms over her head. Her life flashed before her eyes and she felt deeply put out that she had survived so much since The Fog only to perish in such a cartoonish manner.

Death never came.

Constance opened her eyes to see the mottled tree suspended ten feet overhead. On the other side of the road, taller than a house, stood a black and silver werewolf. He held the trunk aloft in one giant paw.

She blinked.

Of all the incredible things she'd seen and done since The Fog, this creature was the most phenomenal. Her mind balked. She stared, uncomprehending. He, she assumed it was a he, existed someplace beyond myth, beyond stories.

The myth in question, looking vaguely annoyed, waved a paw in the international signal to "move along."

Constance shook herself out of it and pedaled out of range of the widowmaker. The werewolf dropped the tree and she almost fell off the bike due to the shaking ground. She stopped and turned to look. The werewolf leapt to the center of the road and with a mighty swipe of his claw split the trunk. He heaved each half back into the forest.

The beast stalked towards her. The animal part of her brain knew running would be futile. Constance froze. The werewolf fell away as he walked until a human man with waist length salt and pepper hair stood before her. He wore a pink bear bathrobe.

"Hey."

"Hello…" she replied.Chapter 10

"There's a group of evacuees on the Branciforte Bridge about a mile down the road," he said as he used the pink sleeve to wipe soot from his forehead. "The road down the mountain is blocked but we're trying to clear a path. Sit tight there for a while. You'll be safe."

"Okay," she said. "Yes."

Constance nodded. The man transformed back into a werewolf before her eyes and bounded into the flames.

Her heart raced. She had almost died. Her hands shook as she grabbed the bars and pedaled to the bridge. Constance was so distracted at the thought that she soon found herself on the Branciforte Bridge

About sixty denizens of Sunset Cove milled about on the narrow, two-lane, concrete bridge forty-five feet above the Saint Augustus river. A river that was currently reduced to a series of large, barely-connected, puddles. The forest loomed, dense and silent, around them. Constance told herself that enough concrete stood between her and them to keep the fire away. She needed to believe that.

Before she could get her bearings, someone in the crowd yelled and pointed. They turned as one to watch a huge figure glide through the clouds. In the time before The Fog, Constance would have thought she was looking at the biggest airplane in the world, but that would be impossible now. The flying creature broke through the smoke above them. More than a hundred feet long, the shimmering dragon slithered through the sky. Constance stared, open-mouthed, at the scaly belly above her.

The creature passed by and someone in the crowd yelled again.

A raindrop fell on Constance's head.

Then another.

And another.

"Can't be," she muttered. She held out her hand. Sure enough, drop after drop of rain landed there until a tiny pool formed.

Constance laughed – joyful, relieved, exhausted.

The rain fell in earnest, soaking the crowd who laughed and danced in relief. She hugged every stranger who asked. She felt cold for the first time in weeks.

The dragon danced through the heavens spreading rain across the burning land.

The lightning returned. In the flash, Constance saw the dragon's silhouette. It flew without wings. A young, flame-haired woman in the crowd screamed. The lightning struck again and again. Thunder rumbled the air.

At first, she thought the dragon caused the bolts of electricity, but it became clear as it arced through the clouds that the lightning was aimed at the creature.

"Leave him alone!" the redhead screamed, as rain poured down her face.

She need not have worried. The dragon was too fast, too nimble - the lightning struck every place he'd just been. He rollicked through the heavens, spreading rain as he flew. Constance couldn't be certain but she would swear its claws were flipping the bird.

As the rain fell in earnest, turning from a drizzle to a downpour. Constance found a scraggly dandelion in a patch of dirt on the side of the bridge. With a few waves of her hand, the little weed grew tall enough that its leaves offered shelter from the drenching rain. A seven-foot-tall crocodile man growled in thanks.

"Welcome," she nodded. Constance pulled a scarf out of her bag and wrapped it around her shoulders. Her breath caught. A line drawn deep within her chest went taut and shivered.

The rain came too late for Edgar.

The giant werewolf who saved her earlier, now soaking, bedraggled and reeking of wet dog, emerged from the forest and waved to the dragon.

It writhed through the air getting closer and closer. The dragon's face alone dwarfed the massive werewolf. It flew too fast and too low at the bridge. The crowd ducked and screamed – certain they were about to be crushed, but as one claw touched the asphalt, the dragon's form shattered. In its place, stood a good-looking, young Asian man.

Joon landed to a round of ecstatic cheers that he wasn't quite sure what to do with. He half waved and bowed.

"I'm sor –"

Something small, round and perfect that smelled like the forest after a rainstorm flew into his arms.

Erin.

Joon's heart stilled in his chest. He broke out into a cold sweat when he realized that her head was nestled against his heart. He placed his right hand on the small of her back.

"Hi," he said into her red hair.

She muttered something he couldn't understand in response.

"Umm," Joon cleared his throat, "would you like to –"

She tilted her head back and gazed up at him.

"Can I kiss you?"

"What?" Joon's voice broke.

"Can I please kiss you?"

The lingering wood smoke, the shuffling noises of the people on the bridge, the cool sting of rain on the top of his head, all fell away until only the soft pine needle scent of her skin, the low rise and fall of her breathing, the burning heat of her hand on his chest remained.

"Okay," he said, and for years afterward cursed himself for not saying something cooler.

She grinned and kissed him softly as the crowd behind them went bonkers.

No one, not Joon, Erin, or even Constance noticed an eagle staring intently at them from its perch at the top of the light pole in the center of the bridge.

*****

3:26 pm, Nov. 13, 2020, 46 days after The Fog

Sam landed hard on a taupe carpet. The world zoomed in and out of focus as a woman's slender face appeared above her own. She seemed familiar but Sam's thoughts ran from her dying body. Carl shrieked hysterically from somewhere in this white, dry-walled room. Her whole body convulsed like a fish out of water. She gasped, drowning on dry land as her organs shut down. Her wet lungs filled with inky blood.

The woman pried Sam's sword from her clenched fist. Without hesitation, she stood over Sam and said: "I offer my life to The Morrigan so she may heal and be strong. So tomorrow may be a better day for us all."

She took the hilt in both hands and pressed the tip into the pale flesh above her heart. With the tiniest of grins, she shoved the weapon through her body and with a jolt collapsed onto Sam. Her warm, red blood spurted onto Sam's chest, dousing the flames. The woman's breath shuddered and stopped. Sam passed out.

She awoke, dizzy and pissed off, a few feet away from the mouth of the cave.

"Every fucking time," she said as she stood, brushing sand off her legs. She refused to even look at the cavity.

"Took ya long enough."

Sam windmilled so hard that she sat right back down. The slender, auburn-haired woman stood between Sam and the crashing waves. She strode over and gave Sam a hand up. Dozens of white circular scars dotted her forearm.

"Cigarette burns," she replied, noticing Sam's stare.

"I'm so sorry."

"Don't be. It's over now. It will never happen again."

"You're Yvette, aren't you?" Sam asked, trying to find some way out of the knowledge that her body was knitting itself back together because of this woman's sacrifice.

She smiled. Her green eyes twinkled.

"I was Yvette. I'm dead now. Look, I'm only here to give you a message. Then my part of the deal is done."

"Deal?" Sam felt out of control, out of the loop and a little out of her mind.

"I give my life to save yours. I deliver the message and Nyx makes me a star."

"Message? What message?"

"When you are lost and hopeless, come to this cave and you will find what you need. Got it?"

"Wait. What? Is she helping me? Why is she helping me? Why can't she tell me herself? Who is she?"

"Don't know," Yvette said, auburn hair whipping around her head in the ocean breeze. "Don't care. When you are lost and hopeless, come to this cave and you will find what you need. Got it?"

"Yeah, I got it."

"Great!" Yvette turned and strode with absolute purpose toward the ocean. Sam struggled after her.

"Wait, please, I have so many questions."

"Nope, I refuse. I am not waiting any longer to get what I need and I need to be someplace where no one can touch me again."

As her feet hit the water, Yvette's body shimmered and burned.

Of the thousand questions in Sam's mind, one stood out the most.

"What is she like?" she asked in a high pleading voice. "Please just tell me what Nyx is like."

"Terrifying," Yvette's body pulsed like the sun, "and beautiful."

She rose with a flash into the gray sky and glowed for just a moment before disappearing into space.

"Thanks for saving me … I think. Tell Miguel I said 'Hi.'"

*****

4:50 pm, Nov. 15, 2020, 48 days after The Fog

Sam's eyes popped open. She awoke in Yvette's condo, sticky and covered in blood that was not her own. Her savior's body lay half draped over her. Sam turned her head to meet Yvette's dead, filmy eyes. They taunted her with unspoken secrets. Her sword hilt stuck out of her chest and jabbed Sam's right boob. In a fit of pique, she shoved the dead weight off. Then she remembered who she was and apologized to the corpse. Flies buzzed overhead.

The skin, organs and muscles of her chest felt itchy and new. She resisted the urge to push her fingernails through her skin and scratch the fresh, new corner of her lung. Her breath came in rough little gasps but she assumed that would pass.

Sam sat on that blood-soaked taupe carpet. Since The Fog, so many things didn't make sense. It had been easier to chalk it up to "this is how it is now" than face the elephant beside her.

With a sigh of resignation, Sam turned Yvette's body to dust and sent it as high as she could into the atmosphere.

"You okay, Boss?" Carl chirped from his perch on the back of the beige sofa.

She ignored him, and with a pass of her hands, peeled the dried blood from her body.

"Tip top shape, huh, Boss?" Carl asked, his low, gravelly voice getting higher with every syllable. "I knew she worshiped you so I brought … "

Sam squared off to face him.

"Who are you? You showed up after I woke up. I assumed I knew you - that you were one of mine. But I can't see anything about you, Carl. I don't know your true name. I don't know your crime. Why is that? Who are you?"

"Boss…"

He had the good sense to shrink down smaller into the couch.

"Where'd the dagger come from?"

Sam paced in front of the sectional. Her words were like bullets. She fired warning shot after warning shot into the drywall behind him. Her voice got louder as Carl got smaller.

"The one you stabbed me with that somehow magically healed me? What was that about? Why was I was so fucked up from hearing her name? Also, how did you know Dyn would help me find Chiba? Or better yet," she spun around Yvette's living room, "or better yet, how did you know to bring me here? How did you know this woman would give her life for mine? Why do you know things I don't, Carl?"

"Listen, Boss."

He'd shrunk down to little more than a head, peeking above the cushion. She leaned over, tapped his beak with a long, black nail and asked the $10,000 question:

"Who is Nyx?"

He sighed and returned to his full height with a shake of his feathers.

"You are a troublesome child," Carl croaked. His beady eyes and narrow shoulders drooped in exhaustion.

"Excuse me?" Sam reared back in shock. "I am the manifestation of a four-thousand-year-old goddess."

She didn't know that birds were capable of snorting. He jumped to the couch arm, faced her, tucked his wings into his sides and sat down – a grandfather settling in to tell his story.

"Talk to me in a billion years."

Sam gaped at him.

"Oh, sit down before you fall over," he said.

"The hell, Carl?"

"I am Nommo. I, and my twin brother, were the first living beings on Earth. Together, we are Nommo."

And this was his story:

In the beginning, there was Darkness – only Darkness. Then the great god Ama emerged, sleeping in his egg. When he awoke, Ama spun and cast out into space the clay that would become the planets. Then Ama traveled to one of these planets and made his first children, the Nommo. These children were hardy and meant to populate the earth. Ama then created his second children – humans.

But we Nommo have sharp teeth and unquenchable thirst. Our thirst consumes us. It makes the Nommo do terrible things to humans.

To protect his second children, Ama cast us into the Darkness far from the earth.

Sam blinked.

"Well, that was beautiful but that doesn't answer… anything."

"You weren't listening," Carl said with deep disappointment.

"I heard every word. But what does that have to do with…"

"Nyx imprisoned my brother and I. The man who tried to kill you is my brother. He is Nommo."

"Wait, what? You said you both were imprisoned."

"He escaped thousands of years ago."

"Oh, shit!" Sam grasped the couch cushions in shock. "So Nyx is helping me so she can put him back in jail?"

"Not exactly," he muttered. Carl cleaned his wing without looking at her. "That is another matter entirely."

"Then why is she helping me?"

He sighed again.

"You have something of hers. She will help you to ensure its safe return."

"No, I don't," Sam said and knew, in her bones, that was a lie.

"You do. You have something precious to her."

"What is it?"

"You would not survive the hearing of it," Carl said. "The curse you're under is quite powerful."

"Wait, what? Nyx fucking cursed me? Why?"

Carl's shoulders rose to his ears in outrage.

"She did no such thing. You cursed yourself."

"Why would I curse *myself*?"

"That is between you and you. The mere sound of her name nearly broke your mind. Until you are stronger, I will say no more on the matter."

Sam sat on the uncomfortable couch for long moments digesting it all.

"Carl?"

"Yes?" He stopped preening and looked up at her.

"You never said what your crime was."

The deep obsidian pools of his eyes gazed into the middle distance. His body rocked side to side with his words.

"Where there is life, there is need – need for food, shelter, water, love, care, new experience, health, rest." The lines of him were fallen and sad. "More. Always more. If left unchecked, that need will burn through the world. The first of us were born with an unquenchable thirst for life."

Sam didn't understand. She shook her head.

"You have met my children. You call them werewolves and vampires. They inherited a fraction of my thirst."

Sam covered her mouth.

"Continents ran red with blood. Slaughter doesn't begin to describe the horrors I committed. I didn't know, you see. I didn't understand that my prey suffered – felt pain. In many ways, I still don't. I accept my punishment but I would do it again were I released from this prison. I cannot control my thirst."

He tucked his beak beneath his wing in shame. Sam reached across the couch and stroked the sleek top of his ebony head. He leaned into her hand.

"I would destroy you before I let that happen. You know that, don't you?"

"Thank you." He relaxed and met her eyes. "My brother does not care. He will not stop. His thirst will consume this place."

Sam studied Yvette's condo. She hated it – the too dark, too large wood beams across the ceiling, its nothing walls, atrocious beige carpet and whispered threats of violence lingering in the air. The layout in the living room was similar to that of the Learys' but what it lacked in joyful chaos it made up for in Nazi paraphernalia. Yvette had pulled Michael's Third Reich flags from the walls and burnt them in the fireplace. The room was still hazy with smoke.

"You've been working for her this whole time?"

Carl snorted.

"You haven't trusted me for a moment."

"I did expect you to betray me eventually."

Sam paused and considered her dwindling options.

"She's going to destroy me, isn't she? For stealing from her?"

Carl shook his head.

"I will say no more."

"Quoth the Raven," Sam joked because she didn't know what else to do.

ZZZZTTTTT

"Oh, fuck off," she groaned. "Not again."

Sam stood, tore through reality and emerged into a smoldering apocalypse.

White ash floated gently through the barren air. Thick, hazy smoke clogged her lungs, made her eyes burn and muddied her thoughts. Black scorch marks tattooed the trunks of the giant redwoods as they rose into the brilliant, crimson sky. The world was as still as prayer. The birds had gone. No animals scurried in the underbrush. There was no underbrush.

Sam's brain understood that she had failed – all that effort had been for nothing. Her heart, on the other hand, cracked and refused to bear the weight of the world around her.

Wedged beneath the ashy corpse of a fallen tree lay a half-burnt body. Sam sat on the still-warm ground and reached for its hand, but this body didn't have one. Puzzled, she grasped the blackened forearm and found herself in infinite, formless darkness.

Travis's thin arms clung to the fallen log, He screamed as his grizzled mustache flapped about in a silent wind.

"Hey!"

His eyes were screwed shut against something she couldn't see.

"Travis!" She yelled in his face. "Travis!"

With an eye roll that would make Zara proud, she put her foot down.

"Silence! Be calm!"

His hair and clothing stilled. Shaking, he opened his eyes and grinned up at Sam.

"Knew you'd come," he said. "Knew I had to wait. Knew you had to know. So you can fuck em up too."

*****

5:25 pm, Nov. 15, 2020, 48 days after The Fog

Constance picked her way through the smoldering underbrush. The rain had cleared away most of the smoke. Little fires burned here and there. The flames sizzled and snapped as the drizzle smothered and drowned them.

The line in her chest pulled her further and further into the burn area. She passed giant redwoods with open black scars twenty feet up their trunks. Half-scorched deer, raccoon and coyote carcasses dotted the landscape. Constance pulled her wet scarf tighter over her head and mouth to block out the horror. Mud slurped at her black Converse, threatening to pull them off her feet. The acrid stench of burnt and rotting death drifted through the damp air.

She felt as if she were traversing through the insides of a dying creature. The pulse of the forest had slowed to a near halt. The air weighed down on her with its grief.

The forest will come back. It always does.

But this, this was something from a nightmare – blackened corpses of once living trees all twisted and collapsing.

She had to focus. Yank one foot from the muddy ash and then the other. Edgar and Jeff needed her.

The pull got stronger and stronger until she was dizzy. She stopped to drink a little water to get her bearings and then, in this quiet forest she caught the unmistakable, guttural caterwaul of a very, very, very upset Jeff.

Constance followed the sound until she reached a part of the forest cleared away by the fire. Through the gray light she saw a burnt pile of bones next to a very angry sack. She ran, mud splashing up her legs. Within the bones, nestled in ash, protected ever so lightly by a crumbling, blackened rib cage, rested a beating human heart.

Delicately, careful not to disturb the surrounding bones, Constance knelt down and picked up the heart. She sighed to feel its warm life in her hands. She brushed the ash from its red, bloody surface and cradled it to her chest. The small, black spot at the apex remained untouched. She brought the heart to her lips and kissed it gently but fervently.

"You are a ridiculous man," she murmured. "Thank you for this."

She reached out with her free hand and patted the writhing sack. "Hello, Jeff," she said with a sigh.

When she got everyone home, the relief would overwhelm her, she knew, so she set it aside and patted her very, very, very put out cat through the burlap until he calmed enough for her to gather him up in her arms and take them all home.

"Yes, I will get you both fixed up. Yes, Jeff, you will get extra treats."

When they got home, Constance would draw a bath for Edgar, fill it with herbs and place his heart in the center. She couldn't imagine how excruciating it was for him, but in a week or less his body would grow back around him and he would be right as rain.

"Let's go home," she said.

A few miles south of Constance, in a part of the forest near a high school of all things, underneath a dead pine tree, where a man named Jakob Blanc once rested on his way to becoming a god, lay a burnt and shattered pile of bones. His onyx felt hat had, miraculously, survived.

*****

Anahit's Domain, The Liminal Space

Raquel sat at a small wooden table hip deep in medical textbooks. Their thick spines dotted the ground around her. Fig, apple, olive and pear trees surrounded her. Their lush fruit hung within reach. She lazily plucked a ripe honey crisp apple and crunched on it while reading a passage about the role of the basal ganglia in executive function.

In her world, it was always a pleasant late afternoon.

A gun metal gray door appeared. The circular metal lock spun and cracked open. Raquel studiously ignored the large man with obscene muscles when he stepped through.

She turned the page. The apple crunched in her jaws – as juicy and sweet as advertised.

He loomed before her simple desk. The veins in his biceps stood out in sharp relief.

He had to be so dehydrated to look like that, Raquel thought. *Maybe I should offer him water.*

"He wants to deal," the God of War announced without any preamble or pleasantries.

Raquel turned the page to a detailed diagram of the basal nuclei.

"He doesn't have anything I want," she said as she traced the picture of the shell shaped organ. "Thanks anyway."

"He can stop her."

Her finger stilled on the page.

"Who?" Raquel asked, staring at the colorful image.

"Death. He can stop Death – permanently."

She tilted her head up at him.

"How?"

The big man shrugged.

"He says he was there when Death started. He can end her."

Raquel closed the heavy book with a thud.

"When would he like to discuss the terms?"

"Now."

"Let's go."

Raquel stood. She wiped bits of apple off on her scrubs. Her thick ponytail swung across her back as she walked through the over-sized metal door.

SHIT GETS REAL

10:37 pm, Nov. 15, 2020, 48 days after The Fog

Erin walked home in a daze. The feeling of Joon's lips on hers carried her through the forest up the mountain back to her home. Well, technically, Manny carried her through the damp, smoldering forest. She sat on his back as he sprang across water puddles and tore through downed trees like they were flimsy bits of paper. The chill night wind made her ears burn and go numb.

Her mom had pulled off some crazy, last-minute spell to save their house. But, for some reason it made thirty Barbary goats appear. No one, especially not Erin's mom, Laurel, knew what would happen once the goats left, so Dylan was relegated to goat poop shoveler. Erin was just thankful she'd have a warm place to sleep tonight before her date with Joon tomorrow. They were going for a walk on the beach. Maybe her mom knew a spell for getting out goat stench?

A deep sniffling and a soft, mournful awoo pulled her from her reverie.

She patted Manny's shoulder. Erin knew he wasn't ready to talk about the friend he lost today.

They were getting close to home. The terrain shifted into a steep, rocky incline.

Erin clung tighter to Manny's fur and ignored the distinct wet, dog smell.

Something dark and fast hit Manny like a cannonball. The impact sent Erin flying. She tumbled high into the starry night. A hand snatched her out of the air before she crashed into the ground.

Then it flung her into the mud. Dazed, she rolled onto her back. A beautiful woman's face appeared inches from her own. Erin shrieked and jerked backward. Icy water seeped into her jeans and hoodie.

The woman got closer and sniffed her face and hair. She had never been so repulsed by anything. The action was so analytical, so inhuman.

"You smell like the forest," she said, wrinkling her nose, "and young love," she sniffed again, "and dragons."

The woman straightened. Erin was struck by how out of place she seemed. Stiletto heels, a pencil skirt and ecru silk blouse had no place in the middle of the damp forest.

"This is the one."

"Good."

A big man with large muscles emerged from the shadows, dressed like some steroid-fueled leather daddy. One side of his face was just… gone. Erin couldn't believe what she was seeing. His left eye hung from the socket. Four deep claw marks ran from the top of his head down to his chin. She could see his tongue move through the hole in his cheek. Another thick series of dark gashes ran down his neck and across his torso.

"Manny." Erin tried to stand. But a hand clamped down hard on her shoulder and yanked her back. She turned to see a tall, metal man snap chains around her wrists.

"Let's go before it wakes up," the Leather Daddy said.

She watched as the man popped his eye back into the socket. The injuries on his face closed and healed.

"You're scared of a dog?" the woman asked.

He sputtered.

"Of course not."

He picked Erin and the woman up Then he flung them over his shoulders and ran through the night back down the mountain to Sunset Cove.

During the long, cold, motion-sickness-inducing ride to town, before the fear and helpless rage sank in, all Erin thought about was that she was going to miss her date tomorrow.

*****

3:16 pm, Nov. 16, 2020, 49 days after The Fog

Phillip Octavian Claussen had never been a particularly religious or spiritual man. He grew up in Sunset Cove during the late 70s. He hadn't joined a cult or lived in a commune – something that always surprised his peers. He dropped acid in a purple ashram in the Santa Muerte mountains on a whim one warm, late summer evening. Phil saw pretty colors but felt nothing.

The thought of the divine made him shrug. He never understood what any of that tree-worshiping, healing-light, balanced-chakra bullshit had to do with him.

So he let the hippies and born agains pass him by while he went about his business.

Phil got married and his wife gave birth to two girls. The eldest, Lisa, gave him two grandsons, Colson, age fifteen and Michael, age twelve. They were babysitting the boys the night The Fog rolled in. He ushered everyone into the dirt cellar below their blue and white Victorian. As the nightmares seemed to pass them by, Michael disappeared. One minute Phil was staring at the terrified shape of a young boy huddled in the corner and the next the child was gone.

"Michael?" he yelled. "Michael, son, where are you?"

Phil's wife stared at him like he was daft.

"What are you talking about?"

"I don't see Michael," he said.

"He's right there." She pointed at the spot Phil last saw him. "No, he's not!"

"Grandpa." Colson stood and sat in the corner. He put his arms around the empty air. "He's right here."

But Phil could not see or hear his grandson. The sound of little boy laughter disappeared from his ears. The sight of little boy smiles was gone from Phil's sight.

When his son-in-law and daughter didn't return home in the days and weeks that followed The Fog, Phil and his wife took care of the boys – one invisible, one not.

He made Michael wear his old, white dress shirts and baseball caps. The items floated comically in the air around the child's too small frame.

"He doesn't like it," Colson told Phil. "He says it's hot and he trips over it and the hat smells funny."

"I need to see him."

But the lack of sound bothered Phil too, so he made the little boy wear a golden bell on a chain around his neck. He was told to announce his presence by knocking on the walls and to ring the bell as he walked.

This makeshift life worked as best as it could, but Phil needed to fix the child. Wherever he went, he asked for someone to help the invisible boy – to make Phil see his grandson again. They refused. Every healer, witch, soothsayer, shaman and priestess in the county said the same thing, "I cannot undo what The Fog has done."

Phil refused to give up, he knew there was a cure somewhere. He just had to find it.

So he went to the city council meeting with all the stubborn hope in his heart.

What he found that day was so much more than a cure.

As he sat in that excruciating aluminum chair, the bald spot on the top of his head blistering in the afternoon heat, the world split wide open. Phil found faith. The Man in White shone like the sun. He told them that he only punished them with lightning because he loved them so much. The Man in White said they were guilty of consorting with The Shadow Liar, but he would cleanse them of her filth with holy fire. Then he said that because he was the son of the God of Time he could take them all back to before The Fog and keep it from ever happening – he just needed everyone in Sunset Cove to prove their faith to him.

Phil spent every one of the past three days praying and holding vigil at the Eternal Flame. The Faithful sang songs glorifying the name of the holy father and made offerings in his name. Food was plentiful here. He ate his fill.

Phil finally understood what it meant to believe in something greater than himself.

The Shadow Liar appeared in the late afternoon of the third day. She strode through the crowd of thirty or forty believers on a wave of icy fury. The Faithful became restless in her presence.

Dena stood between her and the Eternal Flame.

"My brothers and sisters," she assured the crowd. "Fear not, for he has prepared for this day. If your faith is strong, he will protect you from The Shadow Liar. She cannot harm you."

With a growl, The Shadow Liar shoved Dena to the ground. The Faithful gasped at her cruelty.

"I'm fine," Dena called from the ground. "I'm fine. The Darkness cannot harm me."

Ignoring her, The Shadow Liar stood before the metal men the Man in White created to guard the Eternal Flame. The gray metal men resembled classical Greek statues with their empty eyes and strange inky symbols across their chests. The Flame burned searing white on the circular concrete pad that once was a small fountain.

The Clocktower, like the rest of Sunset Cove, had been cobbled together with spare parts. At its base, three-thirty-foot tall, square, red-brick pillars supported an arched platform where the white spire, clock face and bell, taken from an old Elks' Lodge, stood. The dozen metal men stood shoulder to shoulder with their backs to the Flame. They moved aside to let anyone with an offering pass.

Phil had never seen The Shadow Liar before. He'd heard stories about the wild woman seeking vengeance and wreaking havoc across the county. They were obviously embellished. No mere woman could do what the stories claimed – particularly such an average one.

"You're a whore," someone in the crowd yelled.

"Blasphemer!" another called.

"Deceiver."

The Faithful hurled insult after insult at her. Ignoring them, The Shadow Liar grabbed one of the soldiers by the arm and yanked. The metal man did not budge. She tilted her head in confusion. Then she punched the guard square in the breast plate.

"Motherfucker!" the woman hissed in pain as her fist bounced off the metal body.

The Faithful cheered.

"See," Dena told them. "He prepared for this. The Shadow Liar cannot defeat us. You are safe in the glow of his light."

Without a sound, the woman leapt over the guards. As one, they turned and extended their spears, forming a point above the Flame. A guard reached up, grasped her leg and flung her aside.

The Faithful went wild. They screamed in joy. Women cried. People clapped. Phil had known he was on the side of righteousness but this show of force confirmed it.

The Shadow Liar ran at the guards but was turned back again. Over and over the woman attacked, hacking at their legs with an evil-looking, black sword, pushing her fingernails into their empty eye sockets, screaming and flailing while the overjoyed Faithful laughed at her antics. She drew a circle around the Clock Tower with a wooden staff, then sliced her wrist with her claws and drew symbols of magic in the air as her blood dripped onto the line. A strange bubble appeared and faded into invisibility. In unison, the guards banged their shields against the ground. A high, eerie note rang through the air. The Shadow Liar flinched and doubled over, hands covering her ears. The barrier she erected popped.

Finally, she stopped, breathing heavy, hair a tangled mess. The Shadow Liar stood before the Praetorian Guards, black liquid dripping from her clenched fists, defeat in every line of her body. The ecstatic Faithful didn't notice the darkening sky or the howling wind.

She turned and muttered something no one could hear.

Dena shushed them.

"Let her speak, everyone, please," she said. "He will forgive you, if only you renounce your wicked ways and submit to his will. Please, join us."

The Shadow Liar turned to the Faithful.

"Murderers," she said. Icy fingers settled into Phil's spine.

Dena stepped back.

"I…"

"FILTHY MURDERERS!" she screamed, and a chorus of ravens and crows joined her. Phil hadn't noticed the birds until now – hundreds of dark shapes lined the rooftops around them. Their piercing cacophony made the Faithful go quiet and still.

"Apparently, I cannot stop you from burning innocent people ALIVE, but I sure as FUCK can show you what happens when you do."

Phil burst out laughing at her audacity.

"Crazy bitch," he muttered.

She met his eyes.

He stopped laughing.

"You're in my realm now," she said and spread her arms wide.

The birds clamored and darted above them in excitement. The temperature plummeted. Phil felt a dreadful presence over his shoulder. He spun to find empty air. Some of the Faithful tried to leave but The Shadow Liar had cast a circle around the group. They beat their fists against empty air but none could pass.

"Creatures of Darkness," she called. A strange calm descended upon the gathering. The birds quieted. The cold winds stopped. Her body shook with impotent fury.

"I command you to feast upon the damned," she screamed to the waiting swarm of birds. "Show your new brothers and sisters their future."

"Except that one," she pointed at Phil. "That one's mine."

Phil felt their glee as darkness fell and madness descended. The ravens and crows swooped down onto the Faithful – a black cloud of chaos. An invisible force pulled a shrieking woman in a blue dress ten feet into the air. With a slurp, it folded her in half. Her organs burst out of her back.

The ravens rested on the tops of their victims heads and pecked their eyes out. The crows overwhelmed their chosen meal. They harassed them in the air until they dropped to the ground. Then they tore through clothing and skin with razor sharp beaks.

The Shadow Liar did not move or flinch. Her expression remained serene as a winter's morning while she gazed at Phil – unbothered by the violence she wrought.

Dena crouched down, hands over her head. She rocked back and forth as she muttered to herself.

"You can't touch me. I didn't throw anyone in. I didn't tell them to do it. He said I'm safe. He said I'm safe. You can't touch me."

The Shadow Liar spared her a glance as arterial blood splattered onto Dena's back. She leaned down and brought the distraught woman to her feet.

"Is that what he told you, Dena?" she asked and wrapped her hand around the trembling woman's throat. The Shadow Liar turned her to face the blood bath. "You know, he was right. I can't hurt you. You are not in my realm. Yet. But I can make you watch."

Intestines flew through the air. Screams turned to gurgles. Dena froze. Her hands tucked between her knees as her eyes darted back and forth – her mind trying to escape the horror. Only ten of the Faithful were left. They had not made any offerings.

Through it all, Phil held steady. The Man in White would save him from this animal. Even in death, his faith would protect his soul. He had never been more certain of anything.

The Shadow Liar released Dena and approached him, stepping over a severed leg covered in crows. She moved like the creeping night.

"I'm not afraid of you," he yelled.

She rolled her eyes.

"Only terrified people say that."

"He will protect me," Phil said. "He smiled upon my offering and was glad. He will welcome me in his heavenly army on Olympus."

"I know what you did. I see it on you. The horror. The filth."

"You dare speak of horror!"

"This is justice, old man." The Shadow Liar laughed at him. "You may not understand because it doesn't look like what you're used to, but that's all this is – justice. You took. Now, it's being taken from you."

"I did nothing wrong." Yet he found himself backing slowly away from her.

The Shadow Liar didn't bother to respond. Her footsteps drew ever closer until his back hit the edge of the circle. He turned away and shut his eyes.

"It was an abomination!" he yelled – his last defense. "My grandson was an abomination."

"She was a little girl!" The Shadow Liar screamed.

His ears ruptured at the sound. Something hot and sharp crossed his neck. He put his hands up to it to try and staunch the warm life's blood pumping away. The last thing his fading eyes saw was The Shadow Liar grinning over his dying body.

*****

9:05 am, Nov. 17, 2020, 50 days after The Fog

The day after The Shadow Liar's massacre at The Clocktower, a disembodied yet soothing woman's voice made the following announcement:

"It is with heavy hearts that we mourn the loss of our brave Faithful. The Shadow Liar slaughtered the innocent in her senseless fury. Those brave souls murdered for their faith will never be forgotten. The Shadow Liar is strong, but we are stronger. She cannot stop us from going back. We Faithful will continue to offer up our very lives.

Our true savior offers us eternal life through the Flame. He, and he alone, will save Sunset Cove from the monsters The Shadow Liar has unleashed. He, and he alone, will turn back the clock. He will return Sunset Cove to the way it was before.

That's why your offerings are so important.

Our savior can only return Sunset Cove to its former glory if he receives enough offerings by the Winter Solstice. On this, the darkest of days, he will be the light of our hope."

Every living being in the county, from those who lived underground, to those in the sea and in the air heard the announcement. It played every three hours. The next day, the message changed:

"All good people of Sunset Cove must make an offering. We cannot let The Shadow Liar win."

The Shadow Liar, for her part, had taken up residence on the roof of the hipster coffee shop next to the Clocktower. She perched on a cement ledge and glared at the Faithful. They did not dare toss anyone into the fire with her watching. Instead, they threw themselves into the flames – sometimes a dozen or more in a day. They lined up and spoke the words:

"I offer my life in the belief of Zeus so tomorrow may be a better day for us all."

Sam witnessed every useless death – every man, woman, vampire, fae, undercreature and being from the deep. She stood over them while they passed through the Gates of Death.

Wordlessly, she escorted them to the Hall of Suicides. Sometimes, they hurled insults at her. Other times, they spat and fought. A few cried. They all begged for mercy when they realized they would have to spend eternity staring into a mirror.

With every death, the Eternal Flame grew. It flared white hot, melting the red brick and steel above it. The stench of burning flesh fouled the air for a three-block radius.

The rest of the gods and goddesses of Sunset Cove, for their part, ignored the disembodied messages. Dre sat at his kitchen table and unsuccessfully tried to cajole Sohlie into finishing her peas. Raquel had taken to wandering the homeless camps and abandoned buildings searching for the sick. Manny slept most days. Jakob's bones lay in an unmarked grave in a far corner of the cemetery. Joon, per his agreement with the Man in White, made it sprinkle for fifteen minutes every other day at 3 pm. In exchange, he got to spend five minutes with Erin six days a week and her safety was guaranteed.

But the air felt unripe and sick - fraught with the unanswered and unavoidable threat of the future.

*****

8:42 am, Dec. 21, 2020, 84 days since The Fog

The morning of the Winter Solstice, Raquel walked along the windswept beach near Dre's house. A thirty-foot pile of picked-clean bones was her only company. She crossed the dune to the living wall that blotted out the sun. The day was cold and clear. Raquel wore a puffy white jacket.

"I, Anahit, Goddess of Healing," she announced with a small bow, "seek audience with the Great God Ama. We have important matters to discuss."

The thick green vines parted – making a door. The skittering creatures sat on branches and nodded to her as she passed. Raquel walked, unescorted, through the savanna. Any animal she met bowed in greeting. Her trip was uneventful.

Dre, Sohlie in his arms, greeted her from the sidewalk in front of their little house. The small girl wore a white sweater over a purple taffeta dress with a tulle skirt and sparkly leggings. Her dress rustled in the afternoon breeze. Two happy afro puffs sat on either side of her head. She buried her face in her father's neck and peeked out occasionally to make nonsensical announcements, only to immediately return to her hiding place.

Gracie set out a pot of coffee and a plate of fruit on the picnic table. The garden was positively bursting with out-of-season fruits and vegetables. It was an intoxicating riot of color and scent.

"What brings you all the way out here?" Dre asked as he sat down.

Raquel stared out into the middle distance and sipped her coffee from a chipped mug that said: 'World's Greatest Teacher' in bright red letters.

"Do you remember what you told me when you gave me that gift all those years ago?" Sohlie refused to let go of Dre's beard while Gracie tried to convince her to eat some triangle cut pineapple.

"Which gift? I've given you a few."

"The Mercy of Unconsciousness," she replied.

"Hmm."

"You told me that I would never get a moment's rest," Raquel said. "No second when I cannot sense when they're sick or in pain? That if I accepted this final gift, I would hold their souls within me while they're unconscious?"

Raquel sipped her steaming coffee.

"When I sleep, I dream of ways to heal them. When I talk, my words are shaped to help them. There is no space between me and their sickness. I am in it with them always, in every moment of every day, of every life. I chose this so many years ago and I would choose it again a thousand times over. But I am exhausted, Dre. I need to rest."

"I'm so sorry. I didn't know."

Dre reached out to pat the back of her hand. Quicker than a striking snake, she grabbed it. He face planted onto the picnic table, knocking over his coffee mug that read 'Gardeners Like It Dirty' in big green letters. The hot liquid pooled across the table and dripped over the side. Gracie didn't have a chance to react as Raquel tapped the hand feeding Sohlie. She slumped over the fruit plate. Before Sohlie could screw up her little face to burst into tears, Raquel pulled her from Dre's side. At her touch, the child went limp. Raquel gathered Sohlie up in her arms and made her way back through the savanna.

The souls of this place had disappeared. The living bodies of all the animals that greeted her, the elephants, mountain lions, gazelles, coyotes, bears, every living creature in this realm were there – haphazardly slumped onto the ground. Their essence was gone. The leaves of plants rolled into themselves in thick curls. Flower stalks wilted and fell over. The moss on the trees curled up and retracted.

The garden had fallen silent – no chittering birds, bullfrogs, or buzzing, creaking insects. They too slept without dreaming.

An enormous raven flew high overhead with a live, unconscious snake clenched in its beak.

When Raquel reached the wall, she hiked Sohlie over her left shoulder, pulled her bronze sword from within her coat and hacked wildly through the vines until she got to the other side. Sweat dripped from her brow.

The Man in White and his two children greeted her. With a blank face, Raquel handed the small body over to the God of War. He flung the child over his black, leather-clad shoulder like a sack of potatoes.

"You've done well, my disciple," the Man in White said.

She rolled her eyes but didn't respond.

With his left hand, the Man in White drew complicated sigils across his lips and throat. When he spoke, these words were heard throughout the county:

"My chosen Faithful, we have come to the day when I will defeat Death itself. I will conquer Life. I will turn back the clock. At 2 pm today at the Clocktower, I will meet The Shadow Liar and her so-called brother. They will kneel before me. The monsters that have plagued you will be no more."

*****

The Cave, 9:25 am, Dec. 21, 68,000 B.C.E., 70,019 years before The Fog

The Great God Ama picked his way down the rocky cliff face. The barest hint of a path guided him through waist-high boulders and loose gravel to the cave entrance. The ocean below was a cool blue mixed with emerald green. White caps rose in the distance as the wind tossed around the simple wrap over his right shoulder.

This was his last hope to either appeal to her mercy (of which she had none) or to strike up a bargain (he had nothing she wanted.) But, it was not in his nature to give up.

Ama turned to check that they still followed him – the two women and one man took turns carrying a young girl. His heart swelled with love and pride as he watched them. They wore animal skins and wove shells into their hair.

It had only been a few million years since they stood on two legs. He could not believe their progress or their beauty – their onyx skin glowed in the sunlight. Ama's second children had evolved in ways even he could not believe. The threat to them hung low and heavy in his heart.

They reached the beach before the cave entrance. She was already there. His children started at the sight of a massive woman with pale skin and burning eyes. Ama patted their hands to reassure them. Her arms, in their long, black cloak, were folded across her chest. He could feel the lecture forming inside her mind.

"Would you like me to say it aloud?"

"Nyx…" he began.

"I told you so. There. It is so satisfying to say it. I do enjoy being right."

"My First Children will awaken soon," Ama said. "The Sleeping Flowers are gone from this world. I can no longer hold back their slaughter."

"I said, I said, when you came up with this ridiculous idea," she glared at him, "I said that it would end in tears and blood. Your tears, and their blood, to be specific."

"I am here to beg for the lives of my children." Ama bowed before her.

She ignored him and continued with her rant as she leaned against the cliff side. The mouth of the cave rose thirty feet in the air. Nyx stood half as tall as the entrance.

"I gave you this solar system in the middle of nowhere because you would not relinquish your obsession. Stubborn. So impossibly stubborn. On how many worlds did you plant the Seeds of Life only for me to destroy them? A few million? A billion? I have lost count – which is notable. After you gave me those sad eyes the last time, it occurred to me that I should just let you go through with this insanity. 'Maybe, he will get it out of his system and we can all move on.' Yet, here you are."

"Please imprison my First Children in Darkness so that my Second Children can thrive," he said.

She pointed to the family behind him. They huddled with their backs to her in a circle on the farthest corner of the beach. Their offspring sat in the center of the circle of their bodies. One of the women placed rocks around them as an extra layer of protection. Nyx would have been charmed by the simple magic if their entire existence didn't annoy her. The very idea of life was appalling – so dysregulated, so erratic, so… *messy.*

"I assume you brought them here to appeal to my compassion? To brag about your accomplishment? To show me that they deserve to be saved?"

He brought them for exactly those reasons but he certainly was not about to admit it to her.

The humans huddled closer together. They shivered. Their nearly hairless bodies offered little protection against the shadows and the cool ocean mist.

Nyx became even more irritated at their predicament.

"Please, my Second Children are innocent. They deserve a chance to grow and evolve."

"Do you see? Do you see how it is for them? They're cold. They're terrified. I did not build this universe for them, Ama. I built it from myself – for my own joy. I built it to watch solar winds eddy through empty space, to see a triple moon rise through a planet made of diamonds, to watch galaxies collide and explode. This is *my* creation. Life has no place here. It is only through your insanity that you've managed to take it this far. But to give them sentience, self awareness and the capacity to suffer while eking out an existence where *I* am everywhere, where death is everywhere is a cruelty I thought beyond you, Ama."

"Your creation is cold and dead," he muttered.

"Better to be cold and dead than alive and burning," she shot back. Internally, she added a deep and abiding annoyance with herself for letting him do this, on top of her base annoyance with him.

"Do you not see that I made them from you?" Ama asked. "That they, too, are part of you – are a part of your creation? I took these things you love: the sunlight caught for an infinitesimal fraction of a second inside a diamond, the mad chaos of colliding galaxies, the ebb and flow of a sun's winds and I trapped them in stardust so they could know themselves, so they could know how beautiful they are. They deserve to experience the wonder of your creation too. It was selfish of you to keep it to yourself.

"Nyx, you say death is everywhere in this Universe. I cannot agree. The Seeds of Life are everywhere. You planted them yourself. I simply encouraged them, nourished them – the minerals of a dying star, the frozen seas untouched by sunlight, the molten cores of lifeless planets – these are my gardens."

He paused for a moment. The ocean roared at his back. A thought occurred to him.

"You did it on purpose," he mused. "You did not build this universe for death. You built it for life. The Goddess Nyx does not make mistakes."

"I changed my mind," she said. "The price was too high. You cannot see them, Ama, not the way I do. You cannot see their suffering, their loss, the crimes they commit when they think no one is looking. I see them. I see all of them and it is too much to bear."

Nyx stared into the middle distance at the white caps, increasing and gaining momentum as they chased each other across the blue-green sea.

"You must understand, Ama, neither of us can escape the consequences of what we create here. This life you have nourished will grow beyond your expectations and my control. The suffering we have wrought will find its way back to us both. That is inevitable. For every action, there is an equal and opposite reaction. It is better to end this here and be done with it. To see their pain is more than enough. I have no desire to experience it."

Nyx waved. The rock of the cliff face rumbled. The stone extended to form a half circle around the cowering humans, sheltering them from the ocean mist.

"Lies!" Ama shouted at her. Tears formed at the corners of his eyes. "You have a plan. You *always* have a plan. You wanted to experience the joy that you only watched from afar. You want to feel what they have instead of seeing it. This soil that you created will do only what you designed it to do. There is longing in every molecule of this place, Nyx. I have heard it. I have felt it. I know it is yours. I did not say anything before out of respect. I have only given your longing form and freedom. I know not what you want but your yearning has created life. Not even *you* can stop it."

Nyx sighed. She tilted her head back and glared at the azure sky.

"I am decided," she said. "Life will not continue."

Ama knew her well enough to know the discussion was over. He nodded and wiped away his tears. Then he ushered his Second Children away.

As they turned, Nyx met the gaze of the little girl over her mother's shoulder. The child stared at her with absolute candor and zero fear in her deep, brown eyes. Her chin jutted out in defiance. She looked more than a little irritated about being in the wet cold. As they walked away, she glared at Nyx. Her lower lip set in a pout.

The goddess couldn't help but notice the way she draped herself over her mother's body with complete trust or how the mother kept her hand on the back of the child's head to steady and comfort her. The girl's little bare feet dangled on either side of her mother's hips.

Then the child scrunched up her nose, crossed her eyes and stuck her tongue out at the Primordial Goddess, Creator of the Universe.

A laugh burst from Nyx's chest. She covered her mouth and looked away, trying to suppress the giggles. She snorted. Then caught her breath.

"Wait!" Nyx called after them, raising an imperious hand. "Wait."

*****

1:33 pm, Dec. 21, 2020, 84 days after The Fog

A lone, white, plastic bag tumbled along Mission Street in downtown Sunset Cove. A chill breeze tossed the tattered remnant of a life gone by along the main artery leading to the Clocktower. It floated past the old movie theater, the corner where the Mad Martinelli used to busk and the intersection leading to Mulberry Square.

The bag traveled along the broken concrete beyond the wreckage of Sunset Cove Bookshop, where the giant tree, whose name was Larry, had long since picked up his roots and moved on. It scurried beyond the yellow awning of Benedict's Candy and Ice Cream Shop, Molly's Pub and finally past the dueling coffee shops across the street from each other – Ruby's and the hipster joint that shall not be named, until it finally came to rest, wedged beneath the foot of one of the metal men standing in front of the Clocktower.

What the bag didn't pass was people. Downtown Sunset Cove, for possibly the first time in its history, was almost completely devoid of life – human, magical, fungal, plant, animal or any combination thereof. After The Fog, downtown became a trade hub. Today, it was abandoned. Even the Faithful had disappeared. Gunfighters at high noon had more of an audience.

The only inhabitants – the human manifestations of Life and Death, were hiding from the chill next to the emergency exit of the hipster coffee joint. Dead leaves gathered beneath their feet in the alcove. Neither spoke to, nor looked, at the other. The breeze filled the sky with billowy gray clouds that threatened rain. Sunlight bounced around inside the stifling blanket of clouds, becoming sharp and pointed.

Sam stared through the glass door to the interior of the hipster coffee joint. The gray metal chairs were turned upside down on hand-crafted, rustic, reclaimed-mahogany tables. A disturbing, surreal painting of bulls and clocks took up a large portion of the far wall. The Fog hadn't changed the place at all. It looked ready for some underfed barista to take her order and judge her for a lack of forearm tattoos.

"Fuckers," she growled.

Dre shook his head. He refused to acknowledge her. His rage and heartbreak had devastated the usually joyful peace between them.

You said we could trust her.

"Hey…" Sam said.

With thunderous eyes, he shushed her.

"They're here," he said.

The Man in White, Fiona and Raquel with Sohlie collapsed into her arms strode down Mission toward the ruins of the Clocktower. The brick edifice had melted in the heat of the Flame. It was split into three parts. The brick pillars slumped outward onto the courtyard like a peeled banana. The metal men guarded the Flame among the rubble. Dre and Sam rushed out from their hiding spot to stand between them and the fire. Raquel did not raise her eyes from the ground.

The air crackled with the Man in White's smug triumph. Other than the snap of electrons bouncing off light poles and the gentle breeze, there was no sound, no murmur of parents calling to their children, no discussion of barter between people, or dogs barking, nothing. Sam's hair stood on end, prickling with tension.

Fiona stepped forward. The sharp clips of her six-inch, white heels echoed through the empty space.

She pulled a light gray cloth from her breast pocket and placed it on the ground between them. Fiona carefully unfolded the cloth to reveal two, small, metal, orbs. At her whispered words, the orbs expanded, becoming three feet in diameter. The one before Sam was gold and the one before Dre was black. They were constructed of delicate interlacing bands with ancient sigils inscribed on the surface. Each had an opening that was large enough for a person. Fiona attached long silvery chains to the back of each circle and gave the ends to the Man in White. Raquel stood next to him with Sohlie clasped in her arms. The child's little dress was wrinkled and one of her afro puffs had come out.

"Into the cage," he ordered.

Sam drew her shoulders back and stuck out her chin.

"No," she said.

"Sam," Dre growled.

She reached out and tore a hole in reality with her left hand. Dozens of people, who at a casual glance appeared human but gave off an air of something primal and wild, emerged. This motley group, led by Manny, were dressed in the Sunset Cove uniform of worn hoodies and shorts. Every single one of them looked ready to rip someone's face off.

"I have a plan," Sam said.

The Man in White raised his right hand.

"So do I," he said.

Metal clanged against concrete in perfect time as more guards poured out of every doorway. Hundreds of them surrounded Sam, Dre, Manny and the werewolves. Their shiny bodies gleamed in the dull afternoon light.

"Sam?" Manny asked.

The werewolves stepped back, forming a half circle behind Sam and Dre.

"It's fine," she said. Her eyes glittered with defiant rage. "We can handle this."

"Wait." The Man in White raised his right hand again and drew a symbol in the air.

Projected onto the air above his head, like a movie coming into focus, was a bird's eye view of a metal man hacking his way through the living wall around Dre's house. The God of War stood by the robot's side, a large metal chain wrapped around his left hand. He pulled the chain hard. Erin, hands manacled in front of her, stumbled into him. He turned, looked up, and waved at them.

"Is that real?" Sam gasped.

Dre closed his eyes.

"It's real," he said.

"It was almost clever of you to try to hide them from me," the Man in White said.

The vampires of Sunset Cove, with special dispensation from the Sun God, spent hours, starting that morning, sweeping through the county. Sam used her magic to charm every door and window, no matter how small, to lead to Dre's house. The vampires pushed and shoved every living being they could find through any door, gate, window, or kitchen cupboard that would fit.

The plan had been to keep the Man in White from getting any more hostages. It backfired spectacularly.

The bird's eye view pulled back to reveal thousands of metal men surrounding the wall around Dre's farm.

"Get in the cage and I will spare the girl child."

Sam opened her mouth.

"You're done, Sam," Dre said. "You're done. Give up."

Her mouth snapped shut. Her head hung low in defeat.

"Are you so stupid that you thought I wouldn't notice everyone was gone?" the Man in White sneered.

Sam glared at him as she crossed the concrete street toward the golden cage.

"He can't be trusted, Dre," Manny called.

He and the rest of the werewolves stood between the Man in White and the Flame. Their hackles rose. Each one appeared to have doubled in size. Their hands hung loose as their bodies tensed and prepared for battle.

"What would you do if it were your kid?" Dre asked as he stood before the black cage.

He bent double and brought his knees to his chest. Before crawling inside the cramped opening, he met Sam's eyes. She nodded. Then she crept inside the thin, golden cell. The space was so cramped they had to crouch with their heads down.

"Excellent!" the Man in White clapped as the slender metal ribbons slid across the hole. He tapped his throat.

"Son, go ahead."

"Wait here," The God of War muttered to the mechanical men. "Don't move."

Dragging Erin behind him, he stepped through the magical barrier.

Gracie, machete in hand, long, dark hair and flowing skirt billowing in the wind, was there to greet him.

Raquel, with the blank visage of the damned, handed Sohlie to the Man in White.

He recited the words with glee:

"I sacrifice this child, blessed and beloved by the God of Life and the Goddess of Death, for a better tomorrow for me and my family."

Dre bellowed from within the confines of the cage. He wrapped his fists around the bars and shook with all of his great might. The symbols on both the inside and outside had been carefully chosen to rob him of his strength and power. Sam, equally paralyzed, covered her face with her hands and sobbed.

*****

The Farm, 2:11 pm, Dec. 21, 2020, 84 days after The Fog

Smyth stood too close to Gracie and grinned down at her. He loomed over the slender woman, his teeth great slashes of white in his smug face. She dropped the machete. It stuck upright in the ground at her feet.

*****

The Clocktower, 2:13 pm, Dec. 21, 2020, 84 days after The Fog

The Man in White tossed the unconscious child into the Eternal Flame like so much trash. As her small form tumbled through space into the fire, Manny leapt through the air to catch her. His large hands outstretched, his black and silver hair streamed behind him as his body arched through space.

No one breathes. Life is suspended. This is the moment of transition, where the balance of the future hangs. Time stops.

Without warning or care, it started again.

Missing her tiny hand by centimeters, Manny's fists closed on empty air.

*****

The Farm, 2:14 pm, Dec. 21, 2020, 84 days after The Fog

Gracie, standing on tiptoe, grasped Smyth's face and pulled it close to her own.

"If I kiss you, will you turn back into my prince?"

The God of War grinned. He swung her into his arms and kissed her with everything he had.

*****

The Clocktower, 2:14 pm, Dec. 21, 2020, 84 days after The Fog

As Sohlie's body tumbled through space over the heads of the metal soldiers, the air around it shattered and reformed to reveal the horrified, very awake and screaming body of the God of War. He dropped, like so much trash, into the fire.

*****

The Farm, 2:15 pm, Dec. 21, 2020, 84 days after The Fog

Erin pointedly cleared her throat as Dre kissed his wife. Sohlie's little head, happy afro puffs intact, popped up from behind Gracie's shoulder. She was tucked safely into the purple wrap around her mother's body.

Dre stopped kissing Gracie and pushed an errant strand of hair behind his wife's ear.

"It's good to be home," he whispered.

*****

The Clocktower, 2:16 pm, Dec. 21, 2020, 84 days after The Fog

Dumbfounded at the unfolding scene, the Man in White barely registered the sound of breaking glass. Manny's form dissolved into a million glittering pieces to reveal Sam – the heat from the Flame made the scarlet air around her hair dance.

"Are you so fucking stupid that you actually thought we'd let you take her?"

The air shifted. The Man in White ducked reflexively as a bronze sword missed taking his head off by centimeters.

Raquel, fury etched in every line of her body, swung again.

"You murdered people under my protection, in my *own* temple."

Her blade snapped and fluttered like a hummingbird. It darted at his face, arms and legs – making him whirl and spin to avoid its ferocity.

"You thought I would help *you*?" she shrieked. Her ponytail danced back and forth across her shoulders in a frenzy. "I will rip out your lungs and beat you to death with your nightmares."

He failed to notice the sea water pooling beneath his feet.

Snarling, with tooth and claw, the transformed werewolves ripped the metal men to chunks, clearing a path for Sam to get to the Flame. Shrapnel flew like bullets.

The man in the gold cage tried to remember exactly what she told him.

"Just transform and break it. The symbols on the outside make it indestructible. The ones on the inside make it a cage for us, but only for us. It can be destroyed from the inside super easy."

"What if I can't get out?" He was more than a little claustrophobic. He'd been buried too many times. "I mean it's a cage, right? It's meant to hold Death. It must be impenetrable."

"It's not designed for you," Sam said. "To hold me, it can only hold me – it can only hold a creature of Death and Darkness. Your gift is from both of us. You'll be able to get out just fine. But they have to be destroyed. It's too dangerous to leave them on the battlefield."

"What gift does he have?" Joon asked. They sat at the picnic table by the lake. Joon made jajangmyeon with grilled pork, zucchini and pickled cabbage.

Sam met her brother's eyes over long, silver chopsticks loaded with savory black noodles. They responded in unison. His cells tingled.

"Resurrection."

Jakob pulled the magic of the trees around himself and stretched. His twelve-inch claws pierced the metal. The slender ribbons snapped against the thick, russet brown fur of his back. Jakob huffed and rumbled. He rose up on two feet, stomping the glittering remnants of the cage. He threw his head back and roared. Manny stood next to him. His cage disintegrated beneath his werewolf form.

Fiona's neck hurt as she gazed up at the thirty-foot-tall grizzly bear high-fiving an equally gigantic werewolf. She took off at a fast clip down the side street next to the abandoned bank by the Clocktower. She needed her mommy.

Raquel swung too hard and overbalanced. The Man in White took advantage. He kicked her in the ribs. She fell back hard onto the street. The wind knocked out of her, her sword clattered to the ground. The Man in White gathered lightning between his fingertips and threw it at Raquel. The sea water beneath his feet rose to engulf him. The electricity could not penetrate the three-foot-thick, watery prison surrounding him.

Joon stepped out of the cresting wave and crouched next to Raquel.

"You okay?"

She nodded and gave him the thumbs up but couldn't catch her breath to speak. He patted her back.

"My turn?" Joon asked.

She pursed her full lips and nodded begrudgingly.

Joon stood. He popped the collar of his Hawaiian shirt, cracked his neck in both directions and stepped forward as a dragon. He rushed the Man in White, snatching him up in his claws, dragging him into the air. The sky filled with lightning.

Sam reached out a hand to help Raquel stand.

"I need you to go to the farm," she said.

"I'll be okay," Raquel said, her hands on hips. "Gimme a minute."

"I know, but you're too valuable as a hostage and you're needed there."

"But I want to wear his entrails as a scarf." Raquel pouted. "A really gross scarf."

Sam giggled.

"Are you laughing at me?" Raquel arched a dark eyebrow.

"Never." Sam tore a hole in reality that led to the farmhouse and wouldn't look at her. "It's- it's just that you're cute when you're bloodthirsty."

"So you're flirting with me?"

"Oh-oh, shit, no!" Sam said, but her face turned cherry red. "I'm so sorry. I didn't mean… I'm not trying to be inappropriate. I was just…"

"Huh, that's too bad," Raquel said, before turning on her heel and walking through the tear.

The werewolves were making quick work of the mechanical men. Black oil matted their thick fur. Blood dripped from their snouts as the serrated metal cut through their hides, but these small injuries did nothing to slow their frenzy. The mechanical guardians tried to fight back but their spears bent like toothpicks. They were almost cleared out enough for Sam to get to the Flame. Manny was knee deep in broken parts and bent gears, ripping guts from an unlucky metal guardian when the wind changed direction. A familiar scent caught his attention. He stopped rooting around in sludgy innards and noticed a medium-sized werewolf sheepishly tossing robot corpses around.

The Flame crackled and snapped behind him. It cast an unearthly glow in the cold afternoon – like the fire of a second sun.

Manny leapt thirty feet in the air and landed among the junk with a riotous crash. He turned back into a human and crossed his arms over his chest.

"Offspring," he said.

Dylan tucked his snout into his armpit and batted a stray metal arm.

"Are you supposed to be here? Turn back now please so we can talk about this."

His son whined and put his head between his paws. Dylan returned to his human form with a shake of his blonde head.

"See, Dad, okay, here's the thing…"

"Sam!" Manny yelled over his shoulder.

"Yeah?" She stopped pacing among the ruins to look at him. "Oh, for fuck's sake, what is he doing here? I told him to go to the farm."

"Yes." Manny glared at his offspring. "What *is* he doing here?"

"See, Dad, I'm watching your six. That's watching your back. You won't even know I'm here. I'll be all ninja-like in the back and when you're in trouble, I'll hit 'em when they're not looking. I saw it in a movie."

"Sam!" Manny roared.

"Yeah, on it!"

She gestured and a tear appeared beside them.

Manny grasped his son's shoulders and carried him to the opening.

"No," Dylan whined. "Dad, Dad, you don't understand. I can help. Please let me help. You won't even know I'm here."

Manny set him down in front of the tear. He hugged his son and kissed the top of his head.

"Love you," he said before gently pushing him through the door back to the safety of the farm.

*****

The Farm, 2:29 pm, Dec. 21, 2020, 84 days after The Fog

Ridley Sparklefarts Fluffypants Leary, aka the Ridster, aka Riddy Boy, aka Do Not Eat That, You Asshole Dog, loathed strangers. He hated their new smell, their big, looming shapes and most of all he despised their prying hands.

The scruffy, gray dog had no qualms about planting his toe beans in the ground, puffing his six-inch wide chest up to seven and a half inches and making his abhorrence known with a series of rapid fire barks. If it came down to it, he was not above nipping a detestable hand or two. His humans had brought him to a small area with many intriguing new smells – that he mostly ignored because the place was rife with strangers. Ridley understood that it was his job to guard his family, particularly the puppies, against the eternal menace of Humans He Did Not Know.

His people sat at a picnic table while he paced back and forth between them. Ridley's cursed leash kept him from chasing the abominable strangers. Dozens of them milled about, standing too close while the stench of their anxiety and dread polluted the air. He shook wildly trying to get the scent off. These strangers needed to get the hell away from his people with their rank nonsense.

He yipped and jumped. The tension around him doubled. A stranger growled at him. Another hissed.

"Control the dog, please," his human mother said.

"I'm trying but he's freaking out," his human father replied.

Into this fermenting soup of emotion, a wondrous fragrance appeared. It reminded him of his girlfriend. This aroma was more warm summer morning than his beloved's icy winter's night. The strangers felt it too. Their stench eased and their clenched hands relaxed. Around him, bat wings were neatly tucked away, claws sheathed and tails uncoiled. The simmering waves of rage dissipated. People on the verge of ugly shouting matches smiled shame-facedly at one another. A baby suddenly stopped crying and giggled.

While Ridley would lay down his life for his human family without question, he loved his girlfriend with his whole heart. She scratched his butt whenever he asked. She called him her sweet boy and took him for the longest of walks. Ridley sighed. His butt wiggled in anticipation.

"Oh, hello. Lovely to see you here."

It moved closer. Ridley had smelled this human a few times before. The scent had clung to his girlfriend and human mother.

"Thank you so much for coming. We'll have this all taken care of soon."

The strangers around them smelled… happy, delighted even, at the man's presence.

"I hope your family is doing well. Yes, of course. Your hair is fantastic – love the color."

The strangers parted and the owner of the fragrance appeared. *Ah*, Ridley understood as the pheromones wafted about him. This male human was obviously a litter mate of his human mother and his girlfriend. *Of course*, how did he not realize it earlier?

He leaned over to pet Ridley.

"Hello, you're looking particularly handsome today, if I may say so."

Ridley immediately flopped over and presented his belly. The man chuckled and commenced with the belly rubs. Then he straightened.

"Hey Chibs." He bowed. "I'm afraid I have to steal you away. Our sister requires your help."

*****

The Clocktower, 2:37 pm, 84 days after The Fog

The werewolves had dismantled enough metal men to hold the line around the Eternal Flame. Sam leapt over the wreckage to stand before it. Her proximity reduced the fire to half its size. She closed her eyes and knew in her heart that she had to extinguish this abomination. The sky blackened as she summoned the Darkness. She pulled the threads within her soul and cast all her magic at that cursed fire. The winds howled and thrashed. Even the werewolves shivered in the deathly cold.

The Flame didn't budge.

"The hell," Sam said.

She raised her arm over her head. The Flame was fifteen-feet high now and about five-feet in circumference at its base. Its corrupt nature made her sick.

Sam pushed her claws out of their nail bed. Black ichor dripped from each tip. She took a deep breath and plunged her hands into the inferno. The flames moved away from her. They left a three-foot space between her skin and the white hot fire. She waved her arms back and forth across the base. It jumped and kept right on burning. Sweat poured down her face.

"What the fuck?"

She hopped onto the circular platform and dove face first onto the inferno. The fire split to surround her body but did not extinguish. Sam flipped onto her back. She kicked the air and screamed.

*****

The Farm, 2:39 pm, Dec. 21, 2020, 84 days after The Fog

From what Chiba could glean, several things happened at once. Dre appeared among the morass of bewildered Sunset Cove denizens congealing on his property. He asked her for help. She said she wasn't sure what she could do considering gods were involved. Dre just smiled and told her she was needed.

"But, my girls," Chiba protested. Somehow, she was standing. She'd been sitting seconds before.

Dre searched the sky – gazing at some presence she could not comprehend. He smiled.

"They are very well guarded," he said as he took her hand and wrapped it around his forearm. "I'm sure they'll be safe as houses. She has so many plans, you know."

No, Chiba did not *know* but the instant her hand touched him, she found herself miles away. They arrived at the massive hedge separating Dre's house from the rest of Sunset Cove. Sam had ferried her, Danny, the girls and Ridley past the barrier when the Man in White first appeared and all the black bands disappeared.

"Why don't you just give everyone the bands again?"

"I'm a little unclear on how I did it the first time."

"You're WHAT?" Chiba asked. "Are you joking?

"I am not."

Chiba didn't have a clue what was going on because the answers were more terrifying than not knowing. Sam, after days of Chiba's pestering, said in her darkest tone:

"Chibs, it's so much safer for everyone, and I mean *everyone*, if you don't know."

She tried to believe her.

Chiba did her best to bury the panic attacks that not knowing gave her and enjoy their time on Dre's property. The girls no longer had a healthy fear of large animals but they were having fun.

That morning, without warning, everyone in Sunset Cove just showed up at the farm. Dre and Gracie acted like it was totally normal for put-out, molting harpies, irritated trolls and lost humans to just appear. But Chiba knew this was Sam's doing.

Dre patted her hand.

"I'm afraid we're going to have to take the long way through," he said.

"Dre, what the hell is going on?" She gathered her dark, blue coat closer around her in defense against the winter chill climbing into her bones.

Dre studied her and the overly polite mask dropped away to reveal an endless sadness.

"I'm doing what I always do when extinction threatens my children," he said. "I come get you, and you save them."

He turned and bowed. The mask firmly back in place.

"You're so lovely today," Dre said to the wall. "Would you mind moving for just a moment, please? We'll be right out. I would appreciate it."

To Chiba's amazement, the vines and branches shuffled and parted. She'd seen incredible things since the night of The Fog, but this seemed the most miraculous.

"Thank you so much," he said.

Dre held out his hand and Chiba wrapped her hand around his tattooed forearm.

"I…" she began.

"You're wondering if I've lost my mind," he interrupted her. "I have not."

They entered the living wall and the beauty of it stole Chiba's breath. Impossible flowers bloomed around and above her: velvety, fragrant roses the size of her fists, pale, hanging orchids and scarlet-petaled poppies, drowsy moon flowers, intoxicating angel's trumpet, tiny sapphire-blue irises with fiery, orange throats, a cloud of apple blossom and spiky, delicate, dark columbines.

"This world is alive, Chiba Leary, because a thousand lifetimes ago, you met the most powerful being in all creation," Dre gently moved aside a curtain of wisteria, drooping with scented white flowers. Bees darted over their heads, "and you dared her not to love you, and because you are… *you*, in all your fractured and stubborn humanity, she could not help herself. So, this world was saved."

Chiba breathed in the heady perfume of the flowers. Her head spun from his words, from how quickly the world tilted on its axis. She realized that his arm vibrated beneath her hand. Chiba looked down and pulled away. Dre covered her hand with his own. With a pat, he set it firmly back onto his forearm.

"It's safer if I escort you."

He nodded to the wall of flowers and deep within them Chiba noticed wide, glowing eyes peeking out from the darkness.

"Why?" She gulped. "Why?"

"Did you know that the sun hums? It's very loud. Every planet has its own resonance. This one has a heartbeat – specifically, it has your heartbeat."

Dre nodded to his arm.

"You can't be saying that you have the same vibration as the sun," Chiba said. Everything he'd said was too mind-blowing to fathom so she focused on this random detail. "That's impossible."

Dre raised an eyebrow as a small cluster of light purple lilacs grew and stretched out its petals to brush his cheek.

"Oh, hello gorgeous," he told the flower. "Look how well you've done. I'm very proud of you."

Chiba didn't know where to look or what to think.

"You're saying Sam's the most powerful being in creation?"

"It was wonderful to see you but we must go," he told the flower. "Thank you so much."

His entire being hummed like a streetlight. The flowers around them inched closer and closer. The perfumed air stifled her lungs and if he said one more cryptic thing Chiba was gonna punch him in the testicles.

"I have to get out of here," she said.

"Of course," he replied and they took a few more steps to emerge from the wall. The cool ocean air hit Chiba's face and her head cleared a bit. Then she realized she was face to face with a sightless metal man.

She gasped.

"Don't mind him," Dre said. "He can't see you."

Thousands upon thousands of them surrounded the farm. They stood shoulder to shoulder from the water's edge to as far as Chiba could see. The landscape turned a dull, mottled gray from their presence.

"What the …?"

The tsunami in her mind lifted her up to dizzying heights. The precipice in front of and behind her was a thousand-foot, sheer drop.

"Tell me there's a plan for this, Dre."

"There is, but they are the least of our problems, I'm afraid." He patted her hand like that would somehow reassure her.

Chiba blinked again and found herself at the edge of a melee. Hunks of metal flew through the air. Werewolves the size of tanks shredded metal men into piles. Stretching into the afternoon sky, a bonfire of white hot Flame licked the clouds. A dragon tussled with lightning overhead.

She didn't know where to look – the noise, the roaring, the thunder boomed inside her skull. Chiba cowered into Dre's side.

"May I?"

He placed his hand over hers and the world fell silent.

"How are you doing all this?" Chiba asked. "Please don't say 'because I'm a god.'"

She was balanced at the top of the cliff and everything he said or did pushed her millimeters closer to the edge of sanity.

"We have functions," he said. His voice was the only sound she could hear. Even her own breath was gone. "It might help to think of them as jobs. My job is to nurture and encourage growth. To that end, I must know what every living being needs at any moment in time."

His soft brown eyes didn't leave the Flame.

"That fire is part of me," Dre said. "My son cut a fraction of my soul and polluted it. He made people throw themselves into it in his name in order to feed it and control it. He will use the fire of creation, the hunger for life to destroy all of my children. I cannot put out this fire, but she can and she needs you."

"Dre, I don't understand any of this." Chiba wiped away frustrated tears. "I'm a person. I don't know what you want me to do. How am I supposed to do anything? You're the *sun*, for fuck's sake. There's a dragon and robots and werewolves. I am so … Dre, I'm nothing compared to this. I'm just a person."

She was dizzy from the heights of it all. He grinned at her – a rare, genuine grin full of joy.

"You'll see."

She blinked and they were standing at the edge of the fire. It flared – shooting fifty feet into the sky. Her body felt the pressure and vibrations of the oppressive heat and sound but she felt no pain of burning.

Blood and spittle flew through the stifling air.

Sam stood with her back to them between them and the fire – hair flying in a million directions. Her arms were outstretched as if to embrace the flames. The fire danced around Sam – never getting close enough to burn her.

"Sam," Chiba shouted to no avail.

Dre grabbed her hand and turned her to face him.

"She can't hear you." His mouth didn't move and Chiba realized that his voice had been inside her mind this whole time. "She is … someplace else."

"I don't know what you expect me to do, Dre!"

He grasped her face with both hands.

"You only have to remember that these things must end the way they began. Remember that and this world will survive. Your children will survive. My children will survive. This must end the way it began."

Then he took her left hand and placed it on the back of Sam's exposed neck. Chiba found herself locked in the precipice between life and death. The tsunami flowed away, or rather, she saw the truth of it – that the reality of her love, her kindness, her place in this vast universe dwarfed the mud puddle that had bedeviled her for so long. She laughed and stomped on it. Water droplets flew into the void. She played in the little pond, splashing about. She felt pure joy.

Chiba jumped again but landed hard on her knees on a sandy beach. Before her, stood the mouth of a cave. The brittle corpses of once lush ferns hung low over the entrance. A soft wind blew flakes from their fronds. No birds soared in the sky. No sand flies deviled her. Chiba felt that nothing lived in the water to her left.

She made her way through the dense sand to the cave. The cosmic high she just experienced negated any residual panic from her last visit to a cave.

As she breached the entrance, her eyes adjusted to the darkness. Water dripped along the walls. It was probably fifty-feet across with a low, twenty-foot-high, curved ceiling. It sloped upward towards the mouth. The ceiling got lower, pushing down on her, as she walked further into the cave. The entire place felt lived in and abandoned like a stadium at 3 am after a concert.

A dark pile of rocks sat against the back wall. As Chiba climbed up the slope, her eyes adjusted further and she realized a person sat there.

Sam, her face swollen with tears, her hoodie blossoming around her like the cascading petals of a black hellebore, cradled a handle of vodka in her lap.

She squinted up at her.

"Hey, Chibs, how'd you get in here?"

*****

The Clocktower, 2:47 pm, Dec. 21, 2020, 84 days after The Fog

Fiona ran to her mother who hid on the other side of the bank across from the Clocktower. Her mother, curly, black hair plaited with gold strands, white gown billowing in the crisp winter breeze, then summoned the monsters at her command.

She called them forth from the depths, the most secret gardens, the places too craven and lost to be named. They lumbered, crawled, slithered and flew on corrupted wings to answer their queen.

The Lamia arrived first to the battlefield. Her thick scales left deep grooves in the concrete. She lifted a brindled werewolf in her human arms and tore her in half.

Then the Hydra arrived. It stretched one of its impossibly long necks to the sky and snagged Joon's tail between its fangs. He dropped the Man in White who bounced like a rag doll off the tattered, yellow awning of the candy shop next to Molly's pub. One of the arms of his white suit had been torn off.

The Minotaur appeared. It stood as tall as both Jakob and Manny. It grabbed Jakob around the belly from behind and tossed him high in the air.

Dre turned away from Chiba and Sam to face his errant child.

"You don't have to do this, my son," he yelled over the din.

The Man in White rolled his eyes and brushed the dust from his clothes.

"I should have known that wasn't you," he replied. "You weren't sanctimonious enough."

"This won't end well," Dre said, pushing through metal scrap to get closer.

The Man in White shrugged.

"What do you think you're going to do?"

The Chimera roared in Manny's face. Its venomous tail bedeviled him, striking closer and closer as he tried to move his massive body fast enough to avoid being bitten.

The Hydra loomed over Dre. Nine, seething, drooling maws circled the God of Life's head. Its breath fouled the air.

"No, really," the Man in White said. "I am as my father made me. There is only one being in all the universe who could stop me. You made me to survive any death she could conceive of. But she's not here. Is she? She gave up on this world ages ago. That's why she took the magic – to torture the living."

Dre glanced at Sam and Chiba.

"What do you think that knock-off Celtic trash is going to do?" the Man in White asked.

"She killed you before," Dre said, raising an eyebrow.

"She cheated!" the Man in White screamed. "It was luck that Nyx intervened. She cannot kill me while I am fully imbued with magic and she certainly can't imprison me. Face it, old man. I will burn this world. I will destroy your creation and make it my own. I will have revenge for what you did to me."

The Hydra drew closer to Dre. Saliva dripped from its jaws, splashing on to the street with a caustic sizzle.

"You can't even kill anything," the Man in White circled him. "Death is not in your nature."

"This is your last warning, son," Dre said. "End this foolishness now before you have to deal with the consequences of your actions."

The Man in White doubled over laughing. He held his belly.

"You finally found a sense of humor," he said, wiping a tear away.

"One," Dre said. The Hydra's hot breath ruffled his afro.

"Are you really counting to three right now? Are you going to put me in a time out?"

"Two," Dre said.

"You can't be serious."

"I seriously think your brother got the brains in the family."

"What did you just say?" the Man in White screamed.

"Three."

Dre turned to the Hydra. One head loomed above him. He grabbed the creature's putrid, slimy jaw. Fire erupted at his touch. It ran along the Hydra's body, scorching the meat off its fetid body. Cinders dripped and fell away. The creature squealed as it burned. Eight of the monster's heads disintegrated. The remaining immortal head, shrieking and vomiting, fell at Dre's feet. He kicked it. It rolled across the battlefield, knocking over piles of metal, until it slammed into the Chimera, breaking the creature's back – snapping its wings.

"Never forget, I am the cruelest god. I can make any living creature beg for my sister's kindness."

"That *thing*," the Man in White screamed, pointing at Sam, "is *not* your sister,"

*****

The Cave

"Dre brought me," Chiba said. "He said you needed my help."

Sam gulped straight, room-temperature vodka.

"No offense, Chibs," she said, wincing as the alcohol burned its way down her gullet. "But what does he think you're gonna do? You're human."

"Right!? I told him that like eight times and he said 'these things must end as they begin.'"

"He's gotta be stoned."

"He didn't seem stoned."

"Huh." Sam rested her head against the rock wall behind her. "Did he happen to mention how all this began?"

"He did not."

"Awesome." Sam took another swig and banged her head.

Chiba wandered around the cave. She examined the rock formations. Pieces of broken pottery lined the walls. As a child, she had dreamed of being an archaeologist. Ancient places fascinated her. Something about this cave called to her and somehow, she knew she had time. It felt connected to reality but slower, like light caught in a diamond.

"Honey," Chiba called over her shoulder, "you know I love you…"

"But I shouldn't get hammered on vodka during the apocalypse?"

Chiba paused over the clay fragment mid-examination in the low, shadowy cave light.

"This is the apocalypse?"

"Yup."

Tears leaked from her scrunched up eyes. Sam sniffed and shoved them away with the heels of her hands.

"Fuck, I was hoping I was too dehydrated to cry."

Chiba didn't move from her half-standing position. The word "apocalypse" held her frozen. Her arms hung loose at her sides with her head swiveled towards Sam.

"Shouldn't you…"

"Yeah, I did. I did 'do something.' I did exactly what she told me to do. She said, 'When you are lost and hopeless, come to this cave and you will find what you need.' Those exact fucking words. I'm here. I'm lost. I'm hopeless and where the fuck are you, Nyx? Huh? Where's my hope? Where's my map? Where's my goddamn plan? Huh? Is fucking bullshit – is what it is."

Sam's arms windmilled around her head and then plopped down to disappear into yards of fabric. She pulled the handle from within the folds of her voluminous hoodie and cradled it.

"That's the last time I take advice from a suicidal redhead," she muttered at the bottle.

"Sam!" Chiba found the strength to bolt upright. "What is going on?"

"Oh, I have no fucking clue, honestly," Sam continued talking to the vodka. Her shoulders slumped and her voice was one step louder than a mumble. "I mean, I have theories. I know some things. Not entirely sure how I know them, but that's not new, right? Let's just add my total fucking cluelessness to the long, horrifying list of my failures, shall we? I mean, why not? I am such a fuck up, Chibs. Seriously. Let's just add stupidity to uselessness, ineptitude, thoughtlessness, inability to fucking plan…"

She banged her head against the wall with a resounding thunk. Bits of rock and dust fell down and caught in her hair.

"Such a pathetic failure. Jesus, she was right about me."

Chiba sat on the ground in front of her best friend – as close as the hoodie would allow. She knew those words.

"Sam, your - Olga isn't here."

"Then why is her voice so *loud*?" Sam looked up at the ceiling and exhaled. Chiba reached over and took her hand with kindness in her brown eyes.

"You are not a failure. You're a goddess."

"Am I?" Sam laughed mirthlessly. "What kind of goddess forgets to protect her friends? What kind of goddess lets her family get kidnapped? What kind of goddess lets her town burn? Her people starve? Or lets the whole world burn because she's too weak to put out one godforsaken fucking fire?"

Chiba grabbed her shoulders.

"Sam," she said, looking her dead in the eye, "it's goddess-forsaken."

Sam snorted. A giggle erupted from deep within her chest.

"I fucking love you."

Chiba smiled.

"I love you, too. I'm so glad that worked. I could have made things a lot worse."

"It was a gamble, but it paid off," Sam laughed and cried as she wrapped her arms around Chiba's shoulders. She pulled her in as close as the hoodie would allow. "Dre's right. I needed you. It's too hard to be in this place without you."

"Oh, honey," Chiba rubbed her back. "Are you better? Is Olga gone?"

Sam sniffled and nodded.

"Yeah, she's gone – for now."

"Okay, what the hell is going on? Why is this the apocalypse? What is this place? And also, what the fuck, Sam? What the fuck? I passed through a robot graveyard and there was a dragon. Then I saw eternity – I think. I mean, what the actual fuck?"

Sam chuckled and rubbed her face, trying to get herself back together.

"Yeah, it's a weird day, huh? How are you so chill right now?"

"I got some perspective," Chiba said. "Besides, you need me and you need to stop the apocalypse. So tell me what's going on. What is this place?"

"This place…" Sam snuffled and rubbed her nose. Then she yanked her hair away from her face. Her breath came fast and shallow. She let go of her hair and rubbed her head hard. "Stick to the facts, Samara. Stick to the facts."

Chiba grabbed her hand and held it.

"This place is very, very old," Sam said. "A long time ago, humans were almost extinct. There were only a few thousand of them left. The rest died from starvation and sickness due to climate change. Most of the survivors sheltered in and around this cave and they flourished. This was a real place once. It's gone from our world now. Nyx took this cave out of our reality and suspended it in space and time."

Sam stared at the blinding entrance. Chiba rubbed her hand.

"Why? Why would Nyx do that?"

"Dunno, why does the most powerful being in all creation do anything? Maybe it was a whim? Maybe she wants to fuck with me? Maybe it's an elaborate punishment?"

Chiba's hand stilled.

"Nyx is the most powerful being in all creation? I thought you were."

"Aww, thank you. That's so sweet. But, fuck no, I am not even strong enough to put out the fire outside, let alone…" she gestured to the cave, "do something like this."

"Dre said that the fire was part of his soul," Chiba said. "He also told me that the world is alive because the most powerful being in all creation loves me.'"

"Huh," Sam said and went back to taking swigs from the handle. "At least, she's not stupid."

"You can't say someone is stupid if they don't like me."

"It's the most reliable measure of stupidity I know."

"Most people don't like me."

Sam raised an eyebrow. The handle paused inches from her mouth.

"I rest my case." She took another swig and wiped her lips with the back of her hand. "I kinda pity them though. They don't realize how amazing you are. They don't see how hard you try or how you came out of hell with your heart intact and how incredible that is. I feel bad for them, honestly. But all of them will be dead soon because I can't get my shit together enough to save them... So there's that."

Chiba's buzz was starting to wear off.

"Sam, why this place?"

She looked around and thought she could see the outlines of the ancient people who once called this cave home – their profiles as they talked to each other. The lines of their bodies hung in the air as they walked back and forth bringing in food and game, as they slept on woven mats made of reeds and straw, as they clung to each other in defense of their fear and uncertainty.

"Fuck me!" Sam exclaimed. "What am I even doing with my life? Why didn't I think of that before?" She put the handle down, pulled out a bottle of orange juice and a tumbler from within her hoodie. "I could have been drinking screwdrivers this whole time. Where is my head at? You want one?"

"Sam, why here?"

She didn't look up as she aimed the mouth of the bottle at the tumbler opening. Vodka spilled down the edge of the cup and pooled onto her hoodie.

"Because of that." She pointed with her left hand at the wall over her head.

"That?" Chiba stood and moved to the wall. Her eyes scanned it.

"That," Sam repeated.

Then Chiba found 'that.' Slightly below eye level was a hand print painted with red ochre. She couldn't tear her eyes from it. She held up her own hand for comparison.

"They were so small back then."

"It's a child's," Sam said, still assiduously measuring out cup after cup of vodka as she missed the tumbler entirely.

"How can you tell?"

Chiba peered at it. The print was not just painted onto the wall, but slightly embedded into it. Its edges were rounded and concave in the light brown surface.

Sam laughed in a way that sounded crazy.

"I dunno know. But it hurts." She wrapped her arms around herself and rocked back and forth.

"It hurts like nothing else." The tears began again. "I remember dying, Chiba. I've been stabbed. I've been burnt, but this place and that… that *thing* feels like my soul being shredded through a meat grinder. Whatever I am, whatever horrors I committed, they start with *that*."

Chiba wanted to soothe her, to say the kind words to help make the pain go away, but she was caught by one all-encompassing thought pulsating through her brain:

I made that hand print.

*****

The Clocktower, 3:10 pm, Dec. 21, 2020, 84 days after The Fog

In the end, as the monsters raged and the dusky heavens quaked, it was easy enough for her to slip past them. She was, after all, one small, older woman. In a way, she had disappeared long ago. It was no surprise no one noticed her.

But still, her husband provided a distraction.

"No, really, what is that? One of my brother's children exiled to the Darkness long ago for her crimes?"

He circled his father, getting closer but not too close and always making him keep his back to the Flame.

Dre grinned.

"If you can't figure it out, I'm not going to tell you."

"I already know." The Man in White shrugged. "That's exactly what she is. She followed in my footsteps and stole Nyx's words. It's a coincidence Nyx took the magic when she and I fought."

Dre took two steps to the left.

Typhon, standing at more than 200 feet tall with one hundred snake heads writhing and snapping from his shoulders, lumbered into the battle. Jakob, Joon, Manny and the few remaining werewolves converged on him. Fiona's mother darted beneath the behemoth to reach the Flame. She stood opposite Sam before the fire.

"Why are you bringing it up, son – if you're so confident?"

She pulled the gold cord from her hair. Gray tresses shot through with black fell to her shoulders. Next, she pulled the knot holding her white dress to her body. Naked, the goddess Hera prayed before the Flame. She prayed to her husband – that he would be righteous and triumphant, that the fires he stoked – the first to demoralize and the second to destroy – would succeed. Hera prayed his enemies would fall before him and he would achieve his dream of building a new world in his image.

Typhon snatched Manny up from the street with one hand and straightened to his full height. He reached through the heavens with his other and tried to grab Manny's snarling head. Joon swooped in. He wrapped himself around Typhon's arm and sunk his teeth in the meat of the giant's hand. He roared – a cacophonous snarl, but refused to drop the werewolf.

In the fading light, starry pinpoints appeared one by one in the purpling sky.

Typhon froze. His hand hovered over Manny's head. The monster's body flashed blue. He paused, unable to move and all twenty stories of him vanished.

Manny and Joon tumbled through the air. Joon gathered himself and caught Manny by the calf with the tips of his claws, shredding his leg muscle before he crashed head first into the ground.

The Werewolf King muttered something under his breath about 'show offs.' Then nodded his thanks, begrudgingly, to his brother, twinkling with laughter in the twilight sky.

The Goddess Hera knew it was time. Yet, she hesitated. The flames rose far over her head. The heat licked at her bare legs and arms. It would be painful, she knew. As painful as anything else she'd endured for her husband. In the end, that is what decided her – the inevitability of what she was about to do.

"I offer my life in the belief of Zeus so tomorrow may be a better day for him," she screamed and threw herself into the fire.

The Eternal Flame spat out a shower of sparks. It bubbled and snapped. Hera screamed. She writhed as her skin blackened and evaporated. Goddesses, it seemed, take some time to burn.

Dre cursed his son as the Man in White laughed and laughed.

"Checkmate," he said.

"Retreat!" Dre bellowed. "Everyone fall back! Head to the farm!"

Joon and Jakob were the only ones paying attention. Joon brought forth wave after wave, yanking Manny and the remaining werewolves off their feet into the rising tide. Jakob, with bloody claws, tore a hole in reality and stepped through. Joon gestured to Sam and Chiba.

"Leave them," Dre shouted.

He nodded. The water swallowed him and rushed back to the ocean.

Jakob arrived deep within the woods. He returned to his human form, pulled his guitar from off his back and planted himself at the foot of the Mother Tree – the tallest, oldest tree in the forest.

The Eternal Flame exploded. The hellish blaze poured over its cement pedestal.

It sprinted after the retreating gods. It spread, white-hot and aching, across the streets of downtown. It raced up the Santa Muerte mountainside, down to the southern beaches and farmland, up to the magical lands of the north. Infecting the water, the ocean boiled. A thick blanket of salty mist rose into the air. It burned with such venomous heat that it did not leave ash. The fire consumed everything in its path.

The flames rose over the mountain toward Jakob. They rippled and rushed. The shock wave hit first, shoving him back against the tree trunk and stealing the air from his lungs. He fought for breath, knowing that without it all would be lost. He gasped. The first note escaped as an off-key croak. He sucked in scalding air and sang without words. His song had no rhythm or even a melody. The flames nipped his black boots. Branches above him snapped and cracked as the water within them boiled away.

Jakob held onto the sounds as the fire shredded his concentration. Flames crept up his torso and arms. He needed to keep going, needed to sing. The flames licked his skull. His ears blackened and burned away. The fire crept into his open mouth. It seared his tongue and turned his teeth to ash. Still the notes poured from his throat.

The song was not for him. It was to remind the trees of the forest, as the fire ate away their skin and bones, that they were not alone and that they would return. And that they too, in all their glory, would be resurrected.

The fire slammed into the edges of the county. The magical barrier Kito erected rippled and shuddered. Beneath the Clocktower, she stumbled from the impact. The mural she spent all those painstaking years building, crashed like thunder to the ground.

"No!" Kito dug her hands into the jagged rocks until her blood trickled into the small tide pool in the center of her cave. A blue band hermit crab scuttled away. "I said, no!"

So she sang. She sang with her blood. She sang with her bones, with her memories and her body that ached beneath the weight of those memories. She sang until her lungs withered and her head felt like it was splintering. Kito refused to be silent.

The barrier between Sunset Cove and the rest of the world held … for now.

When the inferno reached the living wall surrounding Dre's farm, it washed up against a different protective circle created by Sam. The metal men liquefied and dissolved in the heat.

The Chimera and Hydra squealed and writhed as they burned.

The Man in White ignored his dying pets. The fire left him and Dre untouched. It gave Sam and Chiba a wide berth, not unlike two magnets repelling each other.

"Hand that *thing* over to me," he told Dre.

They circled each other. The Man in White edged closer and closer to where the women stood. Dre moved with him, staying between him and Sam.

"Give it to me and I'll spare your daughter," he said with a sneer. "Your new family is so sweet. I'd hate to see anything happen to your pretty wife. Such a cute little girl."

Dre smiled. The flames were waist high. Thick soot stained the air. A large raven circled and spun overhead in the blackened thermal eddies. Concrete buildings melted chunk by chunk into viscous bubbling pools.

"You're afraid of her, still? Is all of this for my benefit or hers?"

"Stop protecting her and I won't murder everyone you love." The Man in White's eyes were wild and unfocused. "The little girl dies. Your wife can live – after I rip out her womb."

"Jealous of your little sister?" Dre asked. "I love all my children equally."

"You banished me!" he screamed. "I will burn the world you made. I will tear it down and make it MINE. I will make it in MY image."

He lunged at Sam. Dre caught him by the shoulders.

"Give up and return to the Darkness," Dre said. "End this foolishness. This is not your world. It never will be."

The Man in White shoved him aside.

"Who's gonna stop me? You? That thing pretending to be holy? Hmm?"

He drew a complex sigil with one nail on the skin of his throat.

"My beloved Faithful." The Man in White's voice rang through the county, soaring over the flames, "I am so close to defeating The Shadow Liar, but I need your help. I need your faith. Kill the non-believers. Speak these words and my soul will light your way. 'I pledge my life to Zeus. May my soul light the way to a better world.' You will know those who are not your kind by their darkness."

*****

The Farm, 4:20 pm, Dec. 21, 2020, 84 days after The Fog

Raquel commandeered the picnic table where the Leary's sat earlier that day as an emergency triage. Dozens of werewolves and Joon lay scattered around her in various states of dismemberment, disembowelment and death. The trampled lilac bushes were stained with blood.

Manny sat on the ground next to the picnic table. His right arm dangled from his shoulder by a few meager lengths of sinew. Raquel stood on the table and bodily shoved Manny's arm back into the socket while simultaneously trying to heal the wound. Blood poured onto the top of her head. It pulsed out of him with every heartbeat.

She had just finished up with Joon. Manny insisted, while chuffing hysterically, that she heal the large chunk missing from The Dragon King's ass first.

"Let me knock you out," Raquel begged for the fourth time.

The Werewolf King growled and shook his head. If he were unconscious, every one of his kind would be too. She knew he didn't want to leave people unguarded. Not, Raquel mused, that any one of them could protect an ice cream truck from an onslaught of hungry toddlers in their current condition.

She grabbed the blood-slick appendage again and standing on tiptoe rammed it back into place, trying and failing to get the damn thing to connect.

Manny groaned. His eyes rolled back. She heard his stomach gurgle. His back arched and she heard the deep hacking cough that she feared within the depth of her soul.

"Don't do it," she warned. "Don't you do it."

Jeddah and the half dozen Healers at the triage stepped back.

"Go over there."

Raquel shoved his back, trying to point him to an empty space. Too late, The Werewolf King bent double and spewed his impressive guts. Vomit splashed back up, soaking her shoes.

Everyone groaned. The vomiting continued for long, excruciating minutes. Raquel patted Manny's back. She stared up at the sky and reminded herself that she had signed up for this.

When he finally stopped, gallons of puke pooled at his feet. The stench of it caused sympathy retching from anyone within a forty-foot radius. He looked at her over his shoulder with apologetic eyes and wiped his bloody snout with the back of his furry paw.

"All done? Better now?"

He nodded.

"Good."

She tapped the arm, barely attached to his body. Manny collapsed onto the picnic table with a crash, shimmered and returned to human form. The other werewolves went limp and turned back to humans. Raquel anchored his arm, still clad in his fuzzy, pink bathrobe, into the socket, placed her glowing hand between them and watched as the bones, muscle and sinew knit themselves back together. Then she rolled him onto his side in case he vomited again. The sleeve of the bathrobe hung on by a few threads. Raquel hoped it could be repaired. She knew what it meant to him.

The Man in White's voice rang out just as she was thinking that it was totally worth all the vomit and blood because she could get to make something so beautiful happen. Raquel paused over Manny's prone form and listened to the announcement.

"*Gandeleesh (*Fuck yourself*)*," she yelled.

In the milling crowd, three voices murmured the prayer to Zeus. Raquel leapt from the table top. Her body spun, ponytail swinging wildly. Her bronze sword flashed through the air. Three headless bodies thudded onto the ground.

She held out her sword as arterial blood pumped from a severed neck. It coated the weapon in cherry red liquid. Then Raquel used her sword to draw a forty-foot circle around the triage.

"No one leaves," she said. "You'll be safe here."

"Where are you going?" Jeddah asked as she stuffed intestines back into a young man's abdomen.

"Gotta find Henry."

Jeddah nodded.

Sword in hand, covered in blood and vomit, ponytail swinging with each step, Raquel set out into the chaos that was the last vestiges of Sunset Cove.

*****

The Farm, 4:20 pm, Dec. 21, 2020, 84 days after The Fog

Twenty-feet below the picnic tables, in a hastily dug dirt cave less than five-feet tall and twelve-feet wide, fifteen vampires bickered.

"She might need our help," Tynan said. He rested his head against the crumbling wall. He lounged on the floor of the cave. Technically, he guarded the entrance – a three-foot hole leading to Gracie's root cellar, but his overall vibe was far too relaxed to be mistaken for guarding anything.

Cora obsessively snapped off dead tree roots jutting from the wall.

"She never needs our help," she said. "She told us to stay put."

"I'm getting hungry." Leo sat on the other side of the entrance. He licked his lips and hissed. "Is anyone else feeling peckish?"

After the Man in White's proclamation, the twenty or so Faithful stuffed into the cave with them all murmured their little prayer. Each of their bodies glowed with a strange iridescence. They seemed extremely proud of themselves while studiously ignoring their captors.

"So eat," Cora said with a shrug. "She said if you're hungry, you should just eat."

Leo got on his knees and swayed.

"I hate eating by myself," he said. "Feels sad." He stretched like a cat.

"Fine," Tynan said and shifted onto the balls of his feet and yawned. "I could eat."

One by one, the vampires hissed, swayed and showed their fangs. Then, as if they were a single organism, and without warning, they launched themselves into the mass of the Faithful.

*****

The Beach, 4:20 pm, Dec. 21, 2020, 84 days after The Fog

Sam's circle, inches outside the living wall, overlapped on the beach side with Joon's. The two protective barriers reinforced and fed each other. The ocean outside the barrier boiled. Joon ordered his people to congregate at the palace for their protection.

He wandered around the farm, searching in the soot-blackened light for Erin. The people milling about were exhausted and terrified. They huddled in small groups and stared up at the ash that fell from the sky but didn't touch them. He fought the urge to limp and reflexively grab his ass in phantom pain when the Man in White's voice rang out.

He swore under his breath and rolled his eyes. Joon's body shimmered and he leapt into the air, returning to his dragon form.

Flying low, he kept within the circle's dome. He just crossed the border, past the beach and the still decomposing corpse of the giant goldfish, when the water's surface bubbled. Rising from the depths, the Kraken glowed in the damped light. Water sluiced from the creature's gray head. Hundred-foot-long tentacles slapped the water's surface.

He was still exhausted from his last battle. It only ended like thirty minutes ago.

"Paul, can't we talk this out? Please?"

In response, Paul the Kraken let loose an ear-piercing shriek and wrapped one massive tentacle around Joon's neck.

"Yeah," he said with a sigh. "I thought so."

*****

The Forest, 4:20 pm, Dec. 21, 2020, 84 days after The Fog

A few hundred feet northwest of the farmhouse, Gracie stood at the edge of the forest doing deep knee bends. Sohlie was fussy and the only way to calm her was the soothing motion of her mother's knees creaking as she bent and stood as slowly as possible. She pulled the wrap a little further over her daughter's head and patted her back as she murmured:

"Shh, shh, mi bébé."

In Gracie's right hand was her abuela's trusty machete. Dre had examined it before he left to get Chiba.

"Clever," he murmured, before sliding his thumb along the edge. She gasped and reached for him, certain she saw blood. He held up his uninjured finger and smiled.

"I thought it was sharper," she said.

"Oh, it's deadly, don't worry," he said and kissed her forehead.

Bees floated lazily about as she contemplated that strange interaction. She idly watched the crowd gathered at her house. Gracie still wasn't used to it – being around people and all the ways they'd changed while remaining exactly the same.

One by one, several people in the ground began to glow like porch lights at dusk. Since The Fog, she'd been isolated on the farm. Gracie assumed that this was another byproduct of the magic until a pretty blonde woman in stilettos broke through the crowd, pointed at her and screamed:

"Her! Get her!! Kill her!"

Dozens of luminescent residents of Sunset Cove swiveled their heads to glare at Gracie. They broke from the masses and streamed toward her. The blonde woman led the rampage.

Gracie barely had time to register it all when a gigantic, snarling, pitch-black hound leapt between her and the mob. She grasped the back of Sohlie's head and in blind panic fled into the forest. The wet sounds of rending flesh and gnashing teeth followed her. Sohlie wailed. Little tears pooled on Gracie's shirt as she darted through brambles and over fallen tree trunks. Branches snatched at her hair and she yanked herself free.

Daring to glance behind her, breath rapid and shallow, she saw the angry, glowing shapes following her. As she watched, some of them rose in the air and with a crunch and a slurp, their light went dark.

Gracie didn't know where she was running to. She tried to put her hand over Sohlie's mouth to shush her as she bolted across the soft, forest floor.

The voices pursuing her faded. The iridescent lights disappeared.

Breathless, her chest aching and her skirt torn, Gracie emerged from the forest into a small clearing. Thirty feet in front of her, the living wall rose out of the earth. Beyond it, the inferno licked at the invisible barrier that cast an unearthly pall on the clearing. It was quiet here.

Behind her, a giant thing crashed through the brush. Gracie ran to the wall and turned to face it. She lifted the machete at the creature while subconsciously bouncing on her toes to quiet Sohlie. The black hound materialized out of the darkness of the woods. Blood and gore dripped from its snarling muzzle. It shook its head wildly – tortured eyes gleaming in the incandescent light.

The blonde woman emerged from behind the animal. She wrapped her pale slender arms around its thick neck and jerked. With a grisly snap, the hound collapsed – eyes wide open, tongue lolling from its jaws.

"You," the blonde woman pointed at Gracie with one long, perfectly-manicured nail, "I have to kill you."

*****

The Farm, 4:44 pm, Dec. 21, 2020, 84 days after The Fog

Raven needed to pee… desperately. She locked her knees together and hopped from one foot to the other. The crowd at the farmhouse was too thick for her to cross easily and her need was too urgent. She certainly wasn't going to drop trou in the middle of these strangers – not like that one-armed troll.

Without any good options, she danced her way toward the eastern edge of the house toward several low bushes.

"Excuse me," she said. "'Scuse me. Excuse me. Pardon me. Please excuse me."

She tapped on every shoulder, spiny ridge, furry back, feathered wing and living stone edifice nudging her way ever closer to the beckoning shrubbery.

"Sorry. So sorry. Please excuse me. Pardon. Thank you."

Raven was too absorbed in the ache in her bladder to notice those around her lighting up like streetlights at sunset.

She stood among the low bushes, did a quick scan to make sure no one was looking, then dropped into a quick squat, unbuttoned her jeans and angled just so as not to get any on her boots. The sweet relief was instantaneous. She sighed and crouched for long moments with her elbows on her knees.

When she finished, Raven stood and surreptitiously buttoned her jeans back up. The world had turned to bloody chaos.

The troll swung her good arm wildly, body turning a circle around a small, green, wood nymph who sat crouched on the ground, knees tucked beneath her chin.

"Leave her alone!" the troll shouted.

A half-dozen glowing people circled the pair. Raven heard the raucous sounds of fighting coming from around the farm. She ran forward, shoving her way through the crowd and stood next to the troll. She glanced down at Raven and paused mid-swing. She tilted her angular head – beady eyes gleaming.

"You're one of hers," she said.

"What?" Raven asked.

She pulled Death to her, as much as she didn't want to use it.

"This one belongs to The Shadow Liar," the troll yelled and pointed at Raven.

"Hey! I was helping you."

The crowd shifted to glare at her. The troll picked up the nymph, slung her over her shoulder, muttered sorry and marched off.

Raven found herself surrounded. Their rabid bodies glowed and writhed with a spectral light. Their teeth gnashed as one. She knew they meant to kill her … slowly. She didn't have time to lay down a trap and the Death she could summon would kill maybe two or three – giving the four or so remaining the chance to take her out. Something sharp jabbed her rib cage beneath her taupe jacket. Raven tried to ignore it as the mob pushed closer but the stabbing pain was unbearable. She reached into her jacket, and to her infinite surprise, grasped a handle of some sort. Raven pulled the object hand-over-hand until a seven-foot-tall scythe emerged from the folds of her coat. It had a rainbow striped snaith aka handle and a sparkly, black blade.

Raven leaned back to admire all its fatal glory. Her eyes lit up with childlike joy.

"You are the most beautiful thing I've ever seen," she whispered. "I am going to name you Elvira."

Then she grasped the snaith of her scythe with both hands and swung.

*****

The Farm, 4:22 pm, Dec. 21 2020, 84 days after The Fog

As soon as the Man in White's decree rang out, Danny picked up Malak in one arm, Zara in the other, wrapped Ridley's leash around his wrist and ran to the farmhouse. He hadn't run anywhere in over a decade so really it was more of a wheezy amble.

"Dad, it's fine," Zara said.

Ignoring his normally catastrophizing daughter, he ripped open the heavy, creaky, wooden side door. He let Zara slip to the floor as he locked it behind them.

They found themselves in Dre and Gracie's small kitchen. The sink was in the corner in front of two windows so whoever did the dishes could look out at the garden. A small round wooden table sat in the far corner. Sohlie's purple high chair stood between the hallway to the living room and the table. The room felt a bit vintage but cozy and well-loved.

Behind him, something large slammed into the door. On the other side of the house, he heard more banging. The room shuddered. Ridley went nuts. He planted his fuzzy, gray paws on the yellow, linoleum floor and yapped with trembling outrage.

"Seriously, Dad." Zara blinked up at him, completely unconcerned. "We've got this."

With a crash, the front door let go. The glowing, faceless mob streamed into the kitchen. Danny shoved Zara and Malak behind him. The door at their backs bucked and shook.

Ridley strained at his leash, trying as only a small dog, who is certain, in his core, that he is very mighty, can when protecting his people.

"Ridley, who's a good boy?" Zara asked.

Thick magic filled the air and Ridley, who was small enough to worry about being trampled on, grew and grew until he was as big as he always knew himself to be – a little larger than a Great Dane. His bark became deeper and louder. He stood on his hind legs and bit the closest interloper in the face. Ridley barreled through the enemies, knocking them to the ground. He bit another's arm and shook until it was shredded and gushing.

"See, Dad," Zara said as she stepped out from behind him. "We've got this."

Then she said:

"I invoke Nemain, the Goddess of Strategy, Magic, Inspiration and Protection."

His daughter's eyes fluttered. Her body disappeared in a flash of darkness. A familiar barefoot woman, wearing a plain brown dress, stood in her place. She carried a wooden staff and a resolute expression.

"Sam?" Danny couldn't believe it.

"I am Nemain, Daniel," she replied. She tapped the door behind him with her staff. It thunked with the sound of a dozen steel locks slamming into place.

"Ridley, heel."

The dog let go of his victim and stood at attention by her side. Blood dripped from his curly, gray maw. Danny had never seen him happier.

"Where's Zara? What did you do to my daughter?"

"She's fine," Nemain replied. "She's asleep."

She tapped the floor two feet in front of them. It transformed into liquid sand. The glowing mob sank to their waists.

"Sister?" Nemain turned to look down at Malak who gazed up at her with big, round eyes and half her fist in her mouth.

"Uh, huh?" Malak asked around her fingers.

"Do you remember the words?"

"Uh, huh."

"Can you say them please?"

"Uh, huh."

Nemain waited patiently while the mob clambered over itself to get out of the sand.

"Sister, can you please say the words?"

Malak blinked. Then she grinned.

"I forgot."

Nemain sighed. She hit the fridge with her staff and it tumbled onto the horde.

"Say 'I.'"

"I."

"Invoke."

"What?"

"In. Voke," Nemain gritted through her teeth.

"In what?"

"Voke."

One of the swarm broke free of the sand. It clambered over the fridge. Ridley leapt up and knocked it onto the floor. Another got loose. It swung on Nemain.

"Voke," she repeated. "Voke. Invoke."

She raised the staff to block its fists. It shoved her back against the cabinets.

Danny got down on his knees to encourage Malak.

"She has trouble with her 'v's," he said. "Remember the song your teacher taught you? Bite your lip, exhale…"

"Sister," Nemain said with patience she didn't actually have. "I am *not* a warrior goddess."

She kneed her assailant in the groin. It dropped to her feet in time for another's fist to crash into the white wooden cabinet inches from her head.

Malak screwed her eyes shut and shouted:

"I inboat Auntie Bad Bird."

Danny swore he heard Sam's disgruntled voice mutter:

"Close enough."

Malak flashed out of existence. Sam, with a cool facial scar and rage echoing through her cells, appeared before him.

"Duck," she ordered.

Using his shoulder as a launch pad, she vaulted onto the upturned fridge. Then she jumped on to the counter with a spin. The headless body of Nemain's attacker fell to the floor. Danny didn't even see how she did it.

Nemain tapped the sand. It reverted back to linoleum, trapping their assailants. With the grace of a homicidal ballerina, Badb leapt from shoulder to shoulder. She plunged her gleaming black sword into the top of each skull as she went.

She crossed into the living room, past where Danny could see. Short gasps, the cracking of heads and the splatter of blood followed her movements. The front door slammed open and shut. For long seconds, Danny heard shrieks outside the house until there was a decisive knock on the door behind him.

Nemain tapped it with her staff. The steel locks thunked open. The knob turned. Badb appeared on the other side, leaning against the frame, jet-black sword dripping blood, bits of intestines and brain.

"Ready, sister?" she asked.

Nemain nodded.

"Stay with Daniel, Ridley," she scratched the top of his head, "You are such a good boy."

The sisters exited the farmhouse to the clamor of battle.

Nemain held out her right hand. Badb pulled a dagger from within her cloak. Nemain sliced her left palm, squeezed and with her heart's blood drew three sigils on the door.

"Only friends may enter," she whispered.

Then she strode away from the house into the edge of the battlefield. Nemain took a deep breath and drove her staff into the ground. It hit the earth with the thunderous beat of a drum. She drove it again and again. The unrelenting pulse spread to every heart in the remnants of Sunset Cove.

When she finished, Badb threw back her head and screamed. Her battle cry was heard by every living being in Sunset Cove – making their blood boil.

Nemain glared at her sister.

"What?" Badb asked.

"Right in my ear."

"Sorry."

"Every time," Nemain said. "You do this every time. I am going to lose my hearing."

"I said sorry."

Nemain whacked her arm.

"You're always sorry. Stop screaming in my ear."

Nemain whacked her back. The sisters slapped at each other, neither gaining advantage until Badb pulled Nemain's hair and Nemain ordered her little sister to stop.

"The field is ours," she said, smoothing her hair back into place. "Just go kill something."

"*You* go kill something," Badb shot back.

"I *will*."

Badb rolled her eyes and leapt into the fray.

*****

The Forest, 4:55 pm, Dec. 21, 2020, 84 days after The Fog

Gracie stepped backward. She glanced behind her. The living wall loomed large and impenetrable. Beyond it, a silent inferno raged.

She patted Sohlie's back reflexively. Her child's tears soaked the front of her shirt. The blonde woman stalked her every gesture. Barefoot, she slunk closer and closer. Brambles and thorns had sliced her legs, face and arms. Thin ribbons of blood dripped from the blonde woman's cheeks. Her taupe pencil skirt and silk stockings were shredded.

"I have to kill you," she said.

"You don't, really," Gracie replied. She tried to move to the left, to gain some ground to sprint back into the woods, but the blonde tracked her.

"I have to."

"Don't." Gracie lifted the machete. She never imagined using it on a person. "Leave. Just leave. Leave us alone."

With a shriek, the woman charged, pale legs flashing in the unnatural light. Gracie braced herself. She angled Sohlie away and wrapped her arm across her daughter's tiny back. She tried to cover the little girl's eyes.

The machete sank with a thud deep into the woman's chest. Fiona's eyes widened in shock. She stared with shocked glee down at the simple leather-wrapped handle jutting from her body.

Neither Fiona nor Gracie knew that the machete she carried was, at this moment, the most powerful weapon in human history.

Her abuela's machete was thrice blessed. The Goddess of Death herself provided the second blessing of Intentional Death. The weapon could not harm accidentally, but if Gracie meant to kill, it became deadly. Her husband, the God of Life, blessed it for the third and final time. He used his blood to amplify the second blessing with the power of the sun. Almost nothing could survive against those two blessings.

In Fiona's case, however, it was the weapon's first blessing that proved fatal. Thirty years prior, Gracie's abuela, Maria Teresa Soledad Rios Gutierrez stood in her backyard, using the machete to cut down mangoes for her grandchildren, Graciela and her brother, Hector. She had performed this action a thousand times. Yet, on that day, two hours before her family was set to arrive, she misjudged and sliced open her left thumb.

Maria inhaled sharply at the pain and then sighed at the inconvenience. Her son-in-law had been lecturing her about getting glasses for months now, and this, she feared, was all the proof he needed to drag her to the eye doctor.

She wrapped the old kitchen towel from her fruit basket around the wound and imagined the fuss her son-in-law would make. Maria smiled because she secretly, deep down, enjoyed that her daughter's husband cared enough about her to make a fuss. Her daughter had married a good man.

This blessing of true, selfless, love proved deadly for Fiona.

"I'm sorry," Gracie said. "I'm so sorry. I didn't… I didn't mean…"

She stared at the red stain blossoming from Fiona's silk shirt.

"Help!!" she yelled. "Help! Someone help! Please!"

"Shhh," Fiona said. She put her bloody hand over Gracie's mouth. "Shh, it's okay. It's okay. We don't need help. Shh. This is fine. It's okay."

She took Gracie's hand and wrapped it around the machete's handle.

"First," Fiona said, "take this. Okay? You got it?"

Gracie nodded and held firmly onto the weapon. Fiona stepped backward. The machete slid out of her chest and she stumbled. Gracie dropped the weapon and caught Fiona with one arm.

"I'm sorry," she repeated over and over. "I'm so sorry."

Fiona fell back onto the ground. Gracie followed. She leaned over her as blood poured out of Fiona's chest and her breath came in rapid gasps.

"Shh, shhhhh." Fiona covered her mouth again. "Listen, listen to me. It's okay." She laughed. "I am awful. It's better this way. Trust me. Shhhh, shhh. It's okay."

Fiona rested her hand against the side of Gracie's face.

"It was supposed to be you," she murmured. "It was always supposed to be you, but my dad … did things to me."

Tears spilled from Gracie's eyes, leaving tracks in the blood smeared across her lips and cheeks. Fiona's eyes fluttered closed. Then snapped open. She held Gracie's face with both hands and studied it.

"Hey… you're pretty," Fiona said. "Not as pretty as me, but still… pretty."

Her hands slipped from Gracie's face. Fiona's heart stopped.

"No," she said. She pulled Fiona's limp body to her and patted her cheeks. "No. No. No. No. No. No."

Yequene. (Finally.)

*****

The Beach, 4:56 pm, Dec. 21, 2020, 84 days after The Fog

Priti Tuhina Reddy could no longer run. Her sides ached. Her breath came in rapid shallow gasps. Bone-deep exhaustion and fatalistic acceptance filled her core. They had been chasing her for so long. She sprinted across the farm until she reached the living wall. Priti heard the crashing waves of the ocean beyond it.

She turned to face the relentless incandescent bastards. As she met their blank faces, a whispered rage flowed through her, pushing out any acceptance.

*Who are they to take from you? Hmm? How **dare** they?*

Priti took a deep breath. She clenched every muscle and exhaled an icy breath. The temperature plummeted.

Frost covered her assailants' faces. They stood, feet frozen to the ground. Their glow faded as she held her head up high and swept past them over the hoary ground.

*****

The Forest, 5:01 pm, Dec. 21, 2020, 84 days after The Fog

Gerald Fletcher Nichols ushered the children ahead of him through the woods. There were six of them, including the toddler in his arms. He counted their shapes through the darkness over and over again. When the people in the crowd spoke those awful words, Jerry didn't think too much about it. He saw this group of children without any adults nearby and he just ran with them. The littlest had been scooped into his arms while the older ones ran on ahead.

No idea what possessed him. He didn't have any grandchildren. He was pretty sure he didn't even like kids.

Jerry glanced behind him at the human fireflies stalking them through the woods.

"Shhhhhhhh," he said to the child in his arms. "Shut up. Shhhhh. Keep going straight. The rest of you, go on."

"I can save them," a woman's voice whispered in his ear, *"but there is a cost."*

He turned, but no one was near. This new world took some getting used to. Jerry had just learned what an emoji was the week before The Fog and then he had to be okay with magic.

The fireflies edged closer.

"What is it?"

The woman's monotone voice laid it out for him. Jerry swallowed.

"You got anything else?"

"*I am sorry,*" she said. "*I do not. You are not in position. My sister is too far away.*"

"Why should I trust you?"

There was a moment of silence.

"*I wanted you to have a choice. I could have given you inspiration at the right moment. It did not seem fair.*"

Jerry nodded again.

"Okay," he said. "I'll do it."

"*Good. Get them to veer left.*"

He shooed the children in the direction she told him. He felt the heat of their pursuer's bodies in the chill of the forest night. They were so close. A large redwood stood in the path.

"*It is hollow on the other side. Hide them there.*"

Jerry passed the toddler to the eldest and told them to shush and shush up good.

His bum knee hurt from the cold and the exercise. He limped away from the hollow tree back toward the fireflies.

"You're sure there ain't no other way?"

"*I am certain. My sister will not arrive in time otherwise. This is the only way.*"

"You better be right, lady."

"*I always am.*"

"Little full of yourself, now, huh?" He was nervous.

"*Yes. I am arrogant at times.*"

"Least you know."

"*You have to do it now.*"

He was stalling and she knew it.

"You'll stay here. You'll stay with me the whole time?"

"*Yes, Jerry. I will not go anywhere.*"

"Hey!" He tried to yell but it got caught in his throat. He coughed and jumped up, waving his arm. "Hey!!! Come here!! Here I am!!!"

He caught the fireflies' attention. They circled him faster than a speeding bullet. He kept jumping and yelling to make sure none of them would wander away and find the kids. The fist that connected with his jaw caught him by surprise – even though she warned him it was coming. He dropped to his knees. His head throbbed and brilliant lights filled his vision. The kick knocked him flat on his back. They gathered above him kicking him anywhere they could reach. Dimly, through the bright lights flooding his mind, a jet-black figure fell from the sky. With a slice and snap, the blows stopped.

"Is that you?" he asked the woman in his mind.

"No. This is me."

He turned to see a woman in a plain brown dress with lank hair and strange eyes. She knelt beside him, holding his hand.

"I had a pretty good run I guess," he said to her. "There's worse ways to go."

She nodded and tears ran down her cheeks. She had warned him that the first blow would cause a fatal aneurysm.

"Hey, now," he patted her hand, "I'm supposed to do that."

She nodded again and hurriedly wiped her cheeks. Then she attempted to pull together a smile.

He studied her and blinked.

"You have stars in your eyes, young lady."

"No one ever noticed before," she said with a grin, and he fell. Jerry tumbled through those eyes into distant, blazing galaxies.

*****

The Beach, 5:12 pm, Dec. 21, 2020, 84 days after The Fog

"Mom!"

Erin, her mom, Laurel, and her younger brother were trapped on the beach inside Joon's circle.

"Mom!" she repeated.

Laurel dug through her comically-oversized, zebra-print bag for a lighter as faceless bioluminescent monsters crawled out of the water toward them.

"I need it to think!" Laurel yelled back around the cigarette dangling from her lips.

Erin picked up a five-foot hunk of driftwood that weighed almost as much as she did and swung it menacingly at the creatures slinking along the sand.

"Here." Her brother, Tyler, held out one hand for the bag. "I'll find it."

"I can find it," Laurel said. "I just need a minute, okay? I just need one damn minute when things aren't on fire, being eaten by goats, exploding or fucking monsters crawling out of nowhere. Okay?"

"We don't have a minute, Mom!"

Tyler took the bag from their mother's hand, stuck his hand into its depths and pulled out a white, plastic lighter.

"Here."

Laurel cupped her hands around the cigarette to protect it from the damp ocean winds as Tyler held the lighter. The cigarette caught fire. Laurel inhaled the smoke deep into her lungs. She exhaled, held the cigarette out as if to ash and pondered the situation.

"Well, what in the fuck?" Laurel sagely assessed the situation.

"Mom!" Erin clumsily brandished the log at the crawling pursuers. These creatures could not stand on land.

"I offer the rest of this cigarette to the Goddess of Chaos. My Lady Eris, please help."

The cigarette burnt to ash in a second. The creature's heads and arms flashed out of existence and were replaced with life-sized teddy bear heads and arms.

One of them tried to grab Tyler's ankle but couldn't hold on with its stuffed animal paws.

"Aww," he said. "It's cute *and* terrifying."

Another bioluminescent menace brought its smiling mouth to Erin's ankle and head butted it.

"Is it trying to bite me? Mom? Mom? I think this might be worse. What the hell?"

"Don't look at me," Laurel said, as she pawed through her purse for another cigarette. "It worked, didn't it?"

*****

5:25 pm, Dec. 21, 2020, 84 days after The Fog

It was an unmitigated slaughter.

Of the remaining 189,659 citizens of Sunset Cove, twenty-five percent of them pledged the oath to Zeus. What they lacked in intelligence, strategy or sheer numbers, they made up for in base stupidity.

The Mad Martinelli, sweating through his costume while being hunted through tundra, convinced he was about to suffer a heart attack, suddenly remembered a movie he'd seen on TV and transformed into a velociraptor. He swung round and sliced his attackers to ribbons.

A legless polar bear with one gleaming red eye gleefully tore the heads off of any attackers that came his way. A very large, white werewolf made a show of protecting a group of teenage girls until one of them broke from the pack and proved to be much, much stronger than he was. A nursery of talking raccoons threw rotting fruit and pointed commentary at the glowing interlopers. A gargoyle with a thirty-foot wingspan carried an old, blind woman on his back while he picked up attackers and dropped them from dizzying heights.

Those without hope heard Nemain's whispered plans. Those with exhaustion weighing down their hearts and bodies felt Badb's strength and wrath. Their enemies did not stand a chance.

Most of the glowing idiots simply disappeared with accompanying sounds of cracking and slurping like a starving man at a Vegas buffet.

After leaving the Farmhouse, Raquel passed through most of the battle, healing where she could, but mostly lopping off heads. She ended up in a glen less than a mile from the farmhouse after searching the rest of the circle. There she found Henry at the far end of the clearing, his violin tucked beneath his chin. The light from the fire above illuminated him like a spotlight. His eyes were closed and at his feet, enraptured, sat dozens upon dozens of people. Some of them glowed faintly, but as he played, as his song drifted out of that instrument and struck the night air, the glow faded, then disappeared.

Raquel smiled with pride. She leaned against a nearby redwood and decided to give herself a little time to enjoy the concert. He played an aching song, full of longing for things lost. The high notes reached out to hold but grasped nothing. Over and over again they tried and failed.

Raquel's heart ached. She bowed her head so no one would see her tears and when the fullness of the longing became unbearable, a new, little note snuck in. Played as softly as a whisper, at first it hinted at joy. Raquel couldn't believe she heard it. But he played the chord – louder and stronger this time but still so small in the grand scheme of it all. The longing notes faded only to be replaced so slowly with joyful ones. They edged closer and louder, building into a bright, whirling crescendo until it ended on one solitary note of yearning.

The assembled crowd sat entranced for long moments. They awoke, one by one, as if from a deep and restful dream of home. Then they exploded into applause.

Henry took several bows before putting his violin back in the case and slinging it over his shoulder. He was stopped several times on his way to her by his adoring fans. Raquel finally had to step in.

"I'm sorry but he's desperately needed someplace else, thank you."

His soft eyes searched hers.

"Were we triumphant?"

"We won," she replied.

Henry jumped and spun with happiness.

"But we have patients back at the triage."

He stopped spinning and nodded.

They arrived back at the farm to find patients trickling in for care.

Constance sat on a tree stump with a needle she crafted out of a transformed rose thorn and thread from a cattail. She held up the thread to Manny's pink robe and whispered words to match the color while he held a flashlight over her shoulder.

The vampires had emerged from underground and were dragging bodies to a faraway field to build a funeral pyre.

Joon and Dylan limped to the farmhouse from different directions. Each was supported by Erin and Taylor respectively. Dylan claimed to have a "badly sprained ankle" while Joon's arm was obviously shattered.

Raquel made Jeddah take a break while she dealt with the rest of her patients.

Ridley shrank back to his normal size and finally let Danny leave the house. The scruffy little dog led him out of the side door to a small hollow behind the large pine tree next to the house. Curled up together in the dirt lay Zara and Malak, fast asleep. With a sigh, Ridley rested his head on the crook of Zara's knee and passed out. Danny found an old blanket in the living room. He spread it over his family and joined them for a nice rest beneath the burning sky.

Edgar emerged from the darkness at the back of the property with a small keg under each arm.

"This place has a brewery," he said.

Constance quickly tripled the size of each keg while another witch multiplied them.

Someone started a bonfire in defense against the night's bitter cold and soon the remaining residents of Sunset Cove were getting very drunk, trading mind-altering substances and eating any fruit or vegetable within scrumping distance.

Raquel sat on the top of a picnic table sipping an excellent sour from what she was pretty sure was an over-sized, hollowed-out mushroom. She gazed up at the inferno licking at the invisible dome protecting them.

"How long do you think the fire will last?" Raven asked. Her scythe was stuck upright in the ground behind her like a deadly, glittering pride flag. They were the only ones looking up.

""I dunno," she said. "Could be weeks. Could be years."

"You think Sam's circle will hold?"

"No," Raquel said. "We've got a few more hours."

Raven choked on her beer.

"SERIOUSLY?"

"Yup." Raquel downed the rest of her beer and stood to get another. "Neither of them are strong enough to keep this up."

"Neither of them? Who's the other one?"

"Whoever is keeping Sunset Cove locked up." Raquel shook her head. "Both the barriers are weakening. I can feel it."

"Do you think she'll save us?"

Raquel shrugged.

"Meh, fifty-fifty. Saving people isn't really her deal. Is it?"

She looked at her empty cup and stood.

"I need something stronger than this," she said. "Yo, witchy people! If I describe Tutovka can you conjure some up?"

Deep beneath the remains of the Clocktower, Kito sang. Blood spilled from her eyes and her ears. She gripped the sharp rocks at the edge of the tide pool as she missed a note.

*****

The Cave

Chiba stared at the hand print. It felt inevitable. She couldn't have called the impulse to reach out and touch it by any name – greater than a compulsion and kinder than need. It was half the size of her own. The ghosts whispered ancient secrets. Trembling, she hovered her palm above the mark and lined her fingers up exactly. Then she leaned her whole body against the wall. To her shock, a soft hand pressed back. She gasped. Chiba tried to jerk away but fingers grasped her own and pulled her into infinity.

She found herself, much shorter, standing in the exact spot she stood now. But both Chiba and the world around her were much younger. It was a time before time itself mattered. People moved about at the mouth of the cave. They went about the daily tasks of living – hunting the waters for sustenance, building to ease their workload, sharing meals and trading stories.

None of them dared get close to the wall at the back of the cave. *She* lived there. This cave belonged to *her*. *She* allowed them to stay out of mercy – for *now*.

They whispered stories around the fire at night about the monsters she slayed. Shadows played along the walls as the elders spoke in hushed tones of creatures with sharp teeth and impossible thirst. She destroyed them with her holy words. Her eyes blazed in the darkness.

Chiba desperately wanted to meet her because she had a wish and only this woman could fulfill it. Her elders warned her that was a terrible idea and would never happen and if she had a lick of sense she would stay as far away from that wall as she could – just like everyone else.

So Chiba stood before the wall with her hands on her hips. She was about six years old, with all of Zara's smart ass attitude and Malak's savage fearlessness.

"I would like a sister," she told the wall. "Please give me a sister."

Years ago, a sickness took all the children. Chiba was the only one spared. She had no one to play with.

"She must be funny and kind. We will swim in the ocean. I will love her with all my heart. We will be best friends forever. Please and thank you."

As expected, a small hand appeared from within the wall. Chiba entwined her fingers with the little girl's, grabbed her wrist, and with every ounce of her forty pounds, pulled. A little girl with wild dark hair and strange eyes emerged.

The odd girl put her hands on her hips, imitating Chiba. She giggled. Chiba giggled back. Chiba hugged her.

"I love you," she whispered.

"I love you," the girl whispered back.

Holding hands, they raced out of the cave to play among the waves.

At the time, neither heard the wails on the other side of the wall, but Chiba heard them now. She recognized those sounds. They chilled her bones. She heard those sobs coming from her own throat in her deepest nightmares. Those sounds haunted every second of her waking hours.

Chiba awoke in the present day with terrible knowledge. She looked down at Sam, who held her ankle at an odd angle, unzipped the pouch on her boot, removed a cheerful yellow, paper drink umbrella and plopped it into her half-empty screwdriver. Chiba remembered a thousand lifetimes where a woman with strange eyes and wild hair just showed up and insisted on being her friend.

Chiba cleared her throat and stared at the ceiling, blinking away tears. She didn't have time to cry. She had to save her sister so she could save the world.

"This is just like the axe-throwing bar," Chiba said.

Sam choked on her drink.

"You cannot possibly compare this," Sam's arms windmilled to gesture at everything, "to the axe-throwing bar."

Chiba paced.

"You were so nervous you almost didn't go."

"Flying edge weapons and drunken idiots are a terrible combination," Sam said. "I was not being unreasonable."

"Did you or did you not hit three bulls-eyes that night?" Chiba knelt before her.

Sam glared into her screwdriver.

"What was the name of that place again?" Sam asked. "Wasn't it terrible? I remember it being terrible."

"Sir Axe-a-Lot."

"Ugh! Yes! So terrible."

"Stop trying to distract me."

"Fine."

"Because you're amazing. You can do this, Sam. I believe in you."

"No, you don't, Chiba," Sam said. "You don't believe in anything – least of all me."

She took a swig and wiped her mouth with the back of her hand. The silence between them became dangerous. Chiba felt like she'd been slapped. Her guts dropped to her knees. Sam glanced up at her and swallowed.

"I shouldn't have said that. I'm sorry."

Chiba had never felt so naked.

"You're wrong," she said. Her hands shook as she wiped them against the sides of her jeans. "I do believe in you."

Sam gazed out at the blank whiteness of the cave opening.

"It doesn't matter," she said. "I can't pick up the axe, Chibs." She gestured to the wall behind her. "I know that's a door. I can't open it. I'm not strong enough – for any of it. I've been trying to tell you, I literally can't do this."

She tilted her head to look up at Chiba with defeated tears in her eyes.

"I wish more than anything that I could be more for you, for the girls, for this town, but I'm not. I'm just… not, and I'm so sorry."

Chiba's blood ran cold. Her mind seized up.

This. This was the real reason Dre brought her here.

The world went hazy and lived beyond her fingertips.

"How long?" She gulped. "How long do my girls have?"

"A few hours. Maybe a day."

It made a certain kind of sense. She had a debt to pay. Her feet felt heavy and stuck in the rocky ground. She knew what came next but her mouth was too dry to speak the words. Chiba blinked several times, stalling for time she didn't have.

"I need a knife," she croaked.

"Regular or extra?"

"What's an 'extra' knife?"

"If you barely swipe it at someone it cuts them a thousand times," Sam said, like she was running through a catalog. "Or it's covered in poisonous acid or it's actually a giant snake's fang."

"Why? Why would you need such a thing?"

"I dunno. Maybe you need extra murder? I don't judge."

"Regular is fine."

Sam rummaged around in her hoodie. She pulled out a nine-inch-long, wicked-looking blade, checked the handle and presented it to Chiba.

"You're wrong," Chiba said. "I do believe in you. You might be the only thing I do believe in. You showed me human kindness when so many others… You're the only person I know with the heart to save this place. You're going to fix this, Sam. You're going to save my girls. You just need a little help."

"Yeah?" The yellow drink umbrella was stuck in her hair. "Who's gonna help me?"

"Me," Chiba said and wiped her sweaty hands on her jeans again. "I'm going to help you." If she dropped the knife, she wasn't sure she could make herself pick it up.

"I offer my life in the belief of my sister so tomorrow may be a better day for my children."

Sam's head snapped up.

"No."

Chiba turned and ran – the knife clutched in her hand.

Sam scrambled to follow but tripped over the voluminous folds of her hoodie. Snarling, she pulled the garment to her and ran as fast as she could across the threshold into the light. Sam emerged, too late, back in Sunset Cove to see Chiba plunge the knife into her heart and fall into the flames.

A stone wall within Sam's mind, so deep she hadn't known it existed, higher and wider than the sun, cracked.

The thousand voices of all the women she used to be clamored in the darkness. Her heart expanded. It took up too much room. It squeezed out her lungs. She wheezed and wrapped her arms around herself. Madness beckoned.

I can't do this.

This is all my fault.

Smaller. So much smaller. They take and take until there's nothing left.

Nowhere to go. Nowhere we belong.

This is all your fault.

I don't know who I am without her.

Why can't we do anything right?

What's wrong with us?

This is all my fault.

It would be easy, far too easy to sink into the quagmire of her mind – to give in. Sam wanted to. More than anything, she wanted to float on the currents until they pulled her under but Chiba needed her.

She grasped the sides of her head.

"Shut up! Shut up! All of you. Shut. The. Fuck. Up."

The Man in White pointed and laughed at her through the flames.

"I told you so," he said to Dre. "This is so beyond that thing's pay grade. It's so sad."

Dre held his son's arm to keep him at bay.

"Remember," he whispered. "Remember, Sam. Remember. Please."

Her mind went blessedly quiet, but her heart beat too loud in her ears. She needed to think. She needed to plan.

What do I have that rivals the soul of a god?

Baa-buump

Sam went still. Several thoughts collided and snapped into place.

Wait, what?

Baa-buump

No. It couldn't be. Could it?

Baa-buump

She searched the corners of her mind but there was no other answer. It seemed too preposterous to be real and yet too perfect not to be.

Oh, this is gonna hurt like a motherfucker.

She ran her nails down the front of her hoodie. The fabric separated beneath her fingertips. Sam took several deep breaths and closed her eyes. Then she jabbed herself in her chest with her left hand. She sliced through the cartilage of three of her ribs and yanked them aside. Tearing through the pericardium, she sank her whole fist into the slick cavity. Her lungs fluttered against the side of her hand. Sam rotated her fist slowly.

"What is it doing?" the Man in White asked. "She's killing herself?"

He laughed and wiped sooty tears from his cheeks.

"That's fantastic. What an awful way to die."

Biting the insides of her cheeks to keep from screaming, Sam felt her way to the dozen or so arteries and ventricles pumping blood to her limbs. One by excruciating one, she sliced them apart until her heart separated from her body. She wobbled and almost fell. The cacophony inside her mind remained silent. Her thoughts were her own for the first time in her life and all she knew, in every molecule of every cell, was that Chiba bet her children's lives that she would not fail. Sam steadied herself and pulled.

Her heart beat softly in the palm of her left hand. When Sam opened her eyes, they burned with holy fire. The smoke formed a crown of darkness around her head. She turned to face the Man in White.

The blood drained his face.

"No!" he screamed. He turned to Dre. "Who is that? Who is she?"

Sam gazed at the beating heart in her hand – so small and human, covered in inky blood. Its crevices and cracks, its low thrum, so alien, was a road map to all that she had ever been and all she ever would be.

She met the Man in White's panicked eyes with a cocky grin and squeezed. Her heart exploded on ravens' wings.

Darkness raced to every corner of Sunset Cove. It chased the flames through the streets of downtown, across Midtown. It raced up the Santa Muerte mountainside, pushing the fire down to the southern beaches and farmland. The Flame tried to hide in the magical lands of the north but the Darkness found and crushed it – shrinking it, until the Flame was no more than a desperate spark that leapt to the safety of Dre's open hand.

The black void of his nightmares surrounded the Man in White. Gravity shifted and he was back in that place – where she had trapped him for all those excruciating millennia. He tore at his hair and shrieked in frustration. Thirst clawed at this mind. She was going to take him back to the emptiness, to the endless hunger.

"I am empty!" he screamed at his father. "I have nothing. I am nothing. I am only thirst and you did this to me. I am your child and you made me this way. I can only do this. I can only consume. How dare you act righteous? How dare you?"

With those burning eyes, she advanced on him through the Darkness. He couldn't believe he hadn't seen it – the way she walked – like she owned the universe. That bitch.

He backed away into the nothingness but she hunted him. She would stalk him through eternity until he relented.

"Father, save me," the Man in White begged. "Please don't make me go back. Please. It's torture. You don't know what it's like to need. To need it all, all the time. It's never enough."

He reached for his father and grasped his hand. His father patted his cheek.

"Of course, I know what it's like," Dre said. "Where do you think you got it from?"

"Like her?" he said. "She's…"

Sam's world fell away. The Man in White made sounds with his mouth. She knew they were words about her, about the truth of her, but she couldn't hear them. A high-pitched whine wracked her brain and stole her thoughts.

A million years away Dre and Carl were yelling.

"He knows."

"Do it. Do it now."

Sam couldn't focus. Her mind rebelled. Those words were a virus corrupting her thoughts.

The world drifted in and out of focus.

She heard music – a trilling of high notes and an accompanying thrum.

"Yes?" she asked, because that was her name and she had been taught that it was polite to respond when addressed.

"Do you remember the day we had the blue ice?"

"The blue ice?

It felt soft and powdery against her lips. The coolness dissolved into sweet syrup in her mouth. She touched her lips.

"It tasted like rainbows."

"Yes, you thought it tasted like rainbows." Carl stood, illuminated, on Dre's shoulder. Everything around Dre was bathed in incandescent light. The rest of the world was empty darkness.

"Do you remember what you learned that day?" Carl asked.

A woman's delicate hand etched symbols into a pale, gray rock with her thick, black fingernail. She saw them clearly in her mind's eye.

"Of course, I remember."

She'd done well. The translucent blue ice was her reward.

"Do it," he ordered. He gestured with his beak to the man in Dre's arms. Dre's hand was clamped over his mouth.

Sam blinked and plunged her nails into the Man in White's chest. She held onto the image of the sigils but they wouldn't come through. Lightning sparked around them. Unhinged, it arched through the air connecting with nothing, but singed her arm hair in the process. She ignored it as she tried to focus but something hot and bright blocked her. The Man in White clawed and chewed at Dre's hand, but he held fast.

"Let go of him, Father," Carl said. "She's not strong enough to get past you yet."

"But he'll tell the truth," Dre said.

"I will stop him," Carl said. "Let go."

Dre unwound his arms from the Man in White's torso and stepped back. Carl jumped on his head and clawed at his eyes. He pecked at his brother's teeth and tongue.

"Send him back." His fathomless black eyes met her own.

"But you'll…"

"Do it," he screamed. The Man in White tried to bat him away. Lightning blew through the air. It snapped off one of Carl's wings. He hurled ancient curse words at his brother as he pecked. Blood spattered across his cheeks. One of the Man in White's eyes hung from his skull by the nerve.

The symbols rose again in her mind. Her blood pooled beneath his skin and spread inside his body. The curse appeared as black tattoos across his hands and neck.

The Darkness around them rumbled. Black tendrils emerged from the void. They pierced his body, connected to the symbols and drew him slowly into the emptiness.

"Carl!" Sam said. "Get out of there. I order you, get away from him."

The bird ignored her. He squawked and fluttered, clawing and pecking. The black swallowed them whole.

Sam raised her left hand high. She drew a symbol in the air that she knew, somehow, meant 'return.' The Darkness flew back into her open hand and solidified back into her beating heart.

It was complete and utter devastation. Sam bent double, gasping at the sight. The Eternal Flame leveled every building. It consumed every road. It had burned hot enough to destroy all the plant matter and liquefy the sandy soil beneath.

Sam and Dre found themselves in a distorted hell scape of solid glass. It reflected the crescent moon in infinite odd angles. Millions of stars shimmered above and below them. A swirling, pink galaxy rotated leisurely beneath Sam's feet. The still-living head of the Hydra left a bump in the Alpha Persei Cluster. Miles away, the Mother Tree cast strange shadows against the smooth, alien, translucent mountains.

The ground trembled with the sound of their breath. It reverberated back at an obscene volume.

"No," Sam yelled. She stamped her foot. The glass cracked twenty feet in all directions.

"No," she repeated and wrapped her arms around herself. She sunk to the ground. Her heart beat softly, clenched in her fist. Sam closed her eyes and refused to acknowledge this bleakness. Dre cried quietly a few feet away – his back to her.

"It can't be like this," she said. "I can't leave it like this. I just can't. I need to fix this. How do I fix this?"

In the silence between the beats of her heart, a thought bloomed like hope in the empty dessert. Sam turned to Dre.

"I can't leave it like this."

He looked at her over his shoulder and wiped his cheeks and nose. He frowned.

"What are you talking about?"

She raised her heart so he could see.

"I can't leave it like this," she repeated and stared pointedly at his glowing hand.

His grief cleared away into a brilliant smile.

"You're a genius."

"We'll need the others."

"I'll get them," he said and disappeared.

Sam pulled herself up off the slick ground and made her way to the still breathing head of the Hydra partially sunk into the glass ground. She knocked on the creature's head once with the back of her left hand, ending its immortal life. With her right, she reached into its blackened maw and dragged out the half-burnt body of the God of War.

His left side was perfectly preserved. His right was a charred skeleton. She propped him up against the beast's rapidly decomposing corpse.

She kneeled to speak to him.

"Renounce my niece and you get to die," Sam said.

She caressed his exposed jawbone and smiled with pride at her handwork.

He swallowed, eye wild. She could see half his tongue through his skeleton.

"If I die, without…" he whispered

"Oh, I know what happens if you die without an heir," she said, helping him. "That's the plan."

"No, no, no…"

"No war," Sam said.

"No, no, no, no, no, no."

"You stuck?"

She knocked on his exposed skull. Then she shoved her finger through his empty eye socket and poked his brain. It squished beneath her finger. He screamed. His eye rolled back. Frothy, pink drool ran down his chin.

"No!"

She sat back on her heels. When he came back to himself, he met her gaze.

"No," he said.

"That your final answer?"

He nodded.

She stood.

"Carl!" Sam held out her arm. A large, black raven landed on her forearm. She blinked at the stranger.

"You're not Carl."

The bird bent its wings in a comical approximation of a curtsy.

"No, your Highness," she said. "Carl cannot return. His earthly body was destroyed. My name is Elizabe–"

"I know who you are, Lizzie," Sam interrupted her. She ignored the stabbing pain of loss and cleared her throat. She moved the bird onto her shoulder. Then she sunk her thumb into the God of War's empty eye socket. She shoved her fingers into his blackened maw. She picked up his half burned body and flung him in the direction of the Mother Tree.

"Tell them to eat his tongue first," Sam told Lizzie. "Make it quick. The rest you can take your time on. Don't take his eye. I want him to see the world thrive around him while he decays."

"Understood, your High–"

"I'm not your Highness. Don't call me that."

"I understand," Lizzie said, with a half curtsy. "Then what should I call you?"

"Nothing," Sam replied. "I won't need you for long."

She gazed off into the night sky. Directly in front of her, so close she thought she might touch them, two galaxies split apart. The concentrated amethyst and rose gas at their center exchanged the secrets between the voluminous giants like a dividing cell.

Lizzie nodded and gathered herself up to fly off and follow Sam's orders.

"Wait, I need you for one more thing."

*****

The Clocktower, 6:17 pm, Dec. 21, 2020, 84 days after The Fog

The whisper of Joon's flight through the cloudless night alerted Sam that they were on their way. Dre reappeared beside her. Raquel and Manny rode on Joon's long back. They dropped to the slick ground when he changed form.

Raquel's eyes were as wide as saucers as she looked around.

"Is this real?"

Sam nodded and wouldn't look at her.

"We can fix this?"

Sam nodded again.

"It's … awful," Joon said. "I hate it."

Manny awooed in agreement.

Sam told them about her plan and what she needed. Hours passed. The sun threatened to rise as they hashed out the details.

"But how many parks?"

"We need satellite offices for every ten thousand people."

"Don't forget everyone with special needs – ogres, vampires, mermaids."

"They're lonely," Dre said. "They're all so lonely."

"Better drainage, ponds, public bathrooms."

"No Miguel, you don't get a say … Fine, what do you think?"

Dawn broke, hot and liquid on the horizon in this glass world.

"Ready?" Sam asked Dre.

He nodded.

"Any personal requests?" Dre asked.

Sam made sure the others weren't listening.

"Spineflowers," she whispered.

"What?" Dre whispered back.

"Spineflowers." She leaned in closer. Her eyes darted around to make sure no one else heard her. "You know Ptarmigan Park? They're endangered?"

"Spineflowers?" he asked, too loud for her taste. "Pink-ish, purple, silvery, delicate, tiny, adorable things?"

Sam drew her shoulders back defensively and looked anywhere but his face.

"They're my favorite," she said. "I think they're beautiful. Save them, please."

"Of course." His lips quirked and he loved her just a little bit more for spineflowers.

"You? Any personal requests?"

"One damn comfortable seat at the Civic Center," he said. "I want to watch roller derby without visiting the chiropractor the next day."

"I can do that."

Sam held out her left hand holding her beating heart. She raised up her right. Dre turned away from her. He raised his right hand to meet hers with the bit of his soul burning in his left. The shadow of a new world rose around them. It burned and fell, waiting to be made real. Roaring and melodic, power beyond comprehension rested in the inches between their hands.

"Wait!" Raquel shouted. She tapped her forehead and pulled out a golden thread.

"Here," she said as the thread floated between Dre and Sam's hands, "for health."

Joon smiled. He caught a tear with the edge of his finger and offered it to the future.

"For a rainy day," he said.

Manny ripped some bloody tufts of pink fabric from his robe and gave it over.

"For the pack – whoever they are," he said.

"On the count of two," Sam said.

"Why not three?" Dre asked.

Sam shrugged.

"Why wait?"

"Three leaves room for doubt."

"Okay then, on three," she said.

He nodded and prepared himself.

"One."

"Two…" Sam said and gnawed on her lower lip. "It won't be the same. It will never be the same again."

"No," Dre said. "It won't. And it's okay to mourn what it was, but this will always be home."

She thought about it and nodded. Then she found her last shred of hope and prayed this would actually work.

"Three," she said and took Dre's hand.

The ground exploded. Sand and bits of broken glass swirled around them. Sam tried to hold it all together– the details that made Sunset Cove Sunset Cove – downtown, the sad, sticky dance floor at the back of the Purple Pear, the fraying, red velvet curtains at the haunted Rialto, gorgeous Victorian painted ladies, the cherry blossom trees that lined Mission, the wharf and the boardwalk, the way bookshop smelled, those majestic lighthouses, but everything new kept jumbling away:

Bike lanes and light rail, multi-family dwellings with big kitchens and courtyards for gardens, solar panels and toothbrushes, housing for people with special needs - ogres, vampires, giants and all the rest, mermaids needed underground transit tubes, population stats, room sizes, census breakdowns, harpy roosts, hospitals, schools and composting. The list was endless and it was running away from her.

"Sister?" Dre glowed in the sandstorm.

If it's too different, she might not find her way back. She'll be so scared if she can't recognize anything.

Sam wasn't going to make any single-family homes. People could build them later if they wanted. But her mind settled on a two-story, white house on a cul-de-sac with a "GO AWAY!" welcome mat.

Home.

Her heart disappeared in a puff of Darkness. The sandstorm cleared. The shadows solidified into buildings and roads.

It was a strange mix of modern and ancient. Miguel, it turned out, was a city planning nerd. He had thoughts.

"The *key*," he said while Manny translated, "is neighborhoods."

She made downtown, the boardwalk and wharf exactly as they had been, with one notable exception – on the wall of the hipster coffee joint, hung a three-foot by five-foot portrait of Carl at his most pompous. All the things that made Sunset Cove what it was were remade exactly – including the surfer statue on the cliff, the painted Victorian ladies, the lighthouse up north and the Purple Pear's weird, sticky dance floor.

Using downtown as a starting point, tarmac trails, ideal for walking or biking, branched outward like a tree into hundreds of neighborhoods. Each was centered around a large courtyard with room for a garden, swimming pond, and plenty of tables and chairs. Little streams burbled through every neighborhood. These small areas within the larger towns of Sunset Cove consisted of multiple, two-story buildings with space for a community kitchen, meeting rooms, workshop locations for witches and other craftsmen. She made them into multiple configurations, some consisted of multi-family units while others skewed toward one bedroom or two for singles and married couples. All of the neighborhoods had multiple paths leading in and out, including water access beneath the buildings so members of Joon's kingdom could visit. Each community had lofts for harpies and fifty-story housing for giants and trolls. There was space for a pub or restaurant and plenty of comfortable outdoor seating. Their roofs were adorned with solar panels. She built underground homes for the vampires. Interior lighting glowed soft and quiet. Every building was accessible for every kind of creature.

Sam strategically placed movie theaters, schools, clinics and libraries between the neighborhoods. There were plenty of public bathrooms and no golf courses. She rebuilt the university up in the mountains and the Buddhist temple in the redwood forest.

The buildings were constructed from everything from stone and brick to wood and plaster. Each neighborhood had a distinctive architectural style from across the globe. There was the gleaming limestone from Greece, the quaint, shingled, wooden houses from Norway, arching sloped rooftops from Indonesia, earthen, brick, structures from Africa. Sam, indulging herself, made a gothic neighborhood with obsidian buildings.

Multiple light rail lines connected every part of Sunset Cove, from the Redwood Valley to Midtown to Bonne Chance to the rural areas of the south.

She created a dozen large buildings for miscellaneous use, including a sports stadium. And true to her word, she rebuilt the Civic Center and added one large, plush purple chair a few seats up from center ringside.

No more mansions hoarded the cliff sides. A mile long swath of open space ran along the coast. Every edifice had running water, heat and electricity.

All the living beings in Sunset Cove had a place to call home with room to grow.

When Sam was done, Dre took his turn. The garden plots within courtyards exploded with fruits and vegetables. Dark, shining plums, golden persimmons and velvety apricots, spiky, delicious arbutus, tart barberries and currants, black figs and yellow, freckled apple trees lined every street and path. Pumpkin vine shrouded City Hall. Their dark green leaves hid fat orange and white gourds. Wild leeks, sweet potatoes, and flowering sunchokes sprouted along sidewalks. Chestnut trees cast a silvery shade over library doorways. Strawberries laid in wait for spring, soft. Red thimbleberries were for summer. A mass of blackberries tangled across an empty lot, drawing birds, squirrels and other small, hungry creatures. A dozen varieties of tomatoes grew next to fuzzy-leaved, blue borage with its sharp cucumber smell. Milkweed, wild iris and trilliums grew for monarchs. Yarrow, mint, and bee balm added warm, spicy scents to the air. The kelp forests of Joon's Kingdom were resurrected.

They agreed to keep Mulberry Square mostly as it was but Dre covered the walls in ivy and passionflower. He planted a few mulberry trees in circular holes in the cement. Water flowed gently between the trees, cooling the concrete. Dragonflies, bees, and hummingbirds darted in the air.

Strangely enough, a high percentage of the new buildings were some shade of purple. Conversely, the residents of Sunset Cove would later comment that many of the new decorative plants in their neighborhoods were jet black.

"You did it!" Joon jumped up and down. He hugged Raquel and Manny. Dre sank to the ground with exhausted eyes and smiled up at him.

"We did it," he said. "We all did it. Right, Sam?"

But she was already gone.

A large raven landed on Dre's shoulder. She dropped a thick, vellum sheet of paper into his hands.

I'm sorry.
I had to.

It read, in blocky, nearly illegible letters. On the back was written:

P.S. Take the girls for ice cream from time to time for me.

P.P.S. Please take care of Raven. She needs a home.
P.P.P.S. Thank you all for being amazing.

About twenty feet below where they stood, unnoticed by them all, Kito lay, alive but unconscious in a pool of her own blood. The barrier cutting Sunset Cove off from the rest of the world held.

*****

The Cave

Samara Tomovna Bridger strode across the sands through the entrance of the cave trapped in time. That was not her real name, she knew. Her true name sounded like the thrum of battle drums, the crackle of fall leaves, that sensation right before it rains and the quiet, secret echoes of the moonlit sky.

Her purpose set, she did not indulge in self pity. Instead, she walked right up to the rock wall and placed her left hand on top of the hand print.

She fell forward, jerked along by some unseen force. Howling, icy winds arose, whipping her hair about. This Darkness was both comforting and utterly alien. She moved lugubriously through this space as if dancing through molasses.

Sam emerged into a Victorian drawing room of incorrect proportions. A monstrous oculus held together with a delicate, wrought-iron depiction of the golden ratio took up a third of the space. The brown-tiled floor stretched out for a mile beneath her feet. Thirty feet away, three walls decorated with gilded, rose and gold wallpaper stood upright without a ceiling. Beyond it all lay a yawning, velvety nothingness.

Two figures chatted in the corner with their heads close together. While Sam could make out the particulars of the room – including the giant, liquid, black, human skeleton sitting on a rough-hewn, wooden throne on the far wall, she had trouble comprehending the forms of these beings. One was double the size of the other. Yet, as she crossed the infinite space between them, the larger figure shrank to average proportions. The incoherent forms resolved into the shapes of a statuesque woman and a gangly, bald man. He wore a high-collared black tuxedo with tails.

Something about the woman made Sam walk faster. She half jogged the rest of the way. Neither of the strangers moved until Sam got within a few feet.

"Look at the state of you," Nyx said, rushing to cross the distance between them.

From her frilly, lace sleeve, she pulled out a black handkerchief. Taking Sam's face in her hands, she scrubbed the dried blood and ash from her cheeks and forehead.

Close up, she studied the woman's face. Her gray eyes burned with holy fire. Thick crevasses spread from the corners of those eyes. Dark, wild hair, shot through with silver strands, sat piled upon her head. Errant wisps brushed her temples. She had gone on a girl's weekend with Chiba a few years ago to Yosemite. El Capitan reminded her of this woman – too joyful, too incongruous – just on the edge of driving her mad with awe.

"I told Ama this experiment was a terrible idea," Nyx muttered as she rubbed Sam's cheeks. "'People, free will, chaos, trees and sunlight,' he said. 'It will be brilliant,' he said. 'Don't worry,' he said. Ugh. *What* a bloody nightmare."

Nyx's skin was paper thin. Her hands were warm and soft. Sam did not notice the sheen of tears in those burning eyes because of the tears welling up in her own. Sam's body shook like a rabid dog. A visceral, ancient, impossible need rose up within her. A deep well of loss overflowed until she had to look away.

Nyx smoothed down the thousand flyaway strands on Sam's head and tucked her hair behind her left ear. Then this stone woman held the torn edges of her hoodie as they knit back together. She brushed away the dust and dirt on Sam's shoulders.

"There," she said, "that's better."

Sam ignored the tangled knot of emotions closing down her throat and knelt before the ancient woman. She bowed her head.

"Nyx, I have come to negotiate for the life of my sister, Chiba Leary. I will return what I have taken in exchange for her life. I will give you whatever you want. I'll do whatever you want. So long as you bring her back from the dead."

"Okay," Nyx replied.

Sam's head snapped up.

"Okay? What do you mean 'Okay'?"

Nyx waved her left hand. The left sleeve of her off-white, Victorian-style shirt with a high, frilly, collar had been torn off to reveal swirling, black tattoos that ran from her arm onto her hand, up the side of her neck, down her left leg and onto her bare foot. She wore a loose, jagged, black skirt. The symbols were precise in their lines and spacing. If Sam thought hard enough about them, their meaning emerged from the deepest wells of her memory.

"I mean 'okay,'" Nyx said. "Chiba Leary is alive and well. She is back home."

This was not going how she thought it would.

"...Okay?" Sam asked. "What now? Torture? Immolation? That thing the Vikings did where they tore people's lungs out their backs? Are you just gonna murder me or is there some kind of ritual blood sacrifice?"

Nyx sighed and rolled her eyes.

"Now, we have tea."

She gestured to the table behind her. A multi-tiered, silver epergne, piled high with delicate cucumber and cress finger sandwiches, colorful petit fours, scones with jam and clotted cream, dozens of pastel macaroons and heaps of luscious croissants drizzled with thick, dark chocolate. Wisps of steam rose from a dainty blue and white teapot.

"... Tea?"

Sam stood reflexively.

"Is that a … pie?"

"Yes, it's strawberry rhubarb."

She had never been more bewildered in her life.

"My favorite," she said as she sat at the table in a daze.

Sam had always secretly wanted to go to a fancy tea party. It was the kind of thing ritzy East Coast ladies with names like Hanly and Preston did with their … A terrible word, in screaming bright, red neon, popped into her consciousness. It consumed her brain and blotted out her vision. She clamped her hand over her mouth to keep from blurting it out.

"Yes, I know," Nyx said.

Before Sam could process that tidbit, the butler laid a pristine, cloth napkin across her lap. With a flourish, he poured fragrant tea into her cup. Upon closer examination, he was about as human as Nyx. His skin beneath the sharp, black suit was a tacky, mustard yellow. His shoulders were too broad and slumped over. His mouth was too wide and his lips were too thin for his sunken chin and sallow, bulging eyes. The butler picked up a delicate sandwich with razor-sharp claws and set it on her plate.

"Thank you, Carl," Nyx said with a nod.

"Oh, hey," Sam said. "You have a Carl, too. I have a Carl. I… had a Carl."

The creature gazed down at her with an expectant smile. A jagged tooth poked out from his gummy mouth. He was oddly tall.

"Carl!" Sam yelled and banged on the table when the truth landed. The tableware clattered. She almost stood. "You're my Carl? You're *my* Carl. You're not dead."

"Hey, Boss," he said.

Nyx smiled over her teacup.

"You may go now, Carl," she said.

He bowed, patted Sam's shoulder and disappeared through the archway next to the skeleton.

"That's my Carl," she said to Nyx, pointing to the direction he'd gone.

"Yes, he is," Nyx said. She bit into a croissant. Bits of flaky, beige pastry lodged into the frilly lace of her shirt.

Sam sipped her tea. It was an aromatic Earl Gray. This woman was definitely going to kill her.

"I'm not going to kill you," Nyx said.

Sam's cup rattled back into its saucer.

"You're a mind reader, too?"

"It's written all over your face."

"I- okay," Sam placed her hands on the table. "Why am I here? What could I possibly have that's yours? How do I give it back?"

"You have my word," Nyx said.

Her world tilted dangerously. She gripped the table edges to keep from falling.

"No, I don't," Sam blurted. "I don't have your word. I don't know what you're talking about."

Nyx put down her tea.

"Such a terrible liar," she said. "I am grateful that, at least, has not changed."

Immolation would have been easier.

"I know, right?" Sam couldn't look at this stone woman. She fought for the tiniest sliver of space between them. "If I keep it up, I won't be the Goddess of Truth anymore."

"You were not given that name because you speak the truth, although it is not in your nature to lie," Nyx said. "You are called the Goddess of Truth because you are the truth of me. Just as I am the truth of you."

The crack in the wall in her mind widened to devastating proportions. It could collapse at any second. She scrambled to duct tape and hot glue it all back together.

"It's not possible," Sam said, fighting tears. "That word isn't possible. I don't know why you'd want it anyway, but it's not possible."

Nyx raised her left arm. The room spun without moving and they were immersed in the pulsating tangerine, cobalt and amber gasses of a dying nebula. Forms danced and died in these celestial clouds. Sam lost her breath. It was the most beautiful thing she'd ever seen.

"I am the Holy Darkness," Nyx replied. Her gray eyes glittered with the dust of ancient galaxies. "My bones are gravity. My eyes are the light trapped inside a black hole. The Laws of Thermodynamics are written beneath my left breast. I, and I alone, decide what is possible. My word is not only possible. My word is fact and I have gone too long without it."

Sam stood, knocking over her chair and wrapped her arms around herself.

"You don't want it," she said, as she rocked back and forth. "Please. It's a terrible word. It's the worst word. You don't want it. All the most terrible things come from that word. Please."

Nyx stood and faced her.

"I know my word was used to hurt you. Those who didn't deserve my word picked it up and tried to use it to keep you small, to make you doubt yourself. But understand, I care for what is mine."

Nyx held out her left hand to Sam.

"Please, I haven't heard my word in so long. I miss it terribly. It is my favorite."

Sam scrunched her eyes shut to block out the light as the wall in her mind crumbled into nothingness. It had been easier, so much easier, to split herself apart, to pretend that she deserved the abuse instead of facing the overwhelming truth of who she always was.

Her voice was so wobbly and quiet, so afraid and broken, when she said:

"Mom?"

A soft hand reached through the darkness. It brushed the tears from her face. The deep wound in Sam's chest healed.

"Yes, my holy daughter," Nyx replied.

*****

7:07 pm, Dec. 23, 2020, 86 days after The Fog

And because magic is real, and every little girl deserves a mother who loves her, a black cloud swirled to life in a pocket dimension so close to the real world, you could almost touch it.

A dark-haired woman with a sour expression that hid the love in her heart, stepped out of that cloud onto a suburban street. She ran straight up the driveway, past the doormat that said "GO AWAY!," through a plain, white door, into an average living room where she was greeted by an overjoyed, scruffy gray dog and two ecstatic little girls.

BREAKING NEWS

SEPT. 29, 2020

A 9.7 magnitude earthquake, the largest in recorded history, tore through Sunset Cove county at 7:01 pm last night.

The quake caused unprecedented damage.

According to witnesses, the entire 670 square miles of Sunset Cove county is: "Gone, just gone."

Experts speculate the multiple subduction zones that created the Santa Muerte Mountain Range combined with liquefaction created a massive mudslide that buried the entire county. Areas that survived the mudslide were decimated by multiple firestorms. The blaze is only seven percent contained as of 5 am this morning.

Tremors were felt as far away as Reno.

So far, only one survivor has been found. James 'Jimmy' Huey St. Clair, 34, was found unconscious with burns over one-third of his body. He is in critical condition at San Jose General.

Rescuers have taken to boats in search of survivors, but hazardous conditions including large aftershocks that have caused tsunamis are hampering rescue efforts.

Our thoughts and prayers are with the residents of Sunset Cove and their family members.

We will continue to report on this tragedy as it unfolds.

IN THE GREEN

The Clocktower, 1:32 pm, June 23, 2021, 184 days after The Battle of the Solstice

They agreed to celebrate Sam's birthday and Joon was late. He hated being late.

"A few minutes is not late," Erin mumbled. "My mom once showed up to a party three days after it was supposed to start."

His arm was slung over her shoulder. Her fingers were entwined with his. It was a beautiful, sunny day with a slight, cooling breeze. They wandered down Mission Street. The twelve-block-long road was now little more than a lane. A woman in a short, red dress roller skated by blowing bubbles. Orange and black monarch butterfly wings sprouted from her back.

Vendors lined each side of the road beneath the shelter of cherry blossom trees hawking goods and services for trade. Some of them sat on wooden chairs next to hastily painted signs advertising services like 'pest control,' 'movers,' 'tattoos for health' and 'palm reading.' Others were ornate, multi-level displays of curiosities, oddities, amulets, lotions, potions and plants. There was an ease to this place. No one really needed to sell anything and no one really needed to purchase anything. It was really more of an excuse to gossip and chat with people from other parts of the county.

Erin had stopped by every witch's stall asking them if they made paint. She ran out of a particular shade of lapis before The Fog and was having trouble replacing it.

Joon twitched at her response. He had invited Laurel over for dinner a few weeks ago and she was three hours late. Her excuse was that she couldn't find the right shoes. He broke out into rage sweat at the memory. Seeing her fiance stress glitch, Erin patted his hand and tabled her hunt.

As they approached the park that now surrounded the Clocktower, they heard Henry's mournful violin. The space was now ringed by nine, giant redwoods, each representing a werewolf who died during the Battle of the Solstice. Their names were etched into obsidian plaques at their base.

Henry stood to the right of the path leading into the park. Jakob, who proclaimed loudly, and to anyone who would listen, that he was Henry's biggest fan, leaned against the tree on the other side of the path. His black hat was set on his head at a jaunty angle.

"Hey, man," he stepped away from the tree to hug Joon and Erin, "You're late. Everything okay?"

"My fault," Erin said and held up her hand. "Guilty. The blue paint…"

"It haunts you," Jakob said. "I get that."

They nodded to Henry, who continued playing as they crossed the threshold. The trees and pine needles blunted the sounds outside.

The park was about a quarter mile in diameter and at its center, hovering thirty feet in the air, suspended by pure magic, was the white clock face of the original tower. It showed the standard time clearly no matter where someone stood in the park. Joon always wondered how she pulled that off.

Eight-foot-tall columns in black and white marble stood in a circle around the clock. The names of the innocent dead, along with blank lines representing each betrayer and murderer were etched onto their surface. The columns shone so brightly that anyone standing in front of them caught the outlines of their own reflection.

On the ground directly beneath the clock, sat a large pool ringed with blue-green irises,

Surrounding the pool were eternally-blooming, delicate, pink spineflowers.

"She would hate that they never die," Chiba told Dre during their last ice cream visit.

"She is welcome to come back to us and kill them herself," he said.

Priti had already set up her cart in the southwest corner next to a half-dozen picnic tables. Bees and swallows darted back and forth among the scarlet amaranth, pink hollyhock, white and scarlet opium poppies, Mexican marigold, radiant lavender and black hellebore. Bracken ferns had sprung up at the edges of the park near the redwood trees. Dre had no idea where they came from. Next to the Mexican marigold, an obsidian plaque read, "On this spot, Chiba Leary saved the world."

Almost everyone was already there except Raven and Raquel, including Laurel, Manny and Dylan.

"How?" Joon gaped at them. "How did they get here before us?"

"Chaos, my love, chaos," Erin said and patted his hand.

Dylan carried a shrieking and delighted Sohlie on his shoulders as he chased an equally happy Malak and Ridley. Zara sat a few feet away beneath one of the redwood trees reading *A Swiftly Tilting Planet*.

Dre stood in front of Priti's cart while she finished pouring butterscotch onto his sundae.

"Bless you," he said, making a steeple with his hands and bowing as she handed over the delicacy. "You are a true artist."

He one arm hugged Joon and Erin in greeting.

"How did Laurel and Manny get here before you?" he asked.

"Chaos," Joon whispered. "Pure chaos."

Dre laughed and joined Gracie, Laurel, Manny, Constance and Edgar at one of the picnic tables. Constance and Laurel had become fast friends when they met during the party after the Battle of the Solstice.

Chiba stood about thirty feet away near one of the columns. She faced the only patch of black hellebore in the park. A little wooden fence kept visitors away from the toxic plant. Embedded into the ground between the fence and the flowers were two glass boot prints.

The air was thick with the delicate scent of the solitary, black hellebore. Chasing that were clean, pungent notes of lavender and the earthy, bitter aroma of marigolds. Hollyhocks' faintly sweet, dusty fragrance completed the heady perfume.

She imagined Sam standing in that exact spot as she spoke.

"I understand why it's taking you so long," Chiba said. "I do, but the girls keep asking when you're coming home. They miss you. I miss you. Everyone misses you. Dre's being kinda weird about it. He quit drinking coffee a couple weeks ago. Jakob had to stage a mini intervention. It was … bad. Raven broke up with that one girl we all hated. Now, she's dating some new girl. She says she might bring her today. We're all skeptical. I'm not saying her taste in partners is as bad as yours but it's … bad. Just come home soon, okay?"

Chiba turned to join the others but stopped and turned back.

"Happy birthday," she said.

Dre walked up and gave her a one-armed hug, clutching his sundae in the other.

"How is she today?" he asked.

"Quiet," Chiba muttered. "Too quiet."

Then she joined the others at the picnic table.

Malak ran to where her sister sat.

"Play with me."

Sohlie was playing peek-a boo with Dylan around one of the stone columns.

"I'm reading, Malak," Zara said, not looking up from her book.

"Please," Malak begged as she jumped up and down. "Pretty puh-leeeeeeeeaaaassseeeeeeee."

Zara sighed like a forty year old who just discovered the coffee shop messed up her order. She memorized the page number she was on, put down her book, and stood. She tapped her sister's shoulder.

"Tag! You're it!" Zara yelled and ran.

"Zaaaarrrrraaaa, NO FAIR," Malak yelled as she ran after her.

Dre finished devouring his sundae and very surreptitiously side-eyed everyone to make sure they weren't paying attention. Manny had pulled up a second table next to the first to make room for everyone. Gracie and Constance were trading gardening stories. Laurel listened in and munched on the freshly picked strawberries and blackberry preserves that Constance brought.

"Banana slugs can be negotiated with," Constance said. "But squirrels are outright terrorists."

Manny and Edgar talked about the RPGs they were running. Joon and Erin shared a double scoop lemon and strawberry sorbet. Henry and Jakob idly strummed beneath the trees. Chiba chatted with Priti while she waited for her vanilla waffle cone with caramel drizzle.

When Dre decided no one was looking, he slid away from the table and tip-toed over to the glass boot prints behind the fence. His own glass imprint was a few feet away next to some flourishing lilac bushes.

"Pssttt," he whispered to the place she once stood, the place they all felt closest to her. Then with great care, he pulled a black and white photograph from inside his Hawaiian shirt.

"We're pregnant," Dre said and pointed to the sonogram, "Look at this beautiful nugget. Don't tell anyone. Come home soon and meet my kid."

He delicately tucked the picture back into his shirt.

"Happy birthday," he said, with a bow. Then he went back to Priti's cart for seconds.

Raquel arrived in a fluster.

"I'm so sorry, I'm late," she said as she pulled her bag over her shoulder and sat next to Gracie.

"But there was an emergency," Gracie said dryly over a spoonful of mint chocolate chip.

"No, smarty pants," Raquel said as she brushed her loose hair behind her ears. "I overslept. I went to a party at Dyn's last night."

The table broke out in a chorus of gasps and applause.

"I know," Raquel said. "I'm proud of me too. Anyway," she looked around the park, "is Raven coming? Have we met her new girlfriend yet? Do we like her? Do we approve? I'm concerned. Is anyone else concerned? Do I need to cut a bitch, is basically what I'm asking, because I will cut a bitch."

"I will also help destroy her," Manny volunteered.

"We're reserving judgment," Constance said from the end of the table.

"She's nice," Joon said.

"Yeah," Erin agreed. She and Raven became roommates and good friends after the Battle of the Solstice. "She's a sweetheart. She likes Studio Ghibli movies."

"That doesn't mean she's a good person," Raquel said, crossing her arms.

'Yes, it does," Joon and Manny said in unison. They high-fived. They, along with Jakob, called themselves the 'Cryptid Bros.' Joon had matching t-shirts made.

"And what does the Goddess of Love think?" Raquel asked.

Gracie paused mid-scraping chocolate chunks from her cup. She thought for a moment. Mourning doves flew overhead.

"She's a fine enough match for Raven," she said and shifted in her seat to make herself more comfortable. "She is no danger to her, but Raven's life partner has yet to reveal herself."

Twenty feet below where they sat, Kito painstakingly adhered abalone shells to the walls of her cave with mud and clay.

The End

529

DRAMATIS PERSONAE

Sam Bridger is a transplant to Sunset Cove. The Fog turned her into the manifestation of The Morrigan (the triple Celtic Goddess of Death, Revenge, Justice and Darkness). She is Chiba's best friend/found sister and aunt to Zara and Malak. She is Dre's found sister. Sam grew up in an abusive household.

Olga is Sam's abusive mother.

The Learys

Chiba Leary (aka Chibs) is Sam's best friend/found sister. Danny is her husband. Malak and Zara are her daughters. She was orphaned when she was very young and was raised in the foster system. The Fog did not change her in any way. Chiba is very human.

Zara Agnes Leary is the eldest daughter of Chiba and Danny, Sam's niece, Malak's older sister, a bit of a worrier. She is 7 years old going on forty-five.

Malak Samara Leary is 5 years old, fierce, inquisitive and loyal. She is Chiba's youngest daughter, Sam's youngest niece and Zara's little sister. Ridley is the Learys' scruffy dog.

Daniel Leary (aka Danny) is Chiba's husband and Zara and Malak's father. He is human.

The Farm

Dre Damascus (aka Dre, aka Andre Sussex Damascus) is a brewmaster and farmer. He is the husband of Gracie, father of Sohlie and found brother of Sam. The Fog turned him into the manifestation of Ama (pronounced AH-ma), the God of Life/Creation/Potential of the Dogon people of West Africa.

Gracie (aka Graciela Ines Smith Gutierrez-Damascus) was a kindergarten teacher before the Fog. She's Dre's wife and Sohlie's mom.

Sohlie is the daughter of Gracie and Dre. She's a toddler.

Dashi is Sam's nickname for her elephant escort.

The Goddesses and Gods

Jakob Blanc was a black-clad musician in Sunset Cove before the Fog turned him into the manifestation of Veles (pronounced veh·lez), the Slavic God of the earth, forests and music.

Joon Yong (주윤 aka Yong Zhu Yun) was born in South Korea and moved to the states as a kid. Joon was visiting Sunset Cove when The Fog turned him into the manifestation of the Dragon King. The Dragon King in Korean mythology is a benevolent figure with power over the oceans and rain.

Raquel Ani Poochigian is the manifestation of Anahit (pronounced AN-uh-hid), Goddess of Healing and a nurse before The Fog. Anahit is the Armenian Goddess of Healing in Wisdom. She has also been portrayed as a battle Goddess.

Manny is the father of Dylan, brother of Miguel and boyfriend of Laurel (Erin's mom). He works nights, drives like a maniac. He is the manifestation of the God Xolotl. Xolotl (pronounced SHO-lot) is depicted as a dog-headed man in Aztec mythology.

Miguel is Manny's brother and Dylan's uncle. The Fog turned him into the manifestation of the Aztec God, Quetzalcoatl (pronounced ket·suhl·kuh·waa·tl) Considered to be one of the most important gods in the Aztec pantheon, he was the wisest of men and can take the form of Venus or the Morning Star.

Nyx (pronounced nEEks) is the primordial Goddess of Darkness. She is supremely powerful and created the universe.

Kito (pronounced kiTo) is the guardian of Sunset Cove. She is a member of the Native American tribe that lived in Sunset Cove for thousands of years before colonizers murdered her people and stole their land. She is immortal, sings to the Fog, and is an artist.

The Heirs

Raven Rainbow Renquist (aka Rave) is Sam's apprentice. She was a college student before the Fog. She is Erin's instant best friend.

Kellyman is Raven's raven familiar. He was an Irish mafia enforcer. He's not very bright but he enjoys his job very much.

Dylan Efran Villalobos is Manny's son and Miguel's nephew. He worked at a pizza joint before The Fog. He is 15 years old and overly enthusiastic.

Jamison Henry Montgomery (aka Henry) is Raquel's heir or apprentice. He plays violin.

The Morrigan

Carl is Sam's raven familiar. The Morrigan is often portrayed with ravens or crows as these birds often appeared over battlefields (because they were smart enough to know what happened next and that it usually meant lunch for them). Carl very much does not like his job.

Nemain (pronounced NEY-van) is one of the aspects of The Morrigan. She is the manifestation that is the Goddess of Strategy, Magic and Inspiration.

Anand (pronounced AH-nund) is both an aspect of The Morrigan and one of Sam's past lives. Anand is the Goddess of Abundance.

Arthmael (pronounced ARTH-miel) is the chieftain of a village neighboring Anand's.

Badb (pronounced beyev) is the Goddess of Battle Frenzy and one of the triple aspects of The Morrigan.

The Villains

The Man in White is a transplant to Sunset Cove. The Fog turned him into the manifestation of Zeus. Fiona, the Goddess of Love, Smyth, the God of War and Dionysus, the God of Wine, are his children.

Fiona is The Man in White's daughter, the manifestation of The Goddess of Love, Aphrodite and sister of the God of War and the God of Wine. Technically, she's Sam's ex-wife.

Smyth Delano Sylvanus (aka Smith) is The Man in White's son. He is the manifestation of The God of War, Ares, and brother of the Goddess of Love and the God of Wine.

Dyn (aka Dionysus) is the non-binary manifestation of Dionysus. They are the child of The Man in White and sibling of Fiona, the Goddess of Love and Smyth, the God of War.

Conal Estes Mayeaux Conal was the manager of a big box store before the Fog turned him into a Silver Tongue, or a person who could control anyone with their words.

Michael Seamus Flannery is the leader of the white supremacist group, the Lords of Ire. He worships The Morrigan.

Tanya is a Nazi troll.

The Hospital

Dr. Jeddah Castle Williams is an Australian Healer who has sworn an oath to help heal the sick. She was a doctor before the Fog.

Inoke was a nurse before the Fog turned him into a Healer. He swore an oath to help heal the sick. He was one of Sam's regulars at the brewery.

Pamela Cherie Giancarlo (aka Pam) is a nurse who worked with Dr. Jeddah Castle Williams.

The People of Sunset Cove

Constance and her husband, Edgar, were part of the Battle of The Beeman Building. She is the manifestation of Baba Yaga. In Slavic folklore, the Baba Yaga dwells in the forest in a house that walks on chicken legs. She and Edgar have a cat named Jeff.

Edgar is Constance's husband. They have a cat named Jeff.

Jeff is Constance and Edgar's cat. He has very strong opinions.

Jimmy is a friend of Sam's from work. Ronnie is his best friend. The Fog turned him into a vampire.

Ronnie is Jimmy's best friend. He is a werewolf.

Erin Angelica Fern (aka Erin) meets Joon at a coffee shop before the Fog. She is an artist. Laurel is her mom.

 Dr. Matthew Lanier Cowart is a theoretical physicist who is working in Sunset Cove when the Fog rolls in.

Byron Masaru Tanaka is a recently divorced man who, while searching for a little peace and quiet, became the first person killed by the Fog.

Callie is Dyn's friend. She is a telepath.

Priti is an ice cream maker who gained the ability to control cold in the Fog.

Frank is a honey badger of a man and the post-Fog leader of the Sunset Cove city council.

Kit is a humanoid cat who can talk.

Cora was a college student before the Fog and now she is the de facto head of the vampires.

Tynan is a vampire and friend of Cora's.

Davey McAllister is an old friend, dealer and co-worker of Chiba and Sam.

Melissa worked with Conal at the big box store.

*Travis Herbert Thompson i*s a meth addict and a member of the Lords of Ire.

Dena Marchetti's family owns much of the land in the area and were largely not transformed by the Fog.

Phillip Octavian Claussen (aka Phil) is a Sunset Cove local and a member of The Faithful.

Yvette is Michael Seamus Flannery's wife. She worships The Morrigan.

Persephone Liadan Morpheus Aradia is a self-described witch and colleague of Dr. Cowart's. She worships many Goddesses.

Laurel is a Chaos Witch. She is Manny's girlfriend and Erin's mom.